# THE PHILOSOPHER'S WIFE

**Other Novels by Edwin Wollert**

*Dreamers of the Grail* (writing as Dale Geraldson)
*Packs* (writing as D. T. Kizis)

Each is published by Stone Ring Press.

# The Philosopher's Wife

### Edwin Del Wollert

Copyright © 2024 by Edwin Wollert
Published by arrangement with the author
Stone Ring Press
www.stoneringpress.com

Cover design by Jon Bogart

Library of Congress Cataloging-in-Publication Data
Wollert, Edwin

The Philosopher's Wife / by Edwin Wollert p. cm.

ISBN 978-0-9829712-8-4; e-pub: 978-0-9829712-9-1

1. John Stuart Mill (1806–1873).
2. Harriet Hardy Taylor Mill (1807–1858) – Fiction.
I. Title PS3600.0666 2011 813'.57-dc20 2010940093

*For Kendra, who inspires me as Harriet inspired John*

# Contents

# Author's Introduction

Alternatively, save this for last, but if you're unsure just who these historical individuals were or wondering more about their times, then this will prove a useful place to begin. A couple of tiny 'spoilers' appear here, so skip to the start of the novel instead to keep the surprises.

For fans of history as well as fiction, let me explain some of what I had in mind for this project. My first novels have notable differences from this one: both are published under pseudonyms; and while both contain elements of history, neither qualifies as historical fiction. Indeed, my first work, 'Dreamers of the Grail' (by my first alias Dale Geraldson) represents what my wife calls 'historical fantasy:' it takes place within post-Roman 'Arthurian' Britain, but contains many ahistorical components. As for the second work, 'Packs' (by my other literary moniker D T Kizis), the main story occurs in our own time, with major parts separated by historical short stories, each focusing on a different time and place and culture in which humans and wolves found themselves near each other.

Moving on to this new piece—appearing with my own name attached—I've opted to return to my academic training, having taught philosophy and later also history at the collegiate level for many years. My doctoral dissertation focused on British history, though it considered the Tudor period, still three centuries before my latest protagonists appeared on the scene. So the question became how to blend my fascination with disparate elements of British history and culture (including spelling and punctuation, though I'm a Yank by birth) with the person who is in fact my favourite philosopher and the lady who profoundly influenced him and his work.

That's 'favourite philosopher ever,' actually. Period. Full stop. Try visiting a university philosophy department and asking the faculty members who their most admired thinkers are. As academics, they'll likely chat you up about the merits of different folks, and perhaps even admit to the subject matter (and its author or authors) that appeared in their own dissertations. But to single out one person above others proves unusual, so I'll admit readily here and now that an Englishman named John Stuart Mill was (and remains) my favourite thinker, his flaws included. I admire an assortment of others from differing times and cultures, and have taught the works of these and other influential folks through the ages of whom I might have lower opinions instead—part of teaching fairly includes explaining course materials neutrally, after all—but Mill emerged for me as a grand intellectual who was yet very approachable and who addressed actual social and intellectual problems, issues that remain universal. To make major contributions to ethics, logic, and political thought is a significant accomplishment; to do so and remain readable entails an additional and no less impressive feat.

Yet while doing my master's degrees (one each in philosophy and history), and then teaching selections of Mill's work to my own undergraduate students, I started to notice more connections between what he wrote and how the time and place in which he lived affected him. I also began reading biographies seriously, something I'd not done before, and at the time I'm composing this little introductory summary I've now read close to three hundred of them, about folks famous and of others almost unknown except to specialists, and it was when I encountered one about Mill himself and another about a woman named Harriet Taylor that I remembered nearly forgotten bits I'd heard about this man John Mill years previously.

Those biographies reminded me of something that far too many instructors and professors of philosophy and history either forget or simply choose not to comment on, even in classes intended for grad students: no one's written work ever is created within a social vacuum. Simply put, we are all of us products of our cultures and times and loves and interests and prejudices and traumas and hopes and beliefs and choices. Phrased another way, consider your own preferred thinker / scientist / sports hero or heroine / actress or actor / author / family member / friend / lover / teacher / or whomever else. Now imagine that person growing up in another culture, in a different time and place, speaking another language, acquiring different skills, practicing and following different worldviews. In the case of John Mill, his initial worldview was moulded by much of what he read (too much and too early as it turned out, despite being a child genius). Yet it was also shaped hugely by his developing feelings and relationship with the love of his life, a woman who at the time of their first meeting was wed to someone else, the father of her children.

You can't make this stuff up, though. Imagine 'pitching' a novel or play or screenplay that begins with a love triangle in which a woman feels torn between two men she truly cares about but who both have the same first name: talk about weak writing! And yet this really did happen. I've presented this convoluted love triangle based largely on the writings of the folks involved as well as on contemporary accounts — some supportive, some condemnatory.

All this biographical material of John and Harriet proved fascinating, affecting me deeply and opening up new elements of history as well as a window into the life of John and his work, which I quickly began to realise was very much their work. Initial editions of what they published tended to list both their names; Harriet's tended to get erased from subsequent editions. That, combined with contemporaries and later commentators suggesting that she was just a 'philosopher in petticoats,' helped largely delete her from the records. Such a fate has happened to far too many women, and non-European writers and thinkers, throughout history. Indeed, John Mill and Harriet Taylor were acutely aware their whole lives of how too many around the world were simply ignored or subjugated, and their time witnessed the strongest period of European (and soon American) domination of most of the globe, including the massive political and economic power structure based within their own nation.

This blending of disciplines—philosophy and history, my specialities—reminded me of two other details within academia: first, that philosophy and history remain, even now, often sexist and racist subjects. Additionally, the more you study within subjects that seem different (and thus appear on different lists within different departments within parent universities), the more you come to realize how astonishingly interconnected the wealth of human knowledge truly is. Universities are not in the habit of advertising this, especially since those different departments and different colleges within them remain subject to differing whims in terms of funding and research and prestigious full-time and / or visiting faculty, which contribute (more or less so) to their prestige. If this sounds confusing, consider that the university where I completed my PhD is known for engineering, agriculture, life sciences, and veterinary medicine, all of which tend to overshadow the 'humanities:' history and philosophy (and religion) comprise the same small department at that school.

Anyway, I genuinely hope you enjoy your foray into this accessible albeit sometimes strange past world. Much will prove recognisable: if you like Austen or Dickens, you may feel somewhat at home, while other details may seem more remote. An example lies in the speech of my protagonists, as Georgian and Victorian educated folks really sounded like my descriptions. But these were real and genuine persons; indeed, the only characters within this entire novel of my own creation are a tiny assortment of service personnel ('the help,' as disparagingly called, then and unfortunately sometimes now), the sorts of persons who, ironically, sometimes found themselves ignored even by the hero and heroine of my historical tale.

Cropping up periodically also emerge a pair of further inventions, though I worked to make them plausible. These are diary entries by Harriet and later also by her daughter, Helen, the youngest of her children. Neither woman is known to have kept such (though Harriet proved an astonishingly dedicated writer, preferring letters, articles, and the aforementioned book contributions); yet I wanted to add their own ideas to the story, both to clarify the events they lived through and to keep them from getting overshadowed by the more well-known John.

These introductory notes will hopefully enable you to also keep in mind the 'big picture' of John and Harriet's time and place. Key themes include dismantling of slavery, global effects of colonialism, women's suffrage, and especially individual rights and responsibilities: indeed, the name Mill remains associated with the greatest treatise ever composed about the rights of each person, along with evaluation of when such rights may yet be temporarily checked for the greater good. Theirs was also a rapidly changing time, making it very relevant to our own: Britain moving through its Georgian and Victorian periods becoming a truly world empire, with the other major European powers—plus the nascently powerful Americans—coming to dominate or outright control, by the conclusion of the 19th century, the lands comprising almost all the nations we can count today. Some curious exceptions survived on their own, such as Afghanistan, Persia, Japan, Korea, Abyssinia, Liberia. The Americas, north and south, plus the rest of Africa and the rest of the Pacific Rim, were run by or answered to those of Caucasian ancestry. This novel is in no way, however, a defence for the many blatantly racist and environmentally destructive practices of colonizers during that century.

Finally, the rapid political and ethnic domination of the period was further matched in speed by sciences and technologies that shrank and altered the world: natural philosophy diverging into biology (especially with evolution and palaeontology), chemistry (most notably within medicine and the discovery of elements), physics, geology, and wholly new perspectives for astronomy; and such socially-altering devices as telegraphs, steamships, and railroads, with hints of domesticated electricity and horrible new weapons just around the chronological corner.

So welcome, dear reader. Meet the philosopher and the woman who challenged him in many ways, and learn of the immense influence their combined work had on our moral, logical, political, and mental worlds.

—EDWIN WOLLERT

*July, 2024*

## PROLOGUE

*London — June, 1823.*

S t James' Park lay verdant in the summer warmth, though the young man, some might say still almost a boy, ignored most of it. It was not lack of attention, far from it: John Mill cherished invigorating long walks, regarding himself a rambler, though city parks could prove just as rewarding. Having such spaces open to the masses for free was still new. In his haste John mentally reviewed the history of the Park, a nervous habit he might engage in regardless of setting, this time more pronounced as he grew concerned about running late: former marsh, then medieval leper hospital grounds, then hunting park for Henry VIII and named for one of his endless palaces. And the pelicans — John smiled as one ambled by looking carefree whilst a flock of others casually swam or stood in the pond — were a gift from the Russians to Charles II.

*No, it is time to pick up my pace,* John Mill thought, redoubling his stride. Because when a boy (*no, man,* he reminded himself) has turned seventeen, childhood cares must remain in the background, and he felt eager to keep proving himself a responsible and respectable young man. Indeed, his birthday celebration lay just a fortnight in the past, more a reminder that he was taking up his post within the famed East India Company, largely through the auspices of his famous philosophising father than a traditional coming-of-age event.

Practical utilitarian gifts had been welcomed by his family for his birthday, sweets and frivolity less so, though John appreciated the job security. He would have no time to savour some Grand Tour of the Continent before settling into work, still wishing to see France again, and Greece and Italy, of course. Such explorations had been the aim of young educated men for at least a century, but his time for such would have to wait.

Thus he trod en route to the imposing Company offices on hectic Leadenhall Street, following the meandering walkway, out of sight of the multi-storey buildings surrounding this lovely park, before espying something perhaps trying to hide in the bushes. *An injured pelican?* he wondered, then noted it wasn't moving. Despite a strict upbringing, John typically ranked curiosity over punctuality, even the rigid and imperial timeliness of the East India Company, and so he stepped closer, suddenly aware that almost no other people were in the park this early. It seemed too soon for morning constitutionals, and those having to walk to places of employ often preferred streets to parks, which seemed confusing, since why would someone take urban ugliness over pastoral peacefulness? Yet John started to wonder why he felt vaguely guilty for approaching whatever-it-was, having decided that a lighter blue scrap of cloth was what had given it away, then recalling that pelicans were hardly blue.

The scrap was a blanket, part of one anyway. And as John leaned over he could see that the blanket contained a doll, with a lifelike head now visible. Hoping that it was indeed a doll left by some hurried or frightened child, John knelt down, a slight damp from the park's grasses immediately wetting and cooling his knee, while some improbably detached part of his memory told him that this non-doll could only have been dead a short time, almost certainly abandoned here overnight, as its pathetic cold form had yet to attract scavengers or even many insects. Curiosity or sympathy notwithstanding, John loathed being late, especially for his new job, and looked about the park to see if a constable might be available to help, even if nothing could be done to save a dead baby. He was surprised by how detached he felt by this dreadful encounter, recalling at once the rigid mental control of his unusual education, combined with the weighing of the utility scale envisaged by his godfather Jeremy Bentham and actual father James.

As for the needed constabulary, there were rumours of Home Secretary Peel creating an official police force for both London and Westminster, but in the meantime just a few hundred constables walked about the mighty metropolis, ready to raise the old medievalist hue and cry if needs be. What they might do this morning, in a park away from the crowds, and for an infant who appeared dressed in quite common and shabby clothing, would likely amount to virtually nothing. What evidence of wrongdoing lay here anyway?

So the baby remained, looking peaceful and accusatory at once: pathetic, lifeless, appearing to lack obvious injury. John Mill at once suspected death by smothering, since strangulation required one to get one's hands dirtier, while likely having to look at the victim, as well as leaving tell-tale marks on the throat, and the infant likewise appeared to have suffered neither from the major killers like cholera or consumption, nor from starvation, though the small bundle was nonetheless quite thin. But John was no physician, and while he initially felt some ancient instinct to cuddle and hold even someone dead, he could yet remain detached and analytical while considering possibilities.

And whilst smothering, if the correct conclusion, was of course murder and thus a horrible crime, that same analytical mind recognised the likely impetus behind such drastic action. There existed simply too many mouths to feed, especially amongst the poor. John's dedication to his father's overbearing home tutelage meant that he had studied the work of Thomas Malthus, who had warned that while world food supplies, surely augmented by recent advents in farming and the machinations of the Industrial Revolution of the prior century, could only ever increase food yields numerically, no matter the agricultural improvements. Human population, meanwhile, increased exponentially, food thus failing to keep pace, mathematics outdoing instinct. While John knew that the parents of this little deceased bundle in his arms had almost certainly never heard of a scholar like Malthus, the baby nonetheless represented that alarming logical prophecy in the flesh: those parents probably were already attempting to care for a number of children. One more might be perceived as endangering all of them with starvation, and one could sell one's offspring in England nearly as easily as one might, say, in a land such as that forming the name of John's new employer. Even the old Poor Laws could only do so much. While John felt sympathy for such situations, his own new salary of £30 per annum would hardly yield sufficient leftovers to do much in the way of charity work. It might, if stretched, permit him to wed someday, but then barely.

The more he considered the problem, the more John kept returning to the ideas not just of Malthus, but of his own godfather, the rabble-rousing creator of 'utilitarianism,' Jeremy Bentham. A good friend of John's father, Bentham had gone philosophically back to the ancient Greeks for inspiration, and their interpretation of human behaviours reducing to the pursuit of pleasure and avoidance of pain, and how the understanding of such a model required a certain amount of training. Still, even the poorest parents in London would surely know that one critical extra crying mouth too far would yield more pain, for its family, and…

John's rapid mental sequencing and reorganising was interrupted by a whistle. He looked up, having to turn around to note one of the City's constables running directly towards him, blowing hard on his whistle every few steps. Apparently young men in work suits kneeling in the morning grass attracted attention, or maybe the constable had simply managed a fortuitous view of what John still cradled, or perhaps someone else had already tried to fetch aid.

'What's all this, then?' the man demanded as he strode smartly up to John, looking almost as young as Mill himself, wearing a bowler hat and single-breasted navy blue suit, carrying a cane which might alternate between walking stick and club. The man displayed a thick moustache, seeming to turn prematurely bald beneath the tight-fitting hat, and glared directly at Mill with hostility.

Mill would later feel pleasantly surprised by his ability to remain calm under such a glare, and during such a sad circumstance. 'Hello, Constable,' he responded simply. 'I was just on my way to work and found this, this—' He found that for once he could not quite form the words. *Dead baby*, he thought, *this deceased innocent I just stumbled upon.*

The accusing eyes softened, the head containing them shaking slightly. 'Another one,' was all the constable said. 'I saw you from across the pond and know you didn't do anything wrong. Give it here then, lad. I'll need you to come along and help me make a statement about how you found the wee one.' *It*, thought John. The tiny lifeless bundle is reduced to an 'it.' He supposed such dispassion a requirement for the constable, who must surely enter regular contact with the seedier locales of the Empire's capital. Yet did the babe's parents likewise perceive their vulnerable new offspring as an 'it?'

At least Mill was not finding himself threatened with arrest, though something must be done about too many infants, or the mostly poor people who kept breeding them. He knew what the wealthy did if they felt they had too many children, and they could afford to keep their affairs more secretive, though their unusually timed adoptions, perhaps from 'parents living abroad' or such, were actually more widely known than perhaps some well-off families felt prepared to fully admit. And as he walked along with the constable, who held the lifeless lump in his arms no less caringly than he might a living baby, John realised he would be late for work after all.

*London — March, 1826.*

While she would not learn of John Stuart Mill's macabre find for some years, indeed would not even meet him in person just yet, Harriet Hardy had already been dutifully keeping a detailed if only occasional diary in her home neighbourhood in Walworth Road, a fashionable part of the mighty City. She might have wondered what an alleged radical like young John might have to say about her own father, who practiced, not as a radical philosopher, but as a midwife. Not a physician, but an actual male midwife, having originally trained as a surgeon! Harriet was proud of him, both for working in a 'woman's' ancient field, and for ignoring the equally old bias of the physicians, who had refused to soil their own hands by actually touching their patients for so many centuries, while barbers and surgeons and dentists and midwives did the real labour in caring for those patients. Father was well enough respected and well enough paid in his curious profession, despite oft-tangled hours, for Mother to remain at home to help guide Harriet and her assorted siblings into maturity. Father could prove boorish at home, one of the motivations behind Harriet beginning a diary in the first place, but he loved his children, even doting on them at times. Considering his occupation, he would hardly have fretted about the warnings of old Malthus as John Mill might: babies were wellsprings of joy as well as sources of steady pay, even when Father had to head outside in any weather, at any time of day or night, to bring forth warm, wet, and whinging new life into the world, though Harriet knew not if he worried about said new life being abandoned in public places to die of smothering or exposing.

But as for lighter subjects, today would be worth remembering, Harriet knew, looking forward to a lengthy if perhaps confused or muddled diary entry, given that her own feelings currently encompassed excitement, trepidation, hope, love, relief, and fear. It was the day before the Ides of March, and a different John, a loving John, would become her husband this day, at the Unitarian Church in Islington, not far from home. 'Mrs John Taylor,' she would shortly and irrevocably become, to a man a decade her senior, seeming even older than he perhaps might otherwise compared to her mere eighteen years. He also seemed worldly, impressing her father with his knowledge of medicines and treatments through his own work as an apothecary, and had always been so kind to her, since their first meeting years ago at the church. Father seemed more reticent and perhaps set in his ways when John once broached the subject of using modern medicines to assist with the almost always agonising process of women bearing children, once raving about 'none of that opium den nonsense for my clients, lad! Whatever would their husbands think,' choosing the well-worn hyperbole carefully, not knowing that John Taylor himself used opiates very sparingly, and there could be quite good benefits from offering a bit of laudanum to a fully dilated mother whose senses might be altered by pain. Neither man, in the end, altered his beliefs, and Father remained proud, justifiably so far as Harriet understood such things, of his own usage of medieval wooden birthing stools to encourage his patients to focus on expelling squalling infants straight down. The more modern method of encouraging women to lie down and actually get their legs into the air seemed, well, not only backward but perhaps an anatomical statement about making themselves more vulnerable to men, rather akin to the position by which most women became pregnant in the first place, at least according to Harriet's limited knowledge of human sexuality.

Her face flushed again slightly at the thought, knowing that there existed more ways of becoming amorous with a lover, though she of course could hardly discuss such with anyone. Maybe she could try with Lizzie and young Caroline, and for a moment she wondered if such a delicate theme might be gently pursued with her husband. She hated the thought of men having such power: something as simple and innocuous as birthing stools left women feeling more in control, or so they reported, but men tended to remain steadfast in their beliefs, and Harriet shuddered at the thought of childbirth anyway.

She looked up at the mirror again, attempting to control a pair of sudden tears that should not play havoc with her carefully made-up appearance. There was no drug to help our younger John, though, she thought quickly if bitterly, remembering her younger sibling, two actually, who had not long ago faced the ravages of illness. It spared Thomas but took their little brother John. Harriet just as briefly considered if marrying another John might be a way of both somehow reaching her recently deceased older brother whilst strangely offering the unspoken advocacy of an apothecary, a man who—who knew?—might go on to help create a better treatment or even cure for that malicious disease, consumption, which took so many too quickly. Such was the anger that helped crack the foundations of Harriet's formerly stronger beliefs. Perhaps true faith was more challenging to erode, but she had never experienced such, at least not the surety of religious conviction.

Steadfast beliefs aside, there would be no stuffy Church of England for her forward-thinking family either, Harriet reminded herself while grudgingly admiring her mirrored reflection shortly before the ceremony, and fortunately Unitarians had been welcomed in so much of greater London. There were reports of finally eliminating the archaic statutes limiting options for England's Catholics as well, but the Lords and Commons had yet to vote on that, and Harriet briefly wondered if her casual flitting into the realm of religious faith served merely as a cover for her own rapidly beating heart (what proper bride does not blush on the Big Day? she wondered for the hundredth time), or for her own attitude to such beliefs in the first place. She could hardly confess to atheism now, after all. Well, 'almost-atheism,' she admonished herself again, yet she knew that her own faith was hardly strong, and honestly did not quite know how strong her future husband's was, either. Certain details often simply had to be presumed, and it was not as though John came from a line of un-baptised savages.

Mother adored her future son-in-law as well, of course: an up-and-coming young man full of promise, with a good job, and in a rare admission of honest feeling, she even confessed to Harriet some days earlier how handsome he seemed. Perhaps not with the dashing mystique of Lord Byron nor the blend of innocence and worldliness in the gaze of Shelley: Harriet had seen the famous portraits of the former, heard descriptions of the latter, both poets deceased not so long ago. Yet her future husband nonetheless captivated with the light of his eager brown eyes, curving brows which suggested interest with whomever he might be speaking, and a long narrow nose, thankfully not pointed downward when he spoke, from a softer mouth rarely pursed in judgement. He preferred his dark straight hair closely cropped, with minimal sideburns which, again thankfully!, did not lead into a beard or moustache. Harriet understood the age-old association in so much of the world of facial hair with masculine virility, but having tugged on her father's sideburns more than once as a girl, recognised that such hair could be thick and discomforting.

Most importantly, certainly for young Harriet, was that her future husband respected her, even listened to her, qualities sufficient for her to fall in love, but more responsibly, and not as quickly or foolishly as the girls in the novels by Jane Austen that Harriet nonetheless loved to re-read at times, perhaps only to mock their prudish Georgian class mores. The Church of England might refuse to educate the Hardy brood in the local school, to the annoyance of all members of the family, even Mother, yet Father had made sure, in a style reminiscent of Thomas More and his own intelligent offspring, that his children could read, and write, and do sums, and speak, not just well but in more than one tongue. French remained one of Harriet's other loves, and she took pride in knowing it more thoroughly, with a more accurate accent, than her siblings.

'Are you ready then, my sweet?' Harriet had not even noticed her father standing at the door to one of the back rooms of the church in Islington, poring over her journal as she was. He was the only one who could intrude on her like that: not even John knew of her diary, and Harriet savoured the few if bold secrets of her life. Her father was the one who purchased the little notebook for her in the first place.

'I am, Father.' She glanced up at him, loving how handsome he looked in his new suit: simple medium blue, with a cravat to almost match the silvering of his hair. 'How is the Pastor holding up?' William Fox, old family friend and dependable Unitarian minister, always fretted over handling weddings, which he considered more nerve-wracking than anything else within his job description save funerals, yet he seemed content and confident in his faith whenever at the front of the small unadorned church. He sometimes joked that things must be easier for Catholic priests, since with all their Sacraments, they always had another ritual to talk about.

Father grinned. 'He'll be fine, fret not. Your young brothers are behaving themselves for the non, though I'm sure they're already looking forward to some enchanting desserts.' Thomas Hardy had a known sweet tooth, but never became overweight for love of chocolate, nor the amount of sugar he put into his tea, too much by half according to Georgian sensibilities. 'And little Caroline is just precious in her dress.' Harriet smiled; her baby sister, just five, was an adorable little imp, strong-willed and smart but cute enough to get away with things.

'What of slightly larger Caroline?'

'I told you not to worry, sweeting. Your friends are ready to stand with you, and if I may say so, both look radiant in the dress design you chose.' Harriet liked that just as much, having indeed chosen the same dress pattern for her friends, a new social trend. And such friends came along rarely: Caroline Fox—unrelated to the fretful pastor, more of a little sister, even fellow aspiring diarist, and seemingly older than her tender years, just several beyond Harriet's younger sibling of the same name — and Lizzie Flower — poetess, musician, and all-around supporter, and who herself wholly approved of John, too.

'Thank you, Father,' the bride intoned simply. 'This never could have happened without you.' She recalled her hesitancy to meet John in the first place, an initial 'date' arranged largely by her father, in one of his more controlling moods. Blossoming love had enabled her to get past the initial resentment.

'Oh, do stop, now. John is a fine man, and I've heard it helps everyone when in-laws get along with each other.' Harriet laughed at that, closing and securing her little green diary. 'And I'm proud of all of you, my clever, literate children.'

Harriet glanced once more at her own reflection, knowing it was time, that her special man, very likewise as anxious as she, would no doubt be standing up at the dais with Pastor Fox, looking to the back and awaiting his first glimpse of his future bride dressed in all her finery, modest though it was. She stood, took an appraising glance around the room as though perhaps forgetting something, and took her father's hand so he could escort her to where she needed to be this special day. She could not imagine loving another so much as she adored her special John.

# PART ONE

# A Dinner Party, Children, and an Illness

*1830.*

John Mill felt alive and capable yet still guilty by the autumn of 1830. Work in the grandiose East India Company proceeded apace; the first quarterly copy of the 'Westminster Review'—intellectual periodical for 'philosophical radicals' created by his father and Mr Bentham—had gone to press shortly after his finding the baby and, in truth, the follow-up event still rankled too much to really discuss. John's father James had worked aggressively to both enable the new journal and to hide his son's disgrace and potentially narrowed employment prospects by all that had followed, even though such matters had nothing to do with babies dead or alive, and John felt a mix of relief, remorse, and odd humour over the fact that he continued to work in his father's shadow. Even a knighthood for the old man was rumoured, as all England seemed to revel in or marvel at his father's magisterial History of British India, even though it had gone to press over a decade previously. An appropriately apologetic work, laboured upon by James for some dozen years, John knew from his Classical upbringing that an 'apology' originally meant something quite different from its more generic and modernised use: originally a justification for some policy, perhaps interpreted negatively by some.

John Mill recognised and tried to come to moral terms with the simple irony of his professional existence, part of the source of the guilt, though he believed in the civilising influence of the Company generally. Educated, yes, heavily so: yet the younger Mill, like the equally intelligent Harriet Taylor née Hardy, had not attended a day of formal schooling in his life. Father James and godfather Jeremy, while claiming to admire the ever-greater calls for mandatory public education, something the Americans were dabbling with, felt nonetheless that these new schools did not yet seem 'up to snuff,' as Bentham might say, and John suspected that reverse snobbery might have kept him out of Eton or Rugby. Still, John remained glad he had never been exposed to the hazing—'traditional,' they called such—of classmates and faculty alike at such proud institutions. Yet without a diploma or degree or certification, John honestly wondered where else he might be cut out to work, at least in terms of official qualifications.

The East India Company, meanwhile, had been guaranteed through official Parliamentary Act decades before John's own birth, and now Raj India, so different from and yet so alike the Islamic Mughal India that preceded it, seemed like the crowning achievement of the British Empire, sufficient salve for the loss of other colonies that had gone their own way in New England. (Indeed, the Company dated to Elizabethan times as an early government monopoly to compete on a global stage against the Dutch in particular, as the Spanish had mostly overspent their ill-gotten New World silver and gold by then. It was of course the same corporation formerly wishing to sell its tea to American colonists without having to pay taxes for the privilege that prompted some of those unruly Americans to dump a shipment of it into Boston Harbour). And with India, not only was England determined to not lose another imperial chance, but it could try and rationalise its ever-stricter control over its central Asian domain by showing the inherently superior blessings of European Christian Civilisation.

To that end, John's father had written of the acquisition of India as part god-send and part inevitable step in the long march of 'history' and 'progress,' not knowing or not caring how his son would later rail against this 'Whiggish' self-serving racist and false assessment of the development of human societies. Amid half-hearted and ultimately futile attempts to assist his father's manuscript evolve into something less insulting, John continued to assess the justification of political armed rebellion, something his father's beloved Empire clearly feared yet was prepared as ever to answer. Sometimes it seemed that too many colonies were securing their political and sometimes economic independence from their European masters, surely a sign of troubling times, even if thinkers like James Mill might display other more enlightened views. Within John's own young lifetime, almost all of South America had finally bade farewell to imperial Spain through rebellions led by Simón Bolívar and José de San Martín. A small new 'empire' had been created in southern Africa by Shaka Zulu, as had a new kingdom clear in the middle of the Pacific called Hawaii, itself recently unified by a Polynesian monarch named Kamehameha. Meanwhile, some American former slaves had 'gone back' to old but changed Africa, to the very region where so many of their ancestors had been sold, to create a new nation they were idealistically calling Liberia. And Greece seemed intent on regaining its ancient glory by freeing itself from the Muslim Ottoman Empire, thanks to dreamers and fighters like Theodoros Kolokotronis.

Yet James Mill, among many others, purported to write of what he called a 'backward' culture, even while he criticised the British invasion of India as well as his own employer's monopolistic history. His readers, including those same employers, seemed content to overlook such a critique, since James, despite never having visited or even studied the nation in question, went on to describe how 'under the glossing exterior of the Hindu, lies a general disposition to deceit and perfidy; the same indifference to the feelings of others; the same prostitution and venality,' traits apparently pertaining to both the indigenous Hindus and also the Muslims, the latter of whom had ruled the

land for several centuries before the arrival of the English. Yet James
had gone even further, as had British imperialist interests, with China,
since both Chinese and Indians allegedly tended to be 'dissembling,
treacherous, mendacious, to an excess which surpasses even the usual
measure of uncultivated society.' When young John had first read
that in an earlier draft of his father's manuscript, he could not help
but cringe, unable to resist the almost instinctive conclusion that the
cultures his father said were 'cowardly and unfeeling' had to include
their own as well. Such was the 'apologetic' feel to the whole piece.
But the book sold well, and still did, and Company officials loved it.

And it was roughly this new, multi-cultural, global scenario that
had led James' son John to first question the 'utility' of the whole
enterprise of India and of European and perhaps American influence
elsewhere, even if the sanctioned official monopoly supposedly justified by his father's book had already written his own pay-cheques for
some years. Utility was supposed to enable greater objectivity, even the
asinine assertion of his father that his famed history text was objective
precisely because its author had never visited India and knew none
of its many languages and had no real idea of its religious heritage,
whether native Hindu, exported Buddhism, or imported Muslim. It
felt hypocritical to John, too, considering how his father, with some
help from Bentham, had so insisted that John study Classical languages at an age when most boys were playing or learning sport.

John closed his eyes for a moment, trying not to dwell on where
his intense academic upbringing had led him—almost to a sanatorium!—even if he nonetheless felt grateful for the ability to read the
ancients in their own languages—but then why in Blazes would his
father not even try to bother doing the same for his Asian subjects?
Latin and Classical Greek were not intrinsically superior to Sanskrit
and Ancient Chinese, were they? John could not imagine such to be
the case, so he professed loyalty to his chief employer whilst occasionally questioning its motivations and prejudicial past.

Small wonder he felt so tired now, pleased with his work for its
own sake, underlying politics notwithstanding. Arriving back home

from the grandiose edifice housing the East India Company, John found, in addition to the day's 'London Times,' an envelope of thick paper, its fibres easily visible and denoting its hand-made quality. The other newspapers he read at work, tending to finish each say's assignments quickly though professionally, and he was thus used to the cheaper filmy feeling of mass newsprint. But the envelope was surprising: anyone wishing to reach him would typically know to also do so through the Company, yet this clearly marked a more personal touch, even having been delivered by hand, since his address did not appear on it. Someone either really wished to reach him directly, or could afford staff to run such a mundane task. Often oblivious to other more practical concerns, it simply did not occur to John to wonder about the potential safety risk of someone knowing so easily how to reach him. While he hardly considered himself hidden away some-where, he just did not fret about such.

'To Mr Mill,' it read simply on the exterior, composed in a clear and elegant copperplate hand, though John could not decide whether that hand belonged to man or woman, such was its confident and refined appearance. His own penmanship had never impressed anyone; even Bentham had once chided him for not attending medical school since his handwriting was often nearly illegible, like that of all phy-sicians. So John stood admiringly at the doorway leading to his flat, on the ground floor of a charming if smaller brownstone a leisurely stroll from the Company offices, deciding not to wait to open what must be an invitation. Some received more social engagements than others, regardless of class, and while John had just earlier in the year become a member of the Athenaeum—that group for 'gentlemen of an intellectual bent'—this seemed more a request for a more formal social occasion. If a dinner invitation, it would be refreshing to not have to cook, he mused. Cooking for one always seemed such a morose act, so John usually consumed his largest repast at midday, his lun-cheon purchased somewhere near work. East India had runner boys always at the ready for such tasks.

It was a dinner invitation, confirmed as John lowered his briefcase to the sidewalk and tucked the newspaper under his arm. 'Mr and Mrs John Taylor,' he read silently, 'request the honour of your presence at a gathering for dinner at our home in Finsbury, London.' That would be a relatively new neighbourhood for John, just north of Blackfriars Bridge. A bit far to walk, even for a seasoned ambler like himself, though he supposed hiring a conveyance of some kind might give his hosts the impression of being a man of more means than he truly was. If he recalled correctly, this would not be far from Leadenhall Street, itself one of London's most exciting and interesting avenues, thronged with goods and wares and peoples from all around the Empire, though it was not quite as hectic as the London Exchange, of course, nor the newer Regent Street shops, which traded in the rare, exclusive, and expensive.

But who in Blazes were Mr and Mrs John Taylor? There was some 'Taylor' known to the Athenaeum as a supporter of 'radical thinkers,' though Mill had not met him. John Mill had an exceptional memory, already outstanding as a child, and he had continued to train it since, often mentally connecting things and places and ideas and names into webs of thought which he supposed might be indecipherable to almost anyone else, though he navigated these memory lines freely, having learned of the 'memory palace' technique of the Tudor-period Jesuit priest who went to China. He just about had the name…

John forced himself to re-focus. He knew that what felt natural to him often proved off-putting to others, part of what had always made it so difficult for him to form friendships, and even when friends came along, they were always well-read intellectuals like himself, such as those 'radicals,' Roebuck and Graham. He also knew that his own family members, his father perhaps the sole exception, likewise had trouble simply getting to know him. Trivial banter that seemed to please so many, especially the aristocracy—a practice which John never could reconcile, since they tended to be more highly educated!—often eluded him, giving others the impression that he remained merely aloof, or as elitist as those same aristocrats, or nobles, or clergy, or whomever else seemed remote and unapproachable. Yet John remained genuinely interested in what others thought, even when he disagreed, sometimes especially when he disagreed. He thought it instinctive, not appreciating how rare or mature the trait actually was.

That left his question unanswered, however. And all the neural networks in his brilliant head could not help him isolate the name 'Taylor' into anything meaningful; he had to conclude he simply did not know these persons. But despite his fatigue from work and another day of spare eating, he for once ignored the newspaper, left his brief-case likewise alone near the door as he entered the flat and shut the door behind him, almost forgetting to lock it, again. Instead, he wandered to his bedroom, sought by a different type of memory the room's sole candle and set of matches, and poked about in his humble closet until he located the grey suit with subtle blue pinstripes that he had already decided to wear to this dinner party. He made a mental note to make sure to have the suit pressed and starched soon, then prepared himself for bed.

* * *

Three days later he felt glad for the cool and dry weather. It hardly felt like winter just yet in London, even though the year only had days remaining to it. The bumpy yet exhila-rating ride to the Taylor home was something John would savour for days to come. Not often riding in anything with wheels, at least as an adult, he had opted to hire one of the brightly painted chaise four-wheeled carriages, this one pulled energetically by a pair of medium tawny horses, though they seemed too large for comfortable riding, in his less-than-expert assessment; he'd not ridden horses for years. En route, he had tried to recall the various traditional descriptions of horse coloration, but could not remember anything more useful. All that sprang to mind were his own foibles within the saddle as a lad.

Such minutiae did not bother John nearly as much, however, as his muddled fumbling through his pockets for appropriate payment for his conveyance upon his arrival. He of course knew royal coinage and specie intimately, indeed sometimes was solicited for input regarding official Company stamps of monetary approvals for decisions made thousands of miles away, yet a more common appraisal of what everyday things might be worth— notable exceptions consisting of foods and drinks and books—often eluded him. By the time he finished mumbling a half-apology for his near carelessness in handing out the right amount to the chaise driver, he could feel a twinge of sweat on his neck. Still, he reminded himself that he really did look his best this night, not having been able to ascertain much about the dinner party. He still regarded curiosity as its own reward and justification.

He waved off the driver at last, climbed the few steps to the private home, well-lit from inside, with a quite recent whitewash and medium-blue window shutters. The address was Number 4 Christopher Street, and John had delighted in recognising landmarks along the way. But now he had to exhale anew, confront his trepidations of feeling put on the spot, even if this soirée was not really about him, and knock soundly on the door. It was immediately opened by a grinning middle-aged man in impeccable serving black-and-white. 'Yes, Sir?' he asked eagerly.

John cleared his throat, again. 'M-Mill, please. Mr John Stuart Mill, of Pentonville.' At least the neighbourhood of his birth had a bit of posh to it, better than what he could currently afford, though Father had alluded to a generous Company wage increase coming. He had already gone from the previous £30 to £100 per year recently, an enviable pay scale for the working classes of London.

John was ushered inside, at once admiring the dazzling display of the chandler's art within, then fought back a cringe as he heard his name almost echoing when the butler repeated it for the whole house to hear. He could detect quiet yet sincere laughter from an adjacent room, then warmed to recognition as the form of William Fox materialised from around a corner, looking dapper yet official in the off-duty black sombre garb of a Unitarian minister. 'John!' he announced, walking forward quickly with an outstretched hand. 'Welcome, indeed! When I heard you were coming, I knew I could not miss it. But of course, I would have come anyway.'

Returning the strong handshake, John could only guess. He and Fox knew each other from the Athenaeum, and had already shared fine talks about those always-welcome dinner party topics: religion and politics, plus philosophy, both moral and natural. 'Will, I must say, I hardly knew whom to expect. May I ask how you know our hosts?' John would take anything to give him a social edge when he did not know whom precisely he would soon face.

Fox threw back his head and laughed, in a way clergy seemed never really permitted to do, at least when standing on the dais. 'Yes, yes, it's all been quite hush-hush, what with John and Harriet secretly planning things.' He quickly glanced behind him and lowered his still-pleased husky voice. 'There has been some, er, tension as of late, and we've all been hoping to lighten the mood somewhat. But come. Let me introduce you, even if I am not the host. I assure you, the true hosts won't mind a mite.'

For John this was seeming surreal, but he had no wish to have gotten dressed up for nothing, and his current surroundings offered a gentle rebuke of his own ways. The Company indeed paid better than his flat might suggest, and he could certainly afford a new wardrobe, even after his recent Continental travels, themselves comfortable if not extravagant. And so he absently followed Fox's lead through the warm entry, decorated with fake but tasteful reproductions of Classical busts, and several thankfully small oils on canvas of what were most likely family members of the residents, perhaps the home-owners themselves. Two in particular caught his eye, one showing a man in a dark suit with light-coloured cravat, a slight smile betraying a sense of knowing, as though he had just gotten a bargain from the artist and would prove slow to pay anyway.

The partnered painting, however, revealed a woman seemingly in deep and engaged contemplation, wearing a golden dress, and a necklace featuring a dark gemstone with a pearl draping from it, and billowing white sleeves suggesting wind. The head leaned slightly to its left in the portrait, a thin headband with a tinier jewel almost lost by the round and knowing brown eyes, with hair to match. The hairdo was parted in the middle, the sides vertically curled, the back arranged more tightly, perhaps in a bun. This woman seemed clearly interested in the artist's every move, or in listening to every word an interlocutor might have to say whilst sitting for the portrait.

Mill rudely stopped, standing there agape, not noticing Fox continue to stride towards what must be the dining room. The woman in the painting was simply captivating, yet the sometimes cynical Mill held back a bemused grin as he recalled that Henry VIII could have confirmed how paintings might, if not deceive exactly, then at least tarnish the truth. Maybe the female subject did not have a captivating attitude in mind at the time.

As if sensing something amiss, William turned back to John, tilting his head and linking his hands behind his back like a schoolmaster, knowing that he had something for which to ridicule his young friend, if just for fun. He found amusement in how John often stood just the same contemplative way. 'You seem captivated, Mr Mill.'

'What? Oh, 'sorry, Will. Please, lead on.'

The dining room proved as elaborate and pleasing to the whole sensory apparatus as Mill suspected it might be, as ornate and well prepared as it could, short of offering a table with which to feed and entertain actual Peers of the Realm, and Mill knew that if he had miraculously been summoned by such, less mystery would have ensued. But the tingle at the back of his neck returned upon seeing the assembled guests: first, he was clearly late, despite what the invitation had said; and second, he was at once confused by the makeup of those in attendance. Two old friends sat there, already saluting him with filled wineglasses, but John knew no one else at the long hardwood table.

The paintings back in the entry hall were good likenesses after all. The same slight yet not patronising smile appeared on the man at the head of the table, dressed in hunting green. At his side sat the woman in gold, though tonight she wore a rich deep red, the shade of a fine French wine allowed to breathe in an open decanter to achieve its proper bouquet, and without jewellery. Her gown was more conservatively cut than in the painting, and the same glance appeared there on her face, yet with a deepening of the eyebrows, lending her a slightly sadder expression which offered Mill only the faintest of appraisals before she, too, raised her glass, but not socially. She seemed innocent and troubled, wise and wistful, all at once. And John Mill knew just as quickly that he had never looked at a woman, nor been looked at by one, like this.

Truly she barely seemed to notice her final guest's arrival at all, while Mill himself could hardly help but stare at the remaining free seat. A quick appraisal of the room told him that in addition to the fine place settings and the blazing but not roaring fireplace, along with a different approach to art on the walls—landscapes, both wild and cultivated, mostly done in watercolours by the looks of them—that at least he had not missed the meal.

Only the repartee, which while clearly having started without him, hardly seemed shy. 'Mill!' came the combined shout of the two men he already knew.

Embarrassment almost gone for a moment—though he wondered again at the forlorn woman who was clearly their hostess—John felt amusement and relief alike to see the two old rambling friends sitting there, looking like boys. He'd seen too little of these other members of their self-titled 'Trijackia' lately: John Roebuck, and George John ('Jack') Graham, the only friends who had ever called Mill himself Jack, and only when all together. Still, even they knew nothing of Mill's recent difficulties. 'Jack and Jack,' he returned, speaking quietly since he had yet to be actually introduced. No, wait—yes, I have!

Fox had already gone to stand by his chair, hovering obviously near another young woman, a blonde who had taken her hand away from that of her hostess, too quickly, John thought. Perhaps a friend trying to offer consolation for something? The other friend seemed quite fetching herself: bedecked in an arresting light blue gown, slightly more formal than perhaps was called for but surely nothing deserving of a full ball. A single strand of pearls draped this other woman's neck, and she offered Mill a simple yet lasting glance and appraisal, as if also wondering at his delay.

The minister filled the gap ably. 'Dear John,' he gestured to the man at the head of the table, who stood politely, with almost a military bearing. 'And the equally dear Harriet,' he added, offering a light sweep of his hand towards the hostess, who nodded slightly more cheerfully, seemingly pleased by the interruption. 'May I present master John Stuart Mill,' Fox said, interrupted by a hearty 'Hear, hear!' from Roebuck and Graham, who clearly felt at ease though thankfully not truly inebriated. Mill noticed their own glasses held a light ale rather than a darker wine. 'John,' this from Fox again, his hand stretching out towards the new guest, 'may I present John and Harriet Taylor. Mr Taylor is a recognised local apothecary, and has heard of you through, well, through us, really.' The other John, the new guest, thought he caught just a glimmer from the hostess to Reverend Fox, as though annoyed he had not added any commentary about what she might do, as if by profession. 'John and Harriet: John Mill, son of the great James Mill, godson of Jeremy Bentham, and writer and thinker extraordinaire.'

*Fox can really lay it on thick,* Mill thought as he took his proffered seat. A different servant, this one a young brunette woman, perhaps the butler's daughter, silently strode in and offered John a glass of sweet-smelling wine just a moment after he sat. He equally silently nodded his thanks and approval. He never felt quite sure how to go about conversing with anyone's staff, including those who served his own family.

Raising the glass, he glanced up and noticed the other guests had all quieted, as though ready to hang on his next words. He cleared his throat. Writing is so much easier than speaking! 'Well then, to my gracious hosts, I must begin by begging forgiveness. I truly believed I had the proper time managed for my ride here.'

John Taylor waved him off. 'No, no, Mr Mill. You had the right time, so think nothing of it. Mr Fox here thinks he can get away with anything in front of us, having wed us some years back.' Taylor smiled warmly as he spoke, and seemed amused with his friend Fox, though he looked perhaps pained as he stole a furtive look at his wife. 'Some of our guests merely arrived early, and were clearly in a rambunctious mood.'

Mill found himself warming in return, despite feeling awkward. 'Yes. Perhaps I should apologise for some of them as well, since Messieurs Graham and Roebuck are fellow mad members of the "Society of Students of Mental Philosophy," emphasis on "mental."'

Harriet and the woman near her perked up at that, turning their ears to hear more. 'What do you mean by that, Mr Mill?'

Again the sense of his heart within his chest, as John Mill first heard the mellifluous tone of Harriet Taylor's voice. It must be capable of a nearly perfect alto with the right training, which he suddenly wondered severely if she had ever received.

He forced himself to look briefly at his place setting. Looking down the table at the women, he simply replied, 'Mrs Taylor, these curious young friends of mine meet sometimes at the home of a mutual associate.'

'Grote!' piped in Graham, thankfully not slurring but nonetheless enjoying himself. 'It's been far too long since we last met at old George Grote's, Jack.' Graham neglected to continue, so Roebuck added, 'A banker, and sometime radical philosopher, though how one remains such a part of the gentrified establishment whilst clinging to revolutionary thoughts remains a mystery to some. At least his house has always proved welcoming.' Mill gazed appraisingly at his friends: both dressed a bit sombrely by their own standards, they yet looked the part of charming gentlemen, in similar light beige suits which might each benefit from extra starch. Still, it was difficult to find fault with them, playful yet interesting and caring as both were. Roebuck was actually Canadian, living abroad rather than in 'the Colonies'—going out of his way to speak with an English rather than North American accent—and there were murmurs of Graham becoming more involved with the government, speaking of the 'gentrified establishment' as they referred to Grote. They loved talking and reading radical ideas, and were quite good thinkers, but Mill felt convinced that they, like most, would only go so far in pursuit of what they thought might be a greater good: socially, politically, morally. John Sterling, for one, had recently proved quite different, surely, perhaps even a touch mad. What might he think of this gathering?

But Mill loved his quirky Trijackia fellows nonetheless: they had never quite truly discussed with Mill the notable row they had with Mill's father back in '24. The younger Mill had his suspicions, had defended his friends to his famous father, but never learned much more. Parents could prove daunting to one's friends, especially if said parents had public prestige.

'Indeed, gentlemen. We must catch up with George someday. Can you believe almost eight years have somehow elapsed since we began our "mental philosophy" meetings?'

'And what did you learn during those meetings?' wondered the woman next to Harriet, the one with the pearls.

Fox almost sputtered his wine, all the riskier since he was clearly fawning over that young woman. Mill knew the pastor was married himself, though he could understand why women might find him enticing, and not just the age-old attraction to clergy. William Fox was eager and bright, and gave his whole attention to whomever he chatted with. 'Mill, now you must forgive me. This is Eliza Flower, a dear friend of our hostess.'

'Please just call me "Lizzie," Mr Mill. And I did ask.' Mill easily saw Harriet elbow Lizzie, despite his sitting several chairs away. If he and Roebuck and Graham could act like boys, then at least his hostess and her friend could act like girls.

'As our host said, Pastor Fox, think naught of it. Truly, where would our industrious Empire be if we all had to follow through with our endless apologies?' Mill was finally calmer, even beginning to enjoy himself. 'And as to your question, Lizzie, we more often than not talked about the implications of economics and politics.'

'I fear I may be unqualified to discuss such heady subjects, Mr Mill, but I assure you, Harriet can.'

Mill turned to their hostess, who finally wore the faint inspiration of a smile, something he would love to take credit for, then decided it vain. 'No, Mr Mill,' Harriet Taylor admonished, 'not me, but Ms Martineau here,' and pointed across the table to another woman, who Mill had barely noticed upon entering the dining room. Annoyed with himself for being both rude and unobservant, both unlike him, he almost instinctively stood again, bringing an actual smile from both Mrs Taylor and Ms (Mrs?) Flower.

Taking a fortifying sip of the excellent wine, Mill perused his outstanding memory again and then remembered: so this must be the exceptional Ms Harriet Martineau! He'd read her work. She was good, better than plenty of the men whose journalistic dribble he had seen in print over the years. She was a fine reporter, had a head for insightful explanations of subtle issues, and Mill had sometimes wondered, encouraged by his father, if her name had been some odd pseudonym, since being known publicly as a woman, whether actually one or not, could influence readers. 'I read your piece The Traveller, Mr Mill,' this second Harriet said. 'Your first published item, if I recall?'

For the first time that night, John Mill felt actual pride. 'So it was, Ms Martineau.' He turned to the assembled diners in sequence, vaguely aware that the first course was being brought out, though the details and identities of the staff would have to wait: after all, the Taylors made no mention of these persons, either. Yet the food certainly enticed, no matter who served it. While no true connoisseur, Mill could still detect the tomato based notes of a creamy bisque, with obvious undertones of bacon and perhaps onion, though food could hardly distract this man once he 'got on topic,' as Bentham would say.

'Yes, that is correct, Ms Martineau,' he repeated, organising his thoughts. 'I was attempting to give a useful interpretation of what David Ricardo implied for everyone, and how he differed from Adam Smith or, indeed, from my own father.'

Harriet Martineau had the confident countenance of someone who had earned her place at the table the hard way, which was true, not just with women working outside the home in general but also in a field in which the labourers might have to visit unsavoury places and interview dubious persons in order to add veracity and detail to their news stories. And Mill noticed that this woman, who seemed roughly his own age or perhaps just slightly older, seemed pleased with herself yet not arrogant, intelligent and opinionated but not patronising. 'The values of commodities depend largely upon their associated labour,' she began, paraphrasing Mill's article as much as the dead economist's own views.

'Correct again. Rents clearly favour the landowners, as they did throughout the Middle Ages.' The others were already trying the soup, apparently undecided as to whether they should offer appropriate oohs and aahs over its obvious quality and perfect serving temperature, or join in a conversation which was already waxing philosophical. But no, John fretted silently, let us not turn this into a lecture!

'So perhaps little has changed since those same Middle Ages, other than the shift from owning land to owning factories,' the formidable woman noted. 'Such is the cost, it seems, of this newly industrialised world of ours.'

Mill was tempted to give a rebuttal along the petty lines of the current times at least enabling a few more members of the Fair Sex the chance to earn pay at all, something simply out of reach for most of them, but he held it back, aware that Harriet Martineau did not seem to be criticising him, but rather their shared period of history.

She surprised him again by advancing their seemingly innocuous chat. 'Mr Mill, I would be delighted to speak with you sometime about another project.' She phrased the matter demurely, as though having gotten away with something, which in a sense she had. 'I have recently undertaken some translations of Auguste Comte, which has included his works on positivism, societal development, and his own new term, "sociology." Working for the newspapers, one does not always get the chance to engage in a salon-style talk with anything much heavier than basic politics or our always charming English weather.'

Mill faintly smiled, intrigued, and then remembered his manners. 'That would be my genuine pleasure, Ms Martineau. Perhaps we can speak more after dinner.' But for his part, he continued to wax and wane between anxiety and relief at this odd gathering, since whilst he truthfully looked forward to discussing Comte with someone as apparently well versed as his female English translator, he wondered again how much these guests of the Taylors knew about him, Mill. And how they might have learned such.

Mr Taylor himself proved prescient on that score. 'We appreciate your patience, Mr Mill, and fear we may have you at a slight disadvantage. My wife actually planned most of our little get-together here this evening, and when she heard about you via your friends,' and at this he looked eagerly and quickly at Harriet Taylor, yet seemed to find nothing reassuring in his love's gaze, 'she decided that you simply had to be added to the guest list.'

'You flatter me, sir. As do you, Mrs Taylor.' For just a moment Mill's eyes met hers, which lightened, he could swear, as though she felt relief in such simple appreciation. Planning a dinner party took some work, he assumed—never having put one together himself—yet this appeared to him something more. He swallowed and suddenly decided to sample the soup, which was indeed excellent. He was hardly surprised.

'What might Ricardo have indicated about the Corn Laws?' interjected Fox at that point. During the chat with Martineau and the others, Mill had largely lost sight and sound of Fox and Flower playfully flirting, and yet when Mill glanced back towards Fox to proffer his response, he noted that Lizzie Flower, even more so than Mrs Taylor, gave him her undivided attention with a simple penetrating look, though Mill had too little experience of women to recognise if that look represented boredom with Fox and gratitude for the interruption, interest in what Mill had to say, or some other kind of interest altogether.

'Since Mr Ricardo died a few years back, Mr Fox, we of course cannot know for sure.' It is unlike me to dodge philosophical discussion! What is happening tonight?

The pastor knew an evasive response when he heard one, and corrected Mill for speaking so politely: 'Will, please, John. There's no need to get lost in ceremony among friends.' Fox felt it was like when he asked members of his own church whether they truly believed in a supreme single deity, or salvation, or transubstantiation. As Unitarians, they tended to hedge their bets. 'I mean, do you suppose Ricardo would have favoured such blatant mercantilism?'

Mill continued looking his way, noting how Fox clearly hoped more for a response from Flower than from Mill himself, but he had a personal policy of answering others' questions regardless. 'No, Mr Fox, er, Will, I cannot say I do. Tariffs on imported foods, while designed to keep certain prices artificially high, can only hurt in the long run, both the producers of the food abroad, and the consumers of such here at home. I think Mr Ricardo would have defined such policy as an easy fix and short-term solution.' Actually, Ricardo had personally said something quite similar to Mill, and to his father, almost a decade earlier. James Mill had helped push David Ricardo into publishing in the first place, and the resulting work was regarded as highly as economic pieces by Smith and Malthus.

'And with the opium trade, too, one supposes, eh, Mill?' This was uttered by John Taylor. Mill felt unsure how to respond to this comment from his host, who as an apothecary would have easy access to opiates, especially the popular laudanum, and yet the East India Company had to fend off rumours of a growing renewed illicit opium trade in the Far East. This was despite repeated attempts by the Chinese Empire to ban importation of opium into China. Emperor Qianlong had personally written to King George III over thirty years past to peacefully yet firmly explain that Britain simply had no exports the Chinese were interested in obtaining, so the British Empire sought ways to circumvent that restriction: how to get tea and silk, along with other luxuries including indigo, spices, white ceramic so thin and fine it had taken on the name of the land which produced it, and even cotton, out of China, and get specie in precious metals out of other parts of Asia to pay for it all. If opium then got traded into China in such a convoluted and morally dubious economic triangle, it was not Mill's fault, surely. Such was taught him by his father, with Bentham echoing the sentiment, though the younger Mill wondered whether Bentham's scheme of utility—providing the greatest good or happiness for the greatest number—could really apply so facilely to a convoluted situation like opium and tea and intercontinental relations. Even if just the numbers were brought to bear for Bentham's hedonistic maths, there existed far more Chinese than English whose happiness was collectively at stake, giving them moral advantage in numbers alone.

But John Mill had worked diligently facing up to his recent and catastrophic emotional upset, and host or no, felt no inclination to be brought into a sensitive topic like opium and its uses and abuses. Besides, a practicing apothecary must derive some benefit from the Asian drug trade as well. Even the increasingly abused laudanum was opium mixed with spirits. 'I make no claim to know, Mr Taylor,' he said simply. He went back to the lovely soup, noticing he was the only one who had not finished it. His wine had been replenished, along with a side cup of tea to help ease each person's palate between courses.

The appearance of tea amused him somewhat, considering thoughts of the greatest happiness. The water supply in Britain remained sketchy, with the main exceptions of private wells for those few who could afford such, though they had largely vanished within the City and Westminster centuries earlier. Boiling it was known to make it safe, even if disagreement continued as to why. Perhaps there was something about tea. At any rate, Mill had not noticed the staff keeping beverages supplied, though he did glance up as soup bowls and serving tureens were gathered by silent and mostly expressionless workers in their uniforms of domesticity. The second course smelled delightful: a fruit salad with fresh melon and raisins, with a perfectly garnished steamed whitefish, Mill suspecting cod or bream, served under a light mustard sauce with capers and thinly sliced sautéed onions, and perhaps a touch of ginger. This time he dug in with zestier relish, the others doing likewise.

The relative silence of contented diners might have lingered for a few more minutes without the risqué comedic timing suddenly evinced by Graham. 'So, Mr Mill, if you wish not to speak of opium,

I think our hosts and the other guests would find themselves regaled by the tale of your arrest for the distribution of seditious literature.'

Years later, several of those in attendance would recall this moment with hilarity and fondness, though John Mill felt otherwise at the time. Nor did he notice that dark-haired serving girl check on the guests with a knowing smile on her no longer naïve face, since she had been one of the beneficiaries of such 'literature': she recalled John from the Park one memorable day, and while the reading proved slow-going for her, she digested every word of the pamphlet in question, even acted upon it, never telling her family.

The pamphlets were 'for the edification of the maid-servants,' such was part of their subtitle. And Mr Mill set down his second fork to answer Graham, noticing, if not the serving girl, then at least how all other eyes in the room were upon him. Ms (Mrs?) Flower was clearly bemused, while Mrs Taylor offered the most dazzling smile seen thus far, even revealing dainty teeth that Mill found somehow enticing. That recognition was all that kept him from shouting at Graham for such a forward comment, social graces be damned.

'Indeed, Mr Mill, um, Jack,' added Roebuck. And if all eyes in the place had not been on him previously, they surely were once Roebuck added, 'if memory serves, I never did truly hear the details of your subsequent jailing.'

*Because I bloody well made sure you did not,* thought Mill, who now could not resist adding a barb of his own. 'Does this perchance go back to that little spat we had two years ago about the merits of certain English poets, Mr Roebuck?'

'As Pastor Fox added,' Roebuck replied, adding just a touch of sarcastic slur to the title, 'there yet exists little need for ceremony among friends. And as I recall, 'twas "I wandered lonely as a cloud, That floats on high o'er vales and hills."'

From the far end of the table, that voice again seemed to rescue Mill. "'When all at once I saw a crowd, A host of golden daffodils,'" Harriet Taylor intoned wistfully.

"'Beside the lake, beneath the trees, Fluttering and dancing in the breeze,'" added Lizzie Flower, almost echoing her friend's soothing vocals. Others clearly knew the outstanding 'Lyrical Ballads' besides Mill, the effort by Wordsworth and Coleridge to bring Romantic literature to Britain from the Continent, just a decade after Goethe started it. The individuality of Romantic writing in this newer context, along with a sense of sublimity within mighty and immortal Nature, had appealed at once to John Mill, permitting what had seemed a perfect blending of his prior love of utilitarianism and his adoration of long walks, the latter with an oft-botanic interest as well.

'You know, Mr Mill,' said Harriet Martineau now, 'William Wordsworth acknowledged the influence of his sister when that lovely piece went to press. It reminded me of how William Herschel, for all his fame and contributions to astronomy, even his membership in the Royal Society, admitted that none of those would have been possible without his sister Caroline.'

'An excellent point, Ms Martineau,' quipped Lizzie. 'Tell us, Mr Mill, what woman might similarly inspire you? Perhaps a sister? I write a bit of poetry myself, as does our gracious hostess, even if she tends to not admit so.' Mill tried to think of a witty retort, but kept hearing his own heartbeat within his ears, so he opted to ignore the question yet smiled at Ms (Mrs?) Flower, then at Ms Martineau, not even noticing how Mrs Taylor had flushed crimson at the mention of her poetry. Apparently few things remained off limits at this gathering! He would have to share the details later with Bentham, that aging hedonist.

'You are surely versed in natural philosophy, Ms Martineau,' Mill conceded, though he was also just as anxious to not have to share that story.

'You know, the younger Ms Herschel is still alive, though living back in their native Germany, I believe,' Ms Martineau said. 'I once tried to interview her, though she seems to prefer her seclusion these days, now that her famous older brother is gone.' Mill could only nod his assent, now feeling embarrassed that for all his forays into philosophy, especially logic, ethics, politics, he had little knowledge of astronomy, ancient or modern.

Roebuck threw him a bone: 'It seems you won that little dispute of ours about Wordsworth and Byron after all, John.' And then Graham ruined it: 'Yet we still await your sordid tale of adventures with illicit literature.'

*To Blazes with it*, thought Mill, finally warming to the idea. His parents might be aghast, especially since his father had called in a favour or pulled some strings osr whichever cliché phrase seemed apt at the time, to make sure his son had gotten released from gaol after just two days, a light punishment considering the infraction. The case had been pushed to the office of the Lord Mayor himself, after John had appeared before the magistrate at Bow Street. The charge had been 'Promotion of Obscenity,' a phrase that John had considered attempting to interpret for its obvious ambiguity standing before the bench that day, before seeing the inside of his cell. But if his dinnermates wanted details, so be it.

'Permit me to begin by noting that the "literature" in question was hardly of an "illicit" nature, Jack.' Daring to glance quickly around, Mill verified that he remained under close scrutiny. What was it that attracted people to the forbidden, or at least the vaguely frowned upon? And how had his own nation become so notoriously conservative about such matters in the first place? Just moments before the group had delved into the merits of some of England's superior recent poetry, something in which Mill often took emotional refuge, and now it was back to sordid details of his past. He wondered how the new 'Bobbies' might have responded to his frequenting the northeast corner of Hyde Park, that public space already getting a reputation as 'Speaker's Corner,' had they found him. Secretary Peel had created his City police force after all, a step up from the likes of the young man who had taken the dead infant from Mill years ago.

'Whatever might it have been then, Mr, er, John?' Lizzie Flower expressed her own interest, brows raised in a blend of curiosity laced with shrewd judgement.

Mill sighed, having hoped he could address one of the men more directly, especially about a topic he had trouble putting into speech himself. 'Several of us were handing out simple pamphlets about, well, Lizzie, about contraception.'

Everyone seemed to freeze, though no one gasped aloud like he thought they might. The ladies themselves remained remarkably restrained, Mill thought.

'I say, Mr Mill,' said Mrs Taylor, proud mother of two and hopeful of at least a third. 'I must ask what you were attempting to accomplish with such.'

He saw from the corner of his vision that she at least she did not seem overtly angry. 'Well, Mrs Taylor, we were certainly not attempting to merely annoy the Catholics, though perhaps that was an added bonus.'

William Fox and John Taylor laughed aloud at that, Graham and Roebuck and the ladies remaining quieter but giggling nonetheless.

Not wanting to lose momentum, Mill continued. 'Please understand: it was most assuredly not my intent then, nor indeed now, to jest about the tremendous responsibilities associated with parenting. I feel awed by those who answer the world's most important calling. But those of you who may have read Jeremy Bentham, or especially Thomas Malthus, likely know what each has to say or at least imply about excessive population.'

'Especially amongst the poor, eh?' quipped Graham. Considering his hopeful career choice, he had gained some exposure to the vital statistics of the City, while he and Mill had previously discussed lands further away, including other realms within the Empire. And it proved very difficult to conclude anything other than that birth rates had to be curtailed in some places, or for some periods, or at least slowed, all around the globe. Mill had never forgotten how that dead bundle in his arms was almost certainly just a casualty of insufficient resources, though perhaps of insufficient love and affection as well.

'Perhaps so, Jack. As you all may be wondering: yes, I was arrested for distributing "smut," having likely been denounced by some unimpressed passers-by, whilst some others of my infamous ilk managed to escape unscathed.' Mill wondered if any of the other guests noticed

Roebuck and Graham raising their eyebrows at each other, not altogether innocently.

'So I did get to see the inside of Clerkenwell. Certainly not so grim or unhealthy as Fleet or Newgate Prisons, though not a place I might recommend for a weekend getaway.'

Ms Flower seemed intrigued further still. 'The prisoners must have been interesting, Mr Mill.' She seemed willing to overlook how revolutionary the contraceptive notices truly were, what they represented. Mill took small satisfaction in that: he still fretted that women of 'higher quality' such as Eliza Flower and Harriet Taylor might have more trouble discussing such heady topics as vaginal douching, or the risks of puerperal fever after childbirth, or any other topic of human health that did not directly involve men, not fully accepting that the true obstacle was his own masculine mindset.

'Oh, some not so bad at all, truly, though I had insufficient time and inclination to get to know many of them well.' Some semi-comfortable chuckling accompanied that.

Feeling a touch more confident, Mill opted to drive his point home even further. Roebuck and Graham knew a bit about that other day anyway, and he hardly wanted them bringing it up in some immature fashion. 'This was, in truth, shortly after a day when I might have been arrested on a charge of manslaughter, or at the very least, abandonment.'

This time there came actual titters. 'Surely not, Mr Mill!' sounded Ms Martineau.

'I fear so, madam. While I would never make light of the situation, I was walking to work one otherwise lovely morning and found a recently deceased baby in St James' Park.'

He had misjudged it this time. His hostess, and Lizzie Flower, both gasped aloud and looked spontaneously ashen and crestfallen, and Mill winced his eyes shut and at once regretted what was actually quite a simple comment. But news of dead children, of any age, hardly seemed likely to liven up a dinner party, nor offer reassurance to young parents, especially when their own children might be taken from them at seemingly any time. If the young could make it roughly to the age of five or six, then their chances improved dramatically, but in the meantime, consumption, measles, typhus, typhoid fever, or other illnesses might whisk away the very young just like they might lay claim to the elderly or infirm. Mill stood at once, facing his error. 'Ladies, please, I beg you, forgive my crude and unwarranted outburst.' He considered adding something about young mothers and childcare and doing their best, then decided to keep the unwarranted outbursts to a minimum.

Composing themselves, Mrs Taylor seemed to speak for both herself and her friend. Following an audible deep breath, she said, 'It is all right, Mr Mill. One of the benefits of having a trusted apothecary in one's home is that one never finds the proper medicine wanting.' In response, Mill thought it was the first time all evening that the lady looked at her husband with anything resembling warmth. He privately hoped Mr Taylor was as doting a husband as he could be. This classy woman clearly deserved it.

'Thank you, Mrs Taylor,' Mill said, retaking his seat. A few bites of his dinner remained on his plate, though they suddenly seemed less appetising. A new hush fell upon the large table, encouraging the guests to complete the current course, leaving each alone with their thoughts.

One of the servants arrived back in the dining room to announce dessert, though Mill felt little residual hunger after eating this well, and he had always been something of a spry man anyway. But the proclamation was quickly drowned out by the unmistakable sound of an actual baby's cry, sounding like it came from upstairs. It had not previously occurred to Mill that the Taylors might have children, this being his first time in their surprisingly entertaining company. 'That's little Haji,' said Mr Taylor simply.

'Haji?' Mill asked. 'An unusual name, that; is it perhaps Indian?' His father's magnum opus about India had poked fun at old Hindu names, too, though Mill was intrigued: one's name might reveal much about one's character, as many ancients had believed.

Mrs Taylor smiled, arising herself to accompany the young maid upstairs. Mill admired a woman dedicated enough to her own children to not have 'the help' do all the work, though the younger woman evinced a confident expression, not even pausing to solicit advice from her employers. 'It's our pet name for Algernon, Mr Mill,' Harriet Taylor added, leaving the room.

Since his wife was clearly in a bit of a rush, Mr Taylor added, 'Some of you know, and since others don't, we have in truth been blessed with two lovely children. Haji, or Algernon, and his older brother, Herbert. Harriet calls him Herby.' There seemed something wistful to Taylor's tone, but he seemed otherwise a proud father. He had in fact begun to rise himself and follow the women upstairs to check on his progeny, though his wife glared at him, apparently thinking no one would notice. Mill knew he was not the only one to force himself to look straight forward again at that. He hoped the couple were well: raising a family must surely be an endless source of stress, for all its joys.

He grinned to himself, thinking of Bentham's long-ago assessment of the pleasures of parenthood and how they were logically and necessarily offset by the pains: such was his utilitarian conclusion. Borrowing from Classic thinkers, Bentham had enumerated his own lists of such pleasures and pains, and expected others to appreciate that he had opted to never marry or have children because the logic and maths told him such common desires were just not worth his effort, and while perhaps a mercenary interpretation of human longing, perhaps even instinct, he had likewise never appeared to fail to live up to his own model of happiness, chillingly rational though it was. Mill currently doubted that the Taylors would appreciate his sharing such details of his godfather's odd ways with them.

'I'm sure they're both fine. Sometimes babies just wake up scared. Anyway, Harriet still holds out hope for a daughter, too, so perhaps someday,' Taylor said, and let it go at that, resuming his seat indecisively.

Mill felt sure he had only been in attendance at this fascinating home for a bit less than two hours, yet in some ways it felt like far longer. It was so unusual to find like-minded souls outside his admittedly narrow circle. Personnel at the Company wanted to discuss pay-cheques and policies and the greatness of the Empire, not divulge their true feelings about ideas, especially when such ideas might interfere with or perhaps cast doubt upon those policies. True, Mill found social outlets outside of work, had enjoyed last year's walks in parts of Berkshire and Buckinghamshire, with Graham on both occasions and chats about Bentham and commitment to social change. Mr Graham had interesting ideas about modifying the now dated and less potent Poor Laws. Pastor Fox would no doubt be interested. And if the fellow guests were intrigued by Mill's run-in with the English legal system years ago, they might faint into their dessert dishes if they heard about the Trijackia's curious sojourn to France just a few months previously, including the influence of John Sterling. Mill found himself savouring discussing its implications with this group sometime soon, already warming to the notion that they might be up for it, and even wondering if he should try and host a similar event, forgetting its logistical demands.

By the time dessert arrived, a simple yet delightful apple and blackberry crumble, Mrs Taylor had crept back downstairs, thanking the servant girl, Penny, for her assistance. Apples could be easily grown in newer greenhouses, though the luscious blackberries must have been canned or jarred back during the summer. Once again, the diners dug in. There was something extra reassuring about a very basic finishing course presented after something more elegant, as if to tell the guests that the party might have begun more formally, but they were welcome to behave like casual guests, even like friends, by this time in the evening. Ms Martineau in particular praised the dessert, receiving humble thanks from their hostess, who admitted it was her own, from a recipe 'kept within the family' for at least two generations.

By the end of the dessert course, some of the guests had to rise and excuse themselves for simple hygienic relief, or so Mill thought he heard at least a couple of them say, in of course the most clandestine manner conceivable. Georgian sensibilities notwithstanding, he knew he would have to do likewise soon, though the savoury wine had thankfully not interfered with his thinking or his digestion, and he did not believe he had made too much of a nuisance of himself. He attempted to reengage each person at the table in some degree of conversation again, from Ms Martineau and her guilty love of shopping on Regent Street — the new row of exclusive venues had been deemed a major gamble only a decade past, but were thriving now; to Roebuck and Graham and whether the new electric motors had true industrial applications — their consensus was yes, but they still did not like to admit ignorance about such possibilities; to estimating safety along the new rail lines linking Stockton and Darlington — generally regarded as 'safe' so long as one did not mind inhaling ash and smoke in any class of car.

Mill became especially animated, encouraged by Ms (Mrs?) Flower and Mrs Taylor, when Roebuck mentioned the relatively recent translation of the 'Rosetta Stone' by a Frenchman. French intelligentsia had been attempting a breakthrough with that piece, never mind it had been stolen from the Egyptians during Napoleon's campaign there decades previously, and some French scholar had apparently finally sorted it out. Mill was thrilled by what light it might shed upon Classical history generally, the stone's etchings having been made long ago in three distinct writings, two versions of very old Egyptian, and one in ancient Greek that was newer by comparison. That it had made its way, thanks to another odd blend of international politics, to the British Museum right here in London, only made it more enticing. Mill admitted he had only seen it twice thus far, but smiled inwardly at the thought of seeing it again and reading some of it this time!

Table talk was just showing signs of swinging around to the 'Swing Riots' in the more industrialised parts of Elham Valley in Kent, when the diners truly began to decide en masse that the party probably deserved to come to an end. Mill, intrigued by technology and scientific pursuits, wanted to hear more about the threshing machines new to farm fields, lumbering horse-drawn behemoths that could separate seeds from stalks and husks of agricultural plants, a task done for millennia by hand and far simpler tools such as flails, which almost invariably caused loss of seeds through simple hand-held violence.

But Fox and Flower and Martineau agreed with the locals in Kent who had opted to illegally destroy some of these new machines, those 'Luddites' who comprised a more or less radical and semi-organised group of workers, especially within the textile industry, that opposed technological innovations within their business generally. The Taylors, meanwhile, along with Roebuck and Graham, seemed to more clearly side with those who had invested in the machines to increase agricultural output, 'for a hungry empire,' as Roebuck put it, a bit emotionally for Mill's preference, though Britain of course kept growing and had to therefore keep importing, often including even basic foodstuffs. Mill almost referred to Malthus again at that point, then opted against it, fearing another faux pas about the deaths of the young and destitute.

Whatever the truth of the matter, Mill retained just enough utilitarian grounding to his habitual if logical thoughts to realise that there might be competing truths in the case of the Swing Riots, as with so many others, but he joined the crowd in slowly excusing himself and seeing about getting home. Naturally, he had utterly forgotten to try and reserve his prior driver, and considering the hour, it might prove trickier to hail someone. Still, as he retrieved his coat from the Taylor's butler, his host saw him out at the door.

'Like some of us, Mr Mill, I too hope to support the more radically-minded ideas and causes, despite my concerns about this year's earlier troubles in Kent.' And with that, John Taylor saluted John Mill, along with his other guests, and within the next hour or so, the party dwindled down, and the Taylor visitors slowly made their ways home, all of them thankful for the opportunity to speak freely and so enjoy themselves. And Mill simply wanted to know when he might encounter the likes of such fascinating female company again.

\* \* \*

*From the Diary of Helen Taylor, dated 1875:*
My readers must forgive me at the outset: whilst I have attempted to re-create scenes that pre-date my very existence on this Earth,

I sometimes find myself wishing I could have witnessed such. There was Mr Mill gawking at that portrait of Mother, then gazing over our old dining table—massive, that beastly thing was!—to then gawk anew at Mother in the flesh. Oh, it can still make me smile, though it reminds me of the later harsh caricatures of him in London papers, making him seem preening or judgemental.

Mother's life was lampooned too, of course—though one must never forget that their brilliance shone ever more brightly when in conjunction. One might lead others out of Plato's Cave of Ignorance with a torch, but Mother and Mr Mill offered a conflagration instead—easy to spot and follow yet frightening to the more hesitantly-minded who found the Cave reassuring. Useful and good ideas are ever threatening to many.

Oh, though I do get ahead of myself at times. In truth I began charting my own thoughts in this little notebook years ago, a gift purchased by Mother for, oh let us consider now... my twelfth birthday. And for years my Diary merely acted as a secure repository for whatever my thoughts and dreams and hopes might be. Such years were the warm-up to greater organisation, along with more focus on a systematic chronology that might have made Mr Carlyle himself proud, damn that arrogant, bigoted man.

That was me that night at the first meeting of John Mill and Harriet Hardy Taylor. Well, 'twas a tiny, mousy, embryonic me to be sure, the third Taylor child nurturing there in Mummy's belly, future female upstart to put the lives of my older brothers in disarray. 'Hope for a daughter,' as Father said wistfully that night. The lads were indeed upstairs making too much nervous noise, like they sensed the inter-loper who had just arrived at that fascinating dinner party on which I would have to make notes later, even many years hence interviewing Ms Martineau and Ms Flower and Pastor Fox and even Mr Mill's curious friends Mr Roebuck and Mr Graham for details according to their memories by then.

'Yes, Harriet initially hoped Mr Mill and Ms Flower would become an item,' quipped Ms Martineau later, in a rare show of interest in more mundane concerns of human relations. 'Well, Ms Taylor,' admitted Mr Roebuck with the gravitas of the Confessional, years after his friendship with Mill withered, 'John Mill was smitten with your mother right from the first. He kept trying to stare at that painting again when your poor parents were ushering us out!'

That was the gist: a lovely dinner which perhaps I heard in utero marked a meeting of sublime and penetrative minds that would scandalise polite society whilst yielding much of the finest moral and political thought witnessed by the nineteenth or indeed any century. Though Mr Mill and Mother would protest if they read my next observation: theirs was truly a great unethical relationship which enabled great progress in ethics.

PART TWO

# In Bentham's Shadow

*1831–1836.*

I n truth, it only took several weeks, with the opportunity fortuitously presenting itself on 28 January, a pleasant Friday, without
Mill having to even do anything to bring the chance about. He
took the same delight in finding a similar envelope awaiting him on
his return home from work just the day before, though it contained
more personal flourishes — 'We genuinely savoured your company
during the previous occasion, Mr Mill,' — so some Georgian formality remained, and Mill ignored that being English, both he and they
would never shed it completely, such forms of polite address being
bred into British citizens from the time they could first speak, — 'and
again request the pleasure of your presence —'

He liked that it was signed by both Taylor and his wife, Harriet.
Mill sighed like an errant schoolboy, even though he'd never been
such and thus could not quite empathise with their ilk. The note
also mentioned specifically the presence of Monsieur Desainteville,
whom Mill had never met previously, or at least he convinced himself
of that after another of his long-term memory-checks. Apparently

Pastor Fox would attend as well, though the invitation included no mention of the fetching Elizabeth Flower. Mill felt disappointment at first: Ms Flower—definitely Ms and not Mrs, as he'd discovered on his way out of the Taylor home that night, feeling his typical befuddlement over such practicalities as a ride home—had proven just as lovely and interesting company as had Mrs Taylor, and 'Lizzie' was single, even if Mill himself could hardly be described as searching for matrimonial matching.

He was thus further surprised when his gracious hosts, again all smiles as they had been upon his entrance at their prior get-together, suggested that he indeed should 'meet Ms Flower again socially,' and that they seemed to accept their roles as potential matchmakers. Fox would doubtless be crestfallen at this, as Mill remembered Fox and Flower shamelessly flirting with one another previously, though he felt himself a slight pang of jealousy, a sensation with which he had little experience. Yet Mill knew that Fox remained married, albeit unhappily. Perhaps that was the reason for the Taylors suggesting that Mill meet Ms Flower again, a scenario to which he could hardly feel himself averse. And yet his surprise at the suggestion seemed compounded the more he discovered he was experiencing difficulty keeping his gaze on the other guests and off Mrs Taylor. He further felt wholly unsure just what to do with such feelings. She was married and had children—now expecting their third—or so she cheerily announced near the start of dinner, accepting her husband's hand above the table in full view, a more tender gesture than she had seemed willing to express during Mill's previous visit.

The setting proved both more intimate and less formal, and Mill already felt more at ease without Fox or anyone else offering introductions. He made sure to arrive slightly early this time, feeling a touch wiser via simply soliciting his own conveyance, another carriage so like the last one they might have been the same, though he knew he had a different driver. He had even permitted himself to smile more as his ride led him once again through the City's endlessly labyrinthine streets. His fine memory could swear that it proved the same route as last time, and he admitted these drivers certainly knew their way!

The guests dug in this time with gusto, with less help from the servants—just a pair of them, Mill silently chiding himself for wondering how much staff the Taylors had, partly because of that ingrained English focus on class, and partly since some semi-detached sense of himself recognised that he could in fact fund a home now, with service staff, of almost this calibre, with careful planning. He just felt little need, and took pleasure in helping set aside some of his generous Company pay to his own immediate family members, not that they needed much assistance, especially with his father still working. Sometimes it seemed to Mill that 'the old man' might never retire.

'Please accept our apologies, Mr Mill,' Mrs Taylor added once they had settled at the table, their differing seating arrangement this time proffering Mill a view of the immaculate kitchen—it looked barely used, and he wondered how its regular denizens kept it seemingly spotless. 'But dear Lizzie let us know just yesterday she would be unable to attend. We hope you will find the rest of us suitable company.'

'Of course, Mrs Taylor, and please think nothing of it. I did enjoy meeting Ms Flower, and please forward my greetings the next time you meet your dear friend. She seems a lovely and amiable soul.' *Dear God*, thought Mill, *since when do I speak so?*

At least Fox seemed a bit brighter at that, and if Mill had more experience with social nuances he might have noticed their hostess glare at Fox, as though warning him off.

'Since our last get-together,' began Mr Taylor, 'I took the liberty of studying some of what everyone favours, including some of Ms Martineau's articles, as well as your own, Mr Mill. I even managed to find some of her translation work, as with Monsieur Comte. He makes for intriguing reading.' Taylor clearly relished not just being the centre of attention in his own home—justifiable, thought Mill, at least in most circumstances—but also the warmer appraisal he received from his wife whilst summarising.

'At any rate, Mr Mill, I was quite taken with Comte's notion of the pouvoir spirituel, and it made me think of your own work referring to the "spirit of the age," or perhaps the German "Zeitgeist." Am I close, at least?'

Mill was impressed. 'You certainly are, and that latter term comes from the monumentally indecipherable Herr Hegel, indeed a German writer.'

Fox finally showed some amusement at that. 'Now I don't feel so bad, Mill: I found Hegel tough slogging as well.'

The other smiled. 'He did show some fine ideas, though it indeed takes some "slogging" to reach the gist of what he's saying,' explained Mill. 'Some now take him as an expert in history, though he's a dense philosopher, even by the standards of philosophers.'

'Is that a double-entendre, Mr Mill?' asked Mrs Taylor.

'Ha. I see your point, and I don't mean that he personally was dense, and surely not stupid. A large part of what he has to say entails the conflict between new ideas and traditional beliefs and practices.'

'I was unsure if 'e reelly welcomed new ideas,' added Monsieur Desainteville, himself dressed more English than French, with little ostentation. A simple lace cream blouse buttoned up to the man's neck, covered by a leafy-green light jacket, contrasted with dark brown trousers and immaculately shined riding boots. Mill smiled inwardly, his Francophilia reminding of how Continental men adored their longer footwear, and he missed French accents as well.

'Well, he preferred if they came from himself.' Mill enjoyed the pause for the others to express their amusement, something he used only occasionally at work. His family typically found his attempts at humour less endearing. 'The new idea,' he continued, 'was labelled "thesis" by Hegel.'

'If I recall then,' quipped Fox, 'this was met by intellectual and social resistance, which he called "antithesis?"'

'Just so, Will. And such resistance might be political or religious in nature. But this fusion of ideas, this conflict, would somehow result in something of a still-new, slightly modified perspective, or even something of a compromise betwixt the two. Hegel called this a "synthesis.'"

'I think we could do with an example,' Taylor said. Desainteville nodded.

'I can offer one,' his wife said with alacrity. She waited just a moment so that she had their full attention. 'I've been doing a bit of research,' and Mill thought she might have looked guilty for just a moment, as though perhaps not disclosing the full extent of her 'research,' whatever it might entail, 'into the life and even a bit of the times of the old printer, William Caxton. What if the printing press, then still revolutionary and new, itself represented a thesis of sorts? Could an item count as one, not just an idea?'

'I should think so,' answered Mill. Mrs Taylor thanked him for that with a glance.

Fox jumped into the fray, since anything pertaining to religious history interested him automatically. 'And among Caxton's first works were Bibles, later translated and also printed instead of copied, into English and other vernacular languages.'

'Think of that resistance!' said Taylor. 'We all had to study the Reformation, and the amended version of it that began here in England.' He liked how he had learned something of that bit of Tudor history, priding himself on having excelled at grammar school, though he failed to understand his wife's sudden slight tensing. Girls going off for formal schooling, even at the lower levels, remained a novelty for most.

'So the seenthesis in Mrs Taylor's example was, what, then?' wondered Desainteville, with a solid understanding of the English language yet with an accent all his own. 'Releegious freedom? Deefferent interpretations of Christianity?' The man's emphasis on long vowels made Mill yearn again for France.

'I think either could qualify,' Fox said.

'I find myself wishing I knew more about how the Chinese confronted the same issue,' added Mill quietly, 'as with Buddhism and Confucianism.'

Mrs Taylor again: 'How do you mean, John, er, Mr Mill.' No one seemed to notice the slip in address. Hosts were expected to maintain more propriety than guests.

'An inventor in old China created a printing press using movable type, four centuries before it was invented in Europe. That's just one of those small titbits of information one gleans while working for an enterprise with deep interests in Asia.'

They all gawked at him in disbelief. 'Now that might be a thesis right there—that other societies can be and often have been just as creative and progressive as our own.'

'I speak no Chinese,' admitted Fox, 'but think of all the pictograph characters involved in that! It's difficult enough making metal type for European alphabets.'

'Regardless, I appreciate Mrs Taylor's interesting contribution to our discussion,' Mill said. 'And Mr Taylor, you mentioned "spirit" or "Zeitgeist?"' His host nodded.

'There is a term I have been tossing about lately, Mr Taylor,' Mill began. 'Well, in truth I should say we, and actually, William here may have heard it also.' Fox looked eager and at ease without Ms Flower to distract him. 'That idea of Hegel's actually bespeaks the far older tradition of Plato.'

'But I don't recall the Socratic dialogues showing conflict between ideas. Plato often starts with a character asking to clarify what some word means,' this from Fox, 'such as "courage" or "virtue."'

The others seemed to follow along raptly. Mill just lived for chats like this! He wanted to proceed at his own speed, though, not have so much forced so quickly, like his father had insisted. 'For your own good,' he could still sometimes hear his father say when Mill himself was a boy, inundated with Classical languages as though he might have a chance to go back in time to explore ancient Athens or Rome.

This less stressful current environment was much more welcoming, intellectually and emotionally. 'True, Will. And then that speaker would gradually, sometimes patronisingly, point out the mistakes that his fellow discussants offered on the subject, and then tell them what the word or idea "truly" meant after all.'

'So what of this "spirit," then, Mr Mill?' Mrs Taylor continued to watch him, her glance somehow curious and on guard all at once, like a school teacher awaiting the correct response from a recalcitrant student, hardly a description of Mill.

'The original term comes from a recent book about key figures from our own century. The character sketches of these persons read almost like the pilgrims in Chaucer's Tales, though these individuals are genuine, and likewise definitely not travelling together. Coleridge numbers among them, along with William Godwin,' Mill continued.

'The same who wed Mary Wollstonecraft?' interrupted Harriet, earning a reproving glare from her husband, thankfully short-lived. She had read the incomparable Wollstonecraft, who died not long after bearing a daughter who grew up to pen that astonishing critique of industrial 'progress:' 'Frankenstein, or the Modern Prometheus.' The mother had been even more radical, critiquing some key events of the first French Revolution — after having even witnessed some of them! — and writing earnestly and logically of the simple necessity of educating girls and women. Harriet Taylor could recite sections of both women's works by rote.

'Yes, the same, Mrs Taylor,' confirmed Mill. 'And Sir Walter Scott, Lord Byron, Wordsworth, those three all exceptional writers, plus Malthus. Most of them are still with us, so to speak, and in many cases continuing to write.' Mill said it almost proudly. 'Even my god-father, Mr Bentham, appears on that curious list.'

'All men,' noted Harriet, almost to herself.

'And all British, I think, or at least European,' added Fox, also quietly.

'Well, that is true,' Mill admitted hesitantly, 'though that hardly undermines their achievements. And to address Mr Taylor's question most directly, the likes of Hegel tend to describe the "spirit" of our times as one of change, more than anything else.'

'Change?' wondered Taylor himself.

'"Mankind 'ave outgrown old eenstitutions and old doctrines,'" intoned Desainteville from memory, '"and 'ave not yet acquired new ones."' He pronounced the last 'wohnes.'

'Since our times are pregnant with change,' Mill finished, clearly pleased that one of the guests had not just read his piece but recalled some of it flawlessly. And Harriet found herself warming to the word choice, since few things in the world could force change like the arrival of new life, something with which she had some familiarity.

'Yet we 'ave still not 'eard this term that you, and others apparently, 'ave used or concocted for this, Mill,' added Desainteville, sipping his excellent tea and making Mill's name sound like 'Meal.' Mill noted that he drank it straight and hot as possible, no milk or lemon or sugar like the English used in varying combinations.

'Oh. Yes, of course. Do forgive me, I sometimes get side-tracked by segues into history or philosophy. The term was actually "clerisy," although now I confess I cannot quite recall who coined it first. That's embarrassing.'

'An interesting term, Mr Mill,' said Taylor now. 'It almost sounds like "clerical."'

Mill grinned openly. 'I grant that it does somewhat, Mr Taylor. But all it refers to is something of a social and intellectual elite, ideally the most able persons making the most important decisions for a society.'

'It was Coleridge, Mr Mill,' added Harriet. Again that slightly cool, knowing expression on her face: if Mill did not know better, he might be starting to like it. 'As with that list of the members of the Spirit of the Age.'

How could I forget something so obvious? wondered Mill now. That was hardly like him, to be so distractible. And the embarrassment briefly continued, as Fox reminded the group, 'It sounds like Plato's old notion of the philosopher-kings.'

'Or queens perhaps, Pastor,' chimed Harriet.

Mill found an opening. 'You know, Mrs Taylor, in that ancient text, the 'Republic,' Plato specifically says that women may indeed serve in the artisan-merchant class, as well as in the class above them, which is essentially of a military nature, and even among the rulers, though he never describes them as philosopher-queens exactly.'

'Yet the possibility must remain?' she asked, smiling.

'Well, yes, I should think so. I honestly cannot think of any reason why an ably-trained and educated woman should not come to a position of responsibility, even of power.' The two of them openly stared at each other for just a moment. For Harriet it was like reliving the excitement of her idealistic girlhood, when she used to fantasise and role-play with her siblings about queens and female warriors, never mind how her brothers—her now dead brothers, she chided herself, never quite comfortable standing up for herself, even silently—poked plenty of fun at her and her sisters over such themes. The boys were too busy fighting mock battles with wooden swords and toy pistols.

Mill meanwhile made himself break contact, just catching a lingering expression from Mrs Taylor's husband as he did so.

Fox came to the rescue, bless him. 'So, John, how else might we interpret this whole Spirit of the Age idea, then? I hardly think the masses will warm much to Plato, much as they failed to do so more than two millennia past, and in a much more mythic setting than our own hopefully more rational society.' Mill liked that summary, and knew his friend George Grote would, too, being something of a historian focused on the classical Greeks.

'Though the Athenians knew somet'ing of managing an empire,' said Desainteville, 'and they also had to deal with multicultural trade, eenfluence, ethneec tensions.'

Again Mill looked at Taylor, partly since neither quite knew for sure which 'John' Pastor Fox had addressed. But since Mill was the author of the 'Spirit' article, he eagerly took the lead. It was like his response to Ms Martineau weeks earlier: simple joy and pride in discussing his work with someone who admired it, or at least had read it. Mill was already used to the simple truth of the universe that not many folks tended to read, perhaps much less understand, the workings of philosophical minds, but he believed that could be changed.

He thought that his most radical idea. 'To summarise, perhaps, it often feels like each period of history exhibits its own overall feeling, its "spirit," if you will.'

Taylor found that intriguing. 'Do you mean in a religious sense, then?'

Mill understood the reticence. 'Oh, no, not at all, though there have certainly been periods when religion could be said to have defined that feeling, such as with our own European Reformation, or the Muslims splitting into Sunni and Shi'a centuries ago. The Jews and Buddhists and Hindus all have their divisions as well, though I'm neither an expert on any of them, nor a theologian in any sense.'

Desainteville added, in his thick accent that still made Mill long for parts of his childhood near Montpellier, current revolutionary French politics or not. 'So what might the spirit of our own age be, in zat case? Could it be somet'ing more overtly political, as weeth all zose peoples in zee West going on about "freedom" and "liberty?"'

Mill took time to ponder this, looking to his hosts, as well as to Fox, for further enticement. 'I think such ideals provide part of the picture, Monsieur Desainteville, as with this past century or so with our notions of "Enlightenment" thinking, though they can often fall short, too, with so many remaining enslaved.'

He failed to notice his hostess, the only woman present in the room that night other than occasional visits by Penny to continue with the light dinner service, focus her eyes and stare right into him, as if he had just offered some gem of an insight, though the situation of so many around the world was glaringly obvious—few chose to comment on the hypocrisy of failed ideals. 'One supposes zat likewise applies to "political dissidents" closer to home, oui, Monsieur Mill?' Desainteville added.

That no doubt came with the expectation of a further response about France's latest revolution, thankfully far less bloody though no less idealistic than its first, almost four decades past now. 'Sure it must, sir. What troubles me is that there has never been such a thing as a true political revolution, by which I mean a fundamental reassessment of a society by that same society, without a drastic civil war.'

They all paused at that, several of them taking sips of the once again excellent wine. Then, 'What of the Americans?' This from Mrs Taylor, Mill enjoying her forthrightness, though her husband frowned, out of view of her since she leaned forward while asking.

'A true revolution,' Desainteville answered. Many French yet admired Americans.

'And a struggle for independence from another power,' added Mill, as though ignoring that he was well paid to work for an organisation that inadvertently played a notable role in the decisions of people he had never met to strive for that same independence. He knew it—he just remained unsure how to respond to it.

'What then is the difference, gentlemen?' Harriet prodded.

The two other speakers looked at each other, though whether to silently request mutual assistance or to offer each other the opportunity to explain something that most political thinkers thought was rather ambiguous, the young woman did not know.

Desainteville began. 'I think zee objectives an' ideals must begin deefferently—freedom from somet'ing, from a foreign power in zis case, would give "zee people" a common adversary, while a domestic revolution might more directly deevide zee citizenry amongst themselves.'

'Yet that "common adversary" might not be so common, yes?' interjected Taylor, adding, 'As with the Americans, many remained loyal to the Crown, while still others simply wished to get on with their lives, with neither the Monarchy nor the rebel leaders telling them how to live.'

The others nodded. Mill was intrigued by the man's perspective, admittedly having previously felt the bias that an apothecary would not likely take much interest in a dialogue such as this. 'So why then would both get bogged down in the horrors of a civil war?' he asked everyone, though he believed he knew the answer.

He paused for thought, then said, 'Because inevitably the shifting of ideals, of beliefs, does not come easily. Not ever.'

'Indeed. Per'aps zee Americans 'ave been zee lucky exception thus far, though they 'ave clashed weet' themselves over slavery an' other issues, albeit thankfully via nothing more zan minor insurrections or protestations, to my knowledge, about issues of obligation an' especially taxation. Wit' zee Yankees, it always seems about taxation,' Desainteville noted. 'Or, as you've observed, Mill, wit' slavery. Thank God we Europeans 'ave rid themselves of that!'

Fox knew that those same European powers were slowly exploring Africa more deeply than they had during slaving years, the horrendous trade in which had occurred exclusively closer to the coasts, and was about to wonder aloud what that might mean for a new form of exploitation, though his thought was pre-empted by their host. 'But something is coming for them,' said Taylor. 'The Americans, I mean. They formerly had different legislatures, even different currencies, and while there might be a "united" states now, nothing seems to determine a nation's path more than economic considerations. They have countless slaves doing the hard work for them, and a tremendous landscape filled with wild animals and savages, and we had to fight another war with them recently, in part because they took their conflicted idealism and acted as though they could force it back on us!'

Mrs Taylor looked somewhere between embarrassed and proud at her husband's outburst, and in truth Mr Taylor could come across as uptight even by Georgian standards. Regardless, he had a point: the 'colonists' could call themselves 'united' all they wished, and the Taylors and their guests and friends elsewhere could proudly call themselves the citizens of a 'united kingdom,' albeit one composed of several separate nations just within the British Islands, to say nothing of its imperial holdings on five other continents. Yet did that make them 'united?' What of diversity of thoughts and ideals and languages? Such were the issues with which John Mill found himself mentally grappling. A lively conversation like this could only help, even if so many, including his own immediate family members, often shied away from such rousing chats. Though if people gathered at a neutral site like a dinner table could not mutually talk about their interests and the rules—implied as well as codified—that shaped their behaviours, then when else could such be discussed? Most could not afford to attend university to broaden themselves, and many lacked the interest anyway.

'An eenteresting point, Monsieur Taylor,' conceded Desainteville. 'An' I make no claim to understand zee American mind, I should say. Their conflicts aside, whether revolutionary or more representative of freedom from more direct control by zis great nation, they seem to 'ave unwittingly begun a tremendous and ongoing experiment in, what we shall we call it, eh?—human abeelity and potential?'

Mill found himself warming to this even more. It was so much more rewarding than the often dull and trite monologues encountered at work, and he wished more from the Athenaeum could be here. Roebuck and Graham would be in their element!

'At least we live in a time and place when we can freely discuss all of this,' said Mrs Taylor, who had been listening attentively and carefully.

'So true, Mrs Taylor,' Mill replied. 'We are not so long historically removed from periods when discussing the best for a society, for any society, would be fraught with risk.'

She offered a warm smile as a response. 'Do you recall, Mr Fox and Mr Mill, how the last time we met, Ms Martineau seemed to inspire you with some of her written work?'

Fox answered first. 'Of course, Harriet.' Mill felt the slightest pang of envy at his liberty with Mrs Taylor's Christian name, though of course he had wed the young woman to her husband. 'She continues to be a prolific and insightful newspaperwoman.'

'That's quite a term, William,' said Taylor. 'As the Germans do, when you need to create a new expression, often the best way is to combine existing words.'

His wife did not respond to that, explaining instead, if a bit slowly and even sheepishly, 'Gentlemen, I myself am in the process of working on something printable about that old printer and publisher, Caxton, to whom I alluded a moment ago, and,' she paused both for nerves and for dramatic effect, 'my own first printed work will be appearing shortly, and I wished to know what you all think.'

There, it is out now, she thought, deliberately not looking at her husband, whose approval in this regard in fact remained a mystery to her. She was delighted when Mr Mill opted to keep the conversation moving. 'Do you know Caxton loved old legends, printing them first?' he asked playfully.

'Oh, yes. You know, most readers interested in history think that his first foray was with Malory and the 'Morte D'Arthur,' but it was actually—what's so funny, Mr Mill?'

'Hmm? Oh, nothing. I was just fondly remembering the Histories of Troy, which I believe you were about to mention.'

'Indeed. But have you ever seen originals of either of those grand pieces? I hope to do so, and will have to get to the British Museum, or wherever such might be kept. We could truly benefit from a national library, too, don't you think?' She knew she was growing anxious, and became chattier when nervous about what others might think or otherwise respond to her. It would be so much easier were she a man!

Mill looked at Taylor, noticing what seemed perhaps a mix of disgust and regret etched onto his usually handsome face. Not wanting to overstep the bounds of propriety, much less get drawn into whatever tension might exist in this marriage, Mill answered simply, 'A fine question, Madam. I fear I do not recall where such priceless masterworks might lie, at least in our homeland, and have only read inexpensive copies one might find at any neighbourhood bookseller, though I agree with your sentiment about the library.'

Fox, too, detected the tension, and tried to defuse it by reengaging Desainteville in some casual pleasantries about his own travel plans, whilst trying to make light of Mill's latest Continental journey. Fox knew his younger friend Mill had devoted considerable parts of his childhood there, though he confessed he knew few details.

Politely wondering if he should relate the odd tale of his friend Sterling and their risky trek to the Continent, Mill said, 'I must thank you again, Mr and Mrs Taylor, for your gracious and warm hospitality.'

His honesty kept him going. 'I must confess, I may have felt some slight hesitation at accepting your initial invitation, having recently become both busy and perhaps a bit spoiled by participating in what the French still call their salons—'he glanced to Desainteville—'I must tell you about Mrs Grote and Mrs Austin some time.'

He truly did not comprehend the mild rudeness of his comment, though his hosts ignored it. 'We shall no doubt look forward to that, Mr Mill,' Harriet said simply. Mill nodded to her, thankful for the encouragement, and while he did so, could again hardly fail to notice his host's vaguely uncomfortable return gaze, aimed at him instead of at his wife. Mill flushed slightly, and he could tell Taylor did too, and Mill tried his best to sneak a subtle appraising look at his host again, who now stared simply at his picked-over dessert plate, as though he had become simply fatigued or perhaps resigned somehow.

Mill recalled this ambiguous sense of tension between his hosts from his first visit, and while they remained seated next to each other, he thought he could perceive a different kind of distance, something unspoken and strained. Perhaps it had been easier to hide then with a greater number and diversity of guests, though Mill also remembered how relieved Mrs Taylor had seemed while excusing herself to check on the children. Knowing vaguely how couples could become emotionally distant, such a sensation was something Mill had no true experience of, not directly. He still wondered what all the fuss was about 'being in' or even 'falling in' love: to him it seemed more like an affliction than something worthy of celebration, like the medieval writers described. Perhaps Bentham's hedonistic maths had been onto something after all.

Mill sensed a subtle shifting in the atmosphere around the dining table, which itself seemed a touch smaller now, what with attention focused on him as it had been once before, not so many weeks ago. And it had taken him those weeks to forgive himself for his clear faux pas regarding children and the fates which befell some of them, too many of them, as he could attest. So he again found himself walking an emotional tightrope, this time between not wanting to make some insensitive comment—he never did feel quite sure just what a woman might find upsetting, and his own father and Bentham had certainly offered no emotional maps in that regard!—and not wanting to come across as boorish. He cautiously met the eyes of the others, and began, 'Do you recall our odd little trio, the "Trijackia?"' The Taylors smiled, hopefully having enjoyed the never-dull company of his friends, while Desainteville lightly shook his head. 'They know this equally quirky friend of mine, Mr John Sterling, who himself concocted the mad idea of somehow making our way to Spain to assist General Torrijos in his attempt to overthrow King Ferdinand VII.'

Gasps all around, with Desainteville continuing his mild head-shaking, though this time with the faintest of amused expressions betraying itself, just at the corners of his mouth; his eyes gave away nothing. Mill knew little of how the man might feel about what had clearly been an imbecilic plan, political sentiments notwithstanding. He did not yet even know the man's religious proclivities: le République remained at least officially Catholic, as of course did Spain, maybe not so dissimilar from the tensions of so many years earlier, when Henry VIII and Charles V and François I had all vied for dominance of the whole European theatre. Then England was the upstart, recognising it needed a true navy as well as more of a presence in the Americas to make a real go of it. Henry met the first challenge, and his daughter had begun to meet the second, yet even now the major Western powers continued to vie for influence—in America, in Africa, in Asia—and many of imperial Spain's former grandeur, represented in its holdings in the other Hemisphere, had been lost during Ferdinand's bungled reign. History always showed itself to the present and continued to shape it, no matter the denials of many.

Mill knew he must continue, and spoke slowly, with no sense of drama—stupidity offered its own flair for the dramatic in the retelling. He confessed to admiring General Torrijos: a proclaimed political Liberal yet also a soldier, a rare blend. The haphazardly planned coup d'état had ended ignominiously, the General and his men remaining still in a Spanish prison.

'Sterling borrowed a boat owned by his cousin, to take some would-be rebels from Cambridge, including Alfred Tennyson—have you read him? His new "Poems, Mostly Lyrical" is outstanding—well, Sterling and the others eventually thought better of the whole scheme and shortly returned to the safety of home, although he met a lovely lady during this bout of madness.' Mill knew he was starting to babble, yet felt unable to pause. Still, as he glanced around the huge table anew, he could verify continued interest. Mr Taylor chuckled quietly, Mrs Taylor was looking at him with newfound admiration, and the other men, who had not heard the story, simply looked across the table at one another as if to wonder silently about the whole hare-brained scheme.

'Whatever one might say about Sterling, he is a good friend,' Mill added, 'though he remained so infatuated with that lady during the rest of last summer that he missed the Trijackia's more rational sojourn across the Channel to France. We got to see Paris after the Révolution de Juillet deposed King Charles X.' Thank goodness I have been living on my own for a spell, also: my mother and siblings would have no doubt question my very reason had I returned to the family home after all that curious galivanting.

'So once again, French politics remain in flux, Mr Mill?' queried Harriet, stealing a look at Desainteville, who just nodded.

He was pleased to be questioned directly. 'So it seems, Mrs Taylor. We even had the opportunity to meet with the famed Marquis de Lafayette who gave such priceless assistance to the Americans.' Now he was showing off, dropping names like that, though he silently confessed to a certain glee through the raised eyebrows and satisfied countenances of the others. Penny the serving-girl almost spilled a spot of after-dinner tea on Mill at that point, which he hardly noticed, nor would he have possessed the foresight to speak to the young woman to find out that she had relatives living in Massachusetts, ancestors who had attempted to remain Loyalists during the colonial War of Independence, narrowly escaping charges of treason.

'Do you remain concerned zat "zee opinions of masses of merely average men are everywhere becoming zee dominant power," Monsieur Mill?' Desainteville quoted another passage from Mill's recent article. He appreciated the attention to detail, but did not want to get drawn any further into international politics. Plus, he was growing tired.

'Yes,' he answered, simply and finally. 'I realise that sounds elitist, but that is the intended purpose behind the idea of "clerisy": to help ensure that the most able persons fulfil the most appropriate occupations, most importantly leadership of the state.'

'But if I understand correctly, Mr Mill,' said Harriet, 'a person must also possess the freedom, the liberty, to do so. Is that not the purpose of the state itself, ultimately?'

He had to admit he had not quite taken that step yet, though it seemed obvious now with her input. 'It seems it must be so, Mrs Taylor.'

While he and the other guests made ready to depart, Mill puzzled about how while old authors could illustrate love and its accompanying irrational passion, he remembered two details: first, that if love was a form of illness, even madness, it was worth the effort, even if its pursuit might lead to war—as in Homer; or self-destruction or madness—like with Shakespeare; or a social trap—found in Chaucer. And second, many of those producers of what the world regarded as the finest of literary pieces proved to be outrageously sexist and belittling to women. Such were his thoughts a short time later when he found himself sharing some nonsense about the weather prognosis with Desainteville, the pair of them being helped to their travelling coats by the butler—whose name was Jonathan, Mill remembered now—and he was taken aback to suddenly find his hostess near the doorway, without her husband at her side, beckoning him a few steps away for some private word.

Mrs Taylor glanced momentarily behind her, with a clear yet quickly dissipated expression of childlike guilt, and simply said to her guest, 'It would please me if you would call on me again soon, Mr Mill.' The wording was wholly proper, her decorum socially acceptable so far as the occasionally socially befuddled John Stuart Mill could decipher, and yet there remained just the hint of something sneaky, almost illicit, in the way she said it. Nonetheless, the young man looked forward to meeting with this bright and energetic young woman again, even with the expression in her rich dark eyes that almost matched that of her husband, as though crying out for help without really knowing how to do so.

* * *

*From the Diary of Helen Taylor:*
Such was how it began, almost innocuously, with all the decorum and propriety of proffered greetings of Ms Austen's sometimes strong yet socially-constrained female characters — semi-independent thinkers yet relying on the attentions — and salaries — of stronger men. Mother would have hated it. Say what you feel you must, the most rational act of my mother's life was reaching out for Mr John Mill of Pentonville. Not to rescue her — sometimes Mr Mill needed his own type of rescuing! — but to find an intellectual and moral equal who could share thoughts and ideas and morph them into something potent.

Are you surprised, Reader? It surprises me too, the thought of writing to an anonymous readership for posterity, though I pen entries to further elucidate these two souls that so moved my mind as well as each other's. I'm aware of the strangeness, and you shall have to judge these oddly matched lovers as you see fit, along with me, for having yet to even mention my dear Father in this context. Brave, sorrowful man... I do so miss him, along with Mother and Mill.

Whatever moralising one opts for vis-à-vis the blatantly immoral relationship of one Harriet Taylor née Hardy and one John Stuart Mill — there appears that pesky paradox again — they recognised from the outset that they would have to be socially careful and philosophically creative. Never mistake them for a Guenever and Launcelot — too much idealised medieval fine amour, that literary trend which may have elevated women out of the kitchen and nursery but which trapped them instead as cult-objects. See Harriet and John rather for the likes of medieval Peter Abélard and the younger but often more mature

Héloïse d'Argenteuil: sharers of grand ideas from a grand love.

Well, no—of course dear Mill was never castrated by Mum's family for what she built emotionally with him, though the frantic English press would come to castigate them both. We harshly judge relationships that do not fit preconceived moulds, and as the lovely 12th-century lady noted, 'sed plerisque tacitis quibis amorem coniugio libertatem vinculo praeferebam.' She preferred love to wedlock, freedom to chains. Of course Mr Mill knew that quote—how could he not? Yet he conversed with Mum often in French, never in Latin. He would neither condescend nor patronise. Indeed, that was the whole point of their collaborative works.

Besides—Merciful God!—I certainly would never have described Mum as a new Héloïse in her hearing. That brazenly smart, capable woman retiring after the death of Peter to become a nun, even an abbess? Perish the thought!

(A separate leaf of paper appears in Ms Taylor's diary at this juncture in her writing, dated many years later and apparently placed between reminiscences of earlier times. It was composed sometime after the deaths of her parents and Mr Mill. The two following paragraphs comprise its totality.—ed.)

And now here I am again in the Hôtel d'Europe, listening to the elegant tones of the local language carrying softly along the breeze, silently confessing that my ability in that Gallic tongue has waned over the years. Perhaps I simply never wished to pursue it as Mother and Mr Mill did, especially gracious Mr Mill. His Francophilia could at times seem excessive, whereas I feel oft caught between two cultures with an extensive history of mutual antipathy. I surely do not dislike persons and things French but have felt less frustration with my Anglo-ancestry, for all its starts and stops and pains… and its attitude to my own faith. Perhaps Mother and Mr Mill would disapprove of my praying today—in Latin—over their graves.

No, that is not fair to either of them. They in fact would have approved, partly for my adherence to my own individuality, and partly since praying at tombs whilst moving one's lips might seem eccentric to those from my Homeland across the Channel behind me.

\* \* \*

Winter was slow to recede, and John Mill and his colleagues at the Company eagerly anticipated the 'rambling season.' Yet this odd woman, Harriet Taylor, Mrs Taylor, invaded Mill's thoughts in a manner unfamiliar to him. He had never ventured out to 'sow his wild oats' or some other banality which clearly demeaned what might otherwise prove a worthy relation of two souls. And he had to admit that a curious attraction had formed in his mind, though he continued to admonish himself that it must be one-sided: a family woman, who clearly adored her children—and, he made himself remember, had been pregnant again the last time he saw her—would surely not be interested in some intellectual gadabout, who yes, was gainfully and securely employed, and yes, he had to admit, did have some interesting titbits to his background, which comprised a most unusual breadth of education.

That was it, he realised at work one day, finishing his paper forms early as usual, savouring some tea shortly before departing, and staring out the third storey windows of the Company building. Harriet Taylor was intelligent and interesting. Lovely, yes, of course: Mill thought her a rare vision. Yet while he had half come to love—'fallen,' as the poets described, and as he asked himself anew now—her painting, that first image of her, he was beginning to recognise an attraction to women capable of meeting him in level conversation. He had warmed immediately to that other Harriet, Ms Martineau, and recognised something of a kindred spirit, since Mill too wanted to keep addressing the newspapers in order to get some of his views across. Ms Flower was also intriguing company, but something felt off there, like a reticence to engage with Mill philosophically.

He turned from the window, looking back at his desk, then through the window of his office door to the hallway down which his father continued to toil. His dear father, raving political and economic philosopher at large, and his godfather, the irrepressible and sometimes half-mad creator of philosophical utilitarianism, between them never seemed to realise a fundamental truth of advanced thought since the times of the ancient thinkers…

Talking 'down' to others just made them resentful. If you wanted to elicit genuine change, you had to present your grandiose ideas and truths into lingo the masses found acceptable. Elitism would kill the whole project, something of which Mill had remained vaguely aware during each of his newsprint submissions.; yet some of them could speak to the masses as well as create radical ideas.

So a key question of Mill's life remained: how to elicit social change — he had so many good ideas: some left over from utilitarianism; some of his own; some, he had to admit, developing in response to others — without having to endure a childhood of pure study like he had, and for which so few had the time and resources to similarly pursue, even if they had the interest. And the other main issue for his life likewise remained just as pressing and interesting: what to do about Harriet Taylor?

That fine lady was beginning to 'show' the next time Mill stood in her presence — and at an unchaperoned dinner — unless one counted the minimal serving staff, just Jonathan and Penny again — at the Taylor residence. Mr Taylor had opted to devote the evening at his club — Mill asked his hostess which one, and she told him it had more to do with high society and sipping brandy, smoking cigars, and losing money back and forth over cards: nothing, as she put it, like Mill's Athenaeum nor his looser 'Trijackia.' Mill laughed at the latter, reminding Harriet that both were quirky friends meeting for fun and intelligent conversation.

'Yet that is what goes missing from my life the most, Mr Mill,' she told him simply.

'What — fun and intelligent conversation?'

'Yes!' she answered brusquely, actually looking around her as though anyone else might be listening. She had planned this evening carefully, encouraging Mr Taylor to go trotting off to his club, which of course did not admit women anyway, so she hardly had to feel guilty for not accompanying him.

'What would you like to discuss, then?'

And she opened up to him, as they took to strolling about the Christopher Street environs, leaving the still quite young children at home. Harriet knew from her father's occupation that despite what many currently believed, regular exercise was in fact a top priority for pregnant women almost right up until labour pangs began. And this honest talking felt so easy, even natural somehow. It felt as if Mr Mill could almost read her thoughts, or at least her feelings, something her husband, in fairness, had once known how to do. But she could still not get past that perpetual and unforgiving sense of betrayal, and besides, time spent with Mr John Stuart Mill could hardly qualify as indecent or indecorous or whichever jaded and judging term might be used by anyone from her own family to the rest of English polite society, that same society which took so long to rid itself of slavery, and which denigrated women and children and made so many, including those two groups, labour incessantly to perpetuate the grand Empire, and—

Harriet forced herself calm, a gesture noticed though blissfully unremarked upon by her social partner. She resumed walking, and talking about her review of a recent book on Australia, and how her brother fancied a visit to that strange land with its endlessly curious wildlife and indigenous people—and about the love she felt for her little ones, which Mill commented on with undisguised admiration, as though he hoped for children of his own, though she learned in turn he had never come close to marrying.

*There I go again, even with something so simple,* she chided herself, as they crossed through charming little Russell Square, just near the British Museum, and not too far a walk west of the Taylor home. At least, Mill thought it not a long urban trek, not realising that his social partner would have agreed if not for needing to look 'decent' whilst outside with a man to whom she was not related. This decency included two skirts, a petticoat, and a thankfully comparatively loose-fitting corset, which did not quite hide her seven-month status. Harriet was, when not 'in a family way,' thin and petite enough to not feel wholly encaged by the last item, though she knew some women found them horrid, and smiled ironically whenever she recalled that some men wore them, too, and for even more ostentatious and vain reasons: corsets were certainly 'slimming' if restrictive, though the whalebone needed for their precise manufacture was becoming more difficult to obtain.

Like Mill, Mrs Taylor could distract herself mentally, sometimes comically easily. The point was that Mr Mill did not need to wed, necessarily, in order to have children. He could adopt, or, well, she blushed slightly at the thought of the obvious, and silently chided herself a second time for fretting over perfectly natural thoughts of the most basic sexuality.

Thoughts of human sexual practices, licit and otherwise, motivated Harriet to progress with the conversation. 'Tell me more about how you define happiness, Mr Mill,' she said abruptly, as the grand Museum came into view. 'If I understand correctly, you have had something of an intellectual falling out with the utility preached by your father.'

To her satisfaction, he laughed again. 'Preached is surely the correct term in this case, Mrs Taylor,' he answered. 'Made all the more ironic in someone who may well be,' and he glanced around, since it was a busy day on the streets of London, even for a Thursday, 'an atheist,' he finished quietly, pretending to look guilty.

Yet he misread the reason for her sudden stop. 'Forgive me, Mrs Taylor. I did not mean to make light of such a delicate subject.' *What in Blazes made me say that!*

'No, no, Mr Mill. That is not the reason at all, and I in fact appreciate your candour with that same "delicate subject," since so few are willing to even broach the topic of their innermost beliefs. It's just that,' and she took some moments to arrange the words, 'let us simply say that I have known other persons who feel likewise. Perhaps I shall gain the opportunity to meet your father and speak with him about it.' *Since when am I become so forward?* she warned herself. It must be anxiety over responding to his queer discourse.

They again resumed walking. 'Perhaps you will,' he said simply, either ignoring her concern or allowing it to pass without further comment. Whichever the case, she found she appreciated it. 'As to your question, however, I have begun to find utility a bit,' and he too fumbled for the correct phrasing, 'wanting. As a philosophical system, it remains simplistic, especially once one adds ethics into the equation.'

She felt ready. 'I'm not sure I understand how. After all, if I comprehend the gist of the matter, utilitarianism, as formulated by your friend Mr Bentham, is at its core a type of teleology, since it assesses the reason or the purpose of anything under discussion.'

'True, and the word itself refers to "usefulness." So what use, then, exists for ethics, or for that matter religion, or science, or the ducks in that pond, or a grand city like this?'

How easy and relaxing it was to chat with this man! Harriet marvelled at it, forgetting for now the far more serious conversation she would have to hold later with her husband, who, attending his club or no, would nonetheless wonder how she spent her days. In the meantime, she was beginning to ponder how her children might accompany her and her new friend as they innocently grappled with subjects many thought too challenging.

'I cannot account for the ducks,' she said playfully, 'since they are another animal creature like ourselves with a mysterious origin, and I shan't even speculate as to the purpose of either group of us.'

'Well stated,' he offered.

'But this city began as a Roman fort, a place for settlement, trade, security, and has grown over many centuries into a mighty world capital. It's almost like it decides its own purpose, regardless of what Parliament and the Monarchy and the rest of us might say.'

He liked that. 'Again, that is well reasoned. So if I may, what then happens if we consider purposes of things when applied to behaviours?'

'So now we delve into ethics?' It felt somehow appropriate that no one else seemed to be taking an interest in their talk.

He nodded, then noticed she couldn't see him do so. They had just crossed Montague Street from the Square, and the astonishing Museum, with the Rosetta Stone and Roman artefacts and all manner of priceless old treasures from every continent lying within, came into view, itself a marvel of modern architecture. It was obvious to anyone looking at it what the teleology of this edifice was: to both offer a permanent home for so many items of historical and cultural merit—even if some had been 'borrowed,' a friendlier term than 'looted' or 'stolen'—and to remain a grandiose symbol of the might of the surrounding culture, the British Empire, with a vested interest in many parts of those same continents.

'Is that a "yes," Mr Mill?'

He stopped and looked at her. 'Indeed, Mrs Taylor. Now, please consider, if you will. I am convinced everyone loves ethics, as convinced as I am that everyone loves history,' and he gestured towards the whole museum campus, now that they stood outside its open gates. 'It's just that many, too many, are poorly taught or not taught at all in either subject.'

'Agreed. Even our own society needs to further address this surprisingly contentious topic of mandatory education. I hope Commons and Lords alike can reach a suitable agreement on that.'

'I concur. So whether the subject is compulsory schooling, or to steal something from this museum just because it's pretty and might look good in one's drawing room, or to wed and have children, all decisions have moral components. That is to say, regardless of the decisions made, they express moral sentiment and are therefore value judgements.'

She nodded, enjoying the talk, even though several individuals had either paused briefly to listen to this strange man—apparently without his even noticing them in return—or hurried their strides just to get past him, since he might really be strange and therefore risky. And no man should be strolling about with his visibly pregnant wife. At least such would have been the assumptions made by anyone taking a sufficiently close glance at Harriet, but some seemed too taken aback by Mill himself to notice her, or wonder whether they were married at all.

'Well then, while we can perhaps save the rightness or wrongness for another day,' and they each smiled slightly at each other, both clearly hoping for other such days, 'this theory of utility espoused by my sometimes half-mad godfather would say that what matters is the resulting happiness of such decisions: who benefits, and by how much, and do the benefits outweigh the potential drawbacks, and any other details that seem relevant.'

'It sounds like democratic politics, to some degree. It seems almost egalitarian.'

He thought about that. 'So it can be. Yet how often do we actually make lists of the pluses and minuses of our decisions, all the while attempting to take into consideration not just our own values and desires but those of others, indeed of anyone at all who might be affected by our decisions, especially since we cannot know for certain in advance what those possible benefits or disadvantages will even be?'

'Well, surely we cannot consider every possible variable, but does it not remain a useful guideline generally? And again, this surely seems a more beneficent method of making decisions that in fact do affect many, as with my comment about politics, compared to selections made by tyrants or dictators.' Harriet recognised the social chance she was taking now—'Was that not Mrs Taylor I saw discussing God-knows-what with some strange eccentric man, and in public no less?'—yet she found herself warming to these discussions that she knew she would never have with her husband. John Taylor was very bright, an excellent apothecary, a devout member of the Unitarian Church, yet when it came to intellectual pursuits other than those affiliated with potential profit, dull or at least disinterested. *How could anyone find our topic today drab?* she wondered.

And yet Mill had a ready answer. 'Because majority rule is not what it is often purported to be. And because the "public weal" or "the will of the people," while indeed democratic-sounding, is actually a potentially extremely dangerous commodity.'

She thought about this while they strolled slowly up to the Museum's grand entryway, spotting a wide range of the Empire's inhabitants doing likewise: the clearly well-to-do, as well as some whose clothing was mismatched or in need of some patching, and a number clearly from lands beyond Europe—those of African, Indian, and Chinese ancestry—Harriet had only seen illustrations of so many of the world's peoples, yet at least felt some reassurance in her ability to identify certain types, unaware that such categorising formed the loose basis of racism. And she mentally returned to Mr Mill's fascinating and confusing comment: how could the will of the masses prove hazardous?

'What, then, should the basis of rules, indeed of government, be?' she queried.

'Oh, please do not misunderstand me. We are, after all, just a few decades removed from a time when Europe's powerful leaders—Frederick of Prussia—not so deserving of his moniker "the Great," if you ask me—' Harriet giggled at this—'along with Catherine of Russia, Joseph II and Maria Theresa of Austria, perhaps even the more recent self-styled Emperor Napoleon I of France—they all argued for something they called "enlightened absolutism," though Frederick labelled it "benevolent despotism." Some years ago I wrote a piece about Parliamentary reform and asked, "Have a hundred despots ever been found to be less evil than one?"'

Most men would have glowed with pride at such a creative insight, Harriet thought, but this man stated it with what sounded like an odd mix of humility laced with conviction.

'The old "Divine Right of Monarchs," transformed from medieval to modern via two Houses yet with a remnant royal house,' Harriet answered, 'the ludicrous and un-provable assumption that an elite few in power have been granted that power by God himself.' She marvelled at her outburst, even gaining a few passing glances from museum-goers, and actually covered her mouth with her hand, as though able to take back her words. *It is interesting where atheism logically leads one,* she thought.

Mr Mill thought nothing of it. She noticed that he seemed to not notice at all the occasional surprised or disparaging or judgemental look, indeed had thought she had noticed such during their first meeting those few months previously. She had suspected simple vanity at first—how else could someone convey the bodily sense of truly not caring what others might think?—but now he just seemed oblivious, unconcerned, or both.

'It's interesting, you know: the Chinese have essentially that same idea, though they call it the "Mandate of Heaven." And it's equally un-provable, as you noticed, though that hardly relegates it to the detritus of history. So many seem to want that one leader, that single perfect idealistic being, whether religious sentiment comes into play or no. It is somewhat like our earlier talk of Plato's philosopher-rulers.'

'Is not the idea in those ancient models partly the stability of the society?' she asked.

'Oh, indeed so! Part of the underlying logic, such as it is, consists in everyone knowing his,' he looked at her for just a moment, 'or her place. Some have likened this notion to a grand symphonic orchestra, such that if each musician knows their part and has sufficient training in their own instrument, then the orchestra, or society as a whole, if you will, functions together and sounds glorious.'

Harriet wasn't taken in just yet. 'But that in turn suggests each person having his,' and she looked up at him, though he was not so much taller than she, 'or her place within the group, even though that place may not have been freely chosen.'

They shuffled a few steps closer to the grand edifice, still drawing the occasional confused or concerned glance from proper English citizens who had been drilled since early childhood into not staring or otherwise being rude, as though one could create, much less run, a gigantic empire without plenty of rudeness to go around. 'Benevolent' despotism remained very much alive and perhaps not quite well, despite the efforts of hordes of beings, mostly men, such as Mill's own famed father.

'Well, no,' Mill conceded, 'and therein lies the rub, so to speak.

This is truly a major part of what occupies my time.'

'If I may probe just a touch further,' Harriet said, John nodding encouragement, 'did not those ancient thinkers also emphasise that the foundation for human society, made up of both the elite and the downtrodden—so long as all knew their alleged place—had to be the family?'

Mill had hoped to avoid this, never forgetting he was developing feelings for a person with her own family issues. 'Yes,' he admitted. 'The basis has to be the family, so the thinking goes, and it serves as a model for the rest. And alas, that ancient paterfamilias mentality remains with us, West and East alike.'

She nodded. They were about to enter the building, finally. Harriet felt excited at the prospect, having only visited once previously, and then for an insufficient amount of time to truly explore. The collections inside were daunting and massive, and she had heard that millions more artefacts lay in undisclosed secure locations in the basements, giving the curators work for years to come, plus the option to 'rotate' countless displays to keep a curious public returning. She recalled her words about tracking down—or attempting to do so—old copies of works printed by William Caxton.

Yet she was taken aback to note the sign which stated that entrance was free, to 'all studious and curious Persons.' She had forgotten that part, only considering it now since she felt briefly concerned, first, not actually having any loose cash on her person, and second, naively expecting that Mr Mill would cover her admission or otherwise pay for anything which might arise during their time together. She simply had not thought of it at all, and then felt angry, though this was over quickly—anger at herself for leaving home unprepared for even the most basic possible economic necessities, and anger at her husband, who while thankfully adequately enlightened on the subject that he never beat her or their children, and remained a dedicated and capable economic provider, nonetheless hardly expected her to acquire any habit of leaving home just to walk about with friends, especially male friends.

She collected herself, and they joined the queue. The blend of social and racial backgrounds of the visitors made more sense now: how outstanding a decision of the British government to amass this astonishing collection of things that could teach others, and then to cover the cost of the huge edifice, and its maintenance staff, without resorting to some new tax! Harriet felt pride at this. She lowered her voice conspiratorially. 'So then, Mr Mill, since we seem to have decided that the despots, however educated or wise or noble or good their intentions and decisions, must necessarily become one of your endnotes of history, please tell me why the apparent solution, government by the masses, or the collective will, or the people, might become just as hazardous.'

They slowly moved forward in the still-growing queue. Several vendors barked their wares from portable carts just outside the doors: pasties and other pies filled with savoury meats and vegetables; hot tea with any mix of lemon, milk, or sugar, and coffee also; even a baker of playfully shaped gingerbread and buttery shortbread goodies. Attached to the edifice itself were posters and fliers advertising recent acquisition of fresh wonders from Egypt—indeed, it seemed all Europe had become Egypt-mad of late, augmenting the new discipline of 'archaeology,' though the British thought the subject was a piece of history in its own right: using remains other than documents to glimpse the historical record, whilst the Americans classified it as a new sub-field of 'anthropology.' Whichever, Harriet found she could hardly wait, and asked John about the famed 'Elgin Marbles,' which had been recently cleaned and re-prepared for public viewing. They now took pride of place near the Museum's entrance, not far from the Rosetta Stone, itself taken from Egypt and granted to England after the Napoleonic Wars had finally concluded.

Just then a less thoroughly cleaned, and no doubt less for public viewing, sight presented itself. Two women walked by the queue, not so obvious as to actually approach the men standing about, but something about their almost leering expressions put Harriet on alert at once. She had never known any 'working girls'—Heaven and the

English gentry forbid!—but quickly sized up the painfully young women as they passed.

'I tol' you's the truth,' the woman (girl?) in a burgundy well-worn light dress said. 'But Lor,' I's up to so many dodges I gets wha' you may call "confounded."'

Her friend or associate or co-worker giggled, evincing the slightest slink to her stride, offset by a dress as dark as the other's garment, and adding, "E wants me to loo' all nice, like I's a hindustrious needlewoman or summat, not knowin' wha' it's like to get druv into the streets, like.' And they kept right on walking, occasionally eyeing the better-dressed men, and earning glares from some of the women, which made them laugh again.

These young women, probably not out of their teen years yet, could at least find the perverse humour in their 'occupation,' and Harriet hated the whole world for just a moment as she couldn't help but briefly wonder if either of them had once shared an encounter with the man to whom she had sworn her undying love and fidelity.

Even stranger, Mr Mill barely noticed them. He glanced at them in passing, surely, but chose not to comment upon their appearance or their dialect, and it seemed to Harriet that he simply was unsure how to respond. He certainly didn't look like the typical mark, Harriet thought: he wore a crisp dark grey suit, with a cream-coloured linen shirt beneath, itself with just the start of wrinkles. He seemed too proper somehow, but then she silently chided herself for thinking so, and thus missed the mental irony of also wondering if there was a woman at home—mother, sister, lover—who might press his clothing for him.

He finally responded, however. 'The beauteous display we are about to witness, called the "Elgin Marbles" in honour of the nobleman who recovered them just a couple of decades past, represents a sizable portion of what once adorned the very Acropolis itself.'

'In Athens?' she asked. For some reason she had not previously considered the distance, nor the sheer logistics, of hefting something so massive as far as Britain.

'The same. The very place where certain Greek words, like "aesthetics" and "ethics" and "democracy," hail from, and to which "Western Civilisation," whatever it might be or strive to be, owes a tremendous debt. The first truly egalitarian society we know of, at least in any urban sense, came from there. And now this display is here, to remind us of our cultural roots.' Then he whispered, 'Even if stolen.'

They shuffled ahead a few more slow steps. Some persons nearby had clearly taken an interest in what Mill was discussing, and displayed varying degrees of success in hiding it.

'If I recall, though, Mr Mill, that same "egalitarian" society, or "democracy" if you prefer, kept out foreigners, women, and slaves.' Mrs Taylor was not actually meaning to bait him; she was simply attempting to meet the ancients on their own terms.

He was taken aback. 'Well, yes, that is true. Though if once you were a member of the legislative Ekklesia or the elected Boulê in Athens, then you were treated wholly as equal to the other members. The Athenians even had what we might now call "term-limits," so that once you served your office, it was very unlikely you could renew it.'

'Yet the Athenians became empire-builders, just like we nineteenth-century Europeans, controlling new territories as subjugated colonies and sources of new wealth.'

John Mill, who could hold his intellectual own with any debater, seemingly on any topic sensitive or controversial, and do so not to emerge superior but because he remained interested in pursuing truth for its own sake, now felt wholly nonplussed. He actually had no idea what to say to this curious woman.

'The ideals matter, though,' he finally said. 'And you're right: like all empires, it also crumbled, unable to maintain those ideals in the face of simple greed and stupidity.'

Yet Harriet Taylor hardly felt she had 'won' somehow. She too was discovering a growing interest in truth for its own sake. She had two children back home to raise, soon to be three, who would inevitably get stuffed full of polite and prim proprieties, which had their place, at least when they kept folks behaving 'civilly' or at least non-violently, yet she wanted them to also learn of the world, not just the edges and headquarters of the Empire.

'May I ask how you yourself manage such sentiments, then?' she asked, curious yet not wishing to intrude upon this odd man's privacy.

He considered it, reminding himself that here he had no obligation to arrive at the 'correct' answer, one which would satisfy his commercial superiors, including his father. 'I have the perspective, each working day, of peering out through various third storey windows as though looking over all of London, even over the whole Empire, though in truth I can only ever see a few smaller businesses nearby from any one angle.'

She wondered where he might be taking this strange analogy, but he answered soon enough. 'It feels like indirect colonialism, if that makes any sense. What I think I mean is that looking down at something, actually gazing down upon something, can give you the fleeting and immature feeling that you somehow control it, all of it. I know how foolish this must sound, but I try to take the best, most rational and most measured decisions I can, often balancing Company policy and Imperial interest with the needs and potential happiness of the other people who might be affected, and render the best judgement possible.'

'Do you truly wield such control over Company interests?' Harriet had to concede that she still only realised a little about the formerly monopolistic and royally-controlled corporation, and did not believe that the man with her here now made life-and-death decisions for many, though perhaps he did. She began, uneasily, to appreciate why her husband might like him: John Taylor had bragged more than once about how much influence over someone's life an apothecary might have, and that was on a vastly tinier scale.

The revelry was interrupted by a trio of young scamps this time, not quite running about the crowds as though looking for something or someone. Harriet found them innocuous and playful, while Mill watched them more suspiciously, his initial conclusion that they were more likely to be pickpockets and less likely to be students on a school trip to the British Museum.

'Go on wiv' ya, then,' one of them said. He was the tallest of the lot, with sandy hair, worn shoes with no visible socks, and a button shirt that seemed more a pile of martyred fabric exhibiting spots and stains that might have been anything from coal or chimney dust to mud splashed by spoked wheels or shod hoofs.

'Ent nothin,' oroit?' replied one of the others, who might have been younger brothers, or fellow gang members, depending on an observer's prejudices.

Mr Mill and Mrs Taylor had trouble catching the rest, partly for their growing distance and partly because they had each benefitted from just enough of a posh upbringing to remain less in touch with cockney or any other 'common' dialect, though they detected 'not needing to be coals and coke today, lads,' and the apparently more appealing 'gettin' bees n' honey from nobs what can't watch their crowded spaces.' Had they bothered to ask about, this pair of adults more conversant in the King's English might have deciphered that the young trouble-makers were planning, or at least joking about, loose briefcases or suitcases sometimes left insufficiently watched by their owners during busier times of day in the City.

Watching the children go tearing off, Mill seemed slightly distant now. 'You know, Mrs Taylor, the two men who most educated me, my father and godfather, always asked, indeed often still ask: how do our decisions offer the greatest happiness to the greatest number of possible recipients?'

Dawning comprehension began for Harriet. This man understood that the organisation which employed him in truth wielded tremendous power, and not merely of the financial sort, over millions, virtually all of whom lived thousands of miles from where the pair of them now stood. And yet Mill clearly possessed a conscience, as she herself did, considering such hardly the automatic end of 'good breeding,' as proper English persons kept supposing, but of some other type of nurturing, whether it was happenstance or a philosophical education like the one this man had clearly received, she did not dare to guess. 'I am truly unsure, Mr Mill. We do the best we can. Your words remind me of my own readings, I'm sure quite paltry compared to your own, though I have some further ideas regarding property and women and the poor and those who come from other places and worship differently, and, well, forgive me—I can certainly run off a bit when I get excited!' Settle down, Mrs Taylor. But despite her silent admonition, she surprised herself anew: 'You truly must start calling me "Harriet," Mr Mill.'

He blushed at that. And she enjoyed witnessing his response. And then she felt her own face heat when he insisted that she call him 'John' in return, and then she felt brief shame since that was of course the name of the man to whom she had wholly pledged herself years ago and without reservation, the father of her beloved children.

Mill could sense the tension as well, and to his credit understood a woman's discomfiture on at least this occasion, so often befuddled at other times. 'You know, Mrs, er, Harriet,' he began, savouring the consonants as they worked their way through his mouth, 'that wild friend of mine, Mr Sterling, loathes Bentham, and perhaps by proxy my father as well, just for all their utilitarian work. Though Sterling loves Coleridge, and simply the idea of helping what he sometimes calls "Continental dissidents." To him the fiasco I described at your home was less about a true coup d'etat and more about sharing ideals with others.'

She got the message. Whatever their future, these two, it would have reason and philosophy and the noble notion of assisting others at its core. She still felt the keenness of somehow betraying her husband, but while Mr Taylor was a smart and good man, even noble in his way, taking such chances with others seemed beyond his moral capacities.

'So tell me then, John: what gave us the bloody right to take those fabulous marble pieces from Athens and bring them all the way to London?' She knew some strangers were staring at her harsh language, and knew she didn't care. Talking freely was its own reward, and Harriet Taylor was slowly resolving to speak her mind, and with whomsoever she wished, wherever it might lead.

Later, they had to check one of the Museum's clocks to verify the time. Somehow almost three hours escaped them as they studied the relics of past civilisations and reminders of how the human world once had been. Harriet delighted in hearing about John's summary of those views he enjoyed from the windows of his office, comparing its height to the third storey of the grand Museum, though he also commented how the contents of the latter were far more interesting. Still, he knew that his father and others at the Company had 'brought back' various pieces of mixed cultural significance, monetary value, and dubious provenance, from not just India but every nation in which the Company maintained a stake.

John opted not to dwell on that for the present, instead escorting his partner for the day back outside where she could catch a quick ride back home. They debated whether it would be better if he accompanied her that far, and finally decided that for the sake of appearances it made more sense for her to arrive home on her own, given that the hour was late, though the day had hardly descended into darkness, so a solo female passenger would seem more acceptable.

'Merci beaucoup, Monsieur Mill,' Harriet said, as they awaited a carriage. 'This has been a delightful day indeed.'

Mill returned her smile easily and warmly. Did she know of his history of being a Francophile, or did she simply wish to play? *Is this flirting?* 'Il n'y a pas de quoi,' he answered simply, acknowledging her gratitude.

'Perdon,' she continued, 'je ne parle pas beaucoup de français.' There was something about switching to French, even though she had just been honest and did not, in fact, feel wholly comfortable in the language, that made their conversation feel almost illicit. She should feel guilty, yet there could hardly be anything indecorous in devoting her free time with Mr Mill.

'Then perhaps we shall get the opportunity to practice together. Yet I fear I must rise early tomorrow for more work.' Mill recognised he was making excuses, and likely behaving rudely in the process, but no longer cared. Something about this was incorrect, even though he knew—through all his studies of logic, and ethics, and if nothing else, simple English manners!—that the more he wished for this day to not have to end, that such a desire was precisely what made it feel disingenuous.

And he did not present himself that way, though Mrs Taylor hardly noticed, offering Mr Mill his coat herself outside the Museum. 'In that case, bonne nuit, Monsieur Mill.'

It sounded almost perfect coming from her, though Mill was not about to comment on how her vowels remained just slightly too long, like she was imitating Monsieur Desainteville. 'À bientôt, Madame Taylor.'

He was out the Museum door, looking about for a hansom or other cab, and failed to hear her practice saying softly on the wind, 'J'adore ton sourire. Tu es charmante.' It was just as well he was out of hearing range by then, as it was something formerly said to her husband, who himself had no French.

* * *

Mill realised, during a moment of painful yet necessary honesty upon arriving back home, that while he was developing feelings for this wed woman, he nonetheless had to absent himself during the period when she would no doubt be going into her third labour. It sometimes seemed cowardly or callous or both to disappear at such an important time in a young mother's life, but the simple truth remained that she was not his wife, that he had no right to her or probably even to his time with her, much as he cherished such. She had sometimes insisted on joining him on his shorter walks in different parts of the City, all but waddling along as they listened to the larger predator and prey species in the new London Zoo in Regent's Park—the Tower Menagerie creatures had been moved there, and the Zoo was intended as purely a research facility, though there were rumours of the public being able to visit someday, and Harriet—no, Mrs Taylor!—had delighted in trying to guess which sounds matched which wild species.

At other times they ventured even outside the peacefulness of London's outstanding parks, pausing to admire mighty Parliament with its Gothic architecture, and just behind to the sacred grounds of Westminster and its Abbey. Mrs Taylor had wanted to stop and playfully do some paper rubbings from some of the brass memorial plaques, commemorating some of the most intriguing contributors to Britain's Greatness, though Mill sometimes fretted about delaying for too long, not so much for potential activities but rather for being visible in public for too long with a married and now quite obviously expecting woman.

Part of it was loneliness. Having discussed a brave soul like Sterling with the Taylors, he confided to Sterling by letter that, 'By loneliness I mean the absence of that feeling which has accompanied me through the greater part of my life, that which one fellow-traveller, or one fellow-soldier has towards another—the feeling of being engaged in the pursuit of a common object, and of mutually cheering one another on, and helping one another in an arduous undertaking. This, which after all is one of the strongest ties of individual sympathy, is at present, so far as I am concerned, suspended at least, if not entirely broken off.'

He, Mill, usually felt pleased with himself, and even found solace when he exploited this ability to write well and clearly, especially when emotions were involved. Polite Britons remained forever on guard against revealing too much of their souls, something he was reminded of during a painful and awkward confrontation with his former dinner host later in the year, thankfully mediated peacefully by none other than chatty Monsieur Desainteville.

Yet he knew he had genuine feelings for this woman, wed or not, and he believed that these feelings, new to his whole experience, were reciprocated in full. But how could he expect anything from someone who, while becoming a lovely and charming friend, nonetheless had major responsibilities at home?

\* \* \*

*From the journal of Harriet Taylor: December, 1831*
I am become a mother for the third time! How glorious this feels, to hold my baby daughter, and know I am truly blessed to now have three

healthy children. It almost permits me to forget about the permanent divide now in evidence between my husband and myself. Forgive my reticence, Dear Diary—I have not yet reached the psychic strength necessary to explain, even on paper, just what ails me, and my husband, and thus our marriage. I can only hope (pray?—No, that must be left to the faithful, and any Deity willing or able to hear such prayer would no doubt recognise a Hypocrite at once)—that our dear children will in no way suffer the effects of what has befallen me. There must come more on that later.

One must wonder also if I might be safe in sharing as much with Mr Mill as he has already shared with me. Poor soul: he was so unsure of himself confiding in me, especially after my husband confronted, nay, berated him, just at the start of this month as we head into another Holiday season. Monsieur Desainteville, of all persons, having dined with us at the very start of the year, proved himself most worthy for intervening in what might have become a rather uglier encounter. I look over my diary entries from years past, and am able to keep my emotions sufficiently controlled and maintain my rationality to realise and recall that I truly did love Mr John Taylor, Apothecary of Finsbury. At heart he truly is a good man, but I cannot quite forgive him for what he has done to me, to us! I want to blame him, to blame the doxy who must have given it to him, and especially to curse any male doctor who tells his married male patients that whoring is not merely morally acceptable but even a healthy release for them!

As for seeking emotional succour elsewhere—am I just finding fancy with another man simply due to difference? Sometimes, perhaps even always, the new is simply so exciting for no other reason than its offer of respite from the old and mundane that we pursue it automatically, perhaps instinctively, which might seem interesting but must also be rather stupid. The new might prove hazardous, after all, like Mr Mill's assessment of the Will of the People. And yet I cannot honestly picture my husband keeping a patient pace with me in so many varied parts of our mighty Capital, nor taking an interest in its minutiae as can Mr Mill. The latter gentleman tried to summarise a portion of his writing about The Spirit of the Age, as per our prior discussions, in such a charming manner that I committed his dedicated words to memory. A person 'may learn in a morning's walk through London more of the history of England during the nineteenth-century, than all the professed histories in existence will tell him concerning the other eighteen,' he intoned while the dazzling Government buildings rose around us and other people hurried past. That is what stands out—this constant hurrying, as if the citizens of Empire cannot arrive at their next destination, their next project, their next task—trivial or monumental!—quickly enough.

Rome was not built in a day, as that old reminder goes, and when I offered that tired dull gem to Mr Mill during that same walk, he noted something else worth recalling, admitting that for himself, 'I differ from those who ridiculously invoke the wisdom of our ancestors as authority for institutions which in substance are now totally different, howsoever they may be the same in form.' We continued walking, however slowly, whilst I attempted to digest and fully grasp this notion, agreeing with him. I have so many ideas, and find myself wanting to share these with this man.

I must remind myself—again!—of my pride, in telling my husband so early in this new relationship that I could not trust him, had already developed some degree of love for Mr Mill, only to be 'banned' from further discourse with the man. Mill, bless him, took it fairly well—my letter reached him whilst he was otherwise enjoying another of his rambles, first in New Forest and thence about the Isle of Wight—and he promised not to call on me again.

Yet now our shared letters confirm that neither of us can get the other out of our minds. And yet I remain wed to another. And my husband could never compose something like, 'At whatever time, in whatever place that may be so, she will find me always the same as I have been, as I am still.' It took some effort to translate that from the French—part puzzle from dear Mr Mill, part effort on his part to remain semi-clandestine in his affections, still relying on the Help to secret his letters to me despite his promise. Thus how can I forego the love of my dear Friend, despite a husband?

Thus I find myself still tied to the father of my children—again, a good man, mostly, and of course a stable provider for myself and those same dear children, and even quite intelligent, especially when one gets him going with his substantive field of inquiry, but he would never pause to notice the implications of our own Native architecture. Nor, for that matter, can I hope to address my own problem with him, the terrible and cruel irony in that, as an apothecary, perhaps he might help me with it!

I feel myself tensing with the anger of betrayal, and yet find myself actually looking around our lovely drawing room, having to convince myself anew of my privacy away from noisy and needy children or the prying eyes of husbands. What is the literary equivalent of whispering, one wonders, and this strange thought almost gives me anew a smile like those which Mr Mill can elicit from me without seeming to try. Yet now that I know myself fully secure in my own home, my own thoughts, my own diary, I can review.

It started many months past. Dear little Haji emerged into the world in February, and I alternated my concerns with his health, and that of his elder brother Herby, and worry over dear Lizzie and her growing intimacies with equally dear Mr Fox. Lovely souls both to be sure, but I do recall how strange it felt to be discussing something as outrageous and evil as syphilis with Lizzie—why were we not chatting lugubriously about the wonders of new love, even if more or less forbidden, as I felt convinced that allegedly developing between Lizzie and Mr Fox was, though perhaps I must beg their pardon for my judgement.

And then I began to notice some of those symptoms. How could this be? I cried, but alone whilst doing so, since the only possible answer could be my dear husband. Granted, I have a history of occasional mild fevers, sometimes laced with fatigue. Who does not, after all? But once the sores appeared, later replaced by rashes, along with a touch of weight loss that I hardly merited after having borne my second child and not truly exhibiting an extensive history of eating less to appear thinner like some ladies I might mention have done... Deserved atheism notwithstanding, thank God the tell-tale sores did not appear on my mouth! It was alarming enough to find them on, well, how does a proper English woman describe her private lady parts? Part of the rationale, if such a term applies here, of refusing my wifely duties in the marital chamber, is simple embarrassment—how to tell the man I try to still love to just ignore the sores or rashes or possible warts on my, oh, very well, I must at least write it for myself—vagina?

Why are men permitted, nay, encouraged, to tend to their 'needs,' even outside the bindings of 'holy' matrimony, even when sex is clearly a luxury, a biologic imperative for the perpetuation of a species, but in no way other than that a need? Why, further, are women denied the same releases, lest they become labelled as equally horrid things as the diseases which can spread via the acts of love? I must question my new Friend about such.

Lizzie seemed otherwise unconcerned, likely from disbelief, and I know no other women going through this horror, or at least I do not know that I know them. No confusion in these words—we have to maintain our little secrets sometimes. And now I find myself withdrawing—emotionally, physically—from the man who appears in prior pages of this tiny book as my One and Only, something from a faerie tale!

'London Society Woman Contracts Illicit Illness, yet Refuses to Inform own Husband, even Though he is an Apothecary.' One of the less reputable newspapers might publish such a dreary headline, and I've no doubt it would help sell more copies, but the irony is sickening. No, of course I cannot tell my own husband the apothecary! Dear Fox, that bastion of good ideas—ones about his love life aside—suggested none other than Mr Mill's friend Mr Roebuck for aid, though I barely know him. Bless him, though, Mr Roebuck admitted he had none himself, and my secret appears safe for the nonce.

This was after the attempt with 'Dr Tuson's' iodine treatment and cough medicine, which did nothing, and I barely hid the obvious bottle from Mr Taylor in time just before dumping the remainder. It was noxious, to say the very least, almost capable of eliciting the horrid but sometimes necessary gagging instinct, and in truth seemed far more the sort of 'snake oil' that we have, alas, inherited from our American counterparts. It seems anything can be sold and bought in the Colonies — no, States — with almost no regulation, something we shall have to address someday, yet at that hectic moment I felt only relieved that My Husband failed to witness the syrupy loss. 'Dr' Tuson, indeed!

Next came the odder solutions, prior to waxing more serious about my own research — folk may wonder at a woman with babes in tow delving into the medical shelves of booksellers — including tinct of bark, tinct of hops, that awful combination of quinine with sulphuric acid, the old steady of laudanum, despite its clear effects on one's judgement... And I had thought quinine was a New World import which exhibited much promise with malaria, so why it should work on something as dreadful as what I have...

Dear God, wrote the desperate atheist out of habit and rage — but am I to have no more reprieve than the one adage I found during my research, seemingly dating to the end of the Middle Ages which I might have found amusing if not suffering from the illness itself — in reference to men seeking illicit pleasures where they should not, that they might have 'an evening with Venus, yet a lifetime with Mercury?' And why then should mercury, that strangest of metals, prove any more worthwhile a treatment than quinine, or indeed anything else? My clandestine reading suggests that simple mineral baths, the luxurious-sounding 'spa' treatments on the Continent, may prove to offer at least some efficacy, but that would lead to other questions, such as why Mr Taylor's wife suddenly wishes a Continental sojourn, and why she seems disinclined to take her precious trio of offspring along. Bless the little dears — may they never have to know this kind of terror!

I have remained careful to not make a show of purchasing anything from our fortunately amply-stocked book shops — Hatchards is useful, though my cry for a larger national bibliothèque remains!—and despite my helplessness I continue to look forward to the day when I shall take my own children to such a locale to read, much as my siblings and I alike prized any chance to visit, not having access to schoolbooks. But I know shopkeepers—making a show of confidentiality while nonetheless of course noticing whatever tantalising item might be leaving their domains—and I need neither judgemental glares nor any sort of record, gossipy or paper-based, to track my recent intellectual explorations. How to explain to anyone, especially one's husband, why you have texts in your parlour about venereal diseases, or the history of medicines, remains too much for my mind to contemplate.

As with Hatchards, so too with my curious diary: secrecy remains absolutely necessary, and discretion may number among the greatest tests and verifications of true friendship, another thought which calls to mind my quirky yet brilliant and handsome—yes, if perhaps a bit less conventionally so!—new friend. At least he regards me as a confidante, that much is clear, and while I surely hope to return such feeling, I yet shudder at the thought of him thinking me a wanton or a whore or one of countless 'unfortunates' in Southwark, and I find myself wondering anew about which unknown and unknowable woman gave my husband the disease that we once called the French Pox the French called the Italian Pox, and then chide myself at the instant, realising that those same female 'unfortunates' are hardly to blame—no woman enters prostitution willingly or full of idealistic hope that the practice will somehow provide her with a better life! Mr Mill deserves my honesty in return. I hope soon to be able to grant it.

Considering him again, Mr Mill seems rarely to hurry, not even during that fateful morning to which he had alluded even during the first time we met, when he found the poor defenceless infant. I shudder while writing this, thinking of my own precious little ones, likewise as defenceless, and also remembering my dear brothers, Thomas and John, lost to illness. I confess I know not how to act the role of eldest sibling, yet that is what I am become, and I can hardly face even the thought of losing my babes to something so vile.

Still, one must focus on the brightness of life, not always on its clouds or despair. I truly did test Mr Mill's potential interest in Lizzie, partly since she should really not be spending so much time with Mr Fox, much as I love that man—he too is married, the old social trap!—yet Mr Mill's eyes seemingly kept returning to me. I pray—hope—that such does not constitute simple ugly vanity, and considered it quite something indeed when earlier this summer Lizzie seriously questioned whether it was myself or Mr Mill who had contributed a short piece to 'The Edinburgh Review'—a progressively-minded paper, thank goodness!—about Byron. So we seem to think rather alike, or at least others may have cause to believe so. I cannot imagine anyone saying likewise about myself and my husband.

Further, Mr Mill offered some praise of my review of that playful book about life in Australia—one of my younger siblings continues to make the occasional comment about wanting to venture to that far removed continent unto itself—larger than our former imperial set of colonies in North America—and then Mr Mill continued to grant his support of my writing, as with the seemingly never-ending bit about Caxton. He is even considering some of Lizzie's poetry for 'The Examiner,' a more appropriate periodical for such. So I continue to debate the question: how does this fascinating John Mill feel about me, other than our innocent friendship, and how free do I remain to pursue my interests, given that my husband has plagued me, quite literally, such that certain desires remain... unfulfilled? What would Mr Mill's father and godfather, those worshippers of 'utility,' have to say?

Finally, lest I give the unworthy impression of being devoid of the goings-on in other parts of our hectic world, I was disturbed indeed by Mr Mill's mention of something horrid undertaken by the Americans—an 'Indian Removal Act' forcing thousands of the northern Aboriginal peoples out of their homes on a trek westward. I fear I remain ignorant as to where exactly, though the Indians' homes had seemingly been previously in the south-eastern portion of the mighty continent, which included, as Mr Mill discussed, the region named 'Florida' by the Spanish—a lovely name for a beautiful area, no doubt, and one wonders how florid and flowery that region can be—and perhaps part of the Caribbean, too, though I know the Americans—former English colonists—are not involved in that area.

Other distressing news from the 'lost colonies': in Virginia, formerly the original British Crown Colony named for Queen Elizabeth of old—though I cannot care whether she died virgin or no—came recent news of a dreadful slave revolt in August. Mr Mill had asked if the revolt was dreadful for the slaves or for the masters, as though slavery was not already sufficiently horrid, though the news reporting gave the impression that some of the owners suffered a terrible vengeance for the treatment of their 'property.' The papers, including those Mr Mill—John—writes for occasionally, described the uprising as quick and violent. Those poor Africans must have been desperate, even more heinously treated than usual.

We also discussed an article about the 'Black Country,' much closer to home, written by a Scots engineer, though this time the moniker is not racial. I had never realised how dreadful our notions of 'progress' might be, so much of our wealth coming from modern industry. Such country—right here in England, near Wolverhampton!—'is anything but picturesque,' writes the man. 'The district is ablaze with iron furnaces... by day and by night the country is glowing with fire, and the smoke of the ironworks hovers over it...' Worse, he writes how 'only the skeletons' of the area's fair trees now remain, how 'the grass had been parched and killed,' and that in a summation from the Classics like dear Mr Mill enjoys, 'Vulcan had driven out Ceres.' I surely agree that 'we pay a heavy price' for our vaunted supremacy,' especially with 'the loss of picturesqueness and beauty.'

Yet I must insist upon closing this year with two notes of sadness compared with two notes of happiness. The 'Spirit of the Age' that we talked about at our earlier dinner seems indeed morally poisoned by this offense to the landscape, and I am beginning to realise that to maintain both my reason and the health and happiness of my children, I will likely have to confront my husband some time about what he has done to me, even if it was not his fault, as he protests!

And yet pure joy may yet be found in baby Helen—already we call her 'Lily'—and the encouragement of good friends, especially male friends as well as female ones, to keep writing and perhaps even complete more publications...

* * *

*From the Diary of Helen Taylor:*
There I came, fresh into the world, wholly and blissfully ignorant of the family dramas that would ensue and the sense that we were all part of some Glorious Epoch in the history of the world. Vanity to be sure, but such was the attitude of nineteenth-century British Greatness.

Mother once described her labour with me as the easiest of the three she experienced on our behalf, though I've never attempted to confirm this with either of my brothers. Perhaps I wished not to know, though men remain hopelessly at a loss whilst discussing the intimate details of how women's bodies work. Whichever the case, another detail never pursued with my brethren was that issue—common among siblings, naturally—about whether I was Mum's 'favourite' or one of the boys was, and in this case my lack of follow-up on the subject stems more from the atypical moral dynamics of my family.

In other words, how could I become sure how feelings in my blended family were distributed: towards Father, or Mother, or Mr Mill?

Such feelings would have to wait as I mentally ingested the utter shock and horror at reading Mum's words for that entry! Dear God—and yes, my Faith remains strong whilst hers collapsed 'ere I was born—the humiliation of it all, to say nothing of the simple distress of having an illness which, even as I compose this so many years later, knows no cure or legitimate treatment. My own research into this morose medical mystery likely paled compared to Mother's, and even though we now know more about tiny micro-killers than before, thanks to the likes of Messieurs Doctors Koch and Pasteur, cures remain wanting. A 'terror' indeed, to borrow Mother's term.

How did my mother endure those treatments? This question

haunts me still, something I address to her tombstone next to Mr Mill's in this peaceful French town.

What must it have been like to intentionally inhale fumes of mercury known for their toxicity, or survive pressurized scalding 'baths,' or to pass such ordeals only to realize that the illness remained, that one could not speak of it in our refined and polite society, that one could only discuss it at all with one select, dear, trusting, non-judging Friend?

Some yet wonder how my mother could have developed such loving and bonding feelings for John Stuart Mill. I find nothing confusing in such whatsoever. Of course she loved him—he listened and loved her back, gentle unassuming man. His own family never fully appreciated his gifts, beginning with his illustrious father.

And yet seeing those same gravesites again reminds me of the selfish follow-on thought: might this disease have passed on to the children of Mr and Mrs John Taylor?

\* \* \*

*1832.*

'Today, Mrs Taylor,' Mill began, knowing he should keep addressing her thusly, regardless of his feelings or her encouragement otherwise, 'we will conduct a simple social and moral experiment, as we savour this delicious ice cream.'

Harriet laughed between laps of the rare frozen treat, something she had only ever enjoyed several times previously. It was difficult to keep, though the Taylor house had a sturdy ice box in which to preserve foodstuffs. They had already joked over how the Americans had businesses which chopped up ice in the Northeast, packed it in sawdust and then wooden crates, and finally shipped it to wherever it might be useful. John and Harriet found further amusement in how wealthier ancient Romans, desperate for enrichment as boring rich people have always been, sometimes showed off to their neighbours by having ice brought to the imperial capital by slaves, only to eat it plain, just because they could. Such were the ways of empires.

But cream mixed with ice here, flavoured with various additions, proved so much better! 'Let the grand experiment commence then, Mr Mill!'

Harriet could hardly wait for the children to be old enough to accompany them like this, and remained grudgingly pleased that her husband had once again made time 'at his club,' or wherever else he might be, to leave them alone. It was amazing what simple guilt could work sometimes, though she did not wish to use such as a weapon: it was cowardly and often dishonest, so she appreciated her husband sometimes absenting himself specifically for her time with friends, especially John Mill. She knew he carried his own guilt, indeed had visited his own medical care providers for other opinions, rather than more of the doxies like the one who had contaminated him, and thus their marriage. Until then, she could enjoy eating at a small private table in the glorious outdoors with a friend.

'Very well. Consider, please, what fine ingredients went into the creation of this magnificent treat.'

'How dramatic.' She considered them. 'I do truly love this chocolate flavour,' and she smiled at him as he enjoyed his own vanilla. She was less taken with the addition of fruits or lollies to ice cream, wondering if she had become some snobby purist. Mr Taylor preferred strawberry. 'All right, then. The chocolate comes from cacao beans, plants not indigenous to our own clime, nor indeed to anywhere in Europe, so far as I know.'

'I concur. Those large beans are indeed tropical.'

'Further,' she added, 'I think the liquor, as their buttery fluid is called once the beans have matured and fermented, is quite bitter, so we add rather a lot of sugar to the mix.'

'Itself another tropical product in need of import,' added Mill. Today, they had been striding about St James Park prior to stopping for their snack, which Mill still savoured visiting, blissfully never suffering from feeling haunted by the memory of the dead child, though he never showed Mrs Taylor quite where he found the body. 'So we have a base of chocolate, the beans coming from South America, into

Central America and Mexico, and now also the Caribbean, such as that part of the British Empire known as Jamaica. Plus, we have a further base of sugar, itself traditionally far more reliant upon slave labour, also including the Caribbean. The historic demand for rum only made that dependency worse.'

Harriet suddenly felt devastated, trying to conjure a way to lighten the mood. 'I was just trying to enjoy my ice cream,' she added tamely.

'And so I genuinely wish you to do so. There is no guilt here, my dear Mrs Taylor, only recognition of what is. As David Hume himself once said, since he was a better philosopher than historian, there exists a moral space between what is, and what ought to be.'

'An "is-ought gap?"' wondered Harriet aloud.

'That's precisely what he called it!' He was impressed, she knew, briefly wondering what else she might take a fancy to reading. 'Now then, what about other ingredients?'

'Well, the cream itself, no doubt. And,' she almost regretted saying it, knowing at least a detail or two about the history of this one, 'salt.'

He grinned, enjoying anew the sweet chilly flavour of the creamy white treat as he licked it from the tiny spoon, letting its subtle scent fill his attentive nostrils while simultaneously enjoying the taste on his tongue. 'My friend Grote could compose an entire history of the salt trade—how it used to be mined, even used as currency—before people understood how strangely common it truly is.'

She liked seeing him so enjoy himself. They lived in a culture which evinced such pride in its 'stiff upper lip' mentality—a notion which Mill's compatriot George Grote could trace back to the stoic Romans, who believed it a mark of distinction to give onlookers the impression that nothing bothered them. The most direct complication was that it also tended to denigrate expressions of genuine feeling, including the childlike simplicity of enjoying ice cream.

'How about the cream, then?' she asked.

'Well, I do not actually know directly in this case, but considering the very short life span of dairy products, one hopes that it's both fresh and local.'

'Would that mesh with our dinner conversation about the economic works of Ricardo or Malthus?' she teased, this time provoking actual laughter from this taciturn man.

'You remember! That's wonderful, Har-, um, Mrs Taylor. The major economists would favour the purchasing of basic food items from local producers, contributing a bit to national pride in the process.'

Harriet wondered for a moment about the additional need for international trade, and where the economic thinkers might draw the cultural line between the two ideals, but she held her tongue. 'Very well. So now that we have our major ingredients,' she said, 'moral and political implications notwithstanding, we can proceed to the rest of your example.'

John had been glad of the distraction, truth be told. His own family members also loved the occasional treat like this, but it often came with statements of guilt regarding its cost, and that was part of his intended discussion today.

'The chief advantage in performing a simple "thought experiment," Mrs Taylor,' he began earnestly, 'is that we need not confront the more awkward practicalities of expensive laboratories. Plus, we may consider whatever we can dream, and not be limited by the constraints of what is possible.'

'Do I detect a note of sarcasm, Mr Mill?'

He pretended to look offended, though she could tell he liked their banter.

'Certainly not, madam. Now, my mentor of old, Mr Bentham, created his assessment of pursuing pleasure while avoiding pain, though that is a bit over-simplified.'

'I understand. And when Mr Bentham added that basic insight into humanity to his own views of what constituted happiness, he began calling it utilitarianism.'

'Perfect.' The Park felt cool today, with just a slight breeze. A pair of children ran about with a clumsy yet clearly beloved kite more or less flying behind them. A governess tried to keep up with them, but had trouble running in her skirts and petticoat, and the kids seemed to further enjoy ignoring her warning shouts. Several other families were present, many laughing gaily at having a day off from their labours, and Mill took time to notice their diversity, like at the Museum: mostly local English, but he could hear Scots accents from one small clan, and witnessed a larger Chinese family partaking of this grandiose public space—so many picnicking, strolling, chatting. No one seemed to have any cares this day.

'So, then,' Mill continued. 'if eating an ice cream may be deemed pleasurable—'

'As indeed it is!' interrupted Harriet, as she lapped up the rest of hers, leaving only the small napkin next to the glass dessert dish. She stared for a moment at the wrought iron table beneath, thinking for several seconds about how typically ornate it was, then recalling that cast iron like this could prove surprisingly brittle if struck suddenly and with sufficient force. And the ornate-ness of the curlicued design had itself turned ordinary, since all the tables nearby looked identical.

'Yes, quite.' He took in her adorable if serious countenance for a moment before continuing. 'Then, are there any associated pains?'

'Now I think I'm following you less thoroughly.' Harriet was enjoying talking, though. She made a point of turning her attention from the hard table to the soft face.

'Part of what Bentham meant was that it is unusual, perhaps impossible, to have an experience which is absolutely, completely, pleasurable or painful.' John had to admit this was fun, more so than the last time he'd discussed seriously the implications of all this utility with his pair of mentor—tormentors. Finding amusement in the similarities between the terms 'sovereign masters' of pleasure and pain, Bentham had once described John Mill as 'having the pride of Lucifer,' to which John replied that Mr Bentham should himself know.

Harriet found herself thinking at once of her happy births: three beautiful, promising children; and the pain, while very real and ongoing—Herby, as the eldest, took the longest, something her father had explained to her years ago as typical—the accompanying pleasure of having these youngsters in her life often felt overwhelming, and she could never regret having gone through with the risks. Mr Taylor had of course proffered to assist her with the latest in analgesic agents, but she had refused each anxious time.

She stared back at her empty dish, the spoon resting at its side, realisation dawning. 'That's why you asked about the sources of the ice cream components.' He nodded. 'So, if the sugar came perhaps from slave labour, that horrid practice, even that one example by itself, as we take time to acknowledge it, might notably offset our enjoyment of the final product.'

He nodded again, pleased she had recognised this so quickly. She possessed an adroit mind, capable of independent, rational thought. 'Excellent. Can you think of any others?'

Is that example not bad enough, or is he thinking of the rare vanilla beans or tropical cacao harvest or good English cattle who live alongside our sturdy sheep, source of so much English wealth and prestige for centuries? 'I—I am not sure yet,' she admitted.

He had just finished his own delectable treat. Some children strolling by with semi-attentive parents looked at the empty dessert bowls enviously. Mill smiled at them, even telling them, 'It's excellent.'

Then he turned back to his friend. 'So then—curious glances of delightful children notwithstanding,' and Harriet somehow felt this man would be wonderful with actual children, though that was yet another subject they had never quite discussed, 'what might it be like if any person, of any literacy whatsoever, could apply this little benefit-disadvantage model to, shall we say, any type of moral decision-making?'

She looked away again, then at those children, then back to the mockingly empty dish which lacked both ice cream and answers, pondering, so far always enjoying their little quizzical repartees. But she had to admit, 'I do not understand where you might be taking this, John.' She liked calling him that. She hated the formality of their time, even among married individuals, of addressing each other properly, though her husband had almost definitively, perhaps permanently, become 'Mr Taylor' for her, even in her diary.

Mill sighed, offering her a concerned glance, like he was about to confess something. 'Mr Bentham,' he began, 'seriously proposed, some years back, what might be labelled a "hedonistic equation" or "calculus," which would enable anyone having to make a moral judgement to weigh, numerically, the merits as well as problems with the decision at hand, and make that decision based on how the maths added up.'

Harriet was stunned. 'Do you suggest, then, that Mr Bentham really believed that morals could be so categorised?' It sounded thrilling, and also cheap and demeaning, all at once. What if it were possible, though? What if all the moral squabbling—about how to treat women, about the inequalities in society—the poor, the different, immigrants, Jews, Catholics—or about anything in everyday life, could be reduced to equations? If it could be determined that any particular policy—an individual's pursuing a certain vocation, or opting to not show up to work someday, or a bill put before Parliament, or an international treaty or trade agreement that required multinational support—amounted to judging according to some basic arithmetic...

'I believe that's the countenance I wore when he first explained it to me, too, my dear Harriet,' Mill said, trying to get past the social rules himself. 'And shortly thereafter, it also marked the start of my—whatever shall I call it—falling out, with Bentham's utilitarianism.'

'But what if it could be done?' Harriet queried, still intrigued.

'Thus my simplistic example with our enjoyment of ice cream. Please consider: I enjoyed eating it, of course, and you seemed to as well.' She nodded. 'And then we elaborated the potential demerits of it: it's expensive, so for most people it can only be a rarity for special occasions. Further, we examined the sources of those things that go into its very creation: while some might be gotten locally, others must come from much further afield, with moral implications for persons and environments producing such ingredients.'

'I begin to see,' she added, more confident now. 'Though we have yet to consider other benefits. After all, we did also just contribute to the local economy, as you hinted earlier, and even with the international implications of ice cream—' she appreciated his smile at her unintended alliteration, 'it might still have pleased the great economist Adam Smith himself to have kept that money "in country," to borrow a phrase.' He grinned encouragingly: several decades previously, Smith had wanted it both ways: to practice free market economic interests, without governmental intrusion or regulation, but also with a sometimes impossible emphasis upon keeping wealth solely within one's own nation. It might have been patriotic, but also impractical: even the deceptively simple ice cream exercise had revealed this basic truth of a world recently shrunk even more with modern technologies and trade practices.

Mrs Taylor took another moment to gather her thoughts. 'So tell me, then, Mr Mill,' she began, enjoying a slight slur to the address, as though they must remain in a more formal social standing, 'should I have enjoyed the bloody ice cream or not?'

And John Mill, easily ruffled socially but almost never so intellectually, found himself laughing aloud at this near-outburst from his new special and lovely friend. She joined him in a guffaw, prompting yet another group of children to spontaneously laugh at nothing in particular, to the obvious consternation of their parents, who in turn glared at John and Harriet. And like children themselves, this just made John and Harriet laugh even more.

Harriet felt delighted, reassured really, that they could converse like this. They still had plenty to share: Mr Mill still had yet to learn of her dreaded disease, for example, and Mrs Taylor realised that not only was it challenging to discuss with anyone, even her own family, she remained unsure of what talking about it would accomplish. No one could help her cure it, apparently, not even her drug-expert husband. Her children mustn't ever know, of course! And as for her parents, her siblings—what good could possibly come of their learning, either?

Yet that brought her up suddenly cold, somewhere in the pit of her heart. It was not like she was considering cheating on her philandering husband, right? And if that was not the case, then why bother sharing such a sordid tale with Mr Mill in the first place? He had become the dearest of friends, as close as Lizzie and precocious

Caroline already, and yet he might turn away from her: she felt damaged, not just contagious and spoiled.

Definitely Lizzie and Caroline, then. She had to arrange tea or something with her friends soon! The ice cream had been a delight, but Harriet and John both knew they had to shortly return to their own homes, apart yet constantly wondering about each other. Harriet sometimes regretted that Mr Mill had foregone his former let home to return to live with his family, then thought better of it. He felt a duty in helping with his siblings, and also sought to set aside sufficient income to perhaps wed someday—he'd let this slip out once, not knowing how it made his lady-friend cringe. Still, Harriet felt her own duties, and the temptation to slip into the habit of staying over at a young unattached man's house might have proved too tempting for them both!

\* \* \*

*From the Diary of Helen Taylor:*
I still adore ice cream, too. Some describe vanilla as plain, though I have never forgotten Mr Mill's description of how far those vanilla beans must travel, nor how they fetch a price almost worth their weight in gold. For me there could exist no richer flavour.

\* \* \*

Fortunately, such a meeting was not long in coming, just several more days. Harriet Taylor actually loathed some of the awkward enforced social events to which all in their society seemed to have to subscribe, at least occasionally. Still, a visit with true friends made it easier, such that inane pleasantries about which tea service to use, or even which tea and accompanying tasty morsels to offer, became more bearable. Plus, she knew rather a lot about what her friends liked, and that was part of her interest in soliciting their input.

Lizzie appeared at the Taylor home in dazzling light orange, among her finer worn colours, to highlight her bright bluish eyes, looking youthful and radiant, or maybe Harriet just felt weary by comparison: mothers often felt inadequate or less beautiful next to those who had never brought children into the world. And Caroline, fast becoming an equally dear friend despite her age, alighted just behind her in a shiny medium green, which just as perfectly set off her own slightly darker skin, Harriet wondering if perhaps her friend spent too much time in direct sunlight. Admiring them as they offered heartfelt greetings, she remembered that since both women—well, woman and girl, Harriet referring to the pair as 'her girls'— lived in Harriet's old neighbourhood around Beckford Row and within an easy walk of Mr Fox's Islington Church, they could easily meet, even without Harriet. Harriet in turn promised them she was never jealous, but secretly sometimes felt envious, though when she was more rational understood such sentiment arose partly from her own domestic situation, something about which her two dearest friends could even now just guess. Then she decided she was mentally rambling, like Mr Mill often did, so Harriet silently thanked both her friends as she greeted them for not being gossips like so many bored women, and some bored men for that matter.

'Oh, Caroline, you look so radiant these days,' Harriet said while embracing the girl, who returned the hug wholeheartedly.

'And Elizabeth,' she added, suddenly pulling the third woman into a group embrace, which just felt natural, though group hugs were, by Georgian standards, something for felicitous schoolgirls, and boys who had achieved some meaningless victory in sport.

'When were we last all together, just the three of us?' asked Caroline, as their hostess eagerly ushered them into the home on Christopher Street.

'Come now, Caro,' admonished Lizzie gently, who was the only one who called her that, herself loving playful nicknames more than most. 'You're the grand diarist, so you must have a record of when it was.' The trio took seats at the table in the drawing room, where Mr Taylor and his own friends sometimes played cards, smoked disgusting cigars, and made small friendly wagers on their usually sedate games of faro, or that curious American import, poker. The ladies, meanwhile, sometimes thought cigar smoke was intended to chase women away, never mind that card games of chance were also deemed 'unladylike.'

Harriet caught a quick glance of her old hoop in a corner, along with the bowling stick she formerly used to keep it going down Beckford Row during a gleeful girlhood, then noticed a perfectly carved hardwood top, ebony she thought it was, that she knew had been a favourite toy of her husband before she was even born, and the sight of these common yet dear items struck her heart. Mr Taylor had clearly left them there intentionally, letting their children get used to them, and yet Harriet felt no anger, merely finding herself looking forward to sharing their like with the Taylor children before much longer. Improvised skittles and bowls, glass marbles, kicking about a football, playing at pirates with wooden swords, caring for dolls with miniature clothes, jumping with a rope or down a chalk-drawn hopscotch course without one—Harriet found herself feeling wistful over such simple childhood pleasures, wondering whether her husband or John Mill or herself should be the one to teach Haji and Lily to use them.

Young Herby already loved the football, even though the aggressive nature of the medieval sport left Harriet questioning its safety at times. At least it wasn't as violent as that awful new 'rugby' she had heard of recently, named perversely for the school where the lads had just starting carrying the football and kicking it differently to score. And of course, many children had to work, too, so it was fortunate for them to steal time away to play at all.

Lizzie had caught Harriet staring. 'What is it?' she prodded gently.

'Oh, nothing,' Harriet lied. She detested deceiving about anything, and her friends deserved better. Still, until she had reconciled her own feelings, along with the needs of her family, and found a longer-term solution for her husband, then sometimes friends might need to know a bit less. She summoned Penny instead.

The servant appeared, immaculate and flawlessly groomed in her traditional blue service dress with white trim, as always. 'Yes, Mrs Taylor?' she asked.

Harriet had already learned not to shudder at being addressed by what was, after all, her legal name. 'Just tea and light sandwiches for us, please, Penny.'

'There's apples over from Borrow Market, if ye'd like some fresh, Mum. Cook's bin wantin' to stew some of 'em as well.'

The young ladies all looked intrigued at that. The notion of fruit eaten 'raw' had been gaining ground in recent years, with some advocating that freshness kept it more nutritionally advantageous, while others insisted that anything uncooked, or overcooked, in what Harriet and her husband once laughingly called the 'English fashion'—back when they shared laughter more often—was risky, even dangerous, especially for children.

'Do you mean "Borough Market?"' wondered Lizzie. 'We were just there last week.' Caroline and Harriet both suspected to whom 'we' referred.

Penny blushed for just an instant, looking down as she'd been taught for years, though she had worked diligently at overcoming her provincial accent. Fortunately it wasn't true cockney, whose speakers savoured for its rhyming, sometimes indecipherable thickness, while the better-born scoffed at its apparent meaninglessness, often not understanding how the rhyming slang often poked fun at the ruling and middle classes. 'Yes, Miss Flower, I do. "Bor-ough" Market,' she pronounced carefully.

Lizzie then seemed to note her mistake, not intended condescendingly. 'Forgive me, I—' and she found she was unsure what to say.

'It's all right, Liz,' said Harriet. 'Penny, your idea sounds perfect. Perhaps you could bring us some of that blancmange, too.'

The girl silently padded to the kitchen, passing the pantry to begin gathering the women's snacks and tea, leaving Harriet's friends staring agape at her. 'What sort of afternoon tea is this, then?'

Harriet responded without missing a beat. 'A more interesting one, indeed. Perhaps influenced by the Americans, who have "snacks," and "dinners" or "lunches" rather than our "luncheons." Or perhaps I'm just tired of cucumber sandwiches and scones, even when the scones have extra cinnamon.' *Or maybe because cinnamon is another exotic imported treat.* Blancmange was merely like a custard, served from a mould, and Harriet had already dared to intentionally drop in the likes of raisins or almonds into her own.

They all giggled at that, Penny hearing them two rooms away and taking some comfort in the belief that they probably weren't laughing at her, like some stuffy middle-class folk would. She was actually very thankful to work for the Taylors, even with the recent stress in the home. The children could sense it as well, and while she was not their governess, Penny felt rather attached to the sometimes grubby but always fun and usually kind Taylor offspring.

'So now, then,' Caroline began again. 'When was it last?'

Lizzie caught her meaning. 'We last all met up, just the three of us that is, for that showing of "Hamlet" at Drury Lane.'

'Oh, yes,' Harriet smiled, relishing the memory. She read the occasional Shakespeare play as though it might have been intended like the current 'closet plays'— literature written as plays yet not really intended to be staged. She loved the theatre, just the idea of it—and Drury Lane had been the nation's first to install gas lighting, in this case enabling the tragic monologue of Ophelia hauntingly portrayed, the light lighting and shading different sides of her face simultaneously. The effect proved quite eerie, as much so as when Hamlet himself confronted his own fatal indecision after a visit from his ghostly father.

Caroline opted to venture into the chancy. 'Perhaps you should have Mr Fox take you to the next play there, Liz,' she said. Caroline, with her child's eye—truly, the young women sitting with her often overlooked her age—still believed in romantic fancy, and thought nothing about a woman initiating steps within a romantic relationship. She might be too young yet to truly understand the details involved when romantic became or entailed physical as well, but she liked the independence of her ideas.

Elizabeth Flower meanwhile, for all her insight as a composer and her perceptions as a friend, still offered a blind side to the implications of what she did with good Pastor Fox. 'Perhaps I should, Caroline,' she answered lamely, oblivious to the slight sarcasm.

Harriet and Caroline stole a quick glance at each other. Caroline Fox herself was equally rational, at least in her daily life, and she had compared writing notes and shared ideas with dear friend Harriet Taylor numerous times already, as each of them considered how they might become more influential as writers. That made all three members of the trio writers, in the most crucial sense of the word — Harriet had already compared them amusingly to Mill's 'Trijackia,' though when Mill suggested they should think of an equally entertaining nickname for themselves she was at a loss.

But that hardly erased the concern they could each feel for one another. 'Lizzie,' Harriet began softly, 'have you, well, considered the implications of Mr Fox's wife?'

Lizzie stiffened and sat bolt upright, looking towards the kitchen as though Penny could not be back quickly enough with their snack, or tea, or whatever. In truth, Penny herself was trying not to listen but found the going difficult.

The normally dainty Ms Flower took her time sighing deeply, a sign of guilt and ire alike. 'Far be it from me to call out a friend for rank hypocrisy,' she began, then had to ignore Caroline, the most animated of them all, the one who would lose her temper the last, as she worked to avoid giggling at the sight of her two closest friends sitting as rigid as any contemporary book of proper manners and etiquette would recommend: her friends were attempting control, not wanting to devolve into some stupid infighting.

Harriet must have caught the effort from Caroline, or at least noticed that things could erupt very quickly, and part of what kept her critiquing women of her time and station was the fact that they so often turned on each other, indeed were sometimes encouraged to do so, especially when the honour of men was purportedly involved. She reached out her hands instead to her friend, feeling Lizzie take them. 'We must not do this,' Harriet said, almost whispering.

Lizzie squeezed her hands back, a tear appearing in the corner of each perfect sky-blue eye. 'You're right, Harriet. Oh, both of you are. Why does this hurt so much? And how can I be so stupid?'

Caroline placed her own hands atop those of the other women. 'Because Mr Fox,' she said, then turned slightly to Harriet, and added, 'and Mr Mill,' and she watched as her friends both flushed slightly—Caroline had never felt the stirrings of 'true love,' or whatever nonsense was promised in the wistful literature of their time, with centuries of history behind it—and so did not fully understand the occasional urges to dance for joy or pull one's hair all because of how one person made another feel, but she continued: 'are both handsome, good, intelligent men. There's can hardly be any mystery over what seems so attractive. But Liz, Harriet is right, my dear girl: Mr Fox of course comes with a wife. And Harriet, dear Liz is also correct, and unlike Lizzie, you and Mr Taylor have a family.'

The words cut into the other women, for Harriet more so. And it hardly helped that she and Mill had already discussed, in addition to so many other irresistible topics, how truth was often painful, even agonising, part of what led to the realisation that knowledge truly did represent power. It had to be earned, and most things worth the effort chipped away a bit more at the innocence with which people were born.

And Harriet looked at darling Caroline anew, constantly attuned to her maturity in some arenas mixed with innocence in others. Some explaining had been in order for her to even accept the idea of having this girl in their midst, coming largely on the recommendation of Lizzie herself. This year marked the twenty-fifth birthday for Harriet, the twenty-eighth for Lizzie, who was glad to act as sometime mentor, even though Harriet remained the only one wed, and the only one with children.

Caroline Fox had recently turned thirteen, and already displayed an 'exquisitely chiselled countenance,' as one of her admirers noted to her elder friends. Even now, Harriet marvelled at the curious girl, and her relationship with John had helped in that regard—at least Caroline had not been expected to learn Greek and Latin prior to puberty. As for others, theirs was a time when boys could work sweeping hazardous London chimneys by age eight, the same for the even more dangerous digging for coal in Britain's endless supply of mines. For girls, the alarming 'age of consent'—at least to wed, few commenting publicly about the physical implications of marriages—was still twelve, fourteen for the lads, a tradition Lizzie and Harriet had railed about more than once, not least because this practice had been exported to British overseas holdings, including the New England former colonies. And then Lizzie had further reminded Harriet that Caroline was being raised for intellectual and hopefully social independence: her mother prided herself on instilling rationality and open-mindedness in her three children, and her father was a geologist, sometime inventor, and prestigiously, a member of the Royal Society. Even Mr Mill had been suitably and obviously impressed to learn that. In truth, the girl was benefitting from a rare liberty to pursue her own interests, mostly intellectual, and until the Empire sought to emulate the ideals of female authors advocating education for girls—like England's own Mary Wollstonecraft—London would simply have to grow accustomed to young, curious, diarist Caroline Fox perpetually peeking into its secrets.

Plus, the Cornish Fox clan were Quakers, tending towards the peaceful and seeking the good in everyone. They might seem irresponsibly libertine regarding the daily whereabouts of their daughter, but said child never explored London on her own, and Lizzie had once relayed to Harriet, wide-eyed, about the time Caroline had taken it upon herself to arrange a tour of the Royal Society, still in venerable Somerset House adjacent to the British Museum—even John and Harriet had been unable to visit during their day at the Museum.

Another youngster, Penny the housemaid, just out of sight now, chose this moment as the most opportune to bring the requested refreshments into the room for the women to savour. She set everything down, arranging tea settings flawlessly, even making the correct additions to the base tea that each of the other women preferred, she knew them that well. 'Will there be anythin' else, Mum?' was all she said.

Harriet quickly and silently wiped away a rebellious tear of her own. 'No, thank you, Penny, that shall be all for now.'

As Penny strode out, Caroline found humour in the situation once again. 'It's like asking when we last got together: how often have we lot almost come to blows?'

The others laughed at that, stirring their steaming cups of tea. 'It's amazing what women, and men too, for that matter, can accomplish when we're not fighting,' Lizzie said.

They smiled at that, waiting for their tea to cool, Harriet's guests trying the delicate blancmange as they each also glanced about for further inspiration.

'See here,' said Caroline, picking up the recent issue of the Monthly Repository, then knowingly flipping pages to reach what she wanted. 'Your friend Mr Mill writes, "Whether, according to the ethical theory we adopt, wisdom and virtue be precious in themselves, or there be nothing precious save happiness, it matters little; while we know that where these higher endowments are not, happiness can never be."'

'That's a lovely notion,' said Lizzie, 'and it hardly matters which such "theory" we adopt, does it? I mean, I'm no' a theorist or nothin,' now am I, wot?' She played her way into a cockney accent with the second rhetorical question, not so much making fun of the lower classes so much as verifying, perhaps, that she could identify with feeling undereducated. Indeed, Lizzie still had trouble reading much of anything—Odd that such a one can compose music! Harriet recalled—and one of the details that had enabled her to develop such passionate and fully requited feelings for Pastor Fox lay in his ability to help her improve. A love affair could be strengthened by both parties sharing something such that one could help the other in some way.

Harriet spoke this time, noting the playful then quickly wistful expression worn by Lizzie. 'He could have taught you well, Liz, my dear, and,' she hesitated, leaning in towards both women in a girlish ploy to make sure they were about to share some grand secret, 'do you both know, I at first thought Mr Mill would develop feelings for you, Lizzie!'

All three of them virtually squealed at that. 'Surely not!' exclaimed Caroline, and Lizzie merely tossed her head back and forth, making her hair bounce in what she presumed must be some alluring come-hither manner. While girls and young women of their station were not taught much beyond music and language and perhaps arithmetic, neither did they learn much about being coquettish at one extreme nor seductive at the other.

'Further,' Harriet continued, 'notice the title of that article, Caroline.' Harriet called faithful Penny back over, who offered refills of hot tea to her mistress and pair of boisterous guests. Penny herself enjoyed listening to them, and had already observed her mistress all but swooning just before or immediately after one of her outings with Mr Mill, who seemed an all right chap, to be sure, but Penny also had her own loyalty to the master of the house. *What must poor Mr Taylor be feeling these days?* Penny sometimes wondered.

'Penny, did you hear me?' repeated Ms Flower. 'Might I have one of those heavenly-smelling scones, please?'

'Mmm? Oh, yes, of course, Mistress Flower. Pardon me.' She used a well-polished pair of silver tongs to gently place one of the home-baked ginger scones on Lizzie's saucer. The women had already taken care of two cucumber sandwiches, daintily cut into fourths to make them what was known these days as 'finger-food.' Gluttony was not only a sin, but also a sure way to social embarrassment. Harriet found herself wishing her husband would remain away from home for even longer than usual lately, this time without guilt, since they had already indulged in enough repast to 'spoil' a later supper.

The serving-girl quickly made her way back out of the drawing room as Caroline read out the title of Mill's magazine piece. '"On Genius?" Is that a question inspired by genuine curiosity, or something pompous and bombastic?' The women giggled anew.

'I'm still not sure,' Harriet said, blowing gently over the surface of the fresh tea, then added, almost from behind her fine porcelain cup, 'I memorised the part most relevant to the title: "Whosoever, to the extent of his opportunity, gets at his convictions by his own faculties, and not by reliance on any other person whatever—that man, in proportion as his conclusions have truth in them, is an original thinker, and is, as much as anybody ever was, a man of genius." Or a woman of genius, one hopes.' She set the teacup down, knowing it would do no good to hide her face behind the Taylor family table service.

Caroline and Lizzie exchanged a knowing look, still smiling but no longer snickering. Harriet recognised the gesture at once. 'Oh, come now!' she said. 'I know people will talk, perhaps already are talking, but I need the support of my dearest friends with this.'

'And so you have it,' Caroline said immediately, meaning it. 'Do you know what else he has written?' she asked, again almost in a conspiratorial tone. 'He wanted to know, what is utility, that "usefulness" he considers, as distinguished from actual happiness?'

Lizzie lit up more at that, having heard it from Mr Fox, who himself was clearly quite taken with the work and words of Mr John Stuart Mill. 'I remember that, too: something like, "whose experience can decide that such is the only or the worthy result of human existence," and something else beyond that, but the gist of it was he used a really queer term about conformity, something Mr Fox himself noted since it's almost religious.'

'Crucifixion,' Harriet nodded. 'That's how he described it. He was saying how automatic or mindless or coerced conformity was the real enemy, and part of what he describes as "genius" is the courage and willingness to go beyond that.'

'Is that why we find ourselves on shaky grounds with our relationships?' Lizzie asked, with an innocence—naivety?—that belied her age. Caroline looked down at the floor with its fine rug—a Persian import, a gift from some very appreciative patients of Mr Taylor, whilst Harriet and Lizzie took each other's hands across the small round table, knowing they were each going well outside social norms and niceties in the pursuit of their heart's desires, their perceived happiness, or at least the pursuit thereof as the Yanks might say.

'By the way, Harriet,' Caroline interrupted the little revelry. 'You must, please, introduce me to that odd friend of Mr Mill—Mr Sterling,

I believe? I've been writing something about Thomas Carlyle and his dreary little wife, and would love to interview John Sterling if I could. Mr Carlyle has some intriguing insights about history, especially regarding the French Revolutions—odd that we now have to speak of more than one of them!—though Mr Sterling sounds fascinating.'

'In truth, I've yet to meet him myself,' Harriet answered, 'though during one of our next meetings,' she looked longingly out the room's sole window with its elegant lace drapery, 'I believe Mr Mill intends just that. I understand Mr Sterling has a strong Scots brogue you'll no doubt fancy.'

There were times when her friends were immune to adolescent teasing. 'He could be married, too, for all I care, Harriet. I just want to find out more about him, wholly innocently.'

Harriet so wanted to share something else on her mind, and was now silently chastising herself for the immature comment about Sterling's accent, although he was Scottish, and likewise sympathetic to issues like Irish Home Rule—'Celtic Fringe' peoples sometimes banded together, something they had failed to do when the Romans landed.

Whatever the case, Harriet had in recent months continued to communicate with another of John's friends, Mr Roebuck, whose confidence seemed truly warranted. He had not, so far as she knew, betrayed her secrecy regarding the humiliating and potentially dangerous implications of the mercury treatments, and she had given up on them anyway. The liquid metal was hazardous to work with in any conditions, and as for such horrid diseases—she fervently hoped—almost prayed really, despite her feelings, that a better cure would be enabled by the natural philosophers someday.

Changes to the British Reform Bill were all but sure to go into effect soon, and while her detailed and rational letter to Mr Roebuck—who was in fact running for Parliament for Bath, no less!—as their mutual trust had grown, had confided other personal details to each other, such as a shared belief that the expansion of British suffrage as outlined in the Reform Bill changes should include women. Perhaps only women of some means would be included at first—the same, despite its problems, as pertained to men, though there was continued debate about eliminating such voting requirements as property and literacy and education level or anything else besides citizenry. But women! Harriet still felt elated by her own audacity, having played with the sealed and addressed envelope with its radical letter for days before finally posting it Roebuck's way.

And now Lizzie and Caroline stared agape at Harriet as she relayed this astonishing piece of news to them. 'Women?' Lizzie said simply, with a slightly sarcastic intonation, the sort Harriet associated with disbelieving sexist men.

'Of course,' she answered. 'Imagine it: both of you, and I, having an official legal say in how this country and its empire are run. Envision if you will the three of us strolling arm in arm to a polling station, queuing with other women, and proudly entering the booths to cast our votes like so many more people all over the world should be able to do!'

Harriet sensed at once she'd gone too far. 'But do you think those people, women included, are really ready for this?' asked Caroline. Harriet was more surprised by her response: Lizzie, forward-thinking in some ways, remained remarkably traditional regarding how men and women should interact, never mind her affair with a wed gentleman, a religious official at that. But Caroline? Harriet found that vexing, this odd answer from her rebellious friend who openly confessed no need of and few feelings for men. The other gender was typically a hassle at best, a dangerous predatory menace at worst.

'Yes!' Harriet added defiantly. 'When people have something at stake, some personal investment, they care more. Think of what amazing societal rules we might bring about, starting with protections for women and children, who as you've pointed out before, Caroline, so often suffer the depredations of men.' She found she was almost sweating, deciding she could not allow anger at her husband to colour her views, not with her friends and not about something so important. And in fairness, John Taylor remained a gentle man even now, despite his ongoing sexual frustrations. Harriet found she had trouble even discussing those with her friends.

'Give us some time to adjust, Harriet,' Lizzie said. 'We believe in you,' she added, catching a glance from Caroline as she did so. 'Is this what all that time with Mr Mill has done?' she asked then, though her tone was unmistakably kind.

Harriet smiled. 'Partly, although in this case it's more a matter of me influencing him. What I mean is, for all of Mr Mill's "modern" attitudes and beliefs, the notion that women might number among those who are downtrodden by a majority, or at least by an apparent majority, seems to have largely escaped him.'

Caroline noted how all three of them had leaned in severely while chatting thusly, and they were amused when she pointed this out, like they were engaged in some dubious or even treasonous conspiracy. From the perspectives of many others, that was precisely what they were up to. Then Harriet sighed and said, 'You know, ladies, Mr Mill and I sometimes memorise each other's better passages, whether published or not. He had another letter appear in 'The Examiner' this year, which I think encapsulates this shared view of ours well.' She took in the curious glances of her friends, and continued. '"The test of what is right in politics is not the will of the people,"' Harriet intoned, '"but the good of the people, and our object is, not to compel, but to persuade the people to impose, for the sake of their own good, some restraints on the immediate and unlimited exercise of their will."'

'That stands to apply to a great many, Harriet, as you've noted already.'

Lizzie swallowed the rest of her cooling tea in a couple of quick unfeminine gulps, burping just slightly at the end of it. Caroline and Harriet held out as long as they could, then laughed, not knowing that the Taylor servants, minus Jonathan the butler, had heard them, indeed had been able to hear their voiced thoughts for several minutes now. And Penny in particular beamed when she heard Ms Flower proclaim, 'Mr Mill must then also condone the removal of those other restrictions for voting, like literacy.'

Harriet pursed her mouth at this, frowning slightly. 'I'm truly not quite sure yet, Liz,' she answered hesitantly. 'It would seem obvious, though I admit we have yet to discuss the matter in such detail.'

Yet dear Caroline seemed reluctant to let her concern go. 'Even so,' she started, 'and even if the literacy issue itself gets smoothly resolved—an issue, I would add, which would not apply to the likes of us since we can read—are "we," that is, women and freed slaves and the American Indians and the India Indians and anyone else... are we all ready for the power and implications that voting entails?'

Harriet just stared, aghast. Lizzie looked downward, whether from wanting to contribute more herself, or unsure just how to respond to Caroline, Harriet could not tell. 'How could anyone not be ready to express their own interests, their needs, in a politically protected manner?' she asked at last. The other women did not seem to have a ready response, and Harriet knew that both her friends at least appreciated that the trio already had things better than many women did, in so much of the world as well as in Dear Olde Englande. Perhaps an apparent shift in topic was justified.

'Lizzie,' she looked at her friend, 'I love that you're doing more with your music, like your seasonal songs, and your hymns.' She started to hum a few measures of one, until Lizzie rebuffed her, feeling embarrassed.

Then Lizzie answered, 'My thanks, sweet Harriet, and I shall continue to feel indebted to your own Mr Mill for the favourable review of those same songs in 'The Examiner' not so long ago.' And then she leaned in and whispered to the other women, 'And it further takes plenty of sheer will to avoid reading that awful Comte, whom you mentioned.'

'He writes in French, dear girl,' answered Harriet confidently, a faint trace of a smile playing at the corners of her mouth. Lizzie, the most playful soul of them all, giggled in return, but ability with another language remained a sore spot with Caroline, who in fact had wished to study French for years.

'Now if we were more empowered, you might feel more able to try and get more of your lovely tunes published, and therefore played, so more could savour them. And Caroline, the same applies to your own writings, as it does to mine, as well as to your wishes for continued study.' Caroline looked at her like she was clairvoyant.

And then Harriet took a further chance with their confidence, sharing something she had been working on in her diary and had thus far only hinted at in her ongoing letter correspondence with Mill. 'Happiness is what matters, ladies. "And what is utility as distinguished from happiness? Whose experience can decide that such is the only or the worthy result of human existence, thus bringing every genuine form of mind, that is to say every individual one, to the crucifixion of conformity to rules which apply to every manifestation of mind, the measure which is common to all minds."'

They both looked back at her. 'All minds,' repeated Lizzie. Caroline remained silent, but nodded.

'Think of it,' Harriet continued. 'This is a short life, something my father's work has taught me, since while he truly is an exceptional midwife, or mid-husband as Mother sometimes calls him jokingly—he never seems to mind that!—too many babies enter this beautiful yet terrifying world stillborn.'

'Or the mothers die during the process,' added Lizzie, who, giggling aside, remained terrified by the prospect of childbirth, knowing enough to realise that maternal survivability had barely improved since the later Middle Ages.

'Indeed,' Harriet said. 'And then think of my own brothers,' and she paused for a moment, recalling how death had invaded her own home, and how she thanked Nature—not God but 'Nature,' since the latter term could remain undefined and impersonal—every night as she watched her three children readied for bed. Harriet felt a pair of rebellious tears begin to make their way down her smooth and recently lined yet fetching face, in memory of two elder brothers dead of consumption, the horrid wasting disease which attacked the lungs and then the rest of the body. John, the younger, had almost survived to see his sister wed to Mr Taylor. Thomas, the elder, succumbed almost three years later.

That was the other part of what kept Harriet Taylor née Hardy reading about medicine and disease and health or its lack. Her friends had endured their own losses. They once discussed how through so much history parents waited perhaps a full year before naming their babies, since a non-named—yet hopefully baptised, Harriet could grimly hear so many British citizens cry—child would allegedly create a less severe emotional trauma.

So many had so little time. So what could be the point other than the enabling of one's own happiness, for whatever time one had? It did not have to be ongoing glee: such seemed the province of the mad or the inebriated, but rather the ongoing sense of well-being, of contentment, the notion that maybe one had at least had enough opportunity to help enable the happiness of other living creatures—Harriet reminded herself of the small animals, the occasional kitten or puppy or kit found in the ever-growing mercantilist beast called London, or of just knowing that one had been loved during one's finite breath of time.

Harriet could feel a hand of each of her long friends upon her back, and reached out to pull them into another triadic embrace, feeling their strength and love alike. *These are potent women,* she silently reminded herself, *so full of life and wonder and potential, and there must be newer and better ways of enabling that in others.*

She could feel their faces, smell their lively hair, as she gave breath anew to one of her poems, still unpublished, for she experienced the same trepidations of her friends when it came to attempting to create a name for herself.

"'Tis man, not nature, works the general ill,'" Harriet intoned softly, "By folly piled on folly, ill the heap Hides every natural feeling, save alone Grey Discontent, upraised to ominous height, And keeping drowsy watch o'er buried wishes.'"

'Amen,' said Lizzie and Caroline in unison.

* * *

Harriet slowly, gradually, patiently learned that it was not the unknown infant's death that prompted John Mill's emotional breakdown years before, and that while his honesty about some aspects of his life had gone truly appreciated by her, nothing had prepared her for an admission of what might under just slightly altered circumstances land someone in a sanatorium! Perhaps he had even visited one and remained hesitant to go that one step further and share that with her also, though she was not about to ask, not wishing to pry yet also feeling anxious. And what he called his breakdown was, ultimately, a simple case of overfilling an idealistic young mind with more information and more perspectives than it could emotionally process, a problem in those of genuine genius. In other words, it was an undiagnosed case of too much philosophy!—he had laughed when she offered that conclusion, though such were the risks when one had a famous thinker as a father who had little faith in the fledgling English public school system.

No, John Mill had seemingly weathered the psychic trial of the dead baby rather stoically, and Harriet found herself even admiring how he had handled it, how it might have made him braver, as with his willingness to risk gaol for speaking his mind by informing the public of something necessary, as in the tale he had shared during their first meeting.

But it was so difficult, even with the tacit support of her friends. She silently thanked Caroline and Lizzie for their recent help, and waited for her sometimes surprisingly masculine friend to 'spill it,' as one of the recent slangy phrases suggested.

So he spelled it all out for her. He had seen right through her atheism, or at least her 'hesitancy' as he labelled it, leaving her wondering how she had slipped up, since it remained in one's interest to not mention such, although her talks with this strange man helped her further wonder how enforced silence on any subject contributed to the happiness of the majority. And so he began by referring to one of the 'Trijackia's' get-togethers at the home of their mutual friend, George Grote, whose wife, still another Harriet, apparently quite easily tolerated the intellectually boisterous gathering of idealistic young men who thought they could alter the universe with ideas alone, Mrs Grote playing the dutiful hostess and not really engaging in the conversations directly, though she remained curious.

Mr Grote had written and published a piece almost a decade

earlier, under a pseudonym, that posed this tremendous question: not whether God existed—Grote seemingly took a singular masculine Deity for granted—but whether or not God's existence contributed anything at all to the happiness of the mortals who walked and crawled and slithered and hopped and swam and flew around His Creation.

It was this question of 'happiness,' this quirky, queer, universal yet maddeningly elusive term that was supposed to comfort and justify and soothe—yet Mill found himself irate, even furious, that no one seemed able to define it beyond anything fleeting and pleasurable. And this despite having given so much of his overwrought youth in a bookish quest to comprehend it. Perhaps it was small wonder that he 'cracked,' aged twenty.

Mill laughed at how the Americans, feeling still Revolutionary at the time, had tried to encapsulate the elusive word to justify their own—indeed each person's own—'pursuit' of the mysterious label, which, whenever put to the test, seemed to devolve into prurient instead of more enlightened pursuits. Yet John Mill found it just as frustrating to realise that he had little beyond the philosophy of the ancients he had studied so heartily—in their own languages, which he learned before turning ten—to justify those 'enlightened' or 'noble' interests. After all, who was he, this scion of a radical economic thinker and servant of Imperial economic interests, to tell anyone what form their happiness should take?

Harriet had almost begun to weep more than once during the telling—how her new friend and love had sought refuge in poetry: witness the vehemence with which he had defended Wordsworth!—and he knew his Shakespeare and Coleridge and had found himself warming to the Romantic writers. That made perfect sense: this perpetual walker, at home in the natural world, understood sublimity. But poetry or romantic prose, as Harriet herself knew, could only do so much to heal a reader who had lost faith or never had it. And that was how Mill opted to describe his inner torment, as a 'loss of faith,' despite, like Harriet herself, having no traditional religious belief of which to speak in the first place. For him it was more a faith in the power of reason, in philosophy generally, and particularly with the rational faith of his father and Bentham, who had done so much to advance the ideas of utility, especially as they pertained to happiness. *No wonder John gave so much detail over to that silly ice cream example!* Harriet thought, almost exasperated, then realised the example had actually been profound despite its superficial simplicity.

She hated to say good-bye to him that day, having loved it so, and she remained as yet unaware that he had been keeping her written correspondence, each piece lovingly addressed simply to 'Mr Mill' at his family's residence, after he moved out of his smaller flat and into the Mill home at Vicarage Place. John admitted he loved the site: a former vicar residence, across the street west of Palace Green, which in turn constituted the western edge of beloved Hyde Park. This park was, thought Mill, the best-kept and groomed of all London's greener areas.

Perhaps the oddest part of all was Mr Taylor's plan for a new house for his own family. He understood that his marriage had deteriorated, possibly for all time, and Harriet shook her head at the embarrassing memory, never shared, that on one occasion some nasty guilty part of her had almost wished her husband might actually do something as hopelessly and illegally melodramatic as challenge his erstwhile adversary—his wife's erstwhile partner, even lover, though thus far a lover via a meeting of minds and ideas and not some husky sharer of carnal pleasures which Harriet admitted no longer bothered her as much—to a duel.

*That would have been something!* she mused to herself. Neither of these men in her life was a traditional fighter, Mr Mill even less so than Mr Taylor, and she could hardly imagine either with a pistol at ten paces, while the thought of either with a sabre seemed even more laughable—though John had once alluded to some more physical training during his early years in France—she would have to press him for details on that sometime.

Amusement aside, Harriet thought less of a new house in itself and more of such quirky practicalities as how she and her friend /

lover / confidante / philosophical muse would continue getting letters to her, since having the servants gather mail when some was clearly in John Mill's own squiggly handwriting could certainly fan the fires of gossip; nor did she wish to arrange some ludicrous method of their getting written thoughts to each other via couriers or errand boys or however else spies might operate. She certainly would not consent to using lemon juice or—gasp!—urine as invisible ink, made visible when exposed to heat. At least Mr Taylor had some interesting tit-bits of chemical history to sometimes share from his work, though hopefully he refrained from signing prescriptions with his own waste.

And yet—a new house! Marital duty aside, there was surely something strong to be said about a man offering not just a roof over his family's heads and hearts, but to do so willingly without being asked, and on a more grandiose scale than before, and possibly with access to funds of unknown or dubious sources—oh, how Harriet hated not even knowing the most basic details of her family's finances!—yet how much was John Taylor willing to try to regain his wife's love? Would it work on the children? Were they susceptible to such blatant bribes, or would they perceive such a noteworthy gesture as one of love first and contrition second? The boys at least knew how to show gratitude for gifts of any scale, and she took pride in that—they had both delighted in the surprise basket of personally collected seashells sent to the family by Mill's friend Mr Sterling earlier this year. Haji and Herby adored the beach, any beach, and could frolic along the rockier coast of the resort town of Brighton as well as use their tiny wooden tools to forge magnificent castles out of the sand at places like West Wittering in Sussex, as a whole nation began to appreciate its coastal lands, its citizens slowly becoming more comfortable in purpose-made swimwear.

And now the house, with the boys and Lily, too. Harriet loathed the selfishness, wanting to pursue her intellectual and moral ideals with Mill as well as continue to blame Taylor for poisoning her body, even if he had never intended to do so. She had to believe that—that Mr Taylor had never meant to harm her. But she detested even more the attitude: her medical readings had confirmed that doctors in Europe and America and Asia all somehow stupidly believed that syphilis and other venereal diseases could only be passed under certain circumstances or if lovers took certain irrational precautions. Harriet wanted to be able to take some degree of surety from her own views, to test them out, even if only as thought experiments. She had a sometimes hostile attitude to Mill himself since he seemed to have already moved past the utilitarianism of his intellectual forebears faster than she could, apparently not realising that if nothing else, evaluating utility was a useful way—she meant no silly pun here—to learn to do philosophy and politics and ethics. As for the house, perhaps someday the pair of them would share such a space, as Harriet had already informed him that her legs felt stronger and her stamina improved, during recovery from her third birth and her walking—not fast so much as far—with her loving friend.

Why could people not just admit ignorance? She loved Mill, but he had trouble with this as well. Granted, he was brilliant in several fields, but the practical wisdom of running a household or keeping up with current events—be they slave revolts abroad or the destruction of forests at home—eluded him more than histories of peoples dead many centuries.

Sometimes she could tease John Mill too, and he found he hardly minded, as she played upon his semi-competence with the otherwise simple and common act of hiring a conveyance to get around the City: 'Yes dear I will meet you, in the chaise,' one of her notes read, 'somewhere between this and Southend—the hour will depend on what your note says to-morrow (that is supposing the chaise is to be had of which there is very little doubt.) Bless you dearest! I did not write yesterday. I wish I had for you seem to have expected it. I have been quite well and quite happy since that delicious evening.'

And then Mill himself would sigh longingly at the memory of not just any evening, but all the ones they had enjoyed at the Taylor home: 'I may perhaps see thee to-day, but if not I shall not be disappointed—as for sad I feel since that evening as though I never shall be that again. I am very well in all respects, but more especially in spirits. Bless thee—tomorrow will be delightful and I am looking to it as the very greatest treat so dear—if you do not meet me on your road from Southend you will know that I could not have the chaise Friday.'

John appreciated that colourful chaise, the pair of them thrilling to the energetic wind in their faces as they chased their way through the City. The conveyance reminded John of what he had previously regarded his personal land-speed record, desperately clinging to an ornery and not-to-be-controlled horse by an unsure boy during a childhood sojourn to France, about which he remained more reticent than the 'baby incident,' or assisting Sterling's asinine scheme of supporting radical and violent politics on the Continent. John finally felt able to admit freely to Harriet that he in truth still felt afraid of horses more often than not, realising they mostly just did as they had been trained and commanded. He even alluded to the sturdy gelding leading them in the chaise. 'See,' he began, 'this trusty beast pursues his own freedom, his own happiness, as best he can within his circumstances.'

So Harriet had learned something of how he thought by now. 'Yet though he is cared for—fed, sheltered, watered, groomed and rubbed, and loved in his own way, there yet remain many things he cannot do, including escape London to pursue some fabled grassy field that he has perhaps dreamt of or knew as a foal.' Harriet knew she was putting a sweet face on it to make a point: she hoped that more forthcoming legislation might reinforce the noble attitudes embodied by the Society for the Prevention of Cruelty to Animals, formed in 1824, but legally the non-humans in their midst were property, just as slaves and women and children remained thus.

How did John Mill escape believing all that evil? she wondered anew. *Here is a man raised to respect authority, an active participant in the Empire's control of so much of the globe via his employers, and yet he is the gentlest and most sympathetic man I have ever met!* Harriet sought an answer to this as much as she sought to simply remain in his company. 'That's just the issue, Harriet: when you explain utility too simply, especially if you make reference to "pleasure and pain" like the ancients and now Bentham, then too many will too quickly conclude that it is merely a recipe for hedonism.'

'I know, John,' she answered. 'And we've worked at helping others understand how it is never that simplistic, how indeed the potential variables and confounding factors are, well, hypothetically endless!' she breathed. It was indeed daunting: how could they, even as a brilliant team that got on well together—usually—collaborate to elucidate on questions and issues which affected everyone and everything—ethics, even in its quirky utilitarian form, left nothing out of potential or necessary consideration—and not come across as heavy-handed, or self-righteous, or, during their darker days, often whilst reading negative reviews, though most had been quite positive and encouraging, seemingly mad?

John once told Harriet that being half-mad was essentially a prerequisite to doing philosophy proper. She still did not know if he had meant that earnestly, or whether he perhaps offered self-deprecating comments like that as a way to face the pain and—his word—shame for his breakdown before they ever met. A person had to not just explain and justify, which meant having a knowledge of logic and reason, and with ethics it became trickier, partly since so many—too many by far thought Harriet—either 'just knew' what was right—an extremely problematic assertion—or that ethics came from, indeed could only ever come from, religion.

The world's religions each had their own moral lessons, to be sure, some quite good; but John and Harriet were solid enough students of history to comprehend how many endless times divine beliefs had been perverted into monstrous things, with untold millions losing their lives in the process. And John further, with his non-expert yet working knowledge of various Asian traditions and beliefs, knew well two things: beliefs differed, even with similar messages; and ethics could not hope to do much of anything if it was not universal, if it did not apply to all living things. Critics continually attacked hedonism this way, and the conservatives stuck to their beliefs, secure that religious faith somehow rendered the believer above reproach, as all one had to do was cite one's 'sacred' beliefs—Harriet Taylor's most hated view: she despised that attitude—but it made for bad philosophy and weak ethics. John and Harriet had assisted one another with more concretised justifications.

For justification of all sorts, built on logic, was his speciality. And her own ability to reason had improved exponentially, as he helped her to become a stronger and more coherent thinker, whilst her equally powerful desire to change so many societal aspects from within shaped his work. She sometimes copied bits and pieces of their talks—serious or madcap, loving or public—into her now well-worn journal, and while she hardly wrote in it every day, or even every month, she still had one of her favourites just inside the cover from a letter he had penned to dear Mr Sterling: 'We have to consider, which we can only do together, how much of our story it is advisable to tell, in order to make head against the representation of enemies when we shall not be alive to add anything to it. If it was not to be published for a hundred years I should say, tell all, simply and without reserve. As it is there must be care taken not to put arms in the hands of the enemy.'

Harriet rarely told John how much she relished reviewing his prior thoughts. For the moment, he simply nodded. 'Yes. I quite believe you're understanding why I've moved away from utilitarianism, sweet Harriet.' She adored when he addressed her thus, no longer weepy at how her husband once called her the same. Eventually there were just no tears left.

'I am loved as I desire to be—' she wrote to him once, another of those bits and pieces sneaking its way into her little personal book for private posterity, still feeling a phantom touch of the wind in her dishevelled hair, '—heart and soul take their rest in the peace of ample satisfaction after how much calm and care which of that kind at least have passed forever—oh this sureness of an everlasting spiritual home is itself the blessedness of the blessed—and to that being added—or rather that being brought by, this exquisiteness which is and has been each instant since, and seems as if with no fresh food it would be enough for a long life's enjoyment. O my own love, whatever it may be or not be to you, you need never regret for a moment what has already brought such increase of happiness and can in no possible way increase evil. If it is right to change the 'smallest chance" into a "distant certainty" it would surely show want of intellect rather than use of it.'

This day, however, they contented themselves with walking, sometimes holding hands, sometimes arm in arm, and not caring what others might think.

\* \* \*

John Taylor dreaded chats with relatives in general, with his in-laws in particular, and utterly resented feeling he had nowhere else to go. Yet one fair evening, just after supper but prior to when the Hardys were likely to be in bed—Mr Hardy kept all hours, thanks to his professional calling, and Mrs Hardy seemed to rarely need sleep at all—he found himself knocking on their door. Without Harriet, with no sign of his children, who themselves had already been tucked in for an early night, being read to by Penny, bless her.

Who else was he to turn to at this point? Not his club—nay, the other 'gents' could hardly be trusted to keep certain matters truly secret. Not his children—dear God!—what effect might this have on them? Not Mill himself—damn the man's polite rationality!—who, then, could a man solicit help from regarding a wayward wife, a horrendous disease, and marriage that remained intact essentially for show?

Her own family, of course, though John Taylor miserably. He knew from prior experience that unlike other parties, they would gladly keep certain details private—how dreadful could it prove to be for a man who helped usher children into the world, including the Taylor's own, if word somehow escaped that syphilis had taken hold of part of the family?

Taylor had heard the staff whispering about his domestic situation, and whilst he had briefly been tempted to determine if any interest in a dalliance might be found with Penny—such arrangements with service staff being common, to Taylor's understanding—he never thought it could amount to anything, and her father was likewise in their employ. There was another maid—Madge, whose off-putting looks were more than made up for by her attention to detail, as the Taylor home typically sparkled. Yet it just wasn't worth the effort, and though it pained him dreadfully to countenance it, he also knew what he'd 'given' to his wife. He could seek his own medicinal treatments, like the solution made from guaiacum wood he had created himself: that 'holy wood' imported from the Caribbean.

But it offered no more actual remedy than the horrible mercury that his wife was using, or at least had used. He knew, of course: apothecaries represented a tiny professional world. He had hoped the treatments would work, remembering the heinous taste and odour of the pulpy guaiacum tincture whilst walking up to the door to knock. He hated even more the ugly truth that he could not even advise Harriet about which form of mercurial treatment might work best: the more expensive calomel, with powdered mercury oxide; or heading to the Continent—England had no such spas—to a sanatorium for the intentional inhalation of steam laced with mercury vapours, since the liquid metal emitted its own heady fumes. And the side effects were breath-taking, no pun meant: thank God neither he nor his wife had presented with erethism or such excessive drooling that others might have thought they had much in common with rabid dogs!

Inside the Hardy home it smelled peaceful, relaxing. The Hardys made do with just a pair of servants, two now almost middle-aged women, cousins, Taylor thought, who roughly shared cooking and cleaning between them, such was Mrs Hardy's pride in their 'humbler' home. Mr Hardy could afford more impressive, but he liked to help out with the furthering of his children's educations, plus there was another future dowry for which to save.

After politely declining tea—it would keep him up too late again, Taylor knew—and after the group had settled in the small drawing room, Mr Hardy spoke up with a resigned air of finality regarding his headstrong eldest daughter. 'We have been extremely blessed, John: while the ravages of disease may have stolen our dear Thomas and John from us — our two first-born — we yet have sons living, even besides William here.' William barely glanced their way; he had not felt much inclination to take on any 'traditional' responsibilities of the eldest son, and he had idolised Thomas and John while they'd lived. William's key motivation lay in keeping himself safe from those same ravages of disease, since consumption and cholera continued to take too many young English lives.

His father continued. 'And we have our dear young Caroline, too. Few parents are blessed with eight children, and few children have been brought terrified into this dangerous world with the help of a man who knows his art.' Father had a penchant for calling his work that, William knew, as elder sister Harriet could attest: midwifery, whether done by woman or man, was truly an art, not a craft nor a mere trade, no matter what the conceited physicians said, the ones who refused to get their hands dirty by touching patients.

Mr Taylor knew all this, too. 'Sir, with respect, why do you remind me of this now?'

Mr Hardy exhaled slowly and deliberately, the mark of a pensive man. 'Just to tell you, lad, that I will speak to young Harriet if you wish, find out more about this rapscallion Mr Mill if necessary.' Mrs Hardy audibly bristled at that, the sharp intake of air denoting the opposite of her husband's exhale.

'Thank you, sir, but no, I should think not. I have reason to believe that I remain non-cuckolded as of yet, and indeed that this odd "friendship" with Mill is just that.'

'But it's unseemly,' added Mrs Hardy. 'For a young married woman, a mother no less, to go off gallivanting with whomever she should please. What if they are seen together, which it seems inevitable they must be?'

'Madam,' Taylor spoke just as softly as he had previously, 'I similarly believe there exists little likelihood of that as well.'

'You know,' added Mr Hardy, 'I've met the man's father. James

Mill is something of a radical. I used to admire some of what he wrote in the past, but some of what he calls for is unrealistic. The same for that friend of his, what's his name—?'

'Bentham. Jeremy Bentham,' Taylor said. He'd read some of what these intellectual men had written. He had to admit he rather liked some of Bentham's ideas for penal reform, and knew young William here did, too, making noises as he did sometimes about how the colony in Australia had begun, and wanting to head all the way down there to try his own fortunes. Will had become a bit of a hypochondriac after the untimely deaths of his brothers, and felt the drier atmosphere 'down under' might do him wonders.

'Yes, Bentham,' Mr Hardy all but spat. 'Him, too. Reform is one thing, as with this latest suffrage bill—which I approved of myself, by the by—but radical change just gets you in trouble.'

'Agreed, Sir,' was all Taylor seemed inclined to offer, not wanting to discuss politics. 'In the meantime, I remain with a—usually—lovely devoted wife who may be having second thoughts,' though he refused to say why, precisely. These other persons hardly needed to know anything about that!

'But then why the secrecy?' wondered Mr Hardy. 'Harriet's a fine mum, a—usually—obedient daughter.' He seemed truly flabbergasted by all of this, and, perhaps a credit to his sex, did not himself head off into the Stews or other neighbourhoods of ill repute and outright danger—muggings, rapes, robberies, murders, gambling houses—featuring anything from illegal boxing matches to cockfights to dogfights to untrustworthy cards and dice and other games of 'chance,' opium dens, and prostitutes... He took pride in remaining 'clean' in that sense, and felt his wife was better off remaining largely ignorant of such locales. Some of his acquired knowledge had been gleaned in dirty fashion, too, desperately summoned on a handful of occasions to assist with emergency deliveries of babies to whores or other unfortunates: immigrant, poor, or both, and Mr Hardy sometimes admitted to himself that it was challenging to determine whether such persons deserved their fate or if whatever men appeared in their lives were equally to blame.

Mr Hardy silently prayed again that his son-in-law did not deserve his fate. He had resisted—albeit lackadaisically—the prodding of friends and business associates to 'get a proper marital education' with someone who would never use her sinful and dirty mouth to kiss his children goodnight. Hardy wanted to blame someone, needed to do so.

But—damn it all!—he also thought he and his wife had raised their children, or at least this elder mulish daughter, better than this. To find stress in one's marriage, or in becoming a parent, was part of the equation, surely it always had been. Time and again Hardy had encountered young women on the verge of adding new life to the world who displayed a full range of feelings—from pride to contentment, from anxiety to terror—and these were all natural. But to run the risk of social approbation, and pour shame onto a decent young man in the process, that was something else.

He had to request that Taylor repeat himself. 'I said, secrecy is surely to be prized regarding the sanctity of one's home and marriage, is it not, Mr Hardy?'

'As you wish, lad. I, that is, we,' he looked at his wife, who beamed back at him, appreciative of the inclusion, 'will try and remain out of it all, at least for now.'

Mr Taylor just looked sad and contemplative. His parents-in-law thought his visage betrayed anger at his wife, and had no comprehension that just as much of his frustration he kept aimed at himself. He rose, offered his most courteous thanks, shook the hands of Mr Hardy and William, and slinked off into the night.

* * *

*From the journal of Harriet Taylor: December, 1832*
The next time the family went for ice cream—little Lily still too young, but the boys thrilled, almost as much as they had been when agog over Mr Sterling's gift of seashells—Mr Taylor caught me just staring at mine, almost like it was unsafe to eat, yet he knew how much I love that silly frozen concoction. I burst out laughing again, just like

on that previous occasion, something proper young English wives and mothers simply are not supposed to do, especially in public, then found that as much as I wished to do so, I could not explain to these other important males in my life the source of my laughter. Oh, Mr Taylor would have understood, certainly—as I've noted previously, he's very bright, perhaps sometimes too much by half—but would he want to understand? He eventually returned to spooning up his own favourite flavour, strawberry, whilst I pondered the utility of so much.

Thus, Dear Diary, my dilemmas: how to offer the love and support and education that my children—Mr Taylor's children!—deserve, without any of them ever, one hopes, feeling as though they have been somehow left out, or that they might have unwittingly contributed to our marital distress, or the like. And then, I must query myself: how also to enable my own happiness. I hate this! The whole mess must surely be a forerunner of hell, if I were foolish enough to believe that a loving Deity could punish, often arbitrarily and for all time, 'sins' which might only elicit fines from Earthly powers. Even prison sentences run out eventually, and I am quickly coming round to the opinion that what we do to ourselves can surely be much more devastating than what we do to each other. This is something I know John Mill understands as well: how else could he have plunged into his own psychic hell, having his poor if brilliant head stuffed so damnably full of data from a young age? If I had been made to translate ancient Greek while other boys were still having pretend swordfights, I should imagine a little madness might have crept into my soul as well!

And yet part of that youthful hell is now gone from John. Mr Bentham, that brilliant, maddening, inspiring, vexing champion and critic alike of our strange and continually-changing age, died this summer past, in fact not long after John left me with that ice cream which I shall undoubtedly never forget! Writing radical philosophy; even travelling to the Russian Empire with his brother to study their penal system in an effort to perhaps improve our own; contributing to the 'Westminster Review' all manner of ideas, from equality of the sexes to improving the welfare of all manner of animals to decriminalising homosexuality to always keeping that ideal of 'the greatest happiness' in his mind as a guiding principle; and grounding these projects in what was usually simple yet tight logic—what should one say of such a man? John attended the service, and I of course could not—there would be no way to explain my presence, though I remain sorry I never met the man, the very idea of whom once frightened me. He labelled all 'God-given' things taken as sacred by so many people in this world as legal fictions, as 'nonsense on stilts.' He was brave, if slightly loony. John described him as lovable, though cantankerous; it seems apt, yet how closely can one know another only through one's writings?

And now he may get to scare others instead. I laughed aloud when John informed me that part of Mr Bentham's dying wishes included not only being dissected to assist with our collective anatomical knowledge—one hopes embarrassment dies with the body!—but having what was left displayed, preserved in as studious a position as possible, mind you, in an airtight case outside one of the lecture halls at new University College here in London!

So now, my Diary (my Conscience?), how do I apply that odd 'calculus' of Mr Bentham—whom I felt as though I would know on sight, since John has spoken so much of him, albeit largely to disagree with much of his philosophy!—and also since I have taken the liberty—pun intended?—of reading Bentham's works for myself? More specifically, am I entitled to seek my own happiness, even if it begins to take a rather different form from that which I envisioned as such a young woman those years past, making my innocent if heartfelt vows at the altar, in front of dear Mr Fox and our families and other witnesses?

On the side of the calculus, and what I once savoured with Mr Taylor—sexuality appears to be the manner by which all between human beings reaches the most beautiful within our nature—and we may be unique within the animal kingdom in having the option of touching and sharing our love face to face, and what could be more powerful than that? There is nowhere for the sentiments to hide during such circumstances, so perhaps that is the reason why certain sexual positions are disallowed—by law!—in certain reactionary societies. I even asked John during our sojourn to France if his cultural contacts with India and its fascinating history had included that curious 'Kama Sutra,' and John blushed at my question! Silly, dear, lovable man: what we shared together during that trip will remain with me always, and him too, no doubt—I think I quite surprised him! He yet requires some tutelage in ars amor, and he still seems like an adolescent at times, wanting both Magdalene and lover, as I think one of his friends put it—Sterling, likely. As for chastity, it can be neither virtuous nor vicious; it is merely abstemious, and anyone who avoids an experience intentionally hardly seems able to consider his—or her—actions and decisions in light of the one part of Mr Bentham's philosophy I seem to remain stuck upon, so to speak. Sex may be pure biology—even my children have witnessed rabbits and dogs engaged in 'the act,' and have posed questions which I answer without blushing, a different response from that of my husband, who like most men seems to think people will simply figure things out on their wedding nights or, as with his own degraded case, seek the socially approved 'tutelage' of women of the night. Yet sex, at least for us, could be elevated to among the 'highest' pleasures imaginable—a means of bonding, of honest and vulnerable communication, in addition to the orgasm which our polite society so often condemns, never mind that European thought since the Middle Ages has believed—wrongly, it turns out—that female orgasm is in fact necessary for conception!

What, then, of Mr Taylor: was he entitled to seek his 'utilitarian' pleasures, as so many callous men in our culture are, outside of the devout marriage bed? What of our children: how could they be affected, and how will this shape their own views of marriage and polite society as they age? How will they find their own happiness? What of dear Mr Fox and his doomed relationship with my other dear friend, Ms Lizzie Flower? She remains the only female friend with whom I could share these revealing thoughts, and even she has trouble, still mired in social guilt, surely not helped by the illicit nature of their relationship.

And yet my own with my dear Mill remains at least as illicit—more so, it must be the case, since with me there are children involved, and no one wants to accommodate the offspring of a 'broken' home or marriage. So why can I discuss these things more forthrightly? Am I whore first and wife second, or whore at all? Why are men not labelled whores, no matter their proclivities? But then, one's own happiness, derived from honest self-appraisal, is clearly a condition of all sentient existence. Those rabbits and dogs sought their own happiness too, even if they could not describe it in human linguistics. And yet this is tempered by the fact that our own pursuits of happiness—dear me, now I sound like one of those Yanks!—overlaps with, conflicts with, the similar pursuits of others. One of those dogs chases and kills one of those rabbits for the enjoyment of its next meal, and many puppies and kits will never even reach adulthood... and a wife faces betrayal and goes about destroying that which she once swore to protect, a marriage contract. And as these utility-thinkers and moral writers from time immemorial compel us each to ask the question again: who is entitled to blame whom? Assigning moral blame—or praise—must number among the utmost responsibilities that any of us humans can ever undertake. There is no innocence here; we are all of us judges. That notion hugely drove the late Mr Bentham.

Around and round go these nebulous and troubling thoughts. Bentham's little maths explanation remains wanting, simply because it is too simple. Even the same question, as I recall that delectable ice cream, could yield a different mathematical answer at different times: what if the person did not like that flavour of the dessert—I hate Mr Taylor's cursed strawberry!—what if the money spent on it would be better spent on some necessity, especially for one's child; what if some new competitive frozen treat emerged which did not use the products of our local dairies and orchards, and imported the like from elsewhere, as with the other components...? What-if, what-if: the mind whirls and gapes at the monumental impossibility of it all.

No wonder so many of the great moral philosophers opted to stick to rigid principle instead—I shall have to endeavour to study more of them, though whether for my own edification or to impress my lovely friend, I shall not declare within these pages, at least not at this time.

And still, what then of that self-same rigidity, the unforgiving nature of the moral rule, which can inspire at one moment and terrify or even injure the next? We are used to this already, as citizens of an Empire with its eternal emphasis upon the minutiae of decorum—except for what we do in secret, such as cheat on our spouses, either with harlots or with family friends—and I do know that dear John's 'spirit of the age' might just as easily imply 'the spirit of conformity,' yet I must condemn the latter as the root of all intolerance, for the mere 'opinions' of a society are merely wispy and as phantoms, but then witness the power of those phantoms, no matter how much steely logic may be wielded against them. These opinions, these conformities, evince the power of the many weak against the few strong.

If I may, I went just a touch beyond dear John with his notion of that epoch-spirit, or the German 'Zeitgeist,' as Mr Taylor called it. To his credit and my appreciation, John thought it numbered among the items I should continue to attempt to get into print. As I put it last year, 'The searcher after the origin of the sublime and beautiful wept over the departure of the age of chivalry. Had he lived a few years later he might have hailed the dawn of as prolific an age that of charlatanerie; of which indeed he might have made a worthy leader.' Now the sublime and beautiful are what John—and I now, more often than not, even with my slower gait—find out-of-doors, as he emphasises the syllables, in the natural world among trees and bushes and wild beasts. As for the chivalrous, or those aspiring to such in our time, one notices cruelty and repression as much of the impetus behind their attitudes.

I must add this also, then share it with my 'lovely friend,' as John now refers to me, and I stare now at the words I composed earlier this evening, partly for his consideration: 'The remedy is, to make all strong enough to stand alone, and whoever has once known the

pleasure of self-dependence, will be in no danger of lapsing into sub-
serviency.' That is how I feel lately: emerging from a state of subser-
vience into one of greater moral and intellectual freedom, prompted
as it was by such odd blends of ideas as those of Mary Wollstonecraft
and a philandering, diseased husband, whose own guilt has brought
him to tears in my presence. How do we go on destroying, when all
I wish is to live?

My new beloved—may I call him that now?—continues to live
with his doting if daunting family at Vicarage Place, on Church Street
over in Kensington. One wonders what they might think of all this,
assuming we eventually go more 'public' with our situation. Would
they celebrate their genius son finding love, even if in an unusual and
not-quite-socially-acceptable manner, or condemn him regardless
for interfering with an existing marriage? Would I be taken as harlot
by them, or worse? Admittedly, this seems getting ahead of matters
somewhat, but it is difficult to control where one's mind leads, especially once passions offer much of its motivation.

* * *

### 1833 through 1834.

While strains within marriages may be inevitable—one
already hears those who are wed for longer than a few
weeks snicker—that between Mr John Taylor and Ms
Harriet Hardy, now Mrs Taylor, had evolved into something so
unusual for its time and place and culture that none of the participants—Mr Taylor, Mrs Taylor, nor even Mr Mill nor any of their
avowed friends or those who gossiped about all the drama becoming more challenging to contain—really knew how to navigate it all
properly. Indeed there was no 'proper' in this case, not only since marital vows were getting regularly cast aside in their society—leaving
questions about what marriage might truly be for—but also because
even while new habits had developed, some 'rules' were never codified,
and the love-triangle drama, no doubt worthy of some English fiction

appearing at the time and often asking similar questions, took on the feel of improvisational theatre. The problem was exacerbated by the fact that such theatre remained almost wholly unknown in England, where, just like with its marital regulations, the performing arts had to be done that certain way—rehearsed, rigid, reinforced—perhaps like marriage itself.

Yet to describe it as drama hardly negates the potent feelings of the players, nor their family members who, whether the Taylor children, or the Hardy or Mill siblings, the latter group adults or nearly so by now, allowed their feelings to venture into confusion to hostility to greater or lesser degrees of acceptance. Harriet Taylor was reminded of this the first time she witnessed her love John Mill weep like a new-born, during one of their 'reunions' in London. She actually had thought the new house purchased by her husband was proving beneficial to all: away from the tighter, enclosed society of London proper, with space for the children to play—Herby and Haji loved the duck pond, even swimming in its filthy water on occasion despite parental admonitions to refrain from doing so—thus enabling, oddly, one of those rare moments when Mrs and Mr Taylor could agree on something—and little Lily likewise loved the small grassy field where said ducks and other small wild creatures sometimes had to flee for their dignity, chased by squealing human children.

But the key players, the adults, were not fooled by any of the growing and sometimes farcical pretences. Despite Mr Mill's entreaties—trying to convince the husband of the woman he had come to love that they were strictly intellectual partners—which to a large extent remained quite true, though one would have to ask both him and Mrs Taylor some extremely indecorous questions to learn why—there remained times when Mr Taylor simply did not feel the need to abandon his own home for several hours for yet another cosy night at his gentlemen's club. And sometimes said club's fellow members might jest, though thankfully nothing so piercing as to leave Taylor feeling a wont for vengeance.

'Thank God you've not been seen together in public yet!' he once shouted at his wife, not knowing it was untrue, though witnesses to their outings thus far had either been total strangers, or, to stretch credulity, known associates opting to not gossip. And she gave as good as she got, yelling back, 'Thank God you've not spread your disgraceful disease to our children!' The moments just afterwards marked the closest John Taylor had ever come to striking his wife, or any woman for that matter, and his shame held his hand that day. He would have been within his rights, and some socially acceptable and buried part of his psyche knew that such a move would have only given his wife — his partner, the mother of his children — more intellectual ammunition for these radical ideas about women and society. For that, and for feeling the better man, he took some amount of pride that day.

But he knew so much was his fault. 'Lads' had a long history of patronising places of 'ill repute' in Southwark and Whitehall and the like, and Taylor had even returned to such to try and find the doxie who'd given him syphilis. He had himself checked by his own physician, had begun treating himself in the time-tested fashion — being an apothecary carried certain perquisites, of course, though mercury, according to the academic literature on the subject, such as it existed, had a success rate of dubious reliability. Regardless, he never found the trollop — Rosemary? No, Maggie? — blast it, he could no longer be sure, though he felt confident he would recognise her on sight, only to tell her, what? *Get out of this horrid business, miss, for yourself and before you infect anyone else.* The idea that slumming with any woman also underscored his cavalier attitude to his own marriage was an idea more slowly coming to the otherwise quite intelligent Mr Taylor; his focus lay more with trying to right a different kind of wrong.

Sometimes the guilt did not quite reach the man, who knew he was being cuckolded, at least on that damnable 'intellectual' level, like the bloody Frenchies, and in deference to him he had proved remarkably accommodating — most men, no matter their financial means and acumen, simply did not purchase new homes for philandering wives and confused children in efforts to win them back, and the truth remained that Taylor doted on those children as much as their mother did, though the boys, Herby and Haji, being slightly older, seemed to feel roughly equally comfortable with their true father as with the man who was already described as something of a 'foster' father. Haji called the man 'Uncle,' for God's sake! Lily remained too young to understand much about the situation, though she too liked being picked up and held and cooed to by Mill as much as by her actual father. Mr Mill seemed endlessly patient with the youngsters, Mrs Taylor once accidentally mentioning in front of Haji and Herby something about Mill's 'lost' childhood.

So the complications continued. And it proved easier to escape them, or at least to briefly pretend that they might not exist, by leaving for a time. What better destination could exist for the strangely matched group than the locale most suited to permit Harriet to practice her linguistic skills, especially for idealistic Francophile John Mill? The République had been deemed safer as of late, after the chaos resulting from a restored monarchy. John had kept trying to comprehend why, after disposing of its royals as England had done in the mid-seventeenth century only to restore them after a vicious civil war, said monarchy was dissolved a second time. Harriet gently chided him about that, reminding him that not everything on the Continent was bound to follow English historical archetypes, and that different circumstances had led to France's own revolution and resurrection of its royalty. But when talk turned to Parliament making John's corporate employers the de facto governing body of India—itself exhibiting a quite different history and culture from both France and England—John opted to switch topics and start enjoying the scenery near where he spent so much of that lost childhood.

But that had largely been in delightful Montpellier, far to the south, and Harriet had gone, with her husband's gracious funding, to the capital city instead, finding her own delight in haunting the bakeries, two fruit and vegetable stands, and a butcher, all but glowing as the Parisians lit up to hear her nuanced and not quite fluent but energetic French, spoken better—so the shopkeepers without exception told her—than any of her Rosbif compatriots back home.

By the time John joined her at the end of that delectable summer, she had made real progress on more written works of her own, in a small rented flat a few minutes' walk from the mighty yet tranquil Seine. She had already been twice to the Louvre museum and through fabled Notre Dame cathedral by the time she could meet her partner, feeling totally free as he actually picked her up — small, weak John Mill! — upon reaching her at the immortal and ancient Pont Neuf bridge over the river. Such happenings were clearly worthy of subsequent entry in Mrs Taylor's private diary, and while their first French foray left them feeling a touch guilty, this time they could be more themselves. That the Taylor lads remained at home this time surely helped.

'Now, dear Harriet,' he exclaimed, spinning her a second time before setting her down, 'try to imagine where the French will have to build their rail stations! The Liverpool and Manchester has worked beautifully for three years now, and the time will come when trains link whole nations.' He wasn't even winded, despite his seeming frailty; he was actually full of stamina, sometimes to his lover's chagrin, and not just with walking. Of course he had lost himself in some current exciting thought process en route to her! She herself had become slightly faint more easily several times during these past weeks, and might have to share that with him, but for now it felt too good just to be next to him again. That would take some doing: she loathed how so many women swooned and fell, not, according to her, from actual medical conditions, but from a childish need, emphasised by their society, to be perceived as frail and in need of male protection.

'Dear Heart,' she began to answer, 'it is always sheer joy to behold you anew. Welcome to Paris. Again! You almost made it in time for my birthday.' His being here was gift enough. She still blushed from his greeting, partly from its unadulterated warmth and longing, partly from its, well, she searched for the word, for its public-ness. Polite English women did not tolerate being picked up by anyone, certainly not in full view of so much of a capital city. Yet Harriet knew the French would not have cared, would likely even have cheered them on: she noticed no condescending glances from others strolling about the Pont Neuf. This was a city for love, or so she had been raised to believe. It already felt vastly better than when she had penned to John, in a period of growing frustration over their 'situation,' that 'happiness has become to me a word without meaning.' She had regretted those words almost as soon as she had posted them, though John had thankfully not taken them to heart, or at least never held them against her.

They walked arm in arm, John in a light blue jacket which accentuated his similarly coloured eyes, with beige trousers and darker well-worn shoes that, for all she knew and all he cared, might have previously been utilised by him during one of his rambling excursions. She felt ideally matched, wearing a darker yellow, almost orange, ensemble of light skirt with petticoat and, thank goodness! she thought, no corset, though her husband had never attempted to command her to wear one, among his more endearing if superficial traits.

'Now tell me, my love,' John said, 'what think you of mighty Paris?' He pronounced it, of course, Pear-eeh, the French way. 'You know, I never actually came here as a lad, at least not to stay, really.'

'Really?' she echoed. 'I did not know that. For some reason, I thought you had spent quite some time here.' She could not remember from where she acquired that notion.

She loved the disguised strength in his proffered arm, wanting to rest her head on his shoulder, but preferred to walk a bit faster than that might permit. 'Montpellier is quite to the south of the country, really,' he added. 'It was quite the adventure to get there each time we came over to visit, and I do not think I ever mentioned that while I never became much of a rider, I also often loathed the jarring bumpiness we had to endure in enclosed carriages for any kind to travel. It seemed more romantic to sail southwest from England, enter the Pillars of Hercules, and thence past the Spanish coast to the French.'

She stopped, suddenly but not hostilely, and looked right into those cornflower blue eyes. 'Mr Mill,' she teased — he always knew now she was teasing when she addressed him such, and he sometimes did similarly in reverse — 'you may be the only person I know who would refer to the Strait of Gibraltar by its archaic and mythic name!'

He laughed, squeezing her hand with his, then turned and began to lead her down the bridge again, looking up at the myriad busy buildings. 'It's the romance again, my dear Harriet. A strait is just a drab name for a fascinating sea passage, and Gibraltar is a British name, just one of many to remind us English of how much of the world lay in our grasp. I hear enough evidence of such at work.'

She thought she felt the slightest tensing as he said so, but ignored it otherwise. 'Well then, keep the romance coming. Tell me of Montpellier.'

'Oh, a marvellous place for children, really.' She always—well, usually—liked how he could just keep going once fed a certain topic. 'It's said that children "pick up" languages more easily than adults, which I suspect has some truth to it, as I got to speak in French regularly, as you might imagine. By then, Father already had me reading in Latin and old Greek, of course,' Harriet thought she felt that same torso tension again, 'though one finds fewer speakers of either these days, even if French is derived largely from Latin.'

That was what she thought she had fallen in love with: this uncanny ability of this strange yet perpetually friendly, polite man to link bit after bit after bit of the whole panorama of human knowledge and show without patronising how the bits and pieces were interrelated. To him, the divisions—between man and woman, Whig and Tory, rich and poor, European and African and Asian—had little actual truth and were built far more on artificiality. She attributed this to his willingness to continue working for his even odder corporate employer—surely the handsome pay did not hurt, she admitted—as he remained in a trusted position to affect communications—and thus to some degree decisions—in ways and to locations throughout the Empire which he thought would do the most good. So far as Harriet Taylor could discern, John Mill eased his conscience by trying to behave in as positive a utilitarian manner as he could—though she had already learned not to call him a utilitarian exactly, since he still claimed to hate it, but she thought it was partly the age-old effort of the young to shake off to some extent the teachings of the prior generation — Bentham and the older Mill! — and assert his own independent thinking.

*What did he just say? Oh, yes... Latin and French.* 'Harriet, did you hear me?'

'Of course, Love. I enjoy practicing the language as well.' They indeed called local greetings to total strangers, very un-English-like, as their parents had taught them from the crib. To their delight, the locals greeted them back with no apparent hostility or xenophobia. What would it would be like to live here? Harriet wondered but kept to herself.

They kept walking, sometimes looking up at the few clouds wispy overhead. 'You know, Harriet, I think you would actually quite love the Château de Pompignan all that way south. Despite what I said about riding a horse or a carriage all that way, the trek remains truly worthwhile.'

'You've only mentioned it once, darling,' she answered.

'It's funny: even that far back, I already was getting into trouble with the likes of Graham and Roebuck. They've been good friends.'

Harriet grinned. 'Just what forms does "trouble" take for the cerebral John Stuart Mill?' she teased. It was often easy to get him to blush.

'In the Mill household, "trouble" might have simply meant not finishing one's lessons on time. For all our talks about gender roles, Miss Hardy,' — she liked that, though was still trying to get used to it. Sometimes Harriet liked to pretend she had never wed, despite how much she missed the children back home.

'I remained in some envy of my sisters,' he continued. 'They seemed to have it so much easier, even though learning to play and sing and read — but not to question what was read — was clearly less work and lower stress for them, and I admit I myself remain a mediocre pianist, as well as a hopeless singer.'

She let her hand slide down his arm to hold his hand in turn. 'And down south there, you were spending those months, whole summers, at that property the Benthams owned.'

'True. The Benthams had an outstanding library, though it became something of a terror, constantly having to read in "the great philo-sophical languages," as my father put it.'

He stopped for a moment, looking away, into the Ile de la Cité, perhaps wondering about the medieval conversations that Peter Abélard would have had with his younger love, Héloïse d'Argen-teuil, in one of the great—yet cut short—romantic and intellectual pairings of that period. Harriet could even now recall one of Abélard's Latin phrases John had taught her: 'Haec quippe prima sapientiae clavis definitur, assidua scilicet seu frequens interrogatio... Dubitando enim ad inquisitionem venimus; inquirendo veritatem percipimus,' Peter had said, though Harriet couldn't recall now if that was before or after his love for Héloïse had been consummated, thus prior to Héloïse's overprotective brothers castrating her lover for his forward-ness. Perhaps it was fortuitous that Mr Taylor had no such vindictive siblings! But Abélard never stopped teaching, whilst Héloïse retired to a convent.

Harriet squeezed John's hand anew. He responded, but kept look-ing afar. His return smile seemed forced this time. 'In Montpellier, I hated the family bathing trips and dancing lessons, though Mrs Bentham—that's Mary Bentham, wife of Samuel, thus Mr Bentham's sister-in-law—seemed impressed by my linguistic abilities. And she never condescended to me about them either, regarding the ability to quote Plato's 'Symposium' in Greek more as a study of old thought and less as a parlour trick to please one's parents. My mother still seems to feel it conformed more to the latter. Jobs for philosophers are hard to find, she's always said, often whilst staring at my father, who earns a living otherwise engaged.'

He looked back at her, responding to the smile she offered with a slight tilt of her head—always to her right, like her little daughter was already copying. 'Tell me now, Harriet, did your family make you learn to ride and study the sword as mine did me?'

'Fencing?!' She felt incredulous. She could not envision a sabre in this man's hand, nor him dressed in the traditional whites of the modernised sport, lunging at an opponent or parrying a counter-strike.

His masculinity manifested in his ability to listen and think, and then listen again, and then rethink, and offer a logical answer. Harriet recalled her girlhood 'fancies': always slightly older boys who evinced strength, dexterity, and handsomeness that she had seen chiselled into the virile marble torsos of godlike men from classical Greek and Roman history that day at the British Museum. Had her tastes changed? Had she simply evolved, matured, or was she still envious of women who could obtain such men?

Yet fencing? It was hilarious, and John did not mind her laughing at the thought.

She chided herself: *men are not property, any more than women.* Whatever the case, she kept trying not to laugh. 'Yes, fencing,' he answered, 'and riding, if you could call it that. Vague attempts at cricket, too, though I'm no batsman. It seems best to let Nature have her way, so to speak, and my gifts lie elsewhere. I actually enjoyed the horses, and still do, but could never seem to communicate my intentions to them.' He almost seemed insulted now, but likewise evinced his own trouble keeping a straight face. 'I was terrible, even falling off a time or three. And a good thing your husband has never challenged me to an actual duel.'

Rarely one for nuance, especially with the fairer sex, he again realised his faux pas too late, with Harriet drawing back some. She could not picture a duel any more than he could, and her husband had barely more experience with weapons than her lover, though that was hardly the point. Still, fighting over a lover had its own romance... *Stop it, woman!*

'Forgive me,' John said. 'Let me speak of a wholly different apothecary, a man who even helped me to attend lectures at the Faculté des Sciences. Another Bentham, George, enjoyed those, too—Jeremy's nephew, that is—George has become a botanist.'

She sighed. Love aside, this man remained so fascinating and yet sometimes so damnably exasperating. How did one account for a person displaying stunning brilliance and erudition, who could simultaneously drive one mad regarding social niceties? Harriet felt excited again by the prospect of her boys starting formal schooling: discipline could be harsh—she and her husband would certainly have it out with anyone who tried to 'thrash' their lads—but yet there seemed no substitute for social contact and conversing in groups, with one's peers, whatever one's sex or faith or social circle. 'Tell me about this natural philosopher at Montpellier, please.'

John resumed his quick gate, excitement returned. 'Funny you should use the time-honoured term, love,' he began, she smiling despite herself. 'Brilliant chap, actually—he's even discovered something called "bromine," which might have surgical relevance, and—'

Good communicator or no, sometimes you just had to cut the man off mid-phrase. 'You mean like a sedative, or an anaesthetic?' Harriet admitted her own curiosity. Her father and husband both had confided to her the risks entailed by their patients, and part of what the two men did for a living could be hazardous, albeit not so much to themselves. That midwives, especially their male incarnations—accoucheurs, to borrow the French term for men in her father's occupation— were sometimes viewed as 'medieval' by some professing to cherish 'modern' medical practices, and as for apothecaries—well, her husband knew all too well the insulting terms 'druggist' or 'leech' from his own practice.

'Well, yes, if I understand correctly. It's just a few decades now since Humphry Davy was getting party guests high on nitrous oxide—little wonder it's also known as laughing gas!—but one supposes that this Monsieur has a more sober application in mind. Though he's not a surgeon, of course.'

'And this bromine is likewise different from opium?' Harriet cringed even at the thought. Opium addiction was fast becoming an epidemic in British cities, just as in their Chinese counterparts, and she had perused Mr Taylor's copy of 'Confessions of an English Opium-Eater,' curious and terrified all at once, whilst she continued to research what might be done with her own 'condition.' Nothing much had emerged to supersede the blasted mercury, which left her feeling nauseated and fatigued.

'Oh yes, entirely so. As I hinted, there may prove a surgical usage. In the meantime, it's exciting in itself: a new chemical being identified in situ, as it were, though of course nothing totally pure ever occurs in Nature.'

She stopped again, frowning right at him. 'What do you mean by that, Mr Mill?'

He knew he might be in trouble anew when she addressed him more formally, wondered if she even realised she did it. But he was unaware of saying anything amiss this time. 'Only that whatever we perceive, it is all composed of mixes or blends of things. The gold for sale in that jeweller's across the street behind you might be described as "pure" for purpose of a sale, though it cannot be one hundred percent. There are always tiny amounts of other things, impurities, one might say.'

Harriet's expression hadn't changed, which now began to alarm him. She did not mince her words. 'Does that mean there might exist no such thing as pure love, then?'

They had progressed far enough with each other for him to resist groaning, to treat her maturely. 'No. Love seems composed of other things. I do not know how passion and emotion and reason can be categorised on some table or chart for the natural philosophers to consult, though that Benthamite calculator might have benefitted from such.' That was his dry humour: Harriet knew that very few others would appreciate or even understand the joke. 'But honestly, I likewise do not know what constitutes "pure" love, either.'

Rather than succumb to pettiness or anger, she resumed her curiosity. 'How so?'

He raised a hand and lightly brushed a wisp of hair from her face. She tingled just slightly at such an intimate yet strangely innocent touch. 'I mean, my love, that for all my interest and dedication, we have our own entanglements, and not just you and I specifically. I hardly need remind you of your social state, and while I adore your children and sometimes wish they were my own, in truth they never will be.'

Harriet could feel the subtle betrayal of her face with a pair of tears wanting to escape, but she held them back. 'Forgive me what I said earlier this year, John.' She referred to a row months earlier, when John seemed to suggest that being able to escape to the Continent might somehow give them leeway to flee their prior lives. That surely qualified as romantic—and she had permitted herself a moment to bask in the imagery of a life roaming Europe, making their own Grand Tour as the fashionable had done for so many years—and then she waxed serious long enough to take John's face in her hands, look deep into his waiting eyes, and tell him that she could not shame her family, nor his, nor Mr Taylor's, and especially not the lives and reputations of her children, for such a scenario, dreamy as it might be.

More simply, Harriet wanted to see the mountains that John knew from a full year in France. He might emphasise attending university lectures at age fourteen and gloss over the manlier pursuits, but what stood out for her from his descriptions of that time was his developing adoration of Nature itself, each bit of it, gloriously composed of other things, like with his current examples. He could hobnob with famous expatriates and well-known Parisians enjoying their holidays, and enjoy it all, but his love of the advanced maths coursework he had done at the Faculté des Sciences paled when compared to how he could lose himself—emotionally and geographically—in a French farming village, or an 'empty' field that actually teemed with life, beast and bush alike, or lying back with his giggling sisters, grass stains on their clothes and hilly mud stuck to their shoes, just to watch the mountain-scape, feeling grand and tiny at once.

Harriet could easily envision herself mastering this language she worked at, though never as proficiently as John, but she understood that the best way to learn anew was via constant exposure. John's French fluency had developed that same year, under the tutelage of Bentham's extended social as well as familial group. And she had found it hilarious to hear of the cranky philosopher Bentham himself striding through the town with a worn walking stick he'd christened 'Dapple,' like it was a pet. He must have been quite a sight with his long unkempt blonde hair, and she equally enjoyed the tale of his affixing notes for his current written works in progress to curtains to help organise his thoughts. If not for his intellectual contributions, he might have been labelled 'mad;' as it was, he certainly qualified as 'eccentric,' that uniquely British moniker which might be applied to anyone with different views: usually not dangerous exactly, but still nonetheless vaguely threatening or at least entertaining. Harriet had already decided that the eccentrics were those with ideas and behaviours too challenging for much of society, and considered herself, along with John, to be actively working towards becoming such.

The sun had begun its inexorable and glorious slide away from view again, the pair of them enjoying its fire bringing out a turquoise and pink panorama to what would clearly prove a pleasing and calming evening sky. Harriet knew the view came from the Earth's own turning, of course, but the ancient analogy was more romantic, hinting at the mysterious. She again silently recited that passage by Abélard: 'For this is the first key to wisdom, assiduous and frequent questioning... By doubting we come to inquiry; by inquiry we perceive the truth.' She had no doubt that James Mill and Jeremy Bentham could have recited it in their sleep, though she wondered if John Mill had ever really been allowed by the older men to question their methods for teaching him.

They soon turned into a charming café — in Paris, all cafés seemed charming, at least to travelling British subjects: the United Kingdom already had too much of a reputation for overly boiled and drab foods for its suppers, leading some French — as John himself shortly confirmed over their first shared pot of tea in that quaint establishment with a serene view of the Seine endlessly flowing past — to attribute British alcoholism to simple want of better food. Thus the English dreary pub, according to the Continental stereotype, compared to the elegant French well-lit street-side salon for savouring superb wines, less often to excess.

Over that same pot of tea — the French, alas, had begun going the way of the Americans by developing a dreadful taste for coffee — Harriet silently faced her guilt again. The children had stayed at home, and she had a husband understanding enough to write off the cost of her sojourn overseas, even if just to nearby France.

She regarded the oddest part of their scenario that while she had
trouble reconciling her feelings towards her husband, she did not in
truth feel any loathing towards whomever it was in London's Stews
who had inadvertently left him infected. She honestly hoped the
poor little prostitute—one of the Empire's endless 'unfortunates,'
a patronising term if ever one had been coined—had not suffered
overly for her affliction, especially since she very likely had not been
born with it. *No one deserved this at birth,* Harriet often told herself,
*and further, I am more minded to consider what led this young woman to
such an existence in the first place. No one should have to whore themselves
just to eat and have shelter. What happiness could she ever have, even if
she might be construed as adding to the 'happiness' of the debauched men
who keep hiring her?*

Harriet deliberately considered the question in Benthamite terms,
wondering what that half-mad logician behind so much of John's
ethics would have thought of such situations. She never did have
the chance to ask him. The man who had penned so much rational
improvement for social institutions like prisons—surely just as hor-
rific as life on an unforgiving city's streets and alleys—could only be
known to her through his literary legacy. John had hoped they might
meet someday, but they never managed it, such was their strange,
improvised, and often dishonest schedule.

Still, whatever and wherever to lay the blame for something as
unspeakable as syphilis, Harriet remained elated that her illness had
remained in a remitted stage. The initial vaginal chancres were horri-
fying to behold, prompting fear and anger alike, and the only others
in the world who knew of it included John's friend Mr Roebuck, and
her husband. And thankfully the second stage, the rash that affected
palms of her hands and soles of her feet, obvious to anyone who could
have gleaned a glimpse of them, had blissfully not driven her mad
with itching nor produced any discharge, which she had fretted about.
The symptoms went away, had indeed been remiss for the better part
of a year now, though she sometimes still awoke at any time of night
fumbling for sufficient light to inspect yet again the afflicted parts of

her tenderest anatomy. She knew not whether to thank the disgusting mercury, and had opted to ignore a Stuart-period treatise which discussed the other effects of the liquid metal, including the notion that it was easily fatal.

She would have to tell John about all of this soon, and dreaded it. Would he be like so many, believing like they did in the Middle Ages that those who suffered from diseases deserved their fates? It reminded Harriet of how their medieval ancestors had shunned and forcibly isolated lepers.

She had almost mentioned it to her father, also. That irascible veteran accoucheur had witnessed his uniquely female patients at their most vulnerable, and similarly must have encountered those with varying medical afflictions. But she could never do it. Even within the bounds of matrimony—and Father so prized Mr Taylor, she thought for the thousandth time—there remained topics that simply could seemingly never be broached. It had not been her fault; she had proven a dutiful wife previously. Maybe it was just that she knew she would also admit to offering her heart elsewhere in the years since.

Their waitress came by and asked if they wished for anything else. The tea was excellent, along with the subtle pastries that accompanied it, and Harriet and John enjoyed the relaxed pace of the establishment. *Now here seems an honest occupation,* thought Harriet, waiting on clientele and making sure they enjoy themselves. Then she forced away the thought that rode into her head on that one's heels: yet that description does not in itself separate this young woman from that London whore whose name I shall never know.

Silent companionship, Harriet already knew, could be just as valuable as engaging conversation. She and John simply gazed at each other, occasionally smiling knowingly or chuckling. She wanted to reach out and take his hand again, the one not holding his tea cup, and then remembered she could: this was more open France, and no one knew them here.

John waited for Harriet to answer the young woman in French not quite as accomplished or accented as his own, though the waitress smiled at the effort. It could prove amazing how far one could get in this life with just a bit of humility and effort regarding the cultures of others. The young woman dutifully slinked off, in no more rush than they to move things along. 'Perhaps we can locate another florist after this. I was pleased by your appreciation of those simple roses and daisies from earlier this year.'

'Oh, yes,' Harriet purred. 'They were charming,' though her favourites were pansies, but in fairness her rarely-shared seasonal poetry—John had only been permitted glimpses here and there—did not mention particular species of anything, and described changes more instead. 'Though there seems little need here, love.'

He seemed to see right through her. 'You once wrote, "Welcome, once more, Flower of the pale cold bell, Sure it some spirit is! so chaste and pure Its pendant head, as it would ring the knell Of hoary Winter in his dying hour—" which I truly admired, since it seems wistful but not morose, and recognises things in flux.'

'Thank you,' she noted casually. One detail they both shared, too much so in her opinion, was their emotional difficulty in having certain persons read their written work. More public was less awkward for some reason, Harriet decided.

'I'm also glad to hear of your friend's successes with their publishing ventures,' he added casually, pleasing her for the slight topical change.

'They had some help,' she grinned.

John replied from feigned ignorance. 'All I did was encourage some of Ms Flower's verse. She's quite poetic when she has a mind to be so.' High praise, thought Harriet.

'Yes, but I wonder even now if she would have found the wherewithal to go through with it in the absence of some genuine encouragement.' She lowered her voice and glanced around the café from sheer habit, like someone might be eavesdropping or otherwise prepared to engage in that very human tendency to gossip. Harriet often wondered how bored some persons must be to do such, though she had to admit she had been guilty of sharing clandestine personal information as well. 'I know that dear Mr Fox likewise encouraged her to go forward, and he's impressed by anyone who can write well, but their relationship together will prove disastrous.'

John felt unsure if that was a dig, and opted for what he knew best: honesty. 'Harriet, others will no doubt say the same of us, indeed some already have.'

'I know! And while I still appreciate your efforts with Mr Taylor,' she began, recalling how her lover had taken it upon himself to write privately to her husband to try and explain things, 'it remains quite painful to have certain matters unresolved.' She had not read that letter, nor discussed its contents with either man, but understood that it was apparently blunt without insult, honest without self-righteousness, and above all, firm. Knowing John Mill, it would undoubtedly have additionally been logically concise and valid, and the only detail he had ever shared with her about it was an outline of concern for the welfare of three young children who had yet to comprehend how the vagaries of adult relationships could work.

John waited in responding, something else Harriet liked about him. 'And further, William Fox and Elizabeth Flower cannot, alas, escape to the Continent for their trysts like some can. Perhaps I should loan them the funds to do so, or at least offer them the chance to escape to, say, Scotland. Pastor Fox said he has always fancied a trip north.'

'Have you gone mad?' Harriet queried. And then she calmed just as quickly, wondering if that might actually qualify as a sound idea. William and Lizzie needed something, to be sure. Lizzie Flower and her sister, Sarah, had been orphaned years ago, with the doting Fox couple taking them into their home, for all the unwitting emotional chaos such an otherwise noble act would wreak. Mrs Fox, herself a lovely dutiful woman named Caroline who in truth hardly deserved a philandering spouse, was allegedly considering complaining aloud, to her husband's Unitarian congregation no less, hardly a worse way for the affair to reach public eyes and ears if it had not done so already.

Their domestic situation might ironically be headed shortly for something of a reprieve, since just this past summer, Harriet and John had successfully introduced young Sarah to William Adams, a bright young man and creative thinker: an engineer obsessed with the new railroads and ways they might be improved, especially from the perspective of comfort for those in transit, so naturally John was curious about him. Both Sarah and William had articles published by the Repository, and had met that way.

John nodded. 'So, Scotland,' Harriet continued. 'Perhaps, I suppose. It indeed might do them all some good, at the very least just to get away from home.' She and John locked eyes for a penetrating moment, and knew they had been quite fortunate: him to earn such a comfortable living from the Company, and her to have a husband willing to often absent himself from the situation, and even to fund her own escapes. She did not receive enough pay from a few articles and book reviews and poems to afford sojourns to France, after all, though this year had witnessed her continued work on reviews in particular: Hampden and Domestic Manners of the Americans had both proven enticing reads. But getting lost in books only ever offered a temporary respite from the realities of life.

*Mr Taylor clearly loves me still,* she thought. *And all I can do is go on destroying, though not for revenge. I do not love this man sitting opposite me in some puerile quest to get even. And Mr Taylor knows, further, that the true separation that he seems to wish for might make matters worse for us all.*

A trip to another country could indeed offer serendipitous clarity. *I am trading my childcare and devotion to my lovely children for the ability to avoid still greater public scandal through divorce.* That divorce remained exceedingly difficult to obtain was beside the point, and Harriet sincerely did not want her husband's business damaged, either. He had worked very dedicatedly to secure his own small commercial concern, and a druggist could suffer from a weakened reputation as much as anyone, she reckoned.

Harriet would have to at least mention the notion of travel to Lizzie soon. In the meantime, John just shrugged, still thinking of trips away from home. He'd spent so much of his childhood abroad, the idea of such getaways came easily to him, and despite his emotional breakdown aged twenty, still regarded travel as the best cure for anything of an emotional nature. That, and poetry.

So that was where he returned presently. She knew he loved verse, found inspiration in it, even healing, as he had admitted previously, during his emotional troubles of young manhood—the desire to prevent such for her sons a large part of her drive to get them into one of the newer schools—but John admitted he had no flair for it. His own talent for verse might remain limited to describing her as 'She to whom my life is devoted,' but how could anyone not adore a person so forthcoming as one who could dedicate that in a letter? As with his letter to Mr Taylor, she could have shared that self-effacing directness with the world at large, and yet John knew she would not.

"'I hold the future in my own control,' he started simply, "'A god unto myself—because of steadfast will, That neither Time nor circumstance may change For that the soul of virtuous Life Of useful acts, and lofty purposes in voluntariness,'" and he made to continue, then stopped, noticing the love reflected back at him.

She reached across the table and waited for him to again accept her hand, squeezing it eagerly as she recalled writing that stanza, even reading it aloud to Lizzie and Caroline. 'It's strange, John: poetry is so personal, the most private writing anyone could ever do, and I was thinking of flowers.'

He almost ruined the moment, that damnable wont of his. 'But it's fruit that nourishes?' That he lilted slightly on the final word's tone, indicating it as a question, was what saved him.

'Yes, but the flowers are the ones more renowned for their transient beauty. As you said with that letter you had sent to the house, "Elle ne refusera pas, j'espère, l'offrande de ces petites fleurs, que j'ai apportées pour elle du fond de la Nouvelle-Forêt. Donnez-les lui s'il le faut, de votre part." And no, of course I could never refuse such a thoughtful gift, whether they truly came from the New Forest or no. They were simply beautiful.' He smiled, even showing some upper teeth, which seemed trying for him to do. Closed-mouth smiles were de rigueur for John Mill, though one who smiled too much might also be thought mad in Georgian England. Mr Taylor had of course fairly asked whence the bouquet came, and she answered honestly and immediately. She opted to keep them in her own room, however, managing to avoid shrieking aloud when Lily accidentally knocked over the vase while reaching for them, though blissfully only a mild slosh of water had escaped.

'Oh, I don't know,' and she could tell now John was jesting again. 'Some would claim that a sun-bright orange or shiny crimson apple seem objets d'art in their own right.' John Mill was in truth not much of a connoisseur, never having learned much of haute cuisine during that childhood devoted partly to southern France—certain fine wines excepted—but he proved finicky regarding simple fresh food. Harriet had observed him spending entire minutes deciding upon just the right bunch of imported figs, or fresh cherries grown locally. He'd told Harriet that he constantly heard stories from co-workers about which exotic foods might best satisfy the often austere—bland, if one asked these Parisians—palate of their own culture, even learned sometimes of deliveries due at the City docks from afar and what might be on offer the next day at the open-air markets. Harriet adored Leadenhall Market, so close to John's Company. She treasured shopping for gifts for the children there, or the best cheeses and sweets, and she knew that was where John preferred to check for flowers. As for tea, his tastes were fastidious even by English standards.

'That reminds me,' she finally said. 'We'll have to do some shopping before heading to my flat. One can hardly eat out all the time, and I'd like us to cook again.'

He laughed at that, recalling their abortive attempt to create a simple meal together during the past spring. John liked to credit the experience leading to at least some of Harriet's interest in visiting France with a knowledgeable guide, but the previously fine bread he had purchased months back had burned too easily, and their combined efforts at something which under quite different circumstances might have charitably been described as pot-au-feu—a more refined version of English beef stew—utterly failed, and they'd had to find contentment with a hasty croque monsieur instead, which Harriet described as the best ham sandwich covered with cheese and egg she had ever tasted. His copy of famed cookbook 'Le Maître d'hôtel Française' had not saved him, much as he enjoyed reading about its emphases on just the right sauces. 'Truly?' he asked her between chuckles. 'Perhaps it would be easier to pick up something hot to accompany our flowers.'

She agreed, and it thankfully proved an easy and simple dinner.

The ensuing necessary discussion proved more difficult. Harriet's rented flat was cosy enough, with elegant candle sconces, a pair of sitting chairs for use on a small balcony—with enchanting if slightly crowded views of parts of the city—a sizable bed, a bureau, a tiny round writing desk—no ink or quills—and a large hideous green rug which was offset by its ability to absorb noises of steps, plus the small oven and ice box that were fortunate accoutrements of a let place. Harriet and her guest laughed at their feeling 'spoiled,' both having become more accustomed to the relative luxury of large ice boxes for food storage, though they could hardly complain with the quality of the food close at hand. Some of Europe's finest bakeries lurked down the streets and alleys not far from the flat, and even this late in the day they could detect the residual whiffs of superior French baked goods.

Harriet led John into the flat by the hand, him admitting a certain awkwardness both at being led by a woman—supposedly it was the man's job to lead the woman into a room, especially a bedroom—and his still carrying his heavy suitcases, having left them earlier with the porter, easing the pair of them in one at a time to keep free the hand that never seemed to want to let go of hers.

John could feel his elevated heart rate. He and Harriet had shared certain intimacies prior to this, certainly—stolen kisses near her home, though rarely directly in front of it, since one never knew when curious youngsters might lurk at the windows—or heady embraces with hands exploring each other's clothed bodies without actual groping—gauche, as John would have described it, and Harriet agreed only so far as public exhibitions of physical affection were almost crossing an invisible line, even for her.

He frantically searched his memory for the male equivalent of the term, and finding none, felt his thumping heart rate jump even a touch higher. And here was this matron, this loving, tender woman, who had borne three beautiful children and thus knew what she was doing. John silently chided himself: since his year in France at fourteen when he had been at the peak of early adult masculine curiosity, exploring and refusing to admonish himself for what the sanitised medical texts still described as nightly emissions, he had been so curious, and terrified. He'd always promised himself that his 'first time' would be with someone experienced, so at least one of them would know how in Blazes to perform!

And that was the true trick, Harriet realised, watching her love slowly and deliberately try and find space for his clothes in the bureau. She hid a smile from him: he was constantly slightly anxious with his movements, as though feeling on display—of course this time he truly was so—and while he could meticulously arrange his belongings, like his thoughts, she had come to understand that it reflected his childhood need for order and structure. That part of his upbringing had never left him, and now too, he was shy, having trouble even meeting her glance.

He took a deep breath, holding it, and turned to face her, seemingly naked despite remaining mostly dressed. 'Last year you wrote to me, saying "I am loved as I desire to be."'

She remembered the words, the final version of that letter having gone through several scratchy draughts before she found pleasure in it. '"Heart and soul,"' she continued, '"take their rest in the peace of ample satisfaction after how much calm and care."' She loved knowing that he remembered her words also, but could feel no surprise, considering his prodigious memory.

'"You need never regret,"' he jumped ahead some, still anxious, '"for a moment what has already brought such increase of happiness and can in no possible way increase evil." Do you still feel that way,

Harriet?' He had taken two steps towards her, nearer the bed, and she noticed that he was all but trembling, still having trouble meeting her gaze more directly.

'Of course, love. My attachment to London consists in my children, and my ties to you, and that is all. My siblings have either left home or are trying to do so, and my parents are beginning to act as though they may force my hand. But the other share of my love goes wholly, unreservedly, to you.' She closed the gap between them and drew him close, embracing him.

John finally looked at her, an intellectual tower of a man with a boy's nervous eyes and quiet voice. 'I don't know,' he intoned softly, 'Harriet, I don't know how to—'

'Hush, love,' she drew just her face away, tilting her head gently to appraise him. She could feel her nipples starting to strain beneath her bodice, the most sensitive they'd felt since tiny Helen had last given suck. John was still slightly turned away, and she gently stroked his cheek, encouraging him to look back at her, and then pressed her lips to his. 'We've kissed before this, recall,' she said.

He remembered: stolen, almost chaste kisses here and there, during a bumpy ride through part of the City, or strolling through one of its grand parks when they felt certain no one they knew could be watching. That necessitated some clever legerdemain, and both acknowledged that social stigma itself offered a thrill.

But this felt different now—safe, desirous, unobserved—and John began to respond, ever slowly. Harriet took time to enjoy the kisses, clumsy and guessing though they were, but she could finally feel him start to relax. In his chest, anyway, as he hugged her more tightly; they remained securely locked enough for her to feel him pressing against his trousers, and loved the effect simple kissing could have on him.

Harriet did not, however, want him to become too excited too soon; she'd read of how easily an inexperienced man could reach climax, and of how it typically took women of all levels of experience longer, like they had been biologically programmed to want the act of love to last. She broke away just slightly, taking his other hand,

and leading him to the bed so they were just sitting hip to hip, hands entwined, Harriet leading the way in stroking John's chest, his thin but strong arms, the insides of his thighs.

'My love,' she said, a touch more serious. She'd been dreading this part, and no detail she had ever gleaned from any medical or other science text had made mention of how a person with a venereal disease might go about further enjoying their own sexuality. The unwritten judgement remained: like those of medieval society condemning persons afflicted by plague or leprosy, the notion was that sexual diseases were a form of subtle but inescapable pronouncement—thus have you been cursed for your wicked ways.

'My love,' she tried again, unable to avoid the electrifyingly tingling sensations as he tentatively, and then with just a bit more confidence, began running his hands over her receptive body as well: a soft hand petting her neck just before he kissed her there; the other hand finding her waist, then sliding slowly, teasingly, upward to find and gently squeeze her breast, eliciting just the slightest moan of delight. *O, how I want this man!*

She removed that brave hand of his, decided she hadn't felt quite enough yet, draped it knowingly on her other breast, and then kissed him briefly again, opening her mouth just slightly. His own response felt like exploratory curiosity blended with hints of that remaining shyness. This would really have to be her moment.

'John,' she broke away, though their hands remained on each other. 'We have shared so much, these past glorious years,' she gasped.

'Mmm?' was all he could seem to say, having taken a sudden keen interest in the scented side of her neck. Her hair remained tied up in its usual bun; he had only ever seen it down once. No, twice, Harriet remembered now, though the second time had been blighted for its hectic chaos, as she had seen off Mr Taylor, gotten the children ready for bed without assistance from the servants, and then rushed to answer the door as John had come calling, forgetting the insistence upon women's hairstyles and what they meant. She tried to keep from giggling now, as she felt one of John's fingers wrapping itself in some of that hair now, like he wanted to loosen it all from her bonnet.

This time she put a hand between them. 'John, please,' she said quietly.

He was clearly taken aback. 'Yes, love?' He could feel the ancient blushing come again, a reaction dating to early childhood when he had to concede that he was a poor equestrian, a clumsy sportsman, even a weak public speaker, for all his published works. He sat there forlorn, looking at her like a puppy in training that yet knows it's about to be chastised. Or placed in a different home.

'What I'm trying to say, John, is that while we've shared so many wonderful moments, even intimacies—' and she took his hand again, thinking nothing of placing it on her thigh and holding it there.

He felt he had to say something, anything, to postpone what seemed like inevitable rejection. He also had next to no knowledge at all of how to address—or undress, he suddenly considered, amused at that word working itself into his restless mind—a woman. All he knew on the subject of human intimacy could be laid out in a short clinical pamphlet. 'I know, Harriet. I, well, that is, I have truly never known anyone like you, nor anyone as well as I know you. And you've been the picture of patience with me!'

She winced at that, though he could not determine why, feeling another tight grip from her hand. 'And here I thought you were the one evincing patience for my benefit,' she said, eyes closed. 'Just talking like this helps. My husband,' she began, opening her eyes back up to see if that bothered him, reference to the other man in her life, then deciding that John Mill had been asked to tolerate so much in this relationship. 'My husband,' she repeated, 'while thankfully not one to force himself ever,' and she had to admit again that she could have found herself with a far worse husband, shared illness notwithstanding, 'seems stuck in the past.' She was having trouble explaining this.

John leaned over and kissed her again, right on her welcoming lips, once, twice, then stopped to listen again. She loved how he could gently wait like this. And she wondered how much he knew of simple anatomy and physiology, beyond the mere clinician's perspective. Her own father, bless him, had offered more of an explanation of what enabled him to stay in business so well, though there of course remained a notable gap between understanding how something worked and what it felt like or what it could mean, if the feelings matched. 'What do you mean?' John finally asked.

'I mean he's just so eager to be finished, I guess I mean. Like he has somewhere else to be, or feels embarrassed, or doesn't really want me.'

'I may not know the man well, Harriet,' John said, 'though I cannot imagine the third of those possibilities could be true.'

Trying to speak seriously in such a setting was proving challenging indeed. Here was mention of her sexual past, another man, about whom she cared but no longer truly loved, at least in no intimate sense, and her lovely genius who remained such an innocent in some ways, and the strange saucy combination of these factors reminded her of how long it had been since she had just been touched. She once shocked her husband before her first pregnancy by ambushing him in their bedroom, the servants finished with their duties so the newlyweds would encounter no interruption, and strode out of her dressing closet naked except for the ribbons in her hair which Mr Taylor had purchased for her that week.

She'd been the exposed one, and her husband, while thrilled, as she soon found out, also seemed strangely put out, like she'd done something wrong.

She just had to get this over with. This poor, patient young man at her side was obviously eager, and herself feeling so moistened with longing that she felt sure she could remove every piece of her clothing—and perhaps his, too—one-handed. 'John, I want to share so much with you. I want us to share something close and physically intimate and,' I want this man; I want to teach him what he's been missing, and perhaps I cannot, 'and while inexperience bothers me not at all, I need to be honest about my, um, situation.'

He looked askance, turning the puppy look from moments before into that of a curious dog, the kind that tilts its head at strange sounds. 'Harriet, have you perchance become pregnant again?'

'Goodness and mercy, no!' she cried. Even now she had to pray to forces she did not believe in that her children would remain free of the sickness and scandal that the more sordid details of her marriage might leave on them, feeling terrified most days of any of them developing signs and symptoms of syphilis on their own as they matured. And her husband yet pretended to wonder why she would no longer let him touch her.'

'No, John, I am most definitely not in a family way again. Three have proved delightful, though plentiful,' she tried to joke lamely. 'The "situation" is of course my,'—oh, how she hated saying it!—'my disease. The damned, bloody syphilis.' There. It was out now, even amid cursing. John already knew, had apparently understood, but even now Harriet wondered if he truly grasped what the disease meant for future sex.

'I've been so anxious to talk about this with you!' he cried.

Some comfort that was, she supposed, disarmed. She knew he was sympathetic about her plight, and now their plight, really. 'There are some wonderful, dare I say it, breath-taking things we can still do together, and share,' to which he nodded enthusiastically.

'I must confess, Harriet, this is one arena in which I remain out of my league.'

She leaned over and kissed him again, more cordially than passionately, though she remained clinging to him tightly. He seemed content just to hold her, his surprisingly strong arms refusing to release her. 'Did you read any of those "materials" I recommended?'

That had been such a conversation that it should have made this one easier. It must have just been the in-person intimacy, the thrill of being away from home, their own joyful respite from hectic lives of children and writing deadlines and Company work. 'Yes, I did. I've hoped to chat with you about those as well,' he answered.

He said it as casually as though describing a farmer's almanac or a luncheon menu, rather than pamphlets and short books explaining sexually-shared diseases, and also considerations of the joys and risks of human sexual behaviours. Then again, this man at her side had described during their first meeting his arrest for merely attempting to teach others about similar issues by handing out similar brochures.

'In that case,' she said now, 'just accept,' and she kissed him again, drawing him close, feeling his lips and mouth and hesitant tongue respond, 'that there exist many ways for two lovers to share their most intimate feelings and commitments other than the traditional mode of intercourse.'

He drew back just then, staring at her playfully, a dog considering whether to chase a thrown toy. 'Some of your materials describe many things other than what has come to be known in polite circles as the "missionary,"' he said.

She smiled. 'Indeed, my love. For all your involvement in the history and affairs of faraway India, have you not perused the 'Kama Sutra?''

He had, blushing every time. The Company kept more than one copy in its vaults, each with such direct and unabashed illustrations that sometimes little textual descriptions seemed necessary, even wanted. He leaned into her again. 'Please help me learn, then,' he added. And so she did, without blushing once.

Lying in the bed later, sated, tired, gloriously spent, John knew then he would offer anything to this woman, would defend her from anything—assault, slander, libel, any form of harm he could imagine. He remained as undecided as she regarding the existence of souls, of anything immaterial and non-corporeal that might constitute part of a person, but something he could not identify made him feel as though his core essence—he knew philosophers from all times and cultures had called it soul or spirit or psyche, even 'animal spirits'—had become entwined with hers. He'd studied and translated so many texts describing this joining, but now the ancient prose seemed wanting: how did it feel to recognise our inherent loneliness, whether deserved through divine insult or not; and how might it feel to realise that the Other, the object of your quest to match the subject of your lonely self, might be in the same room with you? Now, lying in bed with you? Looking at you with what you can only think to describe as a heady and intoxicating mix of longing, pleasure, a teasing yet vaguely sad countenance, a simple knowing?

For Harriet, another letter came to mind. She had noted recently in his desk drawer — never one to pry, mind; it was just there — something she had penned back to John after that first time 'the phrase' had been uttered, and there seemed something visceral, almost instinctive, in receiving something written by one's own hand, particularly something passionate... It was as though documentation offered further proof, and while she knew it was rational, that made it no less real.

'I am glad that you have said it,' her letter had begun, now — still? — lovingly tucked away securely in the desk. 'I am happy that you have — no one with any fineness or beauty of character but must feel compelled to say all, to the being they really love, or rather with any permanent reservation it is not love.' She had thought, reviewing it again, that her own insecurities had emerged in a blend of italics and underlined key words, as though she had to emphasise certain things or John would be too emotionally thick to get the point, the latter of which she at least now knew truly was not the case.

She had gone on to describe their potential mutual timidity as a 'disease of the nerves,' shaking her head at the memory of displaying such queer insecurity, then gone on to note how 'You can scarcely conceive, dearest, what satisfaction this note of yours is to me,' and shortly acknowledged that their relationship would require strength — of feeling and of character both, since it would doubtless seem scandalous to many, and then confessed her own insecurity: 'The most horrible feeling I ever know is when for moments the fear comes over me that nothing which you say of yourself is to be absolutely relied on. That you are not sure even of your strongest feelings. Tell me again that this is not.'

And so he had told her. More than once. And she had told him likewise in return.

*When did love and passion become so rational?* she wondered, smiling at the ceiling.

John flexed his arm where it still remained around Harriet's smaller shoulder, until her face met his, then wrapped her about even tighter with his other arm, which together made him feel as though he held—and beheld—the most beautiful and serene person on Earth, feeling her receptive mouth meet his while he compelled his lustful self to remain in that position, to focus on the now and sheer sublimity of the moment.

* * *

Several nights of what Harriet could only describe with one term—bliss—made her reach for her copy of the now almost legendary Mary Wollstonecraft, herself dead less than forty years, whose widowed husband and creative daughter remained, although the younger Mary had been forced to outlive her own idealised partner, that fabulous lyricist Percy Shelley, lost to the stormy sea. Harriet continued to wish that Wollstonecraft had kept to her written ideals about marriage and love so that she might yet be alive instead of having to sacrifice herself on the altar of childbirth—though Harriet acknowledged that was a selfish and stupid thought, since brilliant daughter-author Mary had emerged from that relationship.

She thumbed through the worn copy, itself replete with Harriet's scrawls of marginalia, arriving at one of her favourite sections. 'The being who discharges the duties of its station,' she read silently, still waiting for John to finish re-stuffing his 'touring trunk,' as he called it—though he preferred to haul a rucksack on his back when taking one of his extended rambles, 'is independent; and, speaking of women at large, their first duty is to themselves as rational creatures.' Harriet finally felt pride in her habit of committing favourite sayings to memory, reinforced by John, though nothing could replace engrossing oneself in actual text. John had once described re-reading of a cherished book as akin to welcoming an old friend back into one's home after a protracted absence, and she still loved the strange analogy. There existed so much they could still share—dreams, aspirations, themselves, and perhaps of greatest import—ideas.

She also located a pair of her letters mailed to John, sneaked out of the house clandestinely, like the errand of an errant schoolgirl, she giggled to herself, revelling in the equally youthful glee from knowing that John had kept these items  Plus, he seemed to have taken many of her words to heart.

'This is one thing so perfectly admirable to me,' she read in her own writing, more ornate and curlicued than his, 'that you, never in any mood, doubt the worth of enjoyment or the need of happiness... Does not this prove that you have the poetic principle?'

She remembered underlining the occasional term or phrase like that, as though John could not quite be trusted to infer what she regarded as the most important points, but she knew it unnecessary. She was just used to having her own words go unremarked upon or even wholly ignored, knowing that she had actually been fortunate in that regard, since she received more intellectual attention than most women.

'Yes—dearest friend,' she continued a few lines further down— 'things as they are now, bring to me, beside moments of quite complete happiness, a life and how infinitely to be preferred before all I ever knew! I never for an instant wish that this had never been on my own account, and only on yours if you could think so—but why do I say mine and yours, what is good for the one must be so for the other and will be so always—you say so—and whatever of sadness there may sometimes be, is only the proof of how much happiness there is by proving the capacity for so much more.'

She considered waking him and embracing him at that point, noticing that he must be enjoying a late dream, based on how the sheet was raised below his waist, smiling as she recalled his not making an ass of himself by overly analysing her words: 'happiness,' 'forever,' he had just accepted that someone was in love with him. He had learned years before the Dinner Party that poetry should never be subjected to stiff rationality.

*This could all be so perfect,* thought Harriet again on that last day, with her love about to sail back home, thinking of her unortho-dox—scandalous?—blend of duties as a rational creature: her chil-dren, her lover, her family, continuing to seek a legal and emotionally satisfying resolution to her now 'separated' marriage. *Let Mr Taylor find his happiness where he may, for I cannot return to him despite his financial support.* And she took true pride in John allowing her to add a little addendum to a letter he had just penned to Pastor Fox and dear Lizzie. John's well-meant writing contained no judgement nor warning about the relationship between those two — truth, it would rank among gross hypocrisy for him to do so, since once again there existed a wed third party who, in this case, or at least so far as Harriet understood matters, had done nothing to encourage her husband to pursue another woman, Lizzie's obvious charms and intellect aside. And describing John, Harriet wrote, 'He tells you quite truly our state — all at least what he attempts to tell — but there is so much more might be said — there has been so much more pain than I thought I was capable of, but also O how much more happiness. O this being seeming as though God had willed to show the type of the possible elevation of humanity.'

Thus the praise of an atheist-turned-romantic.

She had left it there several minutes, smiling at the already folded sheet on the worn desk in front of her, then added, 'To be with him wholly is my ideal of the noblest fate for all states of mind and feeling which are lofty and large and fine, he is the companion spirit and heart desire — we are not alike in trifles only because I have so much more frivolity than he, why do you not write to me my dearest Lizzie? (I never wrote that name before) if you would say on the merest scrap what you are talking about what the next sermon is about where you walked to, and such like, how glad I should be! You must come here — it is a most beautiful paradise. O how happy we might all be in it. You will see it with me, bless you! Won't you?'

It was oddly true: Harriet never had written her friend's name before. She had a servant to inform her friends when she hoped to see them, or sometimes occasionally just materialised at their doors. She would have to arrange another get-together for them with Caroline and perhaps others once she got home. In the meantime, she kept feeling like that giddy schoolgirl, or at least how she imagined giddy schoolgirls felt when swooning over boys who might not even realise they had become targets of affection. But John Mill knew; he knew that his own happiness and his own thoughts had come to largely depend on this woman he had met almost by chance.

Thus matters lay by the end of that frantic, lovely year: two persons very much in love, the one feeling genuine adoration for the children of the other, with a confused, often sympathetic, sometimes enraged, and often sad third party feeling caught in the middle. Mr Taylor cared not that John Mill returned to work dutifully at India House in November, whilst his wife Harriet came home from France seemingly refreshed, to find a forlorn looking spouse and their three eager if clingy children, who wanted to know what yummy foreign treats Mummy had brought home with her.

* * *

As though cognisant of their friends' talks of them, pastor William Fox and his paramour Elizabeth Flower had indeed tried their own form of escape to soothe their troubles, perhaps bring them closer, but more concretised plans tended to bring the unforgiving realities of forbidden relationships to the fore, where the participants might not wish to have to stare at them head-on. It seemed the emotional version of peering into the Abyss, and having not Evil reflected back, but rather Honesty—which could prove just as terrifying.

Still, Mr Fox possessed a more enlightened and rational view about the nature of Evil, believing to his core that God did not permit it as such, but that it existed because of the greatest gift He could possibly have proffered Mankind: the gift of choice, which included the ability to reason. Mr Mill had taught him that as no seminary programme, even more enlightened Unitarian ones, could have.

Mill called Fox the 'Utilitarian Unitarian,' something which Fox had once tried to work into one of his own sermons, with little success, he had to admit. Still, it remained a joy just to say as well as contemplate. And he wondered what Mill might think of the new row, between himself, Fox, and his usually loving partner, the always fetching Ms Flower.

Contributions to the 'Monthly Repository' had strangely offered the tinder for this spat; the flint remained Fox's dutiful though understandably progressively more short-tempered wife, who had effectively decided that enough truly was enough. 'All men stray,' she was overheard saying once in the Unitarian Church in Finsbury, not a far stroll north of the Royal Opera House. Its newer location at South Place Chapel was a haven for 'free thinkers,' an unpretentious edifice of a Nonconformist bent, free from stained glass and iconography and socially conservative perspectives generally. Still, slander could rear its ugly form anywhere humans congregated, and there was the additional hypocrisy in the simple truth that William Fox, for all his acceptance of differing beliefs and backgrounds, was yet guilty of an extramarital affair. Marriage might not be a sacrament within any of the myriad forms of Protestantism that had grown in recent decades in Britain and America, but it still included public oaths, and those still counted for something.

So while William and faithful partner Lizzie had not exactly engaged in competitions with their writing — they hardly could, with her poetic and musical compositions, and his keener interests in theology and philosophy — friends and casual observers alike had heard other comments besides, which in turn prompted questions and concerns about the nature of relationships, and even who should fill the role of 'breadwinner' for any couple. As for John and Harriet, they had reached a point at which they just thought it was thankful that there existed no children in this ongoing emotional triangle. The Taylor children might adore and look up to John Mill, but the boys were starting to comprehend that he was not their uncle.

Fortuitously, the pastor and his competent if illicit lover would soon re-join their close friends, Mr Mill and Mrs Taylor, along with some other of Mr Mill's friends. Perhaps then they could start to get their 'wanton' or 'debauched' lives straightened out better.

* * *

The Taylor children, it must be said, enjoyed being out and about in the City as much as their mother and 'uncle,' and few things could elicit squeals of joy more than the still new London Zoo, though the permanent residents of that facility seemed altogether less enthused by the mostly bald and pale apes when they were small and inquisitive and shrieking with unfeigned glee. Lily remained in her perambulator, or 'pram' as many Londoners were starting to call them, though she too kept reaching her hands out whenever the group came close to another of the enclosures, like she could reach out and just grab onto the coat or nimble limbs of strange species she had never witnessed before, but which interestingly seemed to elicit no fear from her.

The boys — Herby was seven, Haji four and of course running to keep up with his brother as best he could — could hardly be controlled, constantly with a 'What's that?' or a 'How many of them are in there?' John loved it all: the Mill family would never have tolerated such diversions when he'd been of such a tender age, even had the Zoo existed then. France had its older Ménagerie du Jardin de Plantes, but he had never seen it, and he knew that part of the impetus behind this new park dedicated to the world's wildlife — and rescuing what creatures remained in one of the dilapidated portions of the Tower, its royal menagerie dating to the Middle Ages — was to compete in yet another arena with the French. Still, it seemed well done, a surprising success despite some loud voices within Parliament about the risks of wild animals, on one occasion prompting a suit against the nascent Zoological Society about 'violation of the rights of individuals.' John inwardly smiled at the incongruity of such claims — no one had asked about the rights of the beasts who had to make this part of Regent's Park their home — and was also tickled about such growing discussions of rights of persons in the first place. All this revolutionary modern talk, in America — North and South — the Caribbean, parts of Africa and Asia, remained quite a new focus, and he wondered, hardly for the first time, how much of his father's and Bentham's utility and greatest happiness ideals had permeated the world.

And now here living samples from so much of the rest of the world were going about their captive days, though John and Harriet took turns commenting on how rather than try to cram so many poor animals into enclosures just to say that the Zoo had this or that species, there had been more emphasis upon larger artificial habitats, and typically not of strict cages so much as groomed and planted ground areas for these creatures to, if not mingle, then at least get up and move about and enjoy what they could.

Herby was quite taken with the larger ungulates. Oval-shaped dark brown sheds with arched high doors and roofs ending in points, initially for 'Indian cattle,' instead held camels from Asia, bison from North America, buffalo and zebras from Africa. The boy loved them all at once, silently yet carefully mouthing some private mnemonic device to distinguish Bactrian from dromedary camels—the former had already suffered significant population losses in their native lands—or plains from mountain zebras, then showing off his new knowledge to his brother, in the glib self-important way that only older siblings can achieve.

It was good to see Harriet so at ease, too, after the trepidations of last year, coming despite their newfound closeness. 'How does the wee lass?' John asked her now. It was the only vaguely Scottish-sounding term he liked to use.

'She's lovely and perfect as always,' cooed Harriet, fussing over her little daughter perhaps more so than the boys. Herby was already of an age to begin to resist 'Mummy's endless attentions,' but John also suspected Harriet coddled Lily simply because she was the girl in the Taylor brood, and knew without doubt that Harriet would ensure that she would grow up knowing how to read, and travel, and speak another language, and ask questions both simple and challenging, even if the mother had to see to such tutelage personally.

They moved on toward the Gothic House, the best known of the Zoo's buildings, all admiring the fearless yet gentle-looking llamas who resided within. John confessed to learning something new as he read about them, the only megafauna species indigenous to South

America, and how useful and valuable their wool was. He wondered if they might prove a suitable substitute for English sheep, which had changed since being introduced to the British Isles back when—he could not remember, knowing it to be centuries.

'Uncle John,' asked Herby with his more trusting tone, and with a protective arm around Haji, 'do scientists come here to the park to do their work, then?'

'Where did you hear that word, Herbert?' asked John in return. He tended to prefer the children's proper names, leaving the nick-names to Harriet. And to their father.

'Park? I've known that word for years.' At his side, Haji—Algernon, thought John—giggled while looking John right in the eyes.

John didn't care. The Taylor children had already learned they could be more playful with John Mill than with John Taylor. They loved their father, but he seemed more remote, not understanding that such alleged aloofness was partly socially bred, partly their father's natural manner, and partly—more recently—his continuing sorrow at what was seeming a permanent inability to mend his marriage. He was no longer sure he wished to do so, all but certain of his cuckold-ing by now. Still, he did not often raise his voice at his offspring, and never struck them, either in anger or from some counter-productive attempt to shape their behaviour, which was more than too many children could expect. 'No, you little scamp,' John attempted again. Haji kept right on giggling. 'I mean "scientist."'

'Oh, that's what Mummy calls them. I think she wants to be one.'

There was no faulting a child for simple honesty, and far too few adults were ever willing to admit that what they called 'being grown up' or 'behaving properly' amounted to simple deception in the name of societal respectability. 'Well, I think your mummy has the makings of a marvellous scientist. Though I wonder,' he turned his gaze from the child to the woman, 'just where she might have encountered such a strange if grandiose term.'

She answered at once. 'It just seems to be more in use these days.'

'I concur. Though what do you suppose it means, boys?'

Haji's expression betrayed appreciation at being included in a more 'grownup' discussion, even though being grown up for him might mean chatting up a ten-year-old. And he had little idea as to a correct answer.

Neither did Herby, so John helped them along. 'Well, the word itself refers to "knowledge." And it comes from a much older Latin word. Someday you both may find yourselves learning Latin.'

Groans emitted from both boys, though John knew by now from their precise intonations that his premonition hardly seemed worth fretting over. And he took some pride in knowing how both boys already loved the occasional picture books he had offered them carefully as gifts. Mr Taylor might be a fine provider—indeed, John had, before the affair with Harriet had even begun to develop, queried Taylor about preferred methods of parenting, wondering then—and now, for that matter—if he would ever have issue of his own.

And then he silently chastised himself for thinking of that sterile 'scientific' term 'issue.' Anyway, the new 'Fabulous Histories' had become an instant favourite of the children, and Herby loved hearing tales about a family of robins alongside those of a family of humans, while John admired its implied moral lessons. John had also taken it upon himself to make a gift of Wollstonecraft's 'Original Stories from Real Life,' partly for all three children so they could 'grow into' the book, and partly to replace Harriet's well-worn copy from her own childhood. Even then, Harriet had cherished the obvious lesson about two girls and how they were educated, even making her own marginalia in that older copy, to the consternation of her parents, who stressed that children should never 'mar up' anything within the home, even their own possessions.

'So if you're a scientist,' this from younger Haji, 'does that mean you're trying to learn everything?' He was pleased at the ability to at least proffer his own question.

They had to stop walking for a moment to laugh, Haji wondering if they were teasing until John knelt at the lad's side to respond. 'That would truly be something, Algernon,' he said, without the slightest condescension. 'The only problem is that no one knows for sure just how much exists out there to learn.' He swept a dramatic arm around behind him as he said this, as though indicating the whole world, the whole universe.

The boy just gaped back at him, gladly taking his hand as John stood up again. Suddenly that hand felt very comforting now, even within the sequestered safety of the Zoo.

As they resumed walking, Haji kept at it, now fascinated and a bit scared. 'So Uncle John, is there anything about which you know everything?'

John and Harriet both laughed at that, John tossing his head back. 'No, lad. I'm still learning, too; that's what makes it interesting. I like to think I'm more of a lifelong learner.'

That would do no good. 'Does that mean we may have to attend one of those schools forever?' wondered Herby aloud.

More adult laughter. Passing them in the opposite direction were other families, more tolerant of public displays of what some would label 'excessive guffawing' since they were with their young ones, and in a place which seemed to encourage frivolity. 'No,' answered Harriet, 'your father and I are still looking into schools, boys, and remain hopeful that all three of you will acquire good educations.'

Herby wasn't fooled. 'But the two of you didn't go to school, and Father trained as an apote-, aputh-, er, chemist after finishing grammar school, or whatever that is.' He always had trouble pronouncing his father's occupation. Harriet and Mr Taylor had fretted that he might have a stutter, but the problem only became noticeable when he was excited and trying to speak as fast as his thoughts ran.

Harriet was prepared. 'Yes, love, but Uncle John and I each would have been very glad to attend school than learn as we did. My own parents had to help me and my siblings learn to read, and there remain notable gaps in what I call my education. As for Uncle John,' she added, then glanced at him. Until recently, he would have waved her off, but had grown more accustomed to answering questions about how he had clearly become so proficient in the various 'liberal arts,' though Harriet also understood that he was yet reticent about others learning of how close he had come to what could really only be described as incipient madness after barely having become a young man. Surely the newer schools would better balance matters.

'Uncle John what?' Herby waited, as Haji had already skipped on ahead to check on the next exhibit. He still loved sounding the words out on the displays, especially the Latin names of each animal species, which were scientific. 'Come on, you lot,' he cried behind him, sounding like a young gruff sailor.

'Well,' Harriet tried, 'he's exceptionally well read, which is the basis of a school education regardless. And you already love to read, as we've established, so I think you can go as far as you could wish as you get older.'

They approached the new pen and exhibit where the lions, among those former residents of the Tower, now resided, seeming much more pleased for having their own outdoor habitat and better food and care. Every living creature thrived when in its proper environment, Harriet recalled reading recently, which encouraged her to maintain her questioning about the 'proper environment' for women and children and most of the world's human population. 'Civilisation' was artificial, for all those who claimed that history was merely the inevitable unfolding and acting out of God's orderly and endless plan.

'Can you pronounce it all, Algernon?' asked John.

Haji grinned. 'Panthera leo,' he responded proudly. 'Look at the size of them!' Four huge felines were visible, and one kept pacing their quarters. Thankfully, the zoo staff had arranged for a mix of trees and bushes, plus some artificial elevated terrain, atop which lay one of the females luxuriating in the early afternoon sunshine.

'How long do you suppose they live?' asked John now.

The boys both kept reading the information sign, with its little outline map of Africa denoting the creature's wild range. 'Oh, here it is,' said Herby.

'No, let me!' cried Haji, in that whingy way that younger siblings often display in their efforts to keep up.

'So say it, then,' accommodated Herby.

'It says, "Lions sometimes live up to ten years in the wild, though in captivity we are still finding out how much longer. The zoo in Vienna once had a lion reach the age of fourteen." That's amazing!' he breathed, pleased both by his reading, if a bit slow, with him still following syllable by syllable on the imprint with a grubby index finger; and further by his ruminating that here was a hunter that might live to more than thrice his current age.

'Now, how long do you suppose lions themselves have been around?' prodded John.

Herby turned round to look at him. 'What do you mean?'

'I mean, how long do you reckon they may have lived, as a species? This is the sort of question a "scientist" might ask.'

'Um,' both boys began, 'Five hundred years?' thought Haji.

'No!' said Herby, no longer wanting to be outshone. 'Ten thousand years?'

'Good guesses both, boys, and we actually still don't know, though ten thousand is longer than some people think the world itself has even existed.'

Harriet groaned inwardly at that. She knew her dear friend Pastor Fox certainly did not follow along with the notion that both Testaments could be somehow dated such that the world might be interpreted as having come miraculously into being in the year 4004 BC.

'On that note,' John added, 'there's a new scientist who's just begun publishing his work in something called geology, and he's suggesting that the world might really be far, far, far older than that.'

It worked: the boys looked wide-eyed, trying to determine whether the lions, one of whom just yawned to reveal a magnificent gaping maw full of dreadful-looking teeth, or their 'uncle,' was the most interesting right now. They didn't have an answer.

'So how much older, then?' ventured Herby.

'Apparently,' John said, glancing at Harriet for her approval and finding it, 'millions of years. Perhaps even longer.' He had in fact discussed this bit of data with her previously, she finding it fascinating and oddly reassuring, the idea that time existed on a truly tremendous scale, meaning that fundamental changes to the Earth and its inhabitants could occur. She already enjoyed the notion that Earth itself was seeming smaller and smaller, not just for recent advents to industry, but also from another perspective of size, as astronomy kept 'growing,' the universe along with it. In the meantime, her boys had to be reminded to blink, such was their amazement. They asked questions of certain adults, but less often of their father and John.

'That's time enough,' John added, relishing the moment for its implications, 'to consider our home planet as it existed even before people, before the creatures living here in this dedicated portion of Regent's Park.' Sometimes he thought he should have become one of these new-fangled scientists, having given so much effort to philosophy in such a comprehensive manner as to make the quest seem the key to understanding all behaviour. He clearly possessed the aptitude and mind for it.

'Wow,' breathed Haji, barely audible. 'You said it,' added Herby lamely, though both boys were stunned by the implications. Lily still clawed amiably at her pram, wanting to reach out to things, mostly living ones, yet her patience remained such that she rarely cried for feeling ignored or unsatisfied. She had the quietest nature of the Taylor family.

Some private part of Harriet remained vaguely glad that no one else had apparently overheard John entrancing her sons with such exciting talk. As with the social stigma facing them more and more—issues which gratefully had not fully manifested, though they had surely created strains in her relationships—open discussion of such revolutionary ideas always seemed fraught with risks of its own. Once upon a time, John would have been persecuted, perhaps burned alive, for such thoughts.

And yet it was John who explained to Harriet that religion and natural philosophy were not intrinsic adversaries, even sharing his belief that philosophy—at least, the logical questioning and arguing and evaluating—had emerged roughly as people had asked more probing queries about what the deities wanted from their moral followers, and that this had all come about some twenty-five centuries earlier, strangely roughly simultaneously, in not just Greece but India and China also.

The children resumed walking, a bit fatigued now. 'You know what else, boys?' Harriet asked them. John opted to take over with Lily, adoring the little coos and gurgles she offered, like she knew him closely. John had done almost everything with the kids except bathe them. Lily, out of the pram, practiced her slow walk while squeaking delightedly as John swung her about, or pretended she was taking grand leaps as he grasped both her little pudgy arms and claimed that she was soaring through the air as he manoeuvred her from just behind himself, through his gangly legs, and then to a new position in front.

'What, Mum?' came the less enthusiastic reply.

They were heading towards the last exhibit: plants always seemed less exciting to children than animals, no matter how unusual or exotic. 'Well, did you know the government set aside fully nine hundred pounds sterling for the new horticultural exhibition ahead of us? Close to two thousand, four hundred different plant species have been brought to England for this, all of them from outside Britain. You'll find them in none of our local gardens, not even over in Kew or the palace grounds.'

That generated some renewed interest, and Herby—when away from his little brother—might confess to being rather taken by botanical studies, partly as 'botany' was quickly becoming condensed into another of the new discrete scientific paths. It already existed as its own discipline—as with Bentham's nephew—and, thought Harriet, it was just that the effort to keep it intellectually separated from chemistry and zoology and the like was new. The age of the polymaths seemed to be ending, which Harriet instinctively thought a good thing: if a person could really only excel in one or two fields of inquiry, then hopefully it would lead to both more overall human knowledge and fewer human mistakes about that knowledge.

'Is that—?' John said now. 'It is!' he halloed to some couple up ahead outside of the huge herbarium, or whatever this new plant home was called. They seemed smartly dressed for the Zoo, with no apparent children in tow.

'John!' he shouted now. Truly, too many Johns existed in Harriet's life. The other 'John' wore a darker blue 'blazer,' those sporty new outdoor jackets first donned a few years ago by the avid rowers at Cambridge, with tweed trousers. The woman allowing herself to be led by his arm was decked out in a dark pink, almost magenta, light-weight dress, cut short enough to keep her socks and shoes from getting muddy if the rain returned, though the fickle London weather had remained pleasing lately.

'And hello to you, John!' the other man returned heartily. John—her John—turned to Harriet and said, 'It's John Sterling, with his wife Susannah.' They were all clearly excited to have chanced upon each other.

John—this time the other John—completed the introductions, and seemed delighted to meet Harriet's children, who mumbled the politest assents they could manage—they were quite well-behaved and glowed upon learning that 'this is the man who sent you those shells, and the other gifts,' which had amounted to a few new volumes to add to their growing personal library.

Harriet noted and liked how John kept shifting eye-contact with both Sterling and his wife, asking where they were coming from. He knew that this good friend of his was a fellow 'wanderer,' as he sometimes described himself and Roebuck and Graham—'traveller,' John had once explained to Harriet, sounded too much like it carried an agenda, like 'tourist.'

As it transpired, Sterling and Susannah had just recently returned from a second, Caribbean home in St Vincent. Harriet was immediately taken by descriptions of a tropical locale—something she'd never witnessed, and part of what lay behind her excitement at shortly seeing the plants on display just steps from them now—and also by the reason for the Sterling's visit: to seek, if not an outright cure, then at least a treatment for the consumption that definitely afflicted Sterling himself, and might or might not be also poisoning the lungs of Susannah. The doctors—useful as always—thought Harriet, continued to debate her diagnosis. She would have to get this woman aside sometime for a private talk.

'Small' talk completed for the nonce, the adults followed the now more eager boys—and slowly yet determinedly hobbling Lily—into the targeted exhibit, with Sterling this time leading the way in describing some of the unusual species therein for the benefit of the youngsters, who now found the contents of this building more interesting than they might have otherwise. John himself, unlike Harriet, found botany intriguing generally, partly from his long rambles and non-European botany in particular, and Harriet found herself warming to learn about plants that provided her husband with some of his saleable unguents and potions and medicinals, somehow surprised that without exception they looked different from what she had imagined. For some reason she supposed most of the world's plants would look like those she knew from proper English gardens.

The sense of warming clouded a bit when Sterling turned to other topics, even if pertaining to their recent sojourn. 'You know, Mill,' he said as the boys went galloping off to follow a rumour that some sort of flesh-eating vegetable species lurked in the building, 'all talk aside, those Caribbean slaves remain decidedly unfit for freedom.'

All Mr Mill had said about that was a comment about the warm weather affecting people's temperaments, since it had seemingly aided the pulmonary systems of Sterling and his wife alike. 'But it's been three decades already since L'Ouveture finished with the revolt in Haiti, not so far from your own second home,' Mill stated, and Sterling seemed to miss the slightly sarcastic slur, 'the only slave revolt in history that actually led to the establishment of a new nation,' he added. Harriet listened carefully: John indeed had been intrigued to study a bit of how a man of African ancestry had helped a growing number of slaves secure their liberty, even switching sides, fighting first for the Spanish opposing the French, then for the French as they opposed the Spanish.

And the English, in that latter case; perhaps that was behind Sterling's clear disdain of the man. 'Yes, but that Negro ended his days as he should have: as a prisoner in France.'

'But that hardly detracts from the man's accomplishments,' Mill tried again.

'John,' stopped Sterling now, 'these people have continually exhibited precious little scruple in committing violent crimes, but if it's any consolation, slavery itself is officially and rapidly ending in the region.'

'That must terrify the Americans to the north,' John answered.

'Indeed. The Yanks have had their own run-ins with slave revolts, though nothing on the scale of what happened in old Hispaniola.' It seemed to Harriet like there might yet lurk some grudging respect there, but Sterling ruined it, noting that 'those Blacks just won't manage to keep things organised on their own. You watch: consider what's happening in Liberia.'

While John Mill typically retained a certain ignorance of more recent events—unless they offered more insight for him into the realm of the moral or political (which Harriet had pointed out meant roughly all the time)—he nonetheless considered the uprising in Haiti an inspiration for any who wished to overthrow their masters, and no one had more clearly defined masters than slaves. He regarded slavery as morally abominable, such that no utilitarian interpretation could possibly hope to redefine it as justifiable or somehow contributing to anyone's happiness—perhaps the owners, benefitting further from the produce that slaves still enabled via backbreaking labour in so much of the world—but the owners were hugely outnumbered.

'So, you think the slaves in America will do likewise?' asked John of John.

Sterling answered immediately: 'Yes, and God help the Yanks when that happens.'

Not being a parent, John Mill had little experience with using children as an excuse for the removal of one's self from awkward social interactions, but he verified that he was learning. He led the way in helping Harriet to extricate themselves from the company of

Sterling and his wife, trying to end on a more encouraging note but wishing them good fortune again with their seeking of treatments: Harriet especially had witnessed too much death, even by Georgian standards, to the dreaded consumption, and thought that at least this other couple did not currently present with symptoms.

Thus they began to amble away, noting the time and that they would soon need to return to the recently purchased Taylor residence at Kent Terrace. Harriet shortly found she could no longer keep quiet about their encounter today. 'John, I must admit, while I like Mr Sterling—and did enjoy meeting his wife, she seems lovely—how does he maintain that racist outlook?'

'I agree, Love. Some might say your own response to it denotes a certain naivety, but I love you the more for seeing through it.'

'It's like that piece we finished earlier in the year on the situation in Ireland,' she added, momentarily basking anew in the shared pride of an article they had composed together, 'and even some of our fellow Englishmen continue to regard their Celtic neighbours as some alien race.' That was hardly all: the situation amongst the Irish poor, which sadly seemed to encompass a sizable majority of the populace, was becoming ever more dire, with malnutrition and other diseases associated with it growing more pronounced, and Parliament wanting to retain control and resist Irish Home Rule but at the same time not wanting to send much if any funding to help alleviate matters.

'Indeed it is,' John concurred. 'I really appreciated your input on that piece, by the way, and how we've moved forth with the 'London Review,'' he noted with equal pride. That was to serve as an independent journal—the perpetual need for revenue from occasional adverts notwithstanding—and among the earlier solo works by John in the new venue included a tribute to the recently deceased Coleridge who, despite his opium addiction, had offered fresh and exciting Romantic interpretations of much of the world, and his own little realm of northern England. John had noted that not only did Coleridge describe that Platonic term 'clerisy' better than John thought he himself had; he noted that 'we honour Coleridge for having vindicated against

Bentham and Adam Smith and the whole eighteenth century, the principle of an endowed class, for the cultivation of learning, and for diffusing its results among the community.' Wollstonecraft seemed vindicated, Harriet had opined upon reading that, having previously written, also during that calamitous previous century, about the critical need for education to resolve social ills.

Thus was it tied to insight about the plight of Ireland. John had previously observed to Harriet that 'There is much to be said about Ireland. I myself have always been for a good stout Despotism—for governing Ireland like India. But it cannot be done. The spirit of democracy has got too much head there, too prematurely.' She had groaned, pointing out in answer both that India too could benefit from more input from its own populace, and also that the Enlightened Despotism model they had spoken of previously was outmoded and cruel—and, she could not resist, hardly conducive to the greatest happiness for the greatest number, especially since there was no way to consult the greatest number that way.

No, Harriet had sent John's attitude about education right back at him: education first and foremost, then a political model to be chosen by the people themselves. John had annoyingly retorted—thankfully this time in a manner less bigoted than before—that her response implied a level of democratic participation that did not yet exist, and thus revealed a paradox, and that what he meant was that power had to be somehow centralised first to avoid anarchy, and then reforms might be evaluated and implemented, to which Harriet answered by noting the lessons of history and how those in power had little impetus to give it up, and on and on it went. She had earlier gotten him to concede that 'There is not a more accurate test of the progress of civilisation than the progress of the power of co-operation.' He had arrived at that observation while writing a commentary about François Guizot's lecture series on 'European Civilisation,' a writer Sarah Austin had reviewed in more depth. And such issues equally pertained to places like Haiti and the southern American states, whose cotton continued to drive English textile machines and feed English workers. John commented how it seemed little wonder that natural philosophers, mostly the ethicists and political writers, had been both busy and hotly criticised of late.

Then Harriet surprised him, loving doing so. 'Are there truly "natural philosophers" left, then, John?'

At first he was unsure just what she meant. He often attempted to be literal with vocabulary, often frowning over each possible nuance of individual words — both in and out of context — and just watching him get flustered could prove amusing. 'Well, yes of course,' was all he could contribute right then. 'But you know me: I'm just a man attempting to transform the artistic and poetic into the scientific.'

Again she could hardly resist. 'What, then, of this recent news of beings known as "scientists" one might read of? And don't venture off into ethics again, which is, I know, the key to understanding your unusual reference just then.' This had been prior to 'the lads' learning of these strange, smart beings.

Harriet had taken such pleasure in this, in the idea of simply getting one 'up' on her lover, but of course it was short-lived. She might educate him more fully about the political and social and economic needs of women, but within the realm of more abstract thought, she could rarely catch him out. 'You mean Dr William Whewell, and his "coining" that term last year at the meeting of the British Association for the Advancement of Science?'

Deflated, she just shook her head. It was one of their little friendly competitions of a sort, though they never kept score. It had grown from wanting to know more about the world, plus, Harriet thought with some justifiable pride, her own influence upon John's increased interest in current affairs, no matter his adoration of thinkers from centuries ago. Still, she pressed on. 'Did you read Mary Somerville's "On the Connexion of the Physical Sciences," then?'

The boys, Herby and Haji, occasionally stole quizzical looks at these queer adults, sometimes playfully shrugging to one another as they had, by now, arrived almost at the exit from the Zoo and could soon hire another conveyance to get home. Herby understood vaguely that his father's recent expenditures precluded a luxury like one's own phaeton or the like, complete with its own horses and a groom to care for them, although the new house had the space. He loved talking to horses, though Haji shied away from them, still scared of anything so massive. Still, at least the family could afford to hire vehicles for many outings, and both boys liked how Uncle John, after some previous embarrassment early on, had acquired more confidence for such tasks, often making a point of chatting up the driver.

'I confess I have not, in truth, though I am curious. I know it was Whewell's review of Somerville's book that seems to have brought "scientist" into parlance. The term has existed previously, but now it seems more official somehow.'

Still refusing to give up the contest completely, though she could tell by John's tone that he was not thinking in those terms, Harriet said, 'I read his review, as well as parts of the book, though I do not yet have my own copy. More directly, do you suppose this means that "philosophers" are now relegated to a backseat in terms of intellectual influence?'

He stared right at her, taking the time to let his non-concession smile curve his thin lips upward. 'Harriet, my love, if I may recall part of a letter I penned to Thomas Carlyle last year, part of what the great thinkers do is "make those who are not poets understand that poetry is higher than logic, and that the union of the two is philosophy." The storytellers and the rational thinkers are the ones who give birth to science. "Scientists" engage themselves in bringing some part of the philosophical quest to life, or if not literal life like Ms Shelley's misunderstood creature, then at least to greater understanding.'

'Do you know, John, that shortly after we first met at that dinner, the first piece of yours I opted to read was your article about "perfectibility"? You said that passions are the spring, moral principles only the regulator of human life.'

They had arrived at the exit now, Herby already practicing his whistle to fetch them all a ride. Haji cried, 'Stop it!' but was really just jealous as he could not yet whistle. Lily, for her part, had wisely taken to her pram some minutes earlier.

John, in the meantime, felt genuinely touched at the thought of Harriet studying his writings, unaware that she and her friends sometimes provided insight and entertainment to their occasional afternoon teas by quoting John Mill and 'other illustrious and illuminating imperial minds,' as Caroline once phrased it. Lizzie had come close to shooting tea out of her nose before realising that Caroline had meant it mostly in earnest.

'What are passions?' queried Haji, regaining pride at correctly pronouncing the word. Herby was now waving at a carriage large enough for them all, a behaviour his mum would have frowned on just months previously, thinking it 'too forward.' His mum's attitude was easier lately, lighter, like she had less to worry about, and Herby just left it at that.

'They're the strongest feelings you can ever have,' Mum answered now.

'Wow. Can they hurt, or are they good?'

'They can be either,' John answered, looking down at adorable Lily, who smiled back at him, always glad for the attention.

Herby tried to process this note about 'passions,' understanding that something was amiss at home, had even eavesdropped on a tense chat in front of the Taylor household between his father and 'Uncle John.' He'd had to ask Penny what 'damnable cad' meant, eliciting a blush yet also an admission from her that 'Mr Mill was fortunate your daddy did not toss him into the street!' Yet the epithet had been answered bravely by Mr Mill, who insisted to Father that he was 'merely acting in accordance with your wife's wishes.'

Tensions grew at home, but Herby had not turned against any of these strange adults who were so central to his life, nor try to sway his younger siblings against any party. His mummy yet felt so often in the middle of the mess, and the still surprising gesture of Mr Taylor acquiring a new home had strangely helped, since it still felt fresh and exciting to them all, especially the children, who still could not be kept from running around the perimeter of the grounds looking under rocks and sticks and dirtying their toys outside. The neighbour children could sometimes be found in the yard as well, one young boy expertly shooting marbles with a thumb near adult strength, and a girl who prized the deceptively simple act of folding up newspapers or old envelopes or almost anything composed of paper into hats or boats, even having learned how to carefully seal her projects with cheap tallow candle wax to waterproof them.

So now Herby, his siblings, and Mummy and Uncle John remained in fine spirits during the ride home, the children both eagerly asking when they could get together with Uncle John again, while also look- ing forward to greeting their father to show them the new stuffed toys they'd obtained from the Zoo.

* * *

*From the Diary of Helen Taylor:*
What matters to me many years later is that dear Mill asked Ms Somerville — she of inspiration for that intriguing word 'scientist' — to be the first signatory on his motion to Parliament to put women's suffrage on the ballot. Remember them both for that. One commen- tator would describe Mill as the 'principal originator of the women's movement,' though neglected to mention Mother in that context.

* * *

The Carlyles: leave it to mere mention of them to get Harriet's blood going. And she and John would have to start avoiding these seemingly harmless dinner parties and soirées, consid- ering how explosive they could become.

Harriet only met Thomas and Jane Carlyle a few weeks previously. Jane seemed a charming wife on that occasion, dressing in ordinary and subtly-coloured clothing which neither showed off finery nor suggested any level of financial struggle. That evening at the Mill's home, she seemed content and almost proud in a modest light dress and plain flat shoes, while her husband had presented himself just slightly more dapper, sporting a casual yet flawlessly starched tweed suit. He worked as a teacher and part-time historian, thereby offering both Harriet and John topics worthy of discussion.

John had begun with loftier ambition than he could live up to, initially claiming to Harriet that he would manage to personally oversee, and even cook, a suitable dinner for the group of them, meeting Harriet's measured response. She thought he'd been joking, but he had arranged to have his family members and service staff out for the evening enjoying themselves. When questioned, it eventually came out that as he could pay for those servants—he kept claiming no desire for them, which Harriet found perplexing—she began to think he remained more focused on privacy than anything.

The Mill home looked lived in and loved, if a touch unimaginative for Harriet's tastes: little colour to the décor, other than a handful of small pastel pieces—done by enterprising street urchins, John had told her before, and he seemed both to genuinely like them as well as have an excuse to patronise the less well-off—and he loved children. Aside from those on the walls—placed in tiny accommodating frames—there was a large globe in the centre of the main room ('in the family for two generations now'); and two round mirrors on opposite ends of the room, each 'overlooking' a round table that could comfortably hold four for dinner or six for an evening of gaming like Mr Taylor oft enjoyed, though such was less to Mr Mill's taste. Harriet wondered if that was simply from a lack of exposure, and the guests were not treated to a full house tour. She'd certainly heard of the Trijackia's more raucous discussions around a similar table, as the Athenaeum and Trijackia alike met at the Grote's home, but while such men would not typically be found sitting in a circle playing card games for 'friendly wagers,' Mr Taylor and his crowd would never be encountered in precisely the same setting having heated if reasoned debates about Romantic poetry, the merits of the novel as an art form, or how to put Ricardo's economics into practice in British colonies.

The chairs for that round table were sturdy though uncomfortable if sat upon for longer than an hour or so. Harriet had joked that such might encourage discussions from becoming ever more heated, and liked how John found humour in that. He and his mother also loved rugs, preferring a mix of smaller ones: each room had its rugs chosen by members of the Mill clan, including John's parents and siblings, so certain rooms benefitted from what Harriet thought a refreshing riot of colour.

Two end tables appeared in the northern corners adjacent the dining area, each with an oil lamp perched upon it. John had argued that whale oil would shortly become more scarce, even in the Americas — he detested the practice, believing whales of all sorts were actually intelligent and dedicated to their family groups — and hated camphine even more, though kerosene was, for him, just marginally better in terms of odour and emitting small amounts of smoke. Honestly, the Mills could afford good quality candles, and Harriet was glad they had adopted the practice of coloured candles, so the house had morphed into something of a gently lit rainbow. The lighting remained subtle, not necessarily drawing attention of visitors to anything in particular, but making the whole place appear like a smaller version of the previous 'collections of marvels' that famous natural philosophers acquired — licitly and otherwise — in their (usually) extensive travels, to show off in their own homes rather than trust the collections to museums. Museums often paid handsomely to obtain such collections, or compete for the privilege of borrowing them for a time. James and Harriet Mill had clearly accumulated some showpieces, though John had complained of how little they travelled any longer, so items from Greece or India or Egypt might have backgrounds of slightly unknown provenance.

John's bedroom — again, the guests did not see those for the family — sported a mattress barely large enough for two — Harriet had yet to try staying there, of course! — with small cameos and sketches of John's intellectual heroes, mostly a mix of classical Greek thinkers, plus a smattering of early modern Continental contributors. Family images remained in the main rooms, and Harriet had never really noticed him noticing them, with a feeling that they might lurk on the halls mostly out of sight and hung at all mostly out of some sense of duty. A quite comfortable sofa lay in that room also, with satin covering done in a medium green. John indicated a distaste for the curlicued ornamentation on so much furniture available these days, often deployed with the unspoken statement among the upper classes that the more ornate, the more expensive, or at least the more refined. Harriet preferred John's simpler tastes, laughing the first time he'd told her, 'My mind is already detailed and overflowing with what feel like endless loops and whorls, one idea or memory into the next, so let my home be the opposite.' His parents favoured the more ornate.

For all that, this was only her third time here: so many of their meetings—'dates,' as some were beginning to call them, though Harriet preferred 'courting'—took place either at public venues where they could also take the children, or at the Taylor home, though even now the latter option had them keeping largely circumspect. They were tired of feeling they had to hide, part of the reason for tonight's little soirée. And John only felt on display when he was with her. This dining room boasted a charming floral wallpaper on the south side, flanking the entrance, with muted golden and lavender irises. On this section's walls appeared pencil drawings—some by John himself, some by an artist friend at the Company, and even a couple by Herby of the new trains, which Harriet loved him for hanging. Moving further into the house, the walls exhibited evidence of the typical English infatu ation with wildlife, with both black and white, and colour renditions of local ducks and deer—all three British species—as well as horses, though John eschewed the Georgian love affair with 'heroic' images of horses charging into battle with their brave riders. John might have proved a deplorable fencer and mediocre rider, but he also hated the very idea of war, finding it repugnant even if rarely necessary, one of the themes which had proven a stressor between him and his father.

The drawing room, to where John planned to lure guests after supper, contained pieces that John described as his pride and joy, including large maps: one of the whole Earth, showing where famed English explorer James Cook had sailed for glory; another of just

the Western Hemisphere, smaller and with far more details, including rivers and mountain ranges and larger cities, along with a hand-
drawn plot of the voyages of a German—Harriet could not recall the
name now, whose work John unabashedly admired, caring not about
international politics. A reproduced image by that scientist, showing
a profile of a mountain and how different species could thrive best
at varying altitudes and locales, reminded John how 'Everything is
interrelated; there is nothing that lives in isolation, anywhere. Ethics
is become scientific after all!'

Mrs Mill preferred that such ornaments as maps only be taken
out for occasional show, and John had put these on display the very
minute he had ushered his family out for their grand evening at his
expense—'on the town'—including the theatre. His younger sisters
had latched onto such a prize without further pleas for explanations.

The idea of the evening had been to broaden minds and perhaps
trouser belts as well, even with John and Harriet's almost fastidious
gastronomic tendencies. But appetites shrank and nerves grew taut
as John and Harriet, and to some extent William Fox and Elizabeth
Flower, who'd also been invited, felt both more on view as well as
more harshly judged. *So much for proud English decorum*, Harriet noted.

'John, it's all well and good to oppose those strange and unrealistic utilitarian views of your father, and Bentham, rest or rot his soul,'
Thomas Carlyle had begun not long after they'd finished their soup.
No one had bothered to compliment John on having worked his way
through his mother's potato soup recipe, which he had informed
Harriet he'd only tried twice before; they were sufficiently surprised
by how he served them, with no assistance! The staff had also been
dismissed to enjoy an evening with their own families.

'As for parliamentary reform,' Carlyle continued, 'or political economy, we'll never get anywhere if we keep expanding suffrage. It's bad
enough we have to deal with these ungrateful wretches feel entitled to
vote just because some of their labour unions are actually legal now.'

Harriet felt herself bristle, thankful she had not donned a corset
for the evening. She could see tension across the table in Lizzie's eyes

too, another young idealistic woman who recalled their chat about the 'fairer sex' eventually voting, and here was Carlyle belittling even the idea of more men doing so.

John was surprised by feeling he might have to defend himself in his family home. He liked the Carlyles, but Thomas, and to some extent Jane too, could prove a bit, well, thorny was how he'd tried invoking them to Harriet whilst preparing for this night.

Fox broke in instead. 'But Thomas,' he said, feeling as entitled as those workers in some ways with the man's Christian name, even having just met the Carlyles for the first time today, 'one could just as easily argue that this is the logical, even necessary, expansion of the very ideals that comprise Parliament itself.'

Carlyle stabbed a piece of the well-seasoned and tender beef roast, accompanied by a homemade applesauce—John had dreamily thought of preparing a beef ragout, then admitted his meagre culinary talents were just not up to the task—and chewed as if it had insulted him. His wife Jane was the only other one eating at that moment. 'How so?' Thomas demanded of the pastor.

'Think of how revolutionary it once was to even include the "commons" at all—and their rights and representations were very hard-won during the Middle Ages.' Fox didn't mind talking politics with anyone—his profession entailed talking about religion, after all—but like his friend John, he knew it could only really work when people engaged with it rationally, and for so many the two topics remained touchy and emotional.

John knew that also, regarding it a personal failing if a person could not have his—or her—beliefs and perspectives questioned, understanding that faith worked best when it was dissected, analysed, then reassembled, but most people regarded such as personal attacks.

'Hmm,' began Thomas. 'So, if I understand you correctly, William, the mob might gain the upper hand if we only accede to their demands?' He seemed to really mean it.

Harriet opted to invent an excuse to head into the large and well-outfitted kitchen, claiming she had forgotten something, then went seeking a fresh bottle of wine, lest she head back to the dining table to puncture Mr Carlyle's insufferable neck with the corkscrew.

'That's not what I said at all,' answered Fox. 'All I meant was we, a whole society that is, get a better, a wider, a truer understanding of the needs of any group within that society the more members of said group have a chance to speak. And there's no more public way to speak up for what one considers important than by voting.'

Thomas chose to finish the last bite with a touch of the applesauce, even at last offering compliments to the 'chef,' and showing mild surprise at learning that John had indeed largely single-handedly prepared this meal, thus its simplicity, for all that it was proving satisfying for those actually bothering to eat right then. Harriet walked back in, assuring them that she 'had only helped peel and slice ingredients.'

'You yourself would have been left out of that earlier representation in the Commons, Thomas,' John said. 'All six of us would have.' He gestured around the table, and was correct: none of them could boast any noble blood or other such ancestry.

'Dear William and John,' Carlyle began, 'please, let's not venture into the truly queer, such as women or Jews or Africans voting; none of those will ever gain credence, believe me. It's terrifying enough that the Catholics regained their rights a few years back.'

John looked up and met Harriet's concerned gaze. 'None of those is the issue, Thomas,' John said, suddenly questioning his choices of friends. Thomas Carlyle was a respected writer, a mathematician, a religious deist, a promising historian, and honestly, a usually warm and humorous man. But he was also a polemicist, and as was becoming ever more apparent, a bigot as well. Perhaps some polymaths yet remained; John wondered if the historical ones he so admired had proved this narrow-minded.

Thomas asked what the issue was, in that case, seemingly peering over his ample beard. John tended to distrust beards, no matter that they remained fashionable these days; they seemed like masks for the dishonest, and he had never grown one.

'The key issue for this evening,' John began his reply, 'has to do

with whether and under what circumstances more and more individuals have the opportunity and liberty to express themselves, and
in what fashion.'

Harriet chimed in with that. 'Or to find their own happiness.'

'There's that American sentiment,' Thomas said. Jane and Lizzie
smiled politely.

'Yes,' quipped William, 'and not so long ago, we lost those
American colonies mainly for refusing to give adequate attention to
their interests.'

Thomas put his utensils down at that, making it sound like they
chipped his plate. John cared little for his parents' collection of dishes
and flatware, and just thought the noise angry. It actually wasn't;
Carlyle enjoyed intellectual disputes like this, seemingly oblivious to
the effect it was having on his hosts.

'It is not that simple, Mr Fox,' this from Jane Carlyle, who up to a
moment earlier had remained content to focus on the food and listen.

'Indeed,' added her husband, taking her cue. 'As an historian,' he
sniffed, 'one carries the obligation to remind others that truly, history
is never as simple as a single issue.' Fox tried to rein him in, gently
reminding him that once again, they were veering off topic, and for
the worst of reasons: the display of emotion that comes from belief.
'And in this case, William, your old friend Ricardo was correct: of
course rents favour the owners; of course workers deserve their just
wages, but not rents nor income from business.'

John found himself willing to remain on a side issue long enough
to at least correct this. 'But even that pertains to this issue of happiness and interests, Thomas. The delineation of social and economic
groups that Ricardo identified are only possible if more people have
the direction and ability to change their statuses, to aspire to more.'

'That sounds marvellous,' Thomas said, remembering his entrée
was done, and taking a sip of wine. He left that alone as another issue:
John Mill clearly was not much of a connoisseur, at least with imbibed
vintages. 'But what of the labour that a society needs to have done for
it?' Thomas said. 'Not everything is or can be mechanised, John. Some

of what needs to be done has to be done by hand, by cheap labour. You don't have to like it. I don't like it myself, believe it or not. Just look at the descendants of those rebellious Yanks, and what a simple thing like that cotton gin is doing. It's making life far better for the owners: the landowners, the capitalists, while the workers continue to hunch over and work till they drop, duped and still enslaved by a new machine intended to save labour.'

John hated to concede the point, and did not do so out loud just yet. But Carlyle was surely correct about one detail: that surprisingly simple cotton gin, invented and patented for the 'right' reasons of easing labour and helping advance the Industrial Revolution, was also contributing to an increased need for the continuation of slave labour, especially in America. Britain needed that cotton, too. Cotton obtained from India and Egypt remained, or so British consumers believed, of generally lower quality—though that may have been a simply racist sentiment—and hardly addressed the issue of how one-sided such trade was, given British control of those other two nations.

How did a society liberate its people, especially its most down-trodden, and what was its obligation to other societies? What of peoples of African or Asian or Jewish ancestry, or women working for pay at all, or children working for pay and missing their entire childhoods to aid their families, in mines or factories or other dangerous locales where even brave burly men feared to tread?

But questions did not justify slavery, especially when it was based on the perpetuation that some peoples, with racial ancestry in certain parts of the world, deserved to be kept down, uneducated, worked to death, as William Carlyle acknowledged. And John pointed this out again now, finding himself losing interest in the very food he had proudly worked on for a sizable portion of the afternoon.

'John, I agree with the principle, but that hardly changes how some are supposed to rule, others to be ruled. In fact, this is actually rather like your own take on that curious notion of, what was it, clercsy, no, no, that sounds too religious. Clersy?'

John just stared across the table at his guest, aghast at how he had been misinterpreted. Maybe this was how Socrates had felt, and John had become just another gadfly, bumping around London like Socrates in ancient Athens, only serving to pester and annoy others and get misconstrued in the process. 'Clerisy,' he corrected. 'Such is the term we have been discussing recently. And a key element of the notion is that it be not mandated via politics or religion.'

That seemed to throw Carlyle off guard. His wife assisted. 'From where then, John?' Jane asked. 'How is it determined, how mandated?'

Harriet continued to follow the exchange, syllable by awkward syllable. 'From anyone brave enough and bright enough to speak out about what's right,' she said. 'The term comes from Coleridge, who was mainly criticising how the astonishing Enlightenment ideas got betrayed. So many noble notions from the past century, and even from our own time, have been perverted into justifying the same old social controls.'

'But John,' this from Thomas again, 'what of how some of those Enlightenment thinkers from the last century, including quite powerful heads of European states—like Joseph II, the Holy Roman Emperor, trying to ameliorate conditions for the serfs; or Leopold, the Grand Duke of Tuscany, who wanted to do away with capital punishment like your old mentor, Bentham? These men were what some have called then and now "enlightened despots," and despotism is something to which you have given both tacit and written approval, John.'

'But I meant it as something temporary, if ever necessary at all, to help a people find their more civilised footing.' *This was even worse,* John began to think.

Harriet wanted to aid John again, knowing how pompous that sounded. She had disagreed with him previously about how those wishing to do well for many tended to cause the most societal damage, using the hideously named Committee of Public Safety and its blood-thirsty, guillotine-feeding Terror during the first French Revolution as her key point. John still had trouble seeing that, and besides, Thomas Carlyle was clearly hitting his stride.

'And Harriet, we could take the example even further. Jane and I,' and he dutifully indicated his wife, who was definitely not cringing like Harriet thought she was herself, 'applaud your emphases on the ongoing contributions of women. We truly do. So what about some of those other recent "enlightened absolutists," such as Maria Theresa of Austria, or Catherine the Great of Russia? We're talking about women with power who knew how to get things done. And there was no talk of this "clerisy" among them. At the most, those in power might summon a respected contributor, like the manner by which Frederick of Prussia took in Voltaire, and later so discredited him that Voltaire had even more trouble reassimilating to his native French court.'

Harriet and John both knew, almost on an instinctive level, that anyone reducing to utter simplicity either the complex reigns of monarchs or their motivating philosophical perspectives would turn out almost surely to be a superficial, narrow-minded demagogue, and somehow the two of them continuing to try and get others to think deeper and rationally was enabling strange, troubling side effects. Part of it remained jealousy: Carlyle, whatever his faults, had become proficient with history, both ancient and much more recent, and John further tended to agree with how the eighteenth-century 'enlightened,' despotic, absolute rulers often improved key features of their societies, never getting mired in committees.

And William was right, Harriet knew: John indeed had endorsed this sort of absolutism—in a non-militant, non-racist manner—on a limited basis, if such were possible. But how could the 'absolute' co-exist with the 'limited?' She'd not considered the incongruity.

'Forgive me,' Thomas began again, in a slightly patronising tone that fooled no one, 'but I do wish to continue our discussion at a later time, and have no desire meanwhile to sully this fine evening.' It seemed mollifying, but he had to get in one last crack. 'And Mrs, um, Harriet,' he said, Harriet not rising to the bait, whether it came intentionally or no, 'the idea sounds as though it may have its merits, but the words of an opium addict like Coleridge can hardly be worth paying extra attention to, if you'll pardon my saying so.'

Harriet rescued John as she saw fit. 'Be that as it may, Mr Carlyle,' she started, 'we still have to resume with our intended issue: roughly greater participation from everyone and the ongoing privilege of their doing so. But since we have not arrived there yet, it might be worth pointing out that Frederick of Prussia took Voltaire's repudiation of him very seriously, and, petty man that the Emperor actually was,' this drew an instinctual gasp from Jane, who had been raised to not question authority in general, and monarchical authority in particular, though Harriet continued, 'part of his vendetta against Voltaire was the latter's relationship with Mademoiselle du Châtelet.'

This time Carlyle looked just a touch befuddled. His wife gazed at Harriet, apparently curious now, while Lizzie grinned, reaching for William's hand beneath the table.

It almost felt to Harriet like a run scored in one of those cricket matches that were beginning to excite Herby. 'Another of the unsung "natural philosophers,"' she crowed now, expounding upon the brilliant young French woman who composed her own—admittedly dense, Harriet knew, even with John's assistance with the technical French—'she refined the work of our own Isaac Newton, no less of a personage, and verifying, if I understand correctly,' stealing a quick glance at John for support, though he continued to look down at his cooling meat that he'd been so proud of moments previously, 'that the energy of a moving object is proportional to its mass and the square of its velocity. It's quite heady material, I assure you.'

And then Thomas Carlyle all but guaranteed that Harriet Taylor would never again wish to remain in the same room with him, as he stated dully, 'Harriet, I remain quite confident that if anyone had truly "corrected" or otherwise refined the work of England's greatest natural philosopher, Sir Isaac Newton, I would know. And to suggest that a woman might have done so, a woman about whom I have never heard previously—and a Frenchie, at that—strikes me as far-fetched, to phrase it as gently as I am able.'

'You know, Mr Carlyle,' Harriet answered just shy of spitefully,

'Mademoiselle du Châtelet even went on to show how something like this new photography—you've perhaps seen some examples in London's galleries?—would be possible, and postulated types of light energy that are apparently not even visible to us, probably not to any other known animal species. And yet my point is that here is a marvellous, relatively recent example of someone—a woman, mind you!—performing with stunning intelligence, and shedding new light quite literally upon a notable scientific issue. And has it occurred to you at all that your lack of knowledge of her might have something to do with your little interest in French culture generally, or not keeping abreast of ongoing contributions in academic literature, or even your own preconceived and, I promise you, wholly unjustified and unjustifiable, notions of women and our capabilities?'

John had witnessed Harriet becoming riled before, though rarely quite like this, and he wondered if his guests had noticed him blushing. If so, they likely had it down to embarrassment, but he felt pride for Harriet, even a form of arousal that he had previously been unfamiliar with. He recalled their joint attempts to decipher the works of Gabrielle-Emilie du Châtelet, John making a segue into the politically revolutionary work of Olympe de Gouges, who had eloquently and reasonably called for true egalitarianism along gender lines during the heady early days of the first French Revolution, only to become herself another victim of the guillotine.

John now summoned a lifetime of tact and patience to not rise to the bait offered—thrown down?—by Thomas, though he understood the underlying issue differently than did Harriet. His first desired response was to attempt to correct Carlyle over his use of an ad hominem attack on old Coleridge, by citing something about his character—even though it was true, and the opium habit probably contributed to the poet's death—but also pointing out that Coleridge had never really hurt others with his painful chemical tendencies, though John recognised that a case might be built concerning those who had cared about the man.

Still, he must not get side-tracked now. 'Thomas,' he commenced, 'you must know that Harriet is quite correct in her assessment, and not just of you.'

Carlyle looked almost flabbergasted, expecting his male friend to come to his defence, and he turned to look inquiringly at William, who just shrugged slightly. Fox in fact felt insulted by the—mostly—unstated assumption up to that point that relationships outside of marriage were intrinsically wrong, while he knew that the Carlyles largely maintained a marriage of convenience, having returned to London after their first several years of the wedded state on a farm in Scotland, quite a far cry from the likes of their prized place in the Caribbean, like the Sterlings had. And the Carlyle marriage revealed signs and symptoms of trouble, Thomas often barking at Jane to keep things quiet so he could focus on his research and writing, which Jane extended to such intriguing lengths as making sure their more urban neighbours tried to minimise or even cancel the crowing of their cockerels in the mornings when Thomas claimed to be at his most intellectually productive.

How did one silence domesticated creatures just being themselves? William found himself smiling as much at that as the current scene in Mill's home. One might as well try to silence mighty and independently-minded Harriet Taylor; Fox believed she had undergone some genuine transformation since he performed her wedding ceremony less than a decade ago.

John continued. 'I mean, I like and trust you, and one of my commitments, both morally and politically, lies in welcoming disparate views even when I disagree with them.' Harriet silently encouraged him; they both knew he possessed a quiet, sometimes squeaky voice, but he had recently read a story to her children about a brave mouse terrifying an elephant, which he'd claimed traced back to tales he'd read in Greek as a boy himself—and for all the elephant's size and strength, it might find itself undone by the resilient tiny mouse. Harriet found herself smiling now also, like Fox.

'But again, the issue at hand simply deals with questions regarding who should be allowed to speak, and now I find myself in the unenviable position of asking you, my guest no less, to shut it for a minute and let someone else make a point.' John still felt deflated, though: he prided himself on an ability to respond to others more rationally.

So reason remained, even amidst obvious chagrin appearing on the countenances of Thomas and Jane Carlyle. 'My friends,' John added, 'as your host, I of course welcome dialogue and will continue to do so, wherever it might lead. But I must take a stand regarding your biases, Thomas, much as I respect you: there is no room anymore, anywhere, for such restrictive views.'

The guest in question remained unmollified. 'I take no insult, John, truly, and welcome the opportunity for intense discourse myself. Are you not the same writer, however, who advocates the curious notion that "offense" is simply not sufficient cause to try and silence someone?'

That was true, and Mill suspected Thomas would try and back him into a moral corner with this. John had just been thinking of the relevant lack of harm done by Coleridge during his too-short and clearly destructive life, literary merits and contributions notwithstanding. And when it came to considering types of damage done by someone, John was still fleshing out how the notion of offense played into it, since so many claimed so easily and quickly that they found certain behaviours 'offensive,' a societal trait he was starting to despise. It was too facile, like Carlyle's descriptions moments ago, especially for a modern state which claimed to admire freedom of expression and of worship and of the underlying beliefs which motivated these. 'You are correct, my friend, and I do not want anyone silenced. That causes too much ill-feeling, and in the correct circumstances can foment revolution, irrespective of whether it may be justified.'

'So in the meantime,' wondered Jane, 'we may have to try and determine who should constitute the members of your "clerisy?"'

'Yes,' answered John, grateful for someone staying 'on target,' as he sometimes silently referred to keeping an issue in mental focus. 'And I remain open to suggestions. Current members of Lords and Commons perhaps need not apply.'

'Hear, hear,' Thomas said, reaching for another sip of wine despite himself, glad also for the sudden levity. Harriet continued to send a stiletto gaze his way, despite the dissipating smile. Thomas kept trying, though. 'There's too much recent shuffling, with our beloved Parliament going from Wellesley to Lamb to Peel and back again.'

'What of their religious proclivities?' asked Jane, to keep discussion going, almost as though hostilities had not erupted. John stood up and reached behind himself for more wine, pleased that the first two bottles had gone down fairly quickly—a sign of a good dinner, so his father used to say, all the while wondering when he should offer tea. He'd have to try and ask Harriet or Elizabeth on the sly.

'Oh, I don't know,' started William, pleased to move into a topic of which he would no doubt prove the expert, at least at this table. 'The Duke of Wellington supported Catholic Emancipation, while Peel initially opposed it before "seeing the light," so to speak.'

'Isn't Lamb, meanwhile, a closet Calvinist?' queried Thomas.

'I'm not sure,' William said, 'though it was quite a scandal when he admitted that his wife had carried on an affair with Byron.' Then Fox clamped his mouth shut: it seemed none of the six persons at this table could long stay away from talk of illicit affairs, four of them clearly guilty of such themselves: the elephant in the room, as in the mouse tale.

Harriet felt quite sure by that moment that she had finished bristling, at least for this day. 'Are you not likewise a Calvinist, Mr Carlyle?'

'Please, Mrs Taylor,' he said, unaware that he'd just fallen into her semantic trap to get him to address her with her legal, if no longer desired name. He did not appear to notice. 'Call me Thomas. And yes I am, though not a "closet" one. The term reminds me of the priest-holes scattered around the country during the Reformation.'

John was about to interject, knowing his lady's religious proclivities—or lack thereof—closely mirroring his own, and then warmed to Harriet's additional comment, which to his mild surprise did not seem to be leading into some religious spat with her history with Unitarianism, represented by William. 'So you adhere then,' she started, 'to this notion that what we call "history" really represents the unfolding of God's Divine Plan?'

John was pleased, but remained unsure of where she was heading.

Carlyle responded more courteously, at least. 'I would say that is a fair assessment.' At his side, he saw peripherally that his wife was nodding. He had no taste or sympathy with the perspective of some backwards cultures, like those from the Far East, for describing history—including the coming and going of great powers, even empires—in cyclical terms. Time existed on a line, beginning with divine Creation and extending until the time at which God, as per His pre-ordaining so, that Creation would come to a cataclysmic end, the worthy and the undeserving judged accordingly.

'Is that why you remain focused on this notion of the "great men" of history? Are they God's agents made flesh, for the furthering of that Plan?'

Harriet was pleased to note how he did not immediately remark upon her strange question, that he seemed to really be mulling it over without seeking aid from the others. Carlyle allowed just the frame of a smirk to appear, comprehending just where this talk might lead. At length he answered, 'Agency seems part of it, surely, Harriet.' She wished he would acquire some consistency in his forms of address. 'It seems rather like Herr Hegel discussed, himself a respected historian. One must be free to develop a grand idea, perhaps even something radical,' and he allowed himself to take in all five other persons at that point. 'But the new will always be met with resistance, and what Hegel called a "synthetic" idea would emerge from that value-conflict. The crucial point however, is that it takes those "great men," as you call them, to initiate the new ideas.'

He glanced for just a moment at his erstwhile friend Mill. 'That is, I think, as utilitarian a phrase as one could ask for.'

John was now almost envious, impressed by Harriet's ability to intellectually hold her own with a refined and educated man like Thomas Carlyle. 'Thomas,' John said now, 'this partly bespeaks why you and I often do agree. You just said that you remain dedicated to the work of Bentham and my father partially since it would seem to offer a utilitarian,' he grinned back, 'explanation of how anyone can become one of those "great men,"' and here he looked to Harriet instead, 'or "great women."Yet you, Thomas,' he turned back, 'would have as your utilitarian great men a Napoleon Bonaparte or an Alexander, who were undoubtedly efficient and took decisions that were usually daring and sometimes helpful for the societies which bred them. But what of the millions over whom they trod? What became of their personal utility, or more importantly, their own liberty? Such tyranny exists on the grandest of scales.'There existed another form of tyranny, Mill knew and continued to grapple with, barely mentioning it to Harriet thus far, but it was subtle at first, and all the more nefarious for that very reason. For now that would have to wait.

As for Carlyle, he still did not look away from Harriet just yet. He wondered what Mr Mill saw in her, this feisty, opinionated, yet highly rational if radical thinker. Mrs Carlyle, while certainly bright and adept in various ways, had proven a more compliant spouse, at least within the collective public eye, though she was not immune to voicing her displeasures at times regarding what she often perceived as a 'loveless' marriage. Thomas resented that: he and Jane had learned from the cradle forward that marriage needed to rest upon a foundation of familial and social duty. Love just muddled matters.

Still, that did not sufficiently explain their own marital difficulties, or how Jane Carlyle understood herself largely as a labourer assisting her husband out of more duty than affection, or how their very marriage seemed 'Platonic' to most outsiders. That revealed some of how Carlyle himself had looked forward to this evening, and had found—despite himself—some enjoyment in tangling with these four members of illicit relationships. He had a promising marriage to an appropriate wife, even if built more on obligation than devotion, yet tonight had served to remind him of what he—and perhaps Jane, too; perhaps he would ask her—had been missing. Fox and Flower doted on each other like newlyweds, even though their affair had been made public in Fox's own church! As for Mill—he came from a famous father, was respected by intellectuals—often including those he annoyed—and had somehow, despite his unimpressive carriage and patrician looks and dubious style despite what must be a fine income—won over this equally interesting young woman, a mother raised by her own successful if less well-known parents.

Thomas Carlyle just did not understand much of this. It was not what he had been taught should be the case.

And neither was the social and moral and economic utility to which he still mainly adhered, which Mill himself had recently gone out of his way to either further refine or else abandon wholesale. 'Mayhaps we seek largely the same goals, John. And Harriet,' Thomas demurred. Turning to the others, he sounded more gracious to ask, 'So what else about this "clerisy" business, then, hey, William? Or Ms Flower? Or you, sweeting?'

Lizzie piped up for the first time in almost an hour. 'That's always the question, is it not, sir: who should lead, and why? Perhaps this would be simpler if we returned to what Mr Locke said over a century past about the "state of nature."'

Carlyle and Fox shared a smile. *God, but it was good to share a table with educated disputants for a change!* thought Carlyle. That was the largest part of what he felt went lacking with their recent sojourn to the Caribbean, despite its beneficial effects for their health, and he remained too recalcitrant to even consider that what he had already concluded about 'the natives' there was logically similar to what their society said about women: they might indeed have trouble 'governing' themselves, but Thomas Carlyle could not countenance that it revealed a self-fulfilling prophecy, a tyranny all its own. Simply put, if you kept as many people as possible undereducated and intentionally ignorant, then of course they were easier to manage. Asking questions—indeed, knowing which questions to ask—always came as both shock and threat to the powers that were. 'Well said, Ms Flower, truly,' was all he stated now, 'perfect freedom, as Locke described.'

Lizzie raised her glass, enjoying the wine that the Carlyles disdained. 'But with no protections, no one to look after your interests save yourself.' Lizzie no longer wished to stay quiet. She remained anxious about being judged—again—for her relationship with her lovely pastor, but it grew apparent that disparate views and beliefs would still be welcomed, even sought, in the Mill home.

'Locke regarded it all about property,' Harriet said now, feeling calmer. 'Why? I mean, I realise each of us is quite fortunate to have what we do, to live in a great nation with a so-named high standard of living, but that's a material standard, not an emotional or spiritual one. What makes personal property the basis of it all? Clinging to physical attachments offers no end of suffering for so many, even though I realise I too need to be grateful for what I have.'

That your husband provides for you, Madam, thought Carlyle bitterly, but did not say. And not one of them felt ready to admit how well they had it, though they all knew.

Especially John Mill, who largely agreed with Locke, even if Mill continued to try and improve his understanding of the labourers who sold him his food, who drove him around this massive metropolis, who maintained the parks and museums and theatres he adored, and who went abroad to promote or protect British interests. More than any of the others, he comprehended how 'civilisation,' dating to the ancient world that he knew so well and often openly admired, required—indeed so often yet necessitated—slave labour, or at least cheap labour via 'classes' of those in service, usually with little to no understanding of how they got there. 'The individual becomes so lost in the crowd,' he once wrote in one of the 'radical' journals, that 'an established character becomes at once more difficult to gain, and more easily to be dispensed with.'

And that was the joke, one his co-workers at the Company never understood: that workers always out-numbered political leaders and business owners and anyone else in control. Yet if the masses called the shots, it would produce a different sort of chaos, the French and Roman version: that of the mob.

'The clerisy would have to represent all,' John said inanely now. He wanted to elaborate, but was feeling tired, and so much remained to be said and done. Each little societal bit was a step. England and France had established more legislative bodies back in the Middle Ages, though both had since revealed flaws and favourites. Britain had unified, but still had troubles at home and abroad, from Ireland to India and to every other continent. America had found material success and was fast becoming an industrial empire of its own, espousing marvellous ideals about equality for all whilst squashing every group it felt was in its way. It still had slaves, and other American nations had only recently freed themselves from Spanish control, only to realise that 'going it alone' was perhaps a bigger challenge, one not realisable without occasional bouts of tyranny.

*Steps,* Mill thought again. Like his own development, from Classics to philosophy to utilitarianism to... His primary fear was that he would be unable to finish his ideas, to get them in print, and Harriet understood that the key factor of his great love and passion for her was her ability to meet those ideas with him, to dissect them, analyse them, rebuild them, and get them ready for others to consider, while refusing to bow to any of them herself. How had he encountered a woman of such power and ability? How many great minds throughout history had benefitted from an able feminine mind behind their work, mostly unknown to history, like Madame du Châtelet? Reverse influence could happen, too: Harriet's near-idol Mary Wollstonecraft had allowed some of her views to be shaped by her near-anarchistic husband William Godwin, but his views never became her own. She had remained too strong for that.

'What's that, John?' asked Jane, feeling a sudden sympathy for their fatigued host, who oddly appeared to be enjoying himself despite the wariness of cooking and entertaining.

'What?' he looked up, bleary-eyed. They were all gazing back at him.

'Have we at least agreed that any "reform" should and indeed must begin with the individual, John?' This from Thomas.

'Hear, hear!' responded William again, raising his glass and now looking around for more wine himself.

Lizzie decided to get in on this, too. 'And here's to such individuals being women!'

'Amen to that,' murmured John. 'On the topic of independent women,' he continued, 'we shall continue to seek good writers for the new London Review shortly. You ladies should keep up the fine work.'

'Some of us remain busy at it already, dear,' answered Harriet. She looked to Jane for confirmation or encouragement, but instead saw a face betraying genuine sadness. Maybe the rumours of their marriage of convenience had some truth to them, since Thomas was the respected writer, with Jane regarded as either a competent authoress but dedicated to caring for her busy spouse, or as just another woman getting above herself.

John still tended to not notice emotional cues even of close acquaintances, facial or bodily and more so when they were female, so he kept talking. 'Do you all know, Harriet here offered a fine panegyric to the late Bentham—going into coherent detail to explain the difference between "self-interest" and "selfishness"—after his death, one of the best pieces she's composed thus far.'

John pretended to not feel Harriet's nudging foot beneath the table, so kept going. 'Her piece about Caxton and the history of early English printing also made it into the more recent Lives of Eminent Persons that I think some of you have perused.'

Jane tried to squelch this a bit herself. 'Well said, John. You and Harriet must both feel quite proud. Oh, and dear Mr Host, I inquired a moment ago about where your mind had wandered off to.'

'I know what it was,' he said. 'Talking of Coleridge,' Carlyle rolled his eyes, though did not appear hostile, 'reminded me that I always sought solace in poetry. It's like the Romantics, or those strange Yanks with their love of the outdoors, taking their inspiration in Creation itself rather than in what we flawed mortals create.'

'That's why you're such an avid walker, John,' Harriet said, still acutely aware that unless she reminded him of it, she might find herself getting left behind during their tramping, even within London itself when they had to dodge the endless traffic of feet, hoofs, and wheels. She hid her occasional difficulties walking as best she could.

'Allow me,' John said, and he got it all out in one contented exhalation. 'Although a philosopher cannot, by culture, make himself—in the peculiar sense in which we now use the term—a poet may always, by culture, make himself a philosopher. Anyway, that seems to sum it up a touch.'

'Well said, John,' quipped Thomas, and he was surprised as any of them as the evening continued in a state of verbal challenge without hostility, repartee without insult. They all felt like they had earned something when they realised how late it had become.

Harriet excused herself first, seeking to leave last. John began picking up the detritus of a strange but to him mostly successful meal. They both hoped to have the cleaning done and Harriet en route home by the time the other Mills arrived.

While hastily using the guest toilet, Harriet thought she overhead Mr Carlyle refer to her as 'vivid,' even 'iridescent,' bragging to his wife how Mrs Taylor was 'very interesting' and 'of questionable destiny,' whatever that meant, but the romantic part of Harriet found it complimentary anyway.

But his wife, seemingly peaceful at dinner, soon met her husband's summaries with venom; apparently she had already heard of the disastrous public 'coming out' of John and Harriet earlier in the year at a well-attended party, which still left Harriet wanting to scream, sometimes doing so into her fluffy down pillow in her own bed. Mr Taylor by now had his own, even though the pair of lofty beds lay in wait in the same bedroom at the home at Finsbury. The 'separation,' a polite term for near-divorce if ever one existed, was now in full force, and rumours persisted of John Taylor seeking physical and emotional solace where he could; he himself confessed to none, though he knew he would never be caught exploring London's seedier, riskier neighbourhoods anymore. Harriet genuinely hoped for his happiness, having absorbed enough of the damnable utilitarianism that Carlyle railed against to hope nonetheless that her husband would not continue to transmit his illness to any other women.

Perhaps his former interest in Southwark would have him back. Syphilis aside, he could still be described as quite a 'catch,' handsome as ever, at least when the unsightly disease symptoms remained in abeyance. *Thank God,* Harriet still wondered at times, neither of us has been *presenting with those symptoms as of late,* then recalled she was an atheist. And she still was ignorant of the fact that her husband had tried two different treatments also, neither of them curing it, whether God was there to care or no, but at least those frightful symptoms had receded.

So for the moment, guests had to leave the Mill abode to return to other homes. And one never knew what else the gossips might discuss.

* * *

*1835.*

'Come now, Caroline,' Lizzie prodded, 'we both agreed that we wanted some professional help with our work, and this is a fine idea with which to begin.'

'But we are hardly beginning,' Caroline admonished back, standing just to the side of the imposing glossy black door. The neighbourhood felt a touch too posh for their like, though these ladies had nothing of which to be ashamed, so they kept reminding themselves.

'Would it help if I was the one to knock?' Lizzie inquired. Caroline nodded. It was not just that they were 'playing at writing,' as their patronising family members—the male ones, anyway—so often reminded them.

It had required over a half hour to ride here, their hired brougham driver at least not put off by taking a pair of young women acting like feckless girls in his single-horse, four-wheeled conveyance. Indeed, he had found amusement in their insecure drivel, though it masked a serious purpose. And this picturesque stretch of York Street, just north of Hyde Park near St Mary's Church at Bryanston Square, and on such a balmy day, might have proven too challenging to resist. If they were insufficiently dazzled after their attempt at a meeting with the woman John Mill referred to as 'Mutter,' despite being of no actual relation, then they would have to see if they could locate the same driver, who'd promised a detour past the Serpentine River for no extra fare. Such might be the fate for a slow Tuesday afternoon, and the duo had already confirmed a generosity of spirit with their gratuity.

That just left the imposing door in a part of the City Lizzie and Caroline barely knew. They had been raised to never visit a home without both an introduction and a chaperone, thus the reason for them travelling together—that, and it was easier to garner one's courage in the company of a friend. They knew little of Mrs Austin's husband, who apparently had grown into something of another of these new-fangled philosophers himself, though the women knew they'd never read him, which seemed rude now somehow.

'Oh no—no one's home,' cried Caroline, feigning anxiety after knocking.

'No, no, none of that now,' Lizzie kept at her. And the extra wide door opened just then anyway, with nary a sound.

A flawlessly groomed butler peered down at them, from his massive height and from their remaining a daunting two concrete steps below his own footing. 'Yes?' he directed, with what could best be described as a monumental absence of curiosity.

Lizzie recovered faster. 'Yes. Good day, sir,' she said with unnecessary formality, though she prided herself on never talking down to 'the help.' 'Could you please inform your mistress that Ms Caroline Fox and her associate, Ms Elizabeth Flower, have come to call on her, as per prior agreement?'

Caroline glared at her: no such agreement existed. They had only met Sarah Austin in passing, and just once. The Mistress was well within her rights to have this hulking doorman toss them out.

Of course, they were not actually in, so, 'Wait here,' the man answered, closing the door on them. His own rudeness seemed to not bother him in the slightest.

'How could you claim that?' Caroline demanded, almost smiling

despite herself and her friend's duplicity; it was all she could do to
keep from giggling then fleeing.

Lizzie already was giggling, still attempting a more serious countenance. Then the door reopened, surprising both. 'My lady will see
you,' the giant informed them. 'Please do come in, and she shall be
but a moment.'

This was going better than they thought, though the moment
came even sooner. 'Ms Flower and Ms Fox, the poetess and the literary apprentice from Walworth Road.' The surprised guests lacked
the wherewithal to answer straightaway, and not just because that was
Harriet's childhood locale.

They barely had time to take in the tastefully and immaculately
decorated home, and tried to remember if the Austins had children. If
so, they were cleaner than Harriet's brood, lovable as they were. 'The
proper response, good girls, is something along the lines of, "Do forgive our strange interruption of your careful work, Mrs Austin," yes?'

Lizzie and Caroline nodded, not daring to look at each other for
the simple British absurdity of the scene. 'Mrs Austin,' Lizzie began,
again finding her voice first, 'do please forgive the interruption, as
you rightly describe it, but we've simply been so looking forward to
meeting with you during a less hectic occasion, and if you'll similarly
pardon us, we, um, we took the liberty of securing your address from
your friend, Mr John Mill.'

Mrs Austin finally cracked a smile of her own, since she was actually glad for the company, and remained no fan of how long it often
took to plan a simple get-together. For women it was even worse:
with whom to travel, possibly needing someone's approval—almost
invariably a man—and then fretting over what to wear, how to make
up face and hair. Friendship should remain spontaneous.

'Do come the rest of the way in, ladies,' the bemused homeowner
finally said. Truly, she was only a decade older than Lizzie, who in turn
could count almost sixteen birthdays more than Caroline. They and
Harriet knew each other's precise birthdates, but never mentioned
years, a new habit among ladies, though Harriet and Lizzie sometimes

teased Caroline for being the 'baby' of their triad. And today Harriet remained at home with her children, apparently with Mr Taylor—her friends had not sought clarification beyond this.

They entered more fully into the home, appreciating the sheer amount of sunlight entering through the well-apportioned windows: the Austins clearly preferred lighter and thinner curtains over heavier drapes, though the latter offered greater privacy and even warmth during a harsher winter. Few illustrations adorned the walls, which gave pride of place more to thinly framed copies of musical scores—the Austins savoured Bach and Mozart in particular—and similarly framed older pages taken from German books. Lizzie and Caroline understood Mrs Austin to be in the process of becoming a noted translator of works from that Continental language. Her husband John, meanwhile, advocated something called 'legal positivism,' which emphasised that laws were the creations of mortal humans and not of divine beings from any religion, and further that the alleged connection between legality and morality was merely fanciful. Naturally Bentham had been a fan.

'Fetch us some refreshment, won't you, Adam?' Mrs Austin instructed her manservant, who nodded, and with surprising quiet for his size trod purposefully out of the foyer. She in turn led the way into the drawing room, itself painted a festive if surprising light orange, chairs and sofa decorated with more of a feminine flourish than the masculine touch that often dominated such rooms. There was likewise a gratifying absence of the lingering smell of cigar smoke. Mrs Austin felt more in command sitting in her favourite chair, it having been reupholstered in light blue, part of her family for several generations.

'Now then, girls,' she continued, 'to business. I actually do not mind interruptions to my day, as you may have heard from young Mill. How is the dear boy, by the way?' She knew intimately, as John Mill remained in regular correspondence with her, though she was partly testing her guests for honesty.

The guests looked at each other for mutual support. Lizzie chose to start. 'He is quite well, Mrs Austin. We last saw him just a couple of weeks back, and—'

'At the Taylor residence, the new one at Kent Terrace?' their hostess interrupted.

Lizzie briefly looked down at the elegant Turkish rug beneath all their feet, equally briefly wondering how much such a lovely piece must have cost. Her beau, Pastor Fox, would never afford such an item on his humble salary. 'The new one, yes, Mum, at 17 Kent Terrace.' She briefly tried to stretch the topic away from Harriet. 'It's a refreshing walk from Regents,' she added, unsure what else to say.

'Yes, quite. I've strolled there myself with my dogs before. And how is your other friend, the ever-exuberant Mrs Taylor?'

This time Caroline tried instead. 'She is also well, Mrs Austin, thank you. And she is truly among the dearest of friends. In fact, it was she who suggested we contact you, based on your familiarity with, er, with Mr Mill.'

Their hostess allowed another smile. 'John Mill is perhaps my protégé, I suppose, though his French remains far better than his German. I've known his family for years, and he does not give his sisters sufficient credit, I think, being the only son. Have you met them?'

Adam, the lanky yet graceful butler, arrived with his mistress' ordered service, silently and expertly arranging tea with biscuits and strawberry jam. He then placed next to it all a small side of heavy whipping cream, all the items contained within pieces of an exquisite set of the thinnest and most delicate Chinese porcelain the guests had ever seen, each piece ornamented with an elegant thistle, making Lizzie think of Scotland and her wish to visit. A small pitcher of milk appeared too, and the ladies had the option of sugar, honey, or lemon as tea accompaniments. They appreciated the openness of options, though knew they would be considered gauche if they selected more than one. And they were almost afraid to touch such service, half believing they might be able to see through its milky near-translucence.

'Now then, help yourselves. The tea is a personable oolong, my favourite, if you've never tried it.' She insisted they go first, then added,

'Poor John—it must grate on him that the love of his life shares a name with both his mother and one of his sisters.'

Caroline and Lizzie were admiring the scented and relaxing steam now emanating from their teacups, Caroline reaching for sugar for hers, while Lizzie had grown fond of the French method, lacing hers with lemon, though she also liked her childhood manner of dripping honey into it. 'No, Madam, neither of us have encountered the other Mill offspring,' Caroline admitted.

'Oh, but you must! And call me Sarah please, by the way. Let's see: there are Jane and Wilhelmina, along with younger Clara and Harriet.'

Lizzie lightly clanked her teaspoon on her cup, stirring in honey and for just a moment terrified she might have damaged the porcelain. 'Mrs Austin!' she started, then hurriedly changed, 'Sarah, forgive my response, but,' and she frantically picked the spoon up from the gorgeous imported rug, silently praying it would not stain. How strong did tea need to become for it to stain fabrics?

'But—?' Mrs Austin pushed, though gently. The smile remained. 'And you mustn't fret about the rug, dear. It is a charming piece, but it's old and has already been trampled by thousands of loving steps.'

This lady had a manner about her for sure, both younger women thought: maternal but not patronising. It reminded Lizzie a bit of her own mum. Caroline knelt down to help, but Lizzie had already rescued the spoon, managed to spill just a drop or three of tea, which she could not even see now, and was surprised anew to sit up and find herself staring further up yet again at the form of the impossibly neat and demure manservant holding a fresh spoon and replacement napkin.

She took them both and mutely nodded thanks. 'But, Sarah, what I was attempting to get at, was... what do you mean, "the love of his life?"'

'Oh, come now, ladies. To begin with, if you see the man—you've both met him more than once, yes?—lately he's had the healthier glow of someone with renewed purpose. It's almost like the male version of being pregnant, one supposes.'

Caroline thought that hilarious, but then she would, being, Lizzie suddenly hoped, too young yet to have such worries. *And when can girls first sacrifice their 'virtue' and become pregnant?* wondered Lizzie this time. Caroline was still just a girl in some ways.

'What I meant was,' Mrs Austin continued, 'his face appears more radiant of late, like it does whenever he finishes a ramble or avoids going home to that stuffy house. Do not misunderstand me, ladies: I rather like John's family, and they are intelligent, if perhaps a bit too forward-thinking sometimes.'

There clearly remained little use in trying to 'cover' for Harriet, nor was that the reason for the younger women visiting. Besides, Mrs Austin seemed forthcoming with her own loyalties, caring about John and likely about Harriet also. Perceptive little Caroline went first this time. 'Too forward-thinking, Mrs Austin? From what we have gleaned of John Mill, he seems to continually want others to "catch up" to him and his ideas.'

Sarah laughed for the first time then. 'Well, in certain ways you're right, my dear.' Caroline felt not at all patronised by the familiarity; usually she remained on guard against any perceived slight, especially if it had to do with gender or age. 'And let me offer you an example of the type of thinking I mean. Adam!' she shouted suddenly, the noise of her deep commanding voice resonating throughout the entire house. 'Fetch us that recent 'London Times,' please.' It may have sounded appeasing, but Lizzie and Caroline could hear the will in that voice; Mrs Austin might have trained for the theatre from the sound of it.

While they waited, she continued. 'You're the diarist, yes?' she queried Caroline, who nodded, suddenly in awe of someone older, wiser, and more commandeering. 'Stick with that: there exist too few smart women writers as it is, though England has recently been "blessed" with some stupid ones, too.'

Caroline felt some tinge of pride. Journaling helped her keep track of her disjointed life. Her parents might be too 'forward-thinking' as well, content to let their daughter run about largely on her own, though they knew Lizzie well and approved.

'And you,' Sarah said, 'I understand you've something of a way with poetry and music, those ancient gifts of the deities. You put to song Sir Walter Scott's own verse, no small achievement, and I realise that his death last year may have put paid to your getting your due. But that's quite an accomplishment, and you should milk it for all it's worth. Scott was a damned fine novelist, even if he was also Scott the Scot.' She seemed amused by her play on words, and Lizzie had heard of her medievalist bias towards the 'Celtic fringe,' including England's northern neighbour. But she truly was proud of her work, having only met the late Sir Walter a couple of times. And she was astute enough to realise that the truth of her ongoing affair with a married minister might not assist with publicity of her labours in a way she approved of, but at least she'd been receiving some royalties.

At any rate, this fascinating woman had taken the time to research her guests. Harriet had only told them she might prove a useful source of inspiration or perhaps additional options for publication, as Lizzie and Caroline alike remained enthralled by the prospects of witnessing their words—and music, in Lizzie's case—brought to life.

'Madam?' came the masculine voice behind its mistress. 'Your newspaper.'

Sarah did not reach round, merely held out a hand to receive the item. 'Thank you, Adam. Does anyone require anything else?' she asked her guests. 'No? In that case, Adam, kindly return in fifteen minutes to clear away the service.' And with that he was gone again.

Making a point of waiting for the servant's full departure, Sarah made a noisy show of opening up the newspaper, offering mumbled hostile criticism to accompany the rustling sound. All Elizabeth and Caroline could truly catch were 'rag' and 'bloody male editors,' Sarah's bickering offering another spot of amused distraction. 'Ah, yes,' she said at last, 'here it is. When first reading it, I kept praying it was a jest, though a bit of looking into has confirmed that this really happened. I'm sure the men involved found their own infantile humour in this episode. Here,' she added, having folded part of the paper down to reveal a short 'interest' piece, the kind intended to titillate. Lizzie and Caroline took the martyred newspaper and read the item together, Caroline doing so aloud: 'Persons assembled in the neighbourhood of Portman Market to witness the sale of a wife. At the appointed time, the husband, accompanied by his wife, entered the crowded arena, the latter having been led to the spot in the usual manner with a halter round her neck. The business then commenced, amid the hissings and booings of the populace, who showered mis siles on the parties... A dustman stepped forward and exclaimed, "I will give five bob." The woman was "knocked down" for the sum and the dustman carried her off.'

'Well, you have to admit,' Lizzie began, 'it does make for amusing imagery, though one hopes the woman elicited more than just five shillings.'

Sarah grabbed the paper back, rolling it up as though she were about to use it to chastise a wayward dog, and almost did, making Caroline titter, somehow knowing that their hostess was in deadly earnest.

'How can you possibly find anything laughable in such a sordid little episode?' Sarah demanded, gesturing with the still rolled-up newspaper.

Suddenly sober, Lizzie responded, 'Forgive me, Mrs, er, Sarah, but it does seem funny. I thought the tone of the crowd was composed a bit sarcastically by the writer, like the hisses and boos were more in jest, aimed at the men.'

'That is hardly what concerns me either way,' Sarah continued in a schoolmarm tone. 'What of the image of any woman being brought in "for sale" to a public place, or to any locale at all for that matter? It's bad enough,' she continued, taking turns looking at her humbled guests, 'that marriage remains more prison than opportunity for women.'

'Forgive us, Mrs Austin,' Caroline intoned, young enough that she still had trouble addressing an older person more familiarly, 'but are you not yourself married?'

The authoritative tone softened some. 'Yes indeed I am, but to a man I chose, and who regards me as an equal, and who understands that I helped pay for this charming sitting room as well as he. And yet we remain surrounded by these, these,' she searched for a word, having a spot of trouble again with self-control, 'these bloody tossers!' she cried finally.

This time Caroline took a moment longer to answer. 'That seems closer to why we came, Madam, truly. We are fortunate to be ever more associated with not just women thinkers, but women writers, women who can make a difference.'

'And do forgive my apparent flippancy, Sarah, if we can pardon your street ruffian vocabulary.'

That elicited an actual laugh from the other two. 'Yes, and you should hear how my husband John speaks whilst reading this supposedly uplifting publication,' she threw the paper down, 'or when he's in his cups, dear man.'

'Though you're right,' Lizzie said again, 'we're here to seek any advice you might offer regarding additional work. We know, for example, of your translation of "Tour of a German Prince" by his Grace,' and she stumbled over the name, 'am I pronouncing it correctly? — and that Harriet truly admires your work, even writing a review of your review, as it were.'

Sarah thought the young woman did a passable job with the foreign pronunciation, though felt some surprise at Ms Flower's apparent missing of Sarah's knowing smirk at the mention of the prince's name. For someone carrying on with a public figure — although the Herr Prince in question was himself thankfully unwed — Lizzie Flower should seemingly know how to spot a fellow, well, what would society call them? 'Whores' was dreadful and inaccurate, but English had no useful term for 'affair-takers' or 'dalliancers' or the like.

'My thanks, Eliza. There remain plenty of Continental writers worth reading, and it's of course far easier to offer up good translations than to ensure that potential writers are bilingual.'

'I wish I was,' Lizzie said, suddenly a touch forlorn.

'What, bilingual?' Caroline asked.

'Certainly. Harriet keeps practicing French, and Mr Mill could easily travel through Greece in addition to France, considering how he used to study.'

'You see, ladies?' Sarah said. 'This is precisely the sort of thing your dear friend Harriet Taylor speaks about. While I make no claim to know just what has gone so wrong in her marriage and will not pry—though I confess I rather like John Taylor, he's a good man, especially since he clearly permits her to be away from home and sometimes working—I do know that the other John in her life is an outstanding influence, the sort of man ready to shake up the old social order, including how the rules apply to women.'

'Does Mr Taylor speak another language?' wondered Caroline this time.

'No, I should say he does not,' Sarah said, 'though he would no doubt acquire more clients for that curious business of his if he did, considering where we live and how many travellers from afar we have visiting our amazing city.' Caroline thought that last comment might have been a touch sarcastic, then decided against it: this woman had several sources of pride, in her work, in her independence, and in her country, for all its flaws.

Mrs Austin felt supportive of their efforts, and found some bemusement with the predicament of Ms Flower in particular. She felt no need to describe to her guests her own rumoured affair with that German prince—true; nor her alleged translations of additional 'classic' German works, such as the strange tales by the Brothers Grimm or the dense idealism of Hegel—false, though she had been intrigued by the former—chilling and dark stories of children getting into all manner of mischief and evil—and put off by the latter, convinced that the only person who could comprehend the mind of Herr Hegel was the man himself, and she was not even sure of that.

But she found herself enjoying the little improvised visit, and would have to reassure her intellectual step-son, as she sometimes called John, that he in fact had others looking out for his interests, even if his own family and alleged friends did not wish to do so.

\* \* \*

*From the journal of Harriet Taylor: October, 1834; updated August, 1835*
There remain times when one actually craves the deceptive simplicity of party politics: while divisive by nature—us versus them—they
can seem analogous to a marriage. The unwritten behaviours suggest
mutual respect, openness, honesty—one can already hear laughter
applying this model to the political arena—the same rules guide
marriage, and further, the complexities and subtleties appear right
from the outset, with the occasional need for deception alongside
the equally occasional disrespect.

O, Diary—perhaps I merely whinge from a need to express frustration, and sometimes the additional simplicity of pen making marks
to paper fails to accommodate. 'Twould be easier, methinks, to describe
my Love Mr Mill railing against the 'do-nothing' Parliament that
awaited us upon our arrival back to England from France, or the symbolically cleansing fire—though this one apparently began through
stupid accident—that roared through Westminster just days ago. And
his disillusionment stems partly from the fact that divorce—should
a young mother of three ever dare wish for such?—at least in this
nation, requires parliamentary decree, but more so from my husband
as well, who continues to resist the inevitable. My shared work with
the man I now perceive as much dearer, in another short but published piece—On Marriage—made the issue more direct, so that 'the
question is not what marriage ought to be, but a far wider question,
what woman ought to be.' We were off to a fine start, almost in thrall
to the late lady writers Wollstonecraft and de Gouges, but then John
turned more to compromise: 'Determine whether marriage is to be
a relation between two equal beings, or between a superior and an
inferior, between a protector and a dependent, and all other doubts
will easily be solved.' Well, almost, my Love: 'tis not quite an easy
solution after all, since my wanted—needed—divorce remains an
illegal course of action.

So I do not fully agree with him in this case. Part of my response included pointing out later, in the same published work—at least I can take pride in knowing I can work, and write and publish, without fear of censure, and even for occasional if low pay—something too few women can speak of presently, that 'in the present system of habits and opinions, girls enter what is called a contract perfectly ignorant of the conditions of it, and that they should be so is considered absolutely essential to their fitness for it!' Dear Creation, I was a mere girl when I wed, though in an effort to remain honest, I was in love.

Dear Mr Mill might have destroyed his support of such egalitarian sentiments, though, when he chided me for not pursuing a divorce. The nerve! I had to chastise him in return, going over these points again to get that sometimes thick head of his to accept certain realities of Life in Modern England.

Speaking to equality, Parliament has had interesting sessions of late, 'do-nothing' or no, from the expanded Reform Bill of two years ago, to the Poor Law Amendment Act of this year, the first revision of legislation dealing with relief for the economically downtrodden since the first attempt way back in, oh yes, since John made sure I would remember: 1601, near the end of the reign of Elizabeth! That is how long it has taken for us to get back to the needs of so many. As John himself noted earlier this year in the 'Monthly Repository,' 'No person who is able to work, is entitled to be maintained in idleness, or to be put in a better condition, at the expense of the public than those who contrive to support themselves by their unaided exertions,' which historically has included so many nobility and clergy. But then witness the violent history across the Channel in John's beloved France, as the Estates General finally met in 1789, for the first time since 1614—indeed, my love's own passion for history is improving my memory for dates, never before my strength—but that was far too little too late. The Revolution came anyway, as too many able or wishing to work could no longer, or at least not for living wages. John's father approved. Ricardo would have too, had he lived to witness it.

And yet dear beloved John Mill still wants some political machinations to move ever faster. Maybe I prefer slower steps, though in fairness, when the topic is something closer to my own heart, such as that damnable divorce requirement, a holdover from the Middle Ages if ever one existed, I too can feel the urge to enable progress quickly and for its own sake.

But change is always disruptive, I can hear Father say. And one never knows for certain the fallout until it has become too late to prevent said change. Perhaps dear John is simply apprehensive over last year's major parliamentary decree, strangely named the Saint Helena Act, which enhances and specifies further the powers of his East India Company within its namesake nation: there is now a Governor-General of India, and the old monopoly of commerce done by the Company these several centuries becomes overtly political as well as economic... done far from home, and upon a very large local populace which must surely include many who disapprove and who did not grant consent to our continued presence and control. This is how empires operate.

It is also how they get destroyed. India will not, cannot invade us, but sufficient numbers—provided they can learn to overlook their different attitudes from regional religious mixes—might expel their European overlords. That same article of John's also mentioned how people 'should help one another; and the more so, in proportion to the urgency of the need: and none needs help so urgently as one who is starving.' There are far more starving in India than England. Yet John is due for another salary increase, and now he must weigh that against the moral implications of foreign dominance and interference. Sometimes I understand his frequent desires for old philosophy, old history, for their lessons and their respite from modern society. He may be in a greater position to begin to put assets—wealth?—into places and hands where it might do genuine good, yet I fear he begins to perceive his salary as 'ill-gotten,' to borrow that horrid term from novels and newspapers. Among my own strongest desires is that which propels me to comfort him, to love and hold and need him as I love and hold and need my own children.

Desires themselves take many forms, of course. It seems appropriate, then, to speak of my—and John's—own, perhaps no more clearly evidenced by my having just waxed hostile over international politics.

I pause now, savouring... how does one then truly put into words one's innermost desires and feelings? What I feel for John, what he feels for me, goes beyond the sweet yet superficial penning of a sonnet or song, and we have proven beyond all measure that physical intimacy can become a reality even under the shadow of social repression, the residual awkwardness of youth... even disease.

Married years now, and more of an emotional veteran than my dear Mr Mill—no, that is also unfair, as he too has endured all manner of emotional distress along with happiness—I wonder sometimes if many couples silently play that childlike game of wondering: who will say the immortal words first, that simple, adoring yet readily abused phrase, I love you? I have difficulty recalling when I last heard it from Mr Taylor, though the children all uttered it to me today whilst we played and scampered about that silly duck pond. My more frequent headaches of late proved particularly difficult during my last encounter with my husband—neither of us ceding a single inch—no, not centimetres either, thank you: they seem so Napoleonic. Regardless, those head pains can sometimes prove dizzying, making me want to lie down and await their passing—which I am usually loathe to do, since I pride myself on being a busy woman, and further because society has already endured far too many 'swooning' women—read: helpless, forlorn.

However, I am reminded anew of John's noble description of my husband, as he wrote to dear Mr Fox how Mr Taylor displayed 'really admirable generosity and nobleness which he has shewn under so severe a trial.' In fairness again I must confess that this remains true, such that while I still cannot entertain the full thought of my husband's sought-for reconciliation, I at least may find some solace in knowing that the dedicated father of my children possesses nonetheless a rare nobility of spirit.

I have to brush away a pair of betraying tears on this page. It's not just happiness, but concern for others, that guides our actions.

\* \* \*

John Mill enjoyed the Chelsea neighbourhood: a posher part of the greater City, and he'd even attended, albeit rarely, the occasional match of the Chelsea Cricket Club at the local Commons area, which was slowly giving some way to further urban construction, at least for those who could afford to live there. But today he was in a troubled hurry, and dreading a visit he could only describe as morally necessary, though he allowed himself to hate the reason for it. And he only had himself to blame. He just hoped that Thomas Carlyle would not begrudge him too much for the sordid episode and prove more on the forgiving side. John felt maybe forgiveness could be mutual, considering how irritating Carlyle had himself been just a few weeks previously, along with that dreary wife of his. Still, Mill knew he was just attempting to rationalise something for which he had taken responsibility. He should have offered to have my father read the damnable thing! John thought now as he picked up his stride, feeling the first few drops of what would hopefully remain just a light drizzle for London today: he had left home so quickly to get this over with that an umbrella simply had not occurred to him.

The address of 5 Cheyne Row lay south of Knightsbridge, on the north side of the Thames, across from the western edge of Battersea Fields. There was talk of turning that spot—many hectares of it—into another public park, which Mill approved of almost instinctively, refusing to acknowledge how utilitarian such a venue would be, though he also thought it a positive solution to an area with a reputation for duelling, of all things! As recently as '29, the Duke of Wellington had gone to 'settle a matter of honour'—even now John cringed at the word which merely masked masculine stupidity—with the Earl of Winchelsea, who had vociferously opposed the granting of rights back to Catholics for the first time since the Tudors. The victorious commander at Waterloo against Bonaparte had been called upon to defend himself and his political ideals against a man who inherited his title and was concerned about 'papistry.'

Again, such were the ongoing thoughts of John Stuart Mill when he was involved with a task, never truly able to shut off his active mind, though he had gleaned the tale of duels from dear Harriet, who'd mentioned it after learning of how poor a blades-man Mill had always been.

*This is why I could only have minimal staff,* he thought again as he kept trying to calm himself. Harriet continued to try and soothe his hurt psyche, though she understood that he would keep berating himself, and in this case perhaps with at least some good reason. He had in fact gone to visit her first, so distraught at the prospect of the requisite impending apology that he'd stopped in his family's own doorway to force himself to remember which Taylor address to actually venture towards, and he was still trying to remain calm about the poor maid, Mary, and her much-too-close encounter between an irreplaceable manuscript and one of John's clean-burning oil lamps. It could have been worse, he now permitted himself to think darkly—the whole house might have gone up! And he felt sorry for the new maid, having hired her just weeks prior to the recent tense dinner he'd hosted for Harriet and four friends, accepting her help with some preparatory work but—probably unwisely—insisting upon the cooking himself, with mixed reviews.

There could be no excuse: John had been entrusted by his friend—yes, he kept referring to the strange—strained?—relation as one of genuine friendship—Thomas Carlyle, with a copy, the only copy so far as he knew, of a manuscript of the history of the French Revolution. Carlyle's work showed promise, it analysed both what people thought of as 'the' revolution by moving past the eighteenth century and advancing to their current time, with the more recent iteration of French revolutions. And now it was ashes. Utterly destroyed. And John was preparing, not to sack his new housekeeper—despite a desperate claim to embark upon such a path, which Harriet recognised as frustrated bluster, such was her knowledge of how he thought—but rather to head straight to the Carlyle home and, what? Try and make amends? Suggest a secretary to transcribe another copy prior to submission for publication specifically to prevent such personal disasters?

He could see the home now, proudly painted bright yellow, offset by an equally brilliant cream door, so it was easy for the Carlyles to offer verbal directions to their house, and the place really did stand out from immediate neighbours. As he drew ever closer, he fretted also about other recent issues that had strained matters, and not just with the Carlyles. William Fox had finally separated from his wife, making the same motion as John Taylor—though Fox was of much more humble economic means—and had done no less than move in with Eliza Flower and his two children. John felt anxious for his friends; he truly thought of the pair of them as almost as much his friends as Harriet's, and had known Fox for longer anyway, but now he fretted for all of them, like a group of home-wreckers or something just as garish.

Almost to the door now, John noticing some late-morning Chelsea activity: servants pushing prams—children's mums would hardly do so themselves in such an exclusive spot; several dozen horses leading vehicles about, in this case either glossy and ornate rides occupied by the well-to-do, or slightly less well kept yet still respectable carriages making deliveries to other posh abodes. John could see no stray animals here, no grubby squealing children—only scrubbed and perfectly dressed ones instead, likely on their way to lessons for anything from music to foreign languages; nor beggars, prostitutes, nor even newsboys on corners selling papers. John slowed his pace, recalling Harriet having tea earlier this year with Jane Carlyle, with their ensuing chat quickly becoming 'constrained,' to borrow Harriet's adjective. It had not helped when he, John, had tried talking with Harriet later that same day about his own fear of becoming 'obscure and insignificant'—his adjectives—and continuing to work on his own writing whilst encouraging hers. She took it as simple jealousy on his part, having by this time gotten almost as many articles into print as he, so maybe there was a spot of envy from him, irrational and inexcusable as he regarded it. Still, he hardly wished to have to defend his relationship with her, or their friends Fox and Flower, to either or both of the Carlyles.

And after all the anxiety, none of it feigned, John simply had to stand in the doorway like a dolt, explaining in a near stutter and near avoidance of tears, to the Carlyle butler, what had happened, and could Thomas please contact him as soon as he possibly could, and whatever other banalities came rushing out of him that depressing morning. Despite John's meticulous memory—so detailed he occasionally felt nearly betrayed by it, since remembrances could feel like curses as much as nostalgic reminders—strong emotions could leave him befuddled after the fact, and such would prove the case when he recalled the events of this day. That he was focused more on the incineration of Carlyle's manuscript and less on the minimal damage to his family home—which might have become catastrophic with less attention from dutiful young Mary—he would have to profusely thank her later—revealed much of his own state of mind.

John chose a long way home. Walking was not just about solace and peace for him, but a way to organise his thoughts. He could hardly wait for the next, to his mind wholly necessary, rendezvous of the Trijackia; it had been too long since their last get-together, and the traditional meeting at George and Harriet Grote's welcoming home could only help.

Graham's presence—Grote's too, for that matter—had gone missing during the recent semi-Trijackia encounter recently in London with a French scholar and aspiring diplomat, whom John had the good fortune to meet first during that strange episode involving General Torrijos and the abortive attempt to restore Ferdinand VII. Alexis de Tocqueville had clearly been sympathetic with that doomed cause—Torrijos and the other prisoners had finally been executed without trial several years ago—but like the Trijackia members, held out more hope for a philosophical revolution instead. De Tocqueville seemed especially interested in the 'American experiment,' as he had taken to calling it, and likewise was becoming a competent historian, which was what made John think of him now. He could hear the posh Norman drawl, probably quipping something about how if Carlyle's history had been worth the effort, Monsieur Mill would 'nevah 'ave been so careless, non?'

Mill had learned from quite a tender age the perpetual need to take personal responsibility, especially for one's own mistakes, well-intentioned or no. His frustration with his beloved nation's less than beloved government came from its parliamentary strengths and history of slowly 'progressive' legislation, yet it could remain stuck in the ancient eternal and infantile game of pointing fingers at other parties. He still felt horrible over what happened, and only slightly relieved by passing on the message, but it would be better when he could speak with Carlyle in person.

John felt slightly better upon arriving home after such days, which had not lasted long yet seemed so, such were his feelings about them. He hated being judged, had caught some grief from his own family, again almost regretting remaining there. As for Carlyle and the destroyed 'script, he would offer to assist in replacing it in any way that Carlyle's honour might demand, including helping with the research or writing or both of a new history text.

\* \* \*

The following year would offer a whole different array of stressors, and one curious couple would need each other to see it through. Matters were hardly helped by the fact that Harriet had to miss two key events of 1836: John's latest promotion at work, to something called 'Examiner of Indian Correspondence'—co-workers thought he was joking when he inquired about what that should entail, since he was unsure and was not convinced he warranted another jump in the ranks anyway. As ever, he would research the position in depth, then find a way to organise his daily work rounds so that he could continue to start with his light breakfast, accompanied by reading a rotating mix of newspapers—several of which he, and Harriet, and Ms Martineau, and that promising young writer Dickens, had

all contributed to. The younger man's first serialised portions of 'The
Pickwick Papers' showed promise, though John actually read little
fiction besides the great epic mythical tales from Classical Greece
and Rome.

The other event, which John desperately hoped was in no way
connected to his new position — he would have resented a pity promotion — was the funeral service for his father. Harriet truly wished
to join John at the Mill 'summer home' that year, partly to soothe and
comfort John, and partly to get to know his family. Thomas Carlyle
had managed to catch up with the family there: John's parents thought
highly of some of his friends, the Trijackia notwithstanding, with
whom James Mill had never reconciled, and neither Graham nor
Roebuck, nor his father, had ever explained what the row from years
ago had been about. John was a man grown, and it was not as though
the Trijackia tried to make a name for themselves by whoring or
drinking or gambling. In truth, John himself had the least inclination
of the trio for the first, the least bodily stamina for the second, and
an utter lack of interest — the same for his two friends — in the third.
Even curious Dickens had defended gaming on Sundays, arguing in
support of the right to pursue one's own pleasures. Reporting on a
clergyman observing a Sunday cricket match, Dickens noted that the
man found joy rather than condemnation in the scene, writing that, 'It
is such men as this, who would do more in one year to make people
properly religious, cheerful, and contented, than all the legislation of
a century could ever accomplish.'

So now John silently cursed himself for feeling some perverse
post-death need to try and justify his friendships, along traditional
Protestant condemnatory lines no less! He'd have to meet Dickens,
see if some of that insightful levity might prove as contagious as that
bloody consumption which so destroyed the lungs. John had found
genuine gladness though, in the three months of leave from India
House that came with his promotion, so, missing Harriet of course,
he had arranged to take sixteen-year-old Henry and twelve-year-old
George, his two 'kid' brothers, on their own miniature Grand Tour,

though just to France. The boys performed at their ablest, John had been sure, relishing in the sights and culture and delighting in hearing their eldest brother speak impressive French.

There had been plans to make it further south, but both boys had sailed off and on for most of the trip, and neither acquired very capable 'sea legs,' despite the Channel crossing being quite short by nautical standards. Regardless, the boys had opted to return home after just the capital city, so Big Brother kept up his travels, claiming they offered the best psychic balm he knew. That Harriet, and Lily, now five, bless her, had been as far as Switzerland at the same time, made his decision easier. John was annoyed by Sterling telling him upon his return to England that Carlyle had written to Sterling—John did not think they were that close—to report Mr Mill once again being in public company with Mrs Taylor, asking, 'Is it not very strange, this pining away into desiccation and non-entity, of our poor Mill, if it be so, as his friends all say, that this charmer is the cause of it?' Nothing—not his own family, not British politics, not the faraway colonial exploitation and bigotry which often travelled with those politics, not failed writing projects or bad reviews or even the horrible stalking consumption—irritated John Mill more readily and rapidly as criticism of the love of his life.

Roebuck and Graham had put him on the spot at their last meeting, again at Chez Grote, as they had all taken to nicknaming their favourite group haunt. Thankfully, Harriet Grote remained wholly amenable to having the strange cohort of intellectual men at her warm and inviting home, joking last time about 'keeping you boys off the streets of Southwark or Whitechapel where you'd just get up to no good.' John had smiled despite himself at that. She knew better, keeping abreast of what these men wrote and produced, once describing John as a 'wayward intellectual deity': how the 'other' Harriet had roared at that, liking the wayward part and distrusting the deity component. John had not repeated his having overheard more of Mrs Grote's commentary, such that Mrs Taylor 'was tired' of her husband, how she 'cared for clever people' instead, noting Mrs Taylor a 'very pretty woman' who had 'fascinated and entangled' John. 'Entangled' was hardly an adjective the said Mrs Taylor was likely to approve, since it might be construed as the sort of feminine entrapment that Harriet loathed and continued to struggle against, insisting like John that women and men alike should be free to create their own voluntary 'entanglements' with as much informed liberty as they could garner from each other.

Families muddled matters, so such thinking also tended to go. So was it too late to make amends with his family, the 'boys' had wished to know of him that day at the Grote's?

'Dear God, how does anyone know?' demanded Mill, knowing he spoke curtly.

George 'Jack' Graham, eldest of the Trijackia though still younger than George Grote, thankfully resisted the inane adage about blood having thickness greater than water—John, during a darker days of his 'depression,' once followed that spurious logic further, recalling that faeces were in turn thicker than blood, so what was the point? Instead, that day Jack answered with something that bordered on the religious for its emotive appeal. 'Family pulls, John. We speak of family "ties," which remains not far off the mark, and we seem to have an instinctive drive to help further our families, no matter what moral wrecks their members have become.'

'And all families consist of said wrecks,' added John Roebuck. 'Believe me: there are reasons why our "polite society" insists upon not discussing certain familial details. I think it comes from simply not wishing to disclose our similar relations.'

'Does it make a difference if you're the eldest?' wondered John aloud. Both Graham and Roebuck were third children, third sons no less, and had worked diligently—feverishly?—for parental approval. Graham once joked that if he and Roebuck had lived during the Middle Ages, their eldest brothers would have been whisked off to study warfare in some knight's manor, and the second brothers—the 'spares'—likely would have ended up as squires in their elder's service, while Graham and Roebuck themselves would have been all but

destined for the clergy. John amused them on that occasion by pointing out that such would have been Catholic clergy, which just made
them wince. 'God, that would make it even worse!' Roebuck had cried.

'I should think not,' responded Graham, earning a nod from
Grote. 'Look, John,' he added, 'plenty of families are simply not that
close, in some emotional sense.'

'But I barely know some of my own blood,' John parried, not
knowing how forward-thinking this attitude of his was. 'Children'
remained mostly small adults: things to become—assuming they
actually survived that first critical year or so without dropping dead
of God-knew-what—apprentices, work for their parents, perhaps get
sold by those parents. The notion that this represented a genuinely
distinct period within the human condition was still new, another
of those pesky 'radical' ideas arrived at by just the sorts of ne'er-do-
wells that John Mill 'always seemed to be associatin' wit,' to borrow
the staccato near-cockney condemnation of his mother.

'But what's to know?' asked Roebuck now.

John did not favour another row right then. Their much earlier
debate about the merits of different English modern writers had been
friendly, almost as though having relied on set rules like traditional
university discourse, though neither Mr Mill nor Mr Roebuck had
proven willing to give an inch, even over something most others found
trivial. The debate was an exercise in rationality; giving in to passion
and shouting meant you had already lost. 'Well, how often do you see
your own families?' he asked lamely.

Graham answered first. 'As you reminded us, John, we're both third
sons, with other siblings to boot. We see each other when we're able.'

That only served to make the interlocutor want to know more.
'Such as when?'

Graham looked slightly exasperated. 'Birthdays. Christenings.
Weddings. Periodic weekends, especially after church services.'

'Good,' John said now, 'that's good. Time was, the local church
served as the centre of village social life. Everyone could meet there,
and now when we study our medieval history we think church was

just a place for accused felons to seek sanctuary.'

Roebuck guffawed at that. 'Perhaps, Mill, but recall: you yourself are hardly the picture of fervent worship.'

John glanced downward, though wearing a disarming smile. 'True enough, Jack.' He was trying to maintain his calm demeanour. John Roebuck, usually tried and true companion, had publicly made unwanted observations about Mr Mill and Mrs Taylor a couple of years previously, during a time when they had already felt their most vulnerable: taking turns trying to bolster each other's courage, John and Harriet had cautiously opted to appear in a semi-public venue. John had eagerly appeared at a casual series of salons, modelled roughly on the French tradition, and attended one with Harriet hosted by Sarah Austin, Harriet Grote, and the wife of a well-known barrister, the very party that Harriet had overheard Jane Carlyle gossiping about after their curious dinner party with Will Fox and Lizzie Flower.

It proved disastrous: Mrs Taylor struggling to hold her head high and ward off tears after entering a room full of judgemental titters, Mr Mill chasing after her, terrified and angry at once, then guilty since whilst Harriet had gone along with the idea, it was originally his own. To his credit, Roebuck—Graham had to work then—had visited Mill at home, attempting to warn him of further ridicule, but Mill had already seen the condemnatory countenances of friends the prior evening, and had welcomed his visitor with a cool aloofness. And now Mill's fretting over the nature of his relations with his own immediate family members had rendered him willing to quiz the ever more estranged Roebuck—and, thankfully to a lesser extent, Graham—about their own experiences with such. Though it was clear they wished to not discuss it.

'Jack,' Mill addressed Roebuck again, 'you were born abroad, in the very country in which my late father took such a profound if biased interest. How did that shape you?'

'Jack,' Roebuck replied, 'I was thrilled to get out of India. We stayed in Madras until I was six, when my own father died, and then came back home.'

This was taking a tack away from family, but Mill remained highly curious, suddenly remembering that the barrister whose wife had hosted that counter-productive evening he had just mentally revisited, had also been born in India. Calcutta, John thought, and the future attorney had also 'returned home' at a tender age. 'You never considered India home, then?'

Roebuck laughed, joined by Graham, who glanced anxiously at the third of the Jacks. 'Goodness no, Mill! It's too bloody hot, the people are different, the food is too spicy, I had trouble with the dialect, England is home, I could go on...'

*Please don't,* John thought suddenly, once again questioning undue English control of India. To him the whole world beckoned, and he sometimes thought the greatest of tragedies was that even with endless resources, a single lifetime could only ever be enough to sample little slices of the world, its cultures—ancient and new—unexplored lands and seas alike, incredibly diverse wildlife—he loved knowing that species kept getting 'discovered,' at least by humans.

That was what the Greeks had taught him—especially Socrates, who had not bothered making notes for posterity—that the point was to keep learning, keep exploring. And here was one of John's closest compatriots, having lived in one of the countries that John Mill knew he might very well never get to visit himself, disparaging the whole experience! Mill thought children of any means should be required to live abroad for a time, at least a good year or so, and preferably in a place which had a differing dominant language. He could only imagine the peace that might result from that. He had only been able to explore and get to know some of western Europe, and understood that he was fortunate to have the open attitude and financial resources to enable even that much.

Others continued to wonder at his strange motivations. He got along with colleagues, even enjoyed some pleasant London walks with them. But when one argued in favour of eliminating Sanskrit, Hindi, and Arabic—all three at once!—from the curricula of the British schools throughout India, John had become apoplectic. The gall of empire! There were times John hated himself for continuing to work for the Company, still insisting he could improve some things from within, and he had to confess that said governmental corporation remained remarkably lenient with the tone of some of 'Mr Mill's writings' in newsprint.

He remained intrigued by these friends, even when disagreeing with them. He wished Sterling could have been there then, but that yet-another-John had been fatigued caring for his own lovely wife. Sterling's first novel, several years old now, had not earned the praise nor funds that he had hoped, but he insisted upon not giving up the fight, as he had phrased the issue, and was at work on new projects. His input would have been welcomed, at least by Mill: the rest of the Trijackia had reservations, but John remained unsure if those heralded from class tension—once, in his cups, Grote had remarked disparagingly upon Sterling's 'common' pedigree—or if perhaps it was simply that Sterling had shown university potential only to leave Trinity at Cambridge without completing his law degree. But he had his own reasons. The practice of law sounded horrid to Mill as well—it seemed more direct, more public, more honest, to write instead, and change minds that way.

John Sterling was something of an 'opposite' for John Mill: half-mad for his ideas—never mind that Roebuck already had a few years as 'Radical MP' for Bath—and simply less afraid of speaking his true mind, whatever the consequences or attitudes of others. And that was precisely what Mill loved most about him.

Mill would come to rely on that truer friendship more and more in the coming years, then start to pull back from it as Roebuck, much more so than Graham, waxed more critical of John's relationship with Harriet. The Trijackia 'meeting' proved pleasant enough, though Mill mentioned—very slowly, locking eyes with Roebuck as he did so—a work with Harriet about logic, growing into a full book; Parliament dabbling with, then retreating from, revisions of marriage laws; winter that seemed to arrive early and with heavier snows; and an outbreak of influenza striking all over Europe, not just Britain.

Interestingly, Mill and Roebuck, even though by this point diverging sharply in their thoughts and ideas, yet shared a moment of fond remembrance and drank a pseudo-toast—just with tea—to the memory of Bentham and how Britain had switched its bear-baiting attitudes from the Tudor years to becoming the first nation with an organisation like the Society for the Prevention of Cruelty to Animals, rumoured to shortly gain a 'Royal' prefix from monarchical approval. As Bentham had put it, 'the question is not "Can they reason?" nor "Can they talk?", but "Can they suffer?"' It was one of few of Bentham's ideals that Mill intended to carry forward: more groups—endless groups—of individuals who merited consideration of their happiness, simply for being alive and able to experience the world. Now he and Harriet had to keep developing their work into how humans could do likewise, just with more emphasis on reason and ethics.

# PART THREE

# Logical and Sexual Utility

*1842–1844.*

I t was true, as the pair of them had learned over a period of years
now: lovers could share meaningful, desirous, lustful intimacy
even without 'regular' intercourse. And of course, their society
was reputed to be the originator of the perhaps instinctive 'missionary' position—odd religious connotations of the phrase aside, as
English and other Europeans took their cultures and beliefs around
the globe—but it was generic, limiting, not very creative, destined
to leave more open and eager lovers seeking more. So it had become
with Harriet and John: kisses themselves could become nearly the
peak of human passion when accompanied or motivated by hungry
curiosity about another person's tongue and mouth, or neck, or ear-
lobes. Or other locales.

John felt his heart rate increase whenever he thought of exploring
Harriet's body with his hands and mouth. Granted, she was his 'first,'
but she no longer had to act as something of an instructress in the
arena of sexual fulfilment. Yet she could still surprise him: ambushing
him in his own home when he had stepped out for a few moments on

some forgotten errand, by shrugging off her jacket at the door to his bedroom to display her unabashed nakedness just for him. A simple and improvised gesture like that could still cause a near instantaneous 'tightening of his drawers,' as he had later tried to describe it to her, which she found hilarious.

Couples had to have fun together. That was one of his most cherished lessons in this life, something with which she agreed wholeheartedly. John had overcome his fears by now: of discovery, though the couple remained shy; of vengeance visited upon him and perhaps Harriet, compliments of a jilted husband; of sex altogether, since polite society still had yet to work past its—religious and hypocritical—judgemental attitudes about sexuality generally; and of himself and Harriet and their occasional encounters with medical concerns.

Besides evading syphilis, thank goodness neither of them had ever begun to present with symptoms of consumption—chills, fever, nocturnal diaphoresis, weight loss from less appetite, constant fatigue—one of Harriet's long-lost siblings had also displayed the frightening-looking nail-clubbing—and yet sometimes John still awoke in a slight night sweat from another source, remembering Harriet's note from '41 describing how she 'could not stand when I tried to get up,' complaining further of being 'nervous' and 'feverish.' Her legs had failed her utterly at one point that summer, losing feeling for a time in the right and struggling with the left. While she could now walk again, a slight shuffle remained omnipresent, and she just could not match him for speed or distance, him so often wishing to accelerate and explore the next hillock, the next avenue, the next copse—like he could not visit each part of the world quickly enough. And the occasional slight numbness or sudden cramping of Harriet's lower extremities had driven her and her lover into some creative sexual positioning.

Even the working women in Southwark often remained ignorant of such methods of pleasure, or ignored them for the sake of convenience and earning a few quick pence. Harriet believed, correctly, that her husband had not returned for years, and she learned he had even taken up a small fund among other gentlemen to help educate some of those 'unfortunates'—among the more hypocritical terms coined by anyone within the Empire—so that they might get more respected parts of the Capital—becoming laundresses, cooks, even an occasional governess—some families asked fewer questions than others—and in one unique case, a teacher!

And John Taylor... poor cuckolded yet oddly honourable John Taylor. A rhythm had developed, and none of them really continued to emphasise the fantasy of so many nights of Taylor partaking of his club. He still went of course, and enjoyed it, and the very masculine fellow members had learned not to chide him for an adulterous wife—he had once bloodied the nose of one of the more foolish ones for arrogantly suggesting matters might be resolved with a duel after all. But still, Taylor had arrived at something of an emotional balance with jealousy, continued dedication to the children, mingled with the occasional dalliance with a younger woman who worked at a haberdashery near his own apothecary shop. There were limits, too: he would never adopt the adventurous spirit of his estranged wife—who had once suggested, back in the old days only to be rebuffed, that they make love behind the shop counter. Gone now were the days when Mr Mill might suggest that Mrs Taylor lacked courage for not leaving her husband or attempting the long, expensive, highly unlikely path to divorce. The adults appreciated the usual stability for the children. Likewise, John Taylor would never bring a mistress back home with him, and certainly never permit the children to meet her, unless...

He could only dream of 'unless.' Despite his silent ravings in the early days, he did not want his wife to suffer or die, nor even Mill for that matter. But he would never pursue friendship with that strange man, despite the temptation to do so dating back to their first meeting. It felt more like decades than individual years. He and his wife had briefly gloried in the faint glimmer of hope represented by the 1836 Civil Marriage Act, but for naught: that legislation, long overdue, was about getting married. The act became, at the wish of those involved, a purely secular act, and no longer had to be officiated by clerical personnel. No, Mr and Mrs Taylor remained legally—and religiously—enjoined, till death would they part.

So here Taylor was again, calling upon his in-laws, relations with whom had become strained. He could not properly blame them, he reckoned: they of course wanted what was 'best' for all their children and grandchildren, as he did for his own offspring, and they seemed to have gained more sympathy for their daughter's 'situation' with Mr Mill—perhaps from simple exhaustion and said daughter wearing them down to becoming more accepting.

But blind acceptance did not rank anyone higher along the hierarchy of courage or chivalry, Mr Taylor thought angrily—again—then let it go—again—and his realisation of that, and the accompanying frustration, was hardly aided by the fact that Mill, for all his blasted logic and reasoning, would have to reach the inescapably same conclusion. Oh, he was always on about the liberty of the individual, and how only individuals could think and reason since groups of people—any people—supposedly lacked such ability. To Mr Taylor, who had read a number of the articles printed in those atrocious newspaper articles—hotbeds of radicalism—Mill seemed yet mired in that stultifying half-philosophy of utilitarianism, which by Taylor's analysis was little other than a clever way to justify one's behaviours, be they motivated by a single person's selfish desires or a group's attempting to get away with crime or war or the maintenance of poverty. If one could make a concise appeal to happiness masquerading as rationality, then anything should be possible!

But Taylor operated under a wholly different agenda this day, enjoying a longer walk and thankful to not have any need for a coat or umbrella, especially after the length of time it took to arrive. No, today he was making an unsolicited appearance at the new Hardy home up north for more selfless reasons: he was sickened by the images that kept playing in his mind's theatre about his wife, who, estrangement aside, continued to display signs and symptoms of, well, just what exactly was part of the impetus for his visit. He hated her disease, hated that she had it, hated how she acquired it.

Taylor had also offered—more than once—to try and assist with the other metaphorical tiger in the kitchen, the deteriorating situation featuring another member of Harriet's immediate family. Such was the case of her sister, another young lady named Caroline, who had gleefully wed one Arthur Ley two years ago in what seemed another storybook tale of love and respect. Yet two details had set alarms ringing for Taylor: Harriet had reached out to him for assistance, and also, perhaps more surprisingly, to Mr Carlyle, despite what had grown now into several years of mutual animosity. The Hardys seemed more resistant to assistance than Harriet herself, thus Taylor's intention to try and win them around today, since when Harriet had recently written to him—to her husband, John Taylor!—she had described 'poor little sister' Caroline having found herself in 'a peck of troubles—but only about domestic arrangements.'

This new period of time, already being hailed as 'Victorian' to differentiate it from the immediately prior—and still largely perceived—'Georgian,' seemed intent upon suffusing simple terminology into even more polite code: Harriet's reference meant that her dear younger sister had begun suffering some form of abuse at the hands of her husband, himself rumoured to be a committed drinker.

Taylor dodged a colourful assortment of residents in this quaint village of Kirkburton about their daily business—including a newsboy acting like an old town crier, mentioning the recent Parliamentary debates about an Income Tax Act but truly shouting vociferously about a Mines and Collieries Act—maybe the lad had friends working in the dreadful mines, one of which lay quite close by, and he mispronounced 'collieries.' Taylor also encountered a fellow apothecary passing by on his left, one who further sold candles and tea implements—Taylor believed shopkeepers should stick to as few specialities as possible, especially in smaller locales like this in southern Yorkshire; plus a pleasing woollen shop, smelling far better as he passed than he thought sheep did themselves—Kirkburton was also known for its tanneries. There were drably-dressed but eager-looking boys making jokes whilst trotting off to school—Taylor wondered if girls were part of that equation, which would have pleased Harriet—and finally, just the sounds and colours of a small community waking itself up for another business day, with faint doorbells competing for attention with the clop-clop of shod horse hoofs on the road stones, the splashing sounds of water being fetched from a central village well mingling with such similar sounds of chamber pots and cooking pans receiving their due cleaning, and the myriad of hues evident in one couple clearly strolling and courting across the street; whilst others, mostly young, made their way to jobs.

Taylor felt for Caroline Ley, he truly did, and while he might be faulted for letting down his own wife, he had absolutely never struck her, and continued in the belief that any man who did so, even while within his rights, was nonetheless a cad and a coward. It was unmanly to exploit the weaknesses of another. And he hated the insecurity of not knowing how to respond to a battered wife's defence of her husband's abuses, as though it came from a desperate need less to exonerate the offending man and more to ward off the trepidation of being abandoned. One of those news articles that Taylor's own wife had penned, with which he had agreed, concerned the need for society to address a range of abuses aimed at women: what recourse wives should have; what rights unwed women should possess; even how women—and girls—should be educated—Taylor admitted he found the latter portion a bit radical for his taste, thinking of his duties to precocious little Lily. Still, these were issues not going away, and if fathers and brothers and husbands could not properly care for the women in their lives, then society as a whole would have to do so. One wondered what witty response Mr Mill might have to these concerns, though Taylor refused to believe that Mill and Mrs Taylor shared their written work with each other, acting as each other's coaches and editors before that work ever made its way into printed media.

And now Taylor felt unsure whether he had the address correct. He took out the scrap upon which he had noted the new Hardy residence, mentally computed that the midwifery business clearly had its perquisites—not knowing the property was inherited— and strode

down the gravelly drive to the imposing two-storey solid-looking vast
stone and brick edifice now confronting him. It showed off a mix of
apple and pear trees, old yews and hardy oaks — Taylor grinned at his
poor family pun, and now his legs were beginning to achingly remind
him that perhaps he should have had his driver let him off a bit closer.
Taylor, in a recent 'civil' chat with Mill, had agreed that this part of
the country would surely benefit from the new railroad services that
kept cropping up all over, and today such would have aided Taylor
with his current quest.

Yet he remained wholly unprepared for the vision which met him
at the door, that instantly knowable voice calling behind her, lovely
even despite its current short tone. 'No! I said I shall come right back,
Father, and then we will resolve whether Arthur can assist us or no,
regardless of whether he is in Australia!'

The door all but slammed behind her, and then there she was,
Harriet Hardy Taylor, dressed in ivory summer wear with painstakingly arranged and stitched pink ribbons and tiny flowers, facing
her husband, who immediately doffed his hat in some inane gallant
gesture. 'Greetings, Wife,' was all he could think to say, such was his
surprise.

'Mr Taylor,' she said, not knowing how to respond, no longer used
to hearing herself utter that name while looking at this man. She felt
herself strangely pleased to see him, feeling cut off and isolated up
here. She liked the new Hardy homestead, but wondered at both the
distance to travel and the wisdom of her parents more or less retiring.
Still, Father kept his business going, steadily finding new clientele
in Yorkshire.

The other John remained south in London, working on articles
covering all manner of topics, as usual. 'I should have sent word,'
Harriet's husband intoned now. 'Forgive me.'

'Nothing to forgive,' she said almost automatically. 'The children
will be thrilled to see you. Our Lily has begun keeping notes in that
little diary you gave her last Christmas.'

He brightened at that, always pleased when one of his thoughtful gifts really touched one of the children. The boys were getting more challenging to shop for: Herby seemed old for toys now, and was up to date with the best cricket gear instead, though Haji still liked little tin soldiers, especially the more expensive painted ones, the best coming from a company in France, little exported. Harriet had graciously picked some up during her last travels there, and Taylor felt strangely relaxed at the image of her there—with him, of course, at least part of the time.

'Are they here today?' John asked about the children.

'Certainly. They're upstairs presently. They still have little taste for witnessing Mummy having words with Grandmama and Grandpère.'

In that case there was a little time to discuss more intimate matters, another topic perhaps not for the ears of the young. 'Then you've yet to see a specialist?'

Harriet turned around, as though family members might come ambling out of the new house that she already hoped to never inherit. Her home was London, where the action was, though York could prove interesting with its equally old history. She stepped forward into the shade of one of the oaks, watching her husband mirror her motion.

'That shall have to wait for now, Husband.' They still addressed each other thusly; their Christian names had come to seem off-limits, an intimacy they no longer played at.

'I would have come sooner, but was unsure whether to wait and visit the new house, and, well,' he looked down at the ground, seeing the upper portions of their shadows touching due to the sun's afternoon angle.

'John,' she slipped. He pretended to not notice. She gestured behind her. 'Those are your parents-in-law,' then pointed upward, 'and those are your children, who adore you.'

'And your parents?'

'They have always liked and admired you. Even now, they evince little knowledge of how to deal with our "situation." Naturally, like all adults past a certain age I suppose, they speak of how no one of their generation would skitter about in extra-marital affairs, and they vociferously complain about Fox and Lizzie, for example, but not about me. Usually.'

Taylor flinched for an instant at the brazen way she pronounced 'affairs,' then let it go. 'Please, Harriet,' he returned the slip, though more intentionally than she had, 'help me understand what you experienced. I was quite frightened for you.'

It had happened last year. It had taken this long for them to have privacy to discuss it like this, though Taylor had known the gist of it. 'It was not a stroke, thank goodness.'

Taylor blinked, then stepped forward, reaching for her hands. She found herself welcoming the simple and so often underrated contact, still annoyed with how their society could make stupid mental leaps from hand-holding to nothing less than sexual positions.

'Though it came on like one,' she continued, looking at him. 'Truly, I had trouble just standing up again, and was glad the children had not to witness it.' She spared him the mention of Mill having been at her side that day; he likely suspected anyway.

'It hurts at night sometimes,' she added. 'I've experienced some paralysis.' He looked horrified, so she tried to reassure him. 'Clearly I can still move, John,' she forgot the 'Mr Taylor' greeting again. 'Though I have still some difficulty walking as long as before, and keeping up with,' again she did not mention Mill, unsure why, since that had not previously been an issue for her, 'with the children. As I say, there are some pains during the night, and my hands have experienced a bit of numbness here and there.' Taylor tried to keep from wincing; his wife's honest appraisal was being presented here in such a typical, dry, English 'stiff upper lip' monologue. But he did not interrupt her.

'A couple of facial aches. The headaches were also bad,' she continued, 'though not as debilitating as the pair of fevers thus far.'

'Good God, Harriet, what have you been diagnosed with?' her husband queried now.

She leaned back, shaking her head, as much to clear her wet eyes as from annoyance. 'That's just it: no one really knows for sure. As I said: no stroke, the fevers passed quickly, I've not had any accidents or spills despite the occasional dizziness... I surely do not have cholera or consumption.' She had lowered her voice some, not wanting family members inside the house to overhear any of this, but she had to get it out.

She felt some surprise by how clinical she could be regarding her troubles, no longer concerned whether or not she was confessing weakness. Harriet had wondered—and published—angrily about how many women did not seek treatment for all manner of potential hurts, illnesses and injuries alike, because they believed they could not do so, or at least were unaware of how to go about doing so. Most physicians were of course male, though one item Harriet thanked her father for—despite their recent run-ins with her current visit to the otherwise lovely new home—was instilling in his children, or Harriet at least, who had asked the most questions about Father's job during her formative years, the confidence to solicit help when necessary.

*And there should be no shame in such,* thought Harriet now. But my dear sister is clearly ashamed. She still recalled that horrid recent letter from Caroline, had briefly tried to keep it intact since receiving it—well, her parents had actually received it—and she withdrew it from her petticoat now to show it to Taylor.

He scanned it quickly, noting a date from weeks ago and glossing over the heading to Caroline's 'dear parents,' before settling upon the part that tried to logically exonerate her husband. Apparently Caroline had missed an annualised cricket match, something Taylor and his club associates often enjoyed, because she had experienced 'some immensely disagreeable fuss' with husband Arthur, and that his sister-in-law 'had one of the fits of excessive crying which are fits and which I only have on very rare occasions and my face was so swollen and disfigured that I did not choose to go to be compared with other more successful women of whom he (Arthur, Taylor easily deduced) has one who follows him everywhere and who by insolence,' and he stopped and gazed back at Harriet. '"Swollen and disfigured?"' he asked dully. 'And are "successful women" just those who manage to avoid being beaten by brutish husbands?'

'Damn it, John,' Harriet all but shouted now—he had only ever heard her curse once or twice before, at his expense—'I can manage myself on my own, and with,' she started, but did not finish. They both knew to whom she almost referred. 'But if you truly wish to help and gain my appreciation, and do something just because it's good in itself, then help me to help my sister!' She was sobbing by the end of this little tirade, and Taylor instinctively stepped forward, found himself holding and comforting his estranged wife. He was surprised she permitted it, and thought she felt a bit thinner than he remembered. And she felt reassured; she had missed the fact that her husband could prove a highly useful sounding board when circumstances demanded.

'Very well, then,' Taylor said at last, forcing himself to release the embrace and step back to look into Harriet's saddened face. 'What has been done to aid your sister up to this point?'

She wiped her eyes, not caring about not using a kerchief to do so. And she laid it all out for him, as she had done so for John some weeks earlier. John Mill remained the best listener she had ever encountered, though he could prove befuddled about actual advice, which speakers—so often women—did not want in the first place. And now she told the father of her children about her attempt to liaise with brother Arthur, himself adapting to life in Australia happily, though of course there remained the time delay in communications. She then summarised other assistance, minimising mention of John, who himself had recommended Thomas Carlyle, of all persons! She'd hated the idea of soliciting aid from the Carlyles, believing their fractured friendship perhaps too far gone to enable repair anymore. And her own sister had barely been speaking to her lately regardless: too much had already been said aloud about that ne'er-do-well husband of hers, and it was becoming a family rift. By comparison, her own affair with John seemed mild these days.

And yet here she was nonetheless chatting amiably with a man she had both genuinely loved and truly hated, on the bad days within the span of a single breath. And he listened just as well. Carlyle was certainly well connected, as Harriet relayed the issue, and knew his share of barristers and solicitors—Harriet let several more frustrated tears loose while acknowledging her ignorance as to which type of attorney might be needed for Caroline's situation, and detested the thought that Britain's lawyers, so far as she knew still without exception men, might prove unwilling to come to her sister's aid at all. She had taken to her usual self-guided research, finding nothing encouraging for battered wives, and even then it might only matter if the couple in question shared some impressive fortune, so the state could feel entitled in taking a slice of it.

Harriet continued her narrative, mentioning how her mother had written a letter to her directly, rather than to Caroline, a key part of the impetus for Harriet's fleeing London with barely a word this time to Mill. She paraphrased now, mimicking her mother's words about how Arthur Ley on that occasion 'had been drinking all day,' and eventually erupted to the point at which he had grabbed Caroline's hair, 'pulling out a quantity by the root, and struck her on the back of the neck where he had before injured her so severely.' Harriet felt nauseated in the telling, then had to convince Mr Taylor that such ill feeling was not related to her other recent ills and symptomology. 'By comparison, her experiences have put paid to my own, like my issue with "broken pneumonic blood vessels,"' she said, not wanting to alarm Taylor any further but likewise not wishing to be accused later of having held information back. And she had loved a recent recuperatory weekend spent with the Flower sisters—Caroline Fox had been unable to attend, being needed at home—and Lizzie's younger sister Sarah had regaled them with a rendition of what she promised would remain the final version of her song, 'Nearer My God to Thee.' The tune and accompanying inspiring lyrics had already been accepted for publication.

Harriet calmed herself anew, taking in her husband's exasperated look once more. 'Mother said that my sister has experienced difficulty with her right arm since the incident, though a later letter implied that it is healing properly after all. That bastard,' she spat, again surprising Taylor with both the choice of words and the vehemence behind it, 'even kicked her whilst she lay on the floor, and "brought on flooding," to borrow my mother's words. That's a phrase Father uses sometimes.'

Taylor just nodded once glumly. The expression about 'flooding,' at least in Mr Hardy's profession, was a euphemism for miscarriage. The children must have heard her weeping, for she could then just make out Herby's inquisitive voice behind her inquire if all was well. Then he noticed his father. 'Papa!' he shouted, which served as a near-instant magnet for his siblings.

John Taylor at once found himself all but tackled by more embraces, revelling in the warm playful touches of the little ones, the boys in truth not so little any more. And Lily herself showed signs of sprouting recently. *Dear God, where did the time go?* He and Harriet had reached an informal understanding regarding scheduling, alternating weeks and weekends and holidays, though the latter typically remained family events, at either the Hardy's or the Taylor's homes. In fact the children had become slightly spoiled by Christmases and birthdays spent with two pairs of grandparents, each of which had little to do with one another: each tended to blame their child-in-law for the no-longer-secret estrangement of the Taylor couple.

The children continued to shriek with delight, though Herby kept trying to make his voice sound a touch deeper than it really was. Haji and Lily could hardly have cared less; it was too much of a relief to have their Papa with them! They loved 'Uncle John,' yet were sometimes silently glad when he had other things to do. Herby had taken it upon himself lately to 'teach' his younger siblings about how adult relationships really worked, the other children listening to him like he was espousing gospel.

'Children,' Harriet finally called, not really minding the fresh grass-stains that would have to be laundered from the children's clothing, and her husband's also, from the looks of things. 'Inside now. Papa will join us for dinner and,' she started, looking to him for a recommendation.

'Good news, everyone,' Taylor added, 'I do not need to return to London until after the weekend.' That elicited fresh shouts of joy from the children, who rushed towards the house, almost knocking over their maternal grandparents, who had emerged to determine the source of the sudden hullaballoo.

Harriet knew that this episode, which somewhat did feel like a homecoming, complete with a new location for them to create memories, would elicit another round of awkward questions from the children, mostly previously directed at Harriet since she had been around home in London more often during the days. Yet the kids also devoted much time and effort to staying with their father when possible, Herby even having assisted several times in the apothecary shop, which clients loved, complimenting him on his flawless manners and growing knowledge of his father's trade. For now, the questions could just wait: Harriet had to fight for her sister's health and for her rights, such as they existed. She simply would not permit that damnable Arthur Ley to drink away what the two of them together had amassed, and she would die before she let the bastard lay his hands on her again!

* * *

*From the Diary of Helen Taylor:*
Dear Father: he died still wondering how girls should be educated, never resolving his own inner conflict about my own advanced reading list—largely self-selected—nor how hazardous it might prove for a society to permit its young females to learn much beyond following the dictates of a husband or developing passable culinary and child-rearing skills.

Did you never wonder, Father, at the contradiction in expecting wives and mothers to act as the initial teachers of the next generation after not having been themselves educated? I refer here not to Mr Mill's fanciful notion of Coleridge's 'clerisy,' which has still never appeared in Mill's and Mother's written works—perhaps tacit acknowledgement that education—for all—must surely precede calls for the best educated to lead.

As for my brothers, Herby thought he was teaching us younger Taylor children about how grown-ups thought and behaved, but Haji and I knew our parent's marriage had become a permanent sham. Herby was the only one who ever called Mr Mill a 'home-wrecker,' interestingly a term otherwise reserved for women.

\* \* \*

Back in London, John Mill continued to fret over Harriet's domestic issue, and suspected that Taylor would likely head north to ingratiate himself. He must know by now, Mill mentally reiterated once more, that reconciliation remained impossible. Besides, he had come to trust Harriet entirely, and never for a second thought she might 'betray' him with the first lover in her life—a curious phrasing for someone who was of course wed to her. Yet Harriet had largely come to accept certain matters, knew that even if divorce was a realistic option husbands almost always received full custody of any children, to say nothing of likely keeping any financial and property assets. Harriet had worked out a seemingly equitable pseudo-custody scenario with Taylor, and she would be damned if she would give up her hard-earned money for having become an occasional but professional writer of articles and reviews for Britain's insatiable customers of regular and inexpensive periodicals. She took justifiable pride in reviews of travel books—including one about Australia, where younger brother Arthur lived—and of books focused more domestically as well as works of poetry. She was gaining a reputation for speaking her mind, not hiding behind being a woman, as a recent review of more of Disraeli's disappointing work helped establish. And she had encouraged other women to be as forward regarding getting their voices heard into print.

As for the main writer in her life, John Mill had considered in print the apparent end of the Opium War with China—something that hit close to home considering his work with Asian cultures generally and since they both had strongly opposed the conflict from its opening; and also, which surprised Harriet at first, a panegyric of the still-new Queen, young Victoria, wed two years earlier and very much in love, having borne two healthy daughters and rumoured to be 'in a family way' again, and having survived two assassination attempts already. Both Johns had been furious over the latter, Mr Taylor complaining of the obvious, how an attack on the royal family implied that attacks on any British citizens could thus be perceived as acceptable, even if the new young queen was wed to a German—though Harriet was bemused how the previous several kings were of overwhelming German ancestry, even if born in England. As for Mr Mill, his concern lay primarily with the notion of murder or attempted murder, directed at anyone, and he had struggled, Harriet knew, with the complicating issues of what a loss of the British monarchy might mean to Britain and to the world. The Union Jack flew proudly over six continents, with these subject states offering homage partly to the notion of a beneficent ruler, even though such rulers had not savoured significant power for centuries now. Ms Martineau, whom Harriet and John still saw on occasion, clearly adored Queen Victoria, had taken to writing articles as though Britain had embarked upon some new golden age.

When Harriet and the children returned from Yorkshire, they would be able to make another of their outings to Hampstead Heath, especially during the weekends. The park offered fabulous views of the City's larger buildings, one of the elevated sites throughout the London area, the kids loving them, though Mill recalled that during their last visit Harriet became more winded than usual on their climb upwards. She adored the restored Kenwood House, while the children had to be kept from shoving each other into the swimming ponds. The boys had once gotten into a near-row and trudged home in soaking shoes and socks, Harriet feigning anger while trying not to laugh the whole way. And Lily treasured the ability to wonder at birds and chase after butterflies, though never with any intent to catch them. 'They only live a short time,' she proudly announced during a separate visit, in her squeaky but firm young voice.

But John found himself fretting all the same, concerned about someone else and her ability to live for more than a short time. He had been taken quite far aback at news of Harriet's symptoms from the past months, which she had tried to make light of, but he also could tell they had shaken her deeply, which included making him promise to not divulge any more than absolutely 'necessary' to the children. But you could never hide details from children: they consistently saw through the charades and carelessness of the adults in their world, far more savvy than said adults gave them credit for being, and Herby, Haji, and Lily would not be fooled very much, nor for very long.

His interactions with his own family had included his own occasional symptoms, including head-aches and stomach-aches — which he put down to stress, and a sometimes persistent eye twitch. He truly grieved for the spring death of little brother Henry, even though they had hardly known one another, at least not in the manner by which brothers were supposed to be acquainted. He knew that Henry had been informed of his older brother's 'collapse' — originally it had been a 'breakdown' — upon reaching young manhood, and nobody wanted to admit to direct blood ties with the mad. And Henry had his own battles to fight, finally losing the most critical to that omnipresent devourer of so many, consumption. John had taken some reassurance within the memories of the French trip the brothers had made earlier, though George remained aloof at his 'famous elder brother' for the most part. John considered the memory of his recently deceased brother, and could comprehend the need to reflect on mortality, Harriet still more so, that John had learned from the Greeks, and the assertion about an unexamined life not being worth the effort.

'There is only one plain rule of life eternally binding, and independent of all variations in creeds,' he'd begun that day as he watched the light of life fading from Henry's eyes, 'it is this — try thyself unweariedly till thou findest the highest thing thou are capable of doing, faculties and outward circumstances being both duly considered — and then DO IT.' He'd been addressing the minister at that moment, and his emphasis had startled all those in the sickroom for sounding like a commandment.

Naturally, as John had half-expected, his family took the message wrong, regarding his comment more representative of a critique of poor Henry, not getting a chance to do more with a life cut too short. His mother—only Henry himself had called her 'mum,' another reminder of family formalities—plus Wilhelmina and Clara, had chided him for making light of a sensitive issue, and John barely tried to defend himself on that count, which only led to matters deteriorating further, as the same sisters then accused him of being too intellectual and aloof both by half, unable "'cause of all that endless philosophisin'" to get in touch with real emotions.

Shortly after Henry died, John took solace in more ramblings, including exploring Pendennis Cavern by the huge fortress castle in Cornwall, and the Mills had proved quite welcoming of the 'Foxes'—little sister Clara Mill and Caroline Fox had become fast and firm friends, partly through shared grief, and John had unwittingly elicited tears from Caroline during another pleasant woodland stroll as he freed her clothing from some annoying brambles, telling her of the 'power of turning annoyances into pleasures by undertaking them for your friends.' She agreed with his assessment that such constituted 'a genuine alchemy.' John consistently felt more at ease with younger persons not related to him.

But Harriet's sister! Now there was a mess in need of direct action. John did not know the 'other Caroline' particularly well, having been unable to attend her wedding, even had he been invited, a gesture certain members of both the Hardy and Mill clans would regard as much too forward and embarrassing. John gritted his teeth, and kept returning to the thought of who at the Company might be able to assist, then kept mentally backing off, having already been told it was not his concern. Harriet had struck far too close to home with her comment about this being a 'family matter,' which wounded John, though he understood the reasoning behind it. Legally speaking, it would not do for another Hardy daughter to be perceived as receiving 'aid' or anything else from the rapscallion John Mill. He had heard in the press bits and pieces about his illicit affair with a wed mother, and wondered again if society might find him more threatening if he had developed into a 'manlier' sort; as it was, some of the press regarded Mill as rather inoffensive, an intellectual and physical near-non-entity. He wondered again which hurt more.

But none of this would make the trusteeship issue go away, and it was already complicated, as Harriet seemed to have put all her faith in her brother—John did not yet know of her effort to speak with Carlyle about it either. As with the Americans recently defaulting on their bond debts to Britain, Harriet's deplorable brother-in-law Arthur Ley continued to assert his access to her sister Caroline's trust fund. It hardly constituted a fortune, but that was not the issue: what mattered to Harriet, and what she adamantly felt should matter to her naïve sister, was the economic control this represented. Harriet could not refrain from grinding her own teeth just thinking about this: the money was from their family, not Ley's, and that he was a hard-drinking bastard—Harriet was getting more used to cursing—could only mean that he was entitled to none of it. The issue did not merely strike close to home, as the adage went, it seemed to encapsulate most of the items on Harriet's list of social grievances: established patriarchy; abuse of women; women in turn lacking power, who were further sufficiently under-educated to believe they had no real option but to live with their abusers. Harriet adored her sister, and it became more difficult to tolerate the trusteeship problem as Caroline Ley kept refusing to acknowledge that any problem existed, despite her obvious injuries. John found it just as infuriating, yet also remained convinced it was more his place to not interfere. In truth he felt unsure of the best resolution regardless: all the involved parties were angry or defensive or both, and such a situation left little space for reasoning. 'Family matter,' indeed!

The delays in communication hardly helped. John might not know of Harriet consulting Carlyle, but was familiar with the effort to consult one Arthur about another: Arthur Hardy loved his new life 'down under,' and his response to brother-in-law Arthur Ley would take time that Caroline Ley might not have. The world felt smaller: John had meticulously calculated that a letter despatched from London should take 12 days to reach New York, 13 to Alexandria, 19 to Constantinople, 33 to Bombay, 45 to Singapore, 57 to Shanghai, or 73 to Sydney, plus another day to get sorted and placed in Arthur Hardy's hands. Those data represented a sea-change—quite literally—in travel and communication times, but having to wait five months for advice while your sister got punched, kicked, and dragged through her own home would test the patience of anyone.

John desperately missed Harriet in those days, trying to ignore that his relationship with her continued to reinforce his isolation from his own family. He enjoyed her letters, though: apparently young Lily—he was now so used to the Taylor children's nicknames that he had to remind himself that she was Helen—had begun a journal of her own, a reflection of her mother's tradition. John had never read a word of Harriet's diary, content to sometimes hear mention of him within its pages, respectful of each person's need for privacy in some form.

What amused him in this regard, though, was the description of a near-row between mother and daughter over some of the newer diary's contents. Harriet—very begrudgingly—was willing to admit that perhaps, with proper guidance, religion might yet offer a solid base for moral education, even if she had long since written off its unprovable assertions that could only be accepted or denied as questions of faith. And yet now she was debating with her own daughter the latter's attraction to Roman Catholicism of all things, and more so even than that, asking questions about something that Mill had learned during his bookish childhood was usually called the 'problem of evil.'

Scholars as early as Augustine had weighed in on this one, and the idea must surely date to much earlier than even that—Mill was among the few to have made the connection that philosophy had partly arisen to try and answer questions about human behaviours according to what deities allegedly wished for mortals—and that the newer more rational way of thinking grew at almost the same time in disparate ancient cultures—and this idea was simple enough. 'Evil'—or very unpleasant events—occurred, affected persons and other living things, perhaps the whole planet, and the perhaps instinctive response was to wonder why. Were 'disasters' or the early deaths of siblings from frightening diseases or abuses of spouses some form of divine retribution? Did people and other animals 'deserve' their misfortunes and tragedies? Were the Greeks correct about their notion of what 'tragedy' entailed, a notion of inescapable fate?

Harriet had not minced words with her daughter. 'The essential wickedness of the character of the Deity,' she described to John that she had related to Lily, 'the atrocious conception... of a Being who creates on the one hand thousands of millions of sentient creatures fore-knowing that they will be sinners, and on the other a hell to torture them eternally for being so.' John knew that just a few centuries previously his beloved would have been offered one opportunity to recant such heretical phrasing, or else been led to a large wooden stake with a pile of faggots ready for burning placed around its base.

But there it was, staring John in the face as he continued Harriet's letter: 'and yet this Catholic tradition may offer a potentially utilitarian basis for moral instruction,' not just for Lily but Haji as well, who himself had recently posed some awkward questions. That bloody word would continue to haunt John: he imagined James Mill and Jeremy Bentham laughing from beyond their graves at his discomfiture! And of course, he would advise Harriet to continue the fine and underappreciated use of reason with her children. He looked forward to seeing them all again, unafraid of their questions. Lily clearly savoured intelligent conversation, though she seemed young to engage in such talks; Haji preferred maths, a form of symbolic logic, and he was already becoming an avid adversary of John across a chessboard as well as his companion during walks that featured botanical observations; and Herby loved just talking for its own sake, liking having 'Uncle John' about, though the 'two fathers' scenario was becoming more challenging for him.

* * *

Receiving a publishing contract felt even better than receiving a job offer, John Mill decided that day in 1843, though in a very real sense they were both variations of the same thing. Of course, he had only really received one genuine job offer before, and that had come largely due to a willingness of a corporate-governmental monopoly to practise nepotism. As for the growing number of news articles, John reminded himself that those too constituted publishing, though they amounted to just a few paragraphs here, a few there. But a full book! That seemed like something else entirely.

'A System of Logic: Ratiocinative and Inductive,' the book was entitled, the joint authors continuing to hope that the sub-title would not prove off-putting. Truly the work was aimed at laypersons and the philosophically educated alike, and John and Harriet had laboured to ensure that almost any reader might learn something, yet favoured a style that tried to be approachable. The last thing they wanted with their first longer collaboration was to be perceived as stuffy or too verbose, which some found hard to believe based on that title.

Caroline Fox wrote of this result of the working collaboration too, noting in her own little diary how John would 'mark out the best passages for me,' after sending a copy to her as a gift. She expressed some reservation at his comment about how 'My family have no idea how great a man I am!'—which might be true, though was hardly endearing. The John Mill who Ms Fox knew believed himself trapped in a perpetual cycle of trying to prove himself, mostly to his father, but now after his death, to the rest of his immediate relatives, perhaps not knowing that such 'circular reasoning'—trying to win their approval, seemingly failing, then analysing their subsequent behaviour towards him as too judgemental, then trying to win more approval—was a fine example of cyclical logic or 'begging the question' that he and Harriet wrote of in their book! Still, Caroline approved of his 'saving up his holidays for a third journey to Italy,' hopefully with Harriet and her children, and then she privately joked how Mr Mill 'had serious hopes of an illness in the winter, but was conscientious enough not to encourage it.' Such an ailment would have perhaps enabled more

Continental time with dear Harriet, but this was still during the earlier pre-publication phase, and then those Americans had their bond
default, and probably no one in the States realised how a certain intellectual 'across the Pond' needed years to financially recover from how
that affected English banking. The Mills were never at risk of losing
their home, but foreign travel costs, with fine hotels and good dining
as John preferred, added up quickly.

"'The regeneration so urgently required, of man and society,'" John
read proudly, knowing where to locate his favourite passages, "'can
never be effected under the influence of a philosophy which makes
opinions their own proof, and feelings their own justification.'"

"'Prejudice can only be successfully combated by philosophy,'"
Harriet added, beaming at him with her own advance copy, sitting
upright though naked beneath John's bed sheets. She no longer cared
that they did not get laundered as frequently as her own, and was glad
her legs were not paining her today. 'Do you know, Love,' she purred,
'one of the pre-publication reviews claims that we are the first authors
to utilise the word "consensus" in print. I wonder if that's really true?'

'I know not, dearest,' John said, himself clad just in cotton drawers and a loose, short-sleeved shirt. He remained shy to remain in the
nude for very long at a go, especially in the Kent Terrace home, even
if it often felt like their own.

She smiled at him. 'You still don't think the book too dry, then?
That it has fewer of your delightful old quips, like that one from the
'20s about how assertion lacking proof is easy and quick, and mis-
representation is typically the same?' That had remained her arching
worry throughout, and she scolded herself for the hundredth time for
fretting over the work seeming too 'masculine,' as though rationality
was the province of the stronger sex.

He looked at her, forgetting for the moment that she always
found him amusing when wearing so few clothes: they enhanced
his thin frame, made him look wiry, neither muscular nor chubby.
She thought he had probably weighed almost exactly the same his
whole adult life. 'Harriet, we've been through this time and again.

The whole point is to offer something of a primer in logic, offering useful examples.' Her paraphrasing of what he'd once written about making misguided assertions and claiming to 'prove' things whilst using little or no actual logic whatsoever was itself slightly off, but he hardly cared, knowing that she understood the material so well. Truly, it was largely her own edgy editing that helped turn the manuscript into something more accessible.

'I know, I know,' she shook her head lightly, trying to act demurely while the motion moved the sheet down to uncover a breast, loving that the man across from her could still find even such a simple tease erotic.

And he wanted nothing more right then than to jump back onto the bed like a bouncy schoolboy, and take one of those succulent full breasts in a hand, the other in his mouth, but he had to finish preparing for work. And he loved this woman all the more for not just helping to pen this curious tome, but to deal with a publisher more than he had the time and inclination to manage on his own. That much of him remained an artiste — hoping, naively, that once the product was completed, he could just sit back, relax, and watch praise and funds arrive at his doorstep.

Harriet briefly let the sheet fall just a bit further, beamed at John, and playfully covered herself back up again as he gleamed back at her, mouth in just the subtlest rictus, like a predator catching a scent. As he continued dressing, she had to concede that they really did try with this logic material. It still perplexed her, though surely not as much as him, how so many persons could in fact prove to be quite rational when it suited them, yet even more quickly would toss all that aside as emotion crept in. The 'closer to home' a topic or talk became, the more passionate most became, and so the pair of them had begun sounding like Hume and Locke before them: human knowledge is mostly — though not entirely, as those earlier thinkers and many of their ilk professed — based on experience. The purpose of reason, the utility — We will never fully escape that strange word! thought Harriet — was to add strength or validity or both to what someone proposed.

Such were the tools that their species used to construct truths, and the most responsible at doing so recognised that those truths were contingent—that 'better'—*More useful?* Harriet thought again—might and often did arrive later.

'You also do not think the criticisms of certain unnamed parties are not overly forceful?' she asked, watching longingly as John fumbled with a cravat. The man simply had little manual dexterity on tap.

'Do you mean Whewell?' he said, knowing that their clear critique of the very man who had managed to get term 'scientist' more or less officially accepted would find himself verbally assaulted for being an 'intuitionist,' which John and Harriet thought was foolish, in that it meant one who held that some absolutely certain truths existed.

The difference for William Whewell—and for that matter for Thomas Carlyle, who shared the belief, and whose own book Past and Present was due out from the presses shortly—was their emphasis on scientific absolute truths rather than religious ones. Caroline Fox had already been informed by an eager John Mill that if this new logic book was 'adopted as a full statement of the truth, the whole fabric of Christian theology must totter and fall!' One could only assume that would include other faiths too.

Maybe some certitude did exist, though Harriet and John questioned that, emphasising instead that the point was to question, and that the most telling criterion for maturity and intelligence alike was the ability to change one's own mind, to alter one's weaker beliefs. She had convinced him to leave out some of the more obscure and older traditions, and the notion that good character habits could be nurtured, even taught, that virtue itself was teachable. In the meantime, John had also utilised another word, this one more truly of his own creation: 'ethology,' which existed between the extreme forms of free will and fatalism, between certainty and the puerile notion that anything was acceptable. And they had made the tightest case they could, consistently attempting to avoid absolutes.

Harriet wondered whether the desire to change one's character, to become a more rational and inquisitive person, could only come from one's own character, so maybe they were slightly guilty of begging the question, but she dismissed it, having donned a loose-fitting robe and helping John straighten the cravat. The sight of it always amused her, and even when he had it placed and tied properly, it often still got knocked askew.

She sighed, recalling his question, seeing it reflect in his eyes while she finished aiding him and looking in the small round wall mirror with him. 'Yes, certainly,' she said, 'the Reverend Doctor Whewell. I know of your dislike. I find him pretentious as well, though many say the same of us.'

He made a face in the mirror, making her smile, then turned to face her. 'He is quite bright. Sometimes I wish we'd begun on better terms.'

Harriet recalled they had in fact only met a time or two in passing. 'What proves most interesting about the man is that he almost single-handedly represents a fusion of what the Americans call "church and state."'

John pretended to adjust the tie around his neck, admiring her handiwork and the quality of the starching in his collar, still preferring to have well-paid servants pick up his laundry and take care of it elsewhere. 'I wholly agree. He practices observation and studies experimentation, yet refuses to give up on that tiny collection of religious "truths" that too many cling to. But like the other "intuitionists," he capitalises whatever seems important: "the Absolute, the True," like he's trying to write in German. Carlyle is much the same.'

After these years of 'mostly' together, Harriet had gratefully stopped feeling the slightest concern that any remarks made about religion in general and Christianity in particular, which sometimes did include praise—as with the spiritual explorations by her children—would be met with his hostility. She knew she could say anything to this man. Perhaps that was what put her most at ease around him. 'It continues to amaze how so many seem to think that religion and natural philosophy—er, excuse me,—science—are necessarily adversarial.' She opted to hold back follow-up comments about Carlyle.

He grinned, finally letting his hands fall to his sides. His arms often seemed anxious at home, his fretting about like some university don always trying to make some critical point. And yet when speaking in front of a group, his hands would remain firmly clasped behind his back, like a soldier or sailor at parade rest. 'I know, and yet they're not.'

While they had left supposedly sensitive issues like this out of the 'Logic,' the closest they had come to acknowledging them lay in a willingness to admit that any argument, any belief no matter how logically supported, had to start with some basic premise—which, in turn, even if it had itself already been largely established, and hopefully by equal reasoning, was taken as a given. This was the same as noting that it was taken on faith. It did not have to be religious faith surely, but represented belief all the same. While readers—and the editorial staff were already gabbing about early promising demand and preparing plenty of copies—might gloss over 'methods of agreement' or 'methods of difference,' where the writing admittedly grew more technical and would probably please as many maths fans as philosophers, knowing that one could be logical about any issue, any question, remained at the top of John and Harriet's wish-list for the future success of the book and its impact.

Put another way, John had mentioned to Harriet during the seemingly endless editing and re-writing that any detailed book required, that, 'There is no such thing as a self-evident truth!'

Harriet had not skipped a single heartbeat. 'Except for the self-evident truth that there are no self-evident truths?' He had glared at her at first, then laughed at his own logical paradox, one he had not intended. 'Those Yanks began their whole "Declaration" last century by claiming that some truths were actually self-evident after all.'

'Rubbish,' he declared. 'If that were true, there'd exist no reason to call attention to them: that's what "self-evident" means. And like us, they're continuing to experiment with what is "true" and what is not, like whether slavery can be morally justified or economically expedient.'

'Or if women and non-Christians can become educated or, dare I say it, vote?'

John loved their banter, even when serious. He stood fully dressed now, looking smart and dapper in a newer suit Harriet had purchased for him, indeed had had it made. That proved anxiety-provoking: Mr Taylor proved far less appreciative of a wife 'interfering with a man's wardrobe.' She nodded at John now, feeling decidedly under-dressed in her skimpy robe, and then said, 'You know, John, Lily is proving a better linguist than I could ever hope to be, better than her brothers or her father.'

'Excellent,' he answered, unsurprised. Whilst Mr Taylor might pay to keep a roof over his children's curious heads, Mr Mill had taken on the task and expense of tutors, but always consulted Harriet, who in turn consulted — well, updated was more like it — Mr Taylor, who in fact was quite proud of his precocious daughter. And Mr Mill was careful to attempt a balance with what Lily was learning, not wanting to 'overdo' it like he had experienced at her age, yet also refusing to endorse the common notion that girls could simply not grasp certain subjects as could boys.

Harriet knew John's attitudes towards the newer public schools, too, still mostly reserved for boys. 'I wonder if Lily would thrive with the more "traditional" instruction for girls of her background?'

John was stuffing too many documents, as typical, into his well-worn though sturdy leather briefcase, a gift for his seventeenth birthday just before his encounter with a too-young corpse. It had become thankfully rare for him to still dream at night of children dead before their time, staring accusingly at him with empty, glossy black eyes. 'What else has she been reading, and has she been getting out more?'

Harriet sighed. Her lovely daughter, sometimes seeming wiser than herself, did not lack for social opportunities, though had few other children to truly call friends. She loved the theatre, thrilling in performances and imagining the discipline needed to bring them to life onstage. She was probably a bit brighter than her older brothers, both of whom perceived her as the annoying kid-sister, and Harriet felt sure that her bias in this regard came not from sympathy for her gender. She avoided the latter question, addressing the first. 'She

loves Mr Carlyle's translations,' Harriet said, not slurring that sur-
name this time, 'of the 'Märchen,' the 'Myths,' by one of the Germans.
She said she "likes them very much," and that "they have a beautiful
mysterious air about them!"'

John turned to her again. "'Mysterious air?"' He liked the phrasing.
'Maybe we should have her read Carlyle's 'Past and Present' when it
comes out,' he suggested, receiving a whack on his behind from his
lover's hand for invoking the name.

It made less of a slapping sound this time. 'Even you said he
confuses the medieval too much with the modern, Love. It is not his
best work.'

'Just his most recent. What about Mr Dickens, then? I've not
yet read his Christmas ghost story I've heard discussed lately. Would
ghosts prove too much for Lily, do you think?'

Harriet shook her head. 'Goodness no, and she's already read it.
She thought you might like it, in truth, thinking you have a jaded
view of holidays.' John grinned anyway, always delighting in hearing
what the kids might be studying. 'She's read that Mary Shelley novel
enough times that I may have to secure her a new copy. She offered
a quite mature interpretation, having to do with a mix of faith and a
critique of all our technological and scientific "progress." Lily thinks
it's not about monsters at all.'

'That's quite perceptive, and I agree with her. Our monsters are
really the shadows we refuse to acknowledge when we stare at our
own reflections.'

She thought that an odd response, but was used to such in principle. Then she kissed him lovingly goodbye. No matter where they
were anymore, no matter how public, these two persons kissed each
other any time they had to say farewell, no matter for how long.

\* \* \*

The next year, 1844, would find the curious trio — John,
Harriet, and Lily — travelling together again, this time to
parts of France with which Lily had no previous experience,

and Harriet not much more so: Normandy and Rouen. Herby and Haji had decided to remain in England with their father this time, eschewing travel in general, though both liked letters and tales from Uncle Arthur, still making his prosperous way in Australia. Only Lily ever expressed any interest in someday perhaps going so far, though for now Continental adventures held her content, and she revelled in them, the only one among her siblings who preferred the company of 'Uncle John' to that of her father, though Haji came down roughly in the middle, admiring the erstwhile uncle's accomplishments: being conversant and a good chess mentor—though he sometimes allowed Haji to win, the boy was sure—along with botany, opera, art history. Haji had never warmed to philosophy and abstract thinking, but showed promise in understanding ethics. Both boys were loath to admit that their younger sister was a better and more avid reader, and perhaps smarter than either of them too.

Young Helen—almost always 'Lily,' now, thank you—as the little scamp sometimes politely reminded children and adults alike, also displayed no sign of decreasing her mostly self-imposed reading load. Mr Taylor might have reservations—though his 'lads' were attending Mr Underwood's School in the City, and doing well with Classics as well as the—thankfully, noted Harriet—less stringent emphasis on Christian theology that most universities continued to insist upon, including medieval Oxford and Cambridge. Harriet had already suggested that both boys attend the new University College in London—where Jeremy Bentham's preserved remains yet sat in their protective case, smiling at students and faculty or judging them, depending upon whom one asked—partly to avoid swearing the tenets of the Anglican Church.

The lads would do fine either way though, and Harriet had learned not to push too much. Haji and young George Mill, not-so-little-anymore brother of Harriet's true love, remained friends, George—as with Lily, no longer 'Georgie,' thank you!—continued to make his own strides at Underwood's.

As John, Harriet, and Lily walked softly along the peaceful beach marking the edge of Normandy, Harriet holding onto her straw hat; Lily giggling — still playful, despite her advanced literary repertoire — and darting about, pointing out seabirds; and John hauling a quite large umbrella and the basket still mostly full of food and Lily's favourite grape juice from their picnic that had to be aborted for the strong winds, John stopped as he noticed Harriet struggling to stay with them.

'It's fine,' she assured them both, though Lily had switched to seeking more shells — she and her brothers took pride in their tiny collections of things that could inspire shared memories while having no cash value, though she had to admit this particular beach offered little inspiration for the like this day — and she barely noticed her mother for searching. 'It's the thick sand,' Harriet said, half-truthfully, as determined as any man, so she thought, to not show weakness, though her legs were pained again. Lily had never felt jealous either of how her father had taught her brothers to carve little toy boats to join the gifts of shells.

'We have plenty of time, dearest,' answered John, content to set down the picnic supplies for a few moments. He knew what Lily sought, and was feeling melancholy. Sterling had cared not for birthdays but had loved Christmas, as witnessed by his sending of comfits and toys and other treats to the youngsters; this new 'Victorian' period, as the whole world already referred to it, had fallen in love with the holiday as never before, following the decorative examples of the new Queen and her Prince-consort, Albert of Saxe-Coburg. Dickens' ghost-tale helped, Harriet enjoyed it all too, and what better way to annoy zealous Christians than to turn one of their central holidays into a time of celebrations and feasts reminiscent of ancient Roman Saturnalia!

John Mill thought of Christmases past now, despite the cool summer they were walking through, turning back to look towards Dover and England, hidden presently by thick and low clouds, though they had thankfully not gotten soaked today by the rains that such clouds portended: probably later tonight.

He missed his friend. John Sterling had died recently, leaving dear companion John Mill contemplating cancelling this trip, receiving grief from his family for going anyway: 'off yet again wi' that wanton Mrs Taylor,' as his mother had phrased matters. But John needed to get away, perhaps more than ever before.

He would have offered to remain behind to help Susannah, but she had died just a few short months before her husband. Consumption, again it was, that took them both! John was so sick of hearing about this dread disease: it had previously claimed his father, his brother, two of Harriet's brothers... And the damnable medical establishment still could proffer no useful treatment, certainly no cure. One had to remain vigilant and not catch it.

'What is it, dearest?' came Harriet's voice. John had not heard her approach, though the sound of the endlessly pounding surf today could mask nearby noises. She suspected she already knew the answer.

He was hesitant to even look her way, briefly wondering if he could convincingly pretend that the tears forming in his eyes could be attributed to irritation from blowing sand. Harriet had seen him tear up before — indeed, had witnessed him weeping — though he carried around enough masculine artificial pride that left him not wishing anyone — especially a woman — see him cry. 'I miss him,' he finally said, weakly.

'Mr Sterling?' she gently prodded, having been right. John Sterling, perhaps John Mill's closest friend — the Trijackia still proved a source of support, but Grote was constantly busy with his banking duties; Graham likewise was always on the go these days, though he enjoyed his work with the Registrar General, tracking data on British citizens; and Roebuck, despite aspirations of professional politics, had almost become too radical in his thinking for even Mill. Sterling had shown signs of wanting to become a revolutionary, but he seemed able to comfort his friend Mill when the latter really needed it; John had once written him to say that his own differences with the likes of radicals and utilitarians alike amounted to differences of principle, not reason.

John nodded. 'He cared so much for Susannah at her end, only to die of the same bloody, infernal, damned disease.'

He finally turned to face her, no longer caring about the tears that he made no motion to hide or wipe away. 'Is this what took your faith from you, Harriet?'

She did not even pause. 'Of course. I like to think that after I'm dead, God and I will have a little chat about His Earthly managerial style.' John briefly smiled slightly at that, suddenly picturing a chastened Deity sitting at a school desk facing ironic nun Harriet Taylor about to rap His knuckles with an all-powerful ruler, and then smiled even more brightly at the mad blasphemy of his imagination.

Harriet turned to see her daughter skipping back towards them, still smiling for the pleasant day, even if the planned picnic had almost blown away into the French countryside. She thought there was nothing wrong other than that the adults had fallen behind. They could be so slow sometimes! 'John,' Harriet said, 'I am so sorry, truly sorry, for the loss. You and I have had to bid permanent farewells to too many of those whom we've loved, and since I have no traditional faith of which to speak, I take my faith in knowing how much we have been able to strengthen one another, for years now.'

'Perhaps,' John started, but could not finish. *Perhaps you should simply go back to your husband. I still have difficulty comprehending what you see in me.*

'Perhaps,' she echoed, 'you—we—can continue to help each other, as you have helped so many already. Just in the past few months, you've obtained gainful employment for your brother at India House.'

John thought of younger brother George. *Yes, love: now he works for a morally dubious monopoly attempting to govern a nation which does not need British 'help.'* John was realising he had not felt this morose since his breakdown so many years ago. *Before Harriet,* he thought. As with the life of our new Queen, people will say, 'Oh, that was just a month before Queen Victoria came to the throne,' or 'it's been five years now since the Queen wed her German prince.' For John Mill, Harriet Taylor was that lifetime milestone.

'And your sister Mary, like so many fortuitous women in your life, has joined the ranks of the published. That item of hers about political economy in the 'Westminster Review' might have made Ricardo himself proud.'

But my charming little sister remains just as frivolous as the others in my family, John thought, barely focused now on Lily still scampering over the sand, not caring how much its thickness slowed her determined steps. She had shed her fine shoes and stockings, loving how chilly seawater felt on her bare skin, how sand felt between her toes as she clenched each foot to take another step. She was now close enough to slow down, having glimpsed the forlorn expression on Uncle John's face.

'You're the one who perceives ultimate aims, Harriet,' he said finally, reaching out and clasping her to him. 'What was it I wanted to say in the Logic's dedication? You remain focused on the "constituent elements of the highest realisable ideal of human life."'

'"Through immediately useful and practically attainable changes to society,"' she finished for him. 'I love that, John, still do. It just struck me as a touch grandiloquent for a logic primer.' She was starting to cry now herself.

He finally smiled again, not yet noticing her sudden response. 'My own attributes lay wholly in the uncertain and slippery intermediate region, that of theory, or moral and political science.' Then he saw it. 'There, Harriet, why are you in tears of a sudden also? It's bad enough I'm making myself a spectacle here!'

She all but whispered. 'I'm so damned tired, John. How many loved ones have we had to lose, gone before their time? And I know what my parents, or dear Pastor Fox, would say right now—that one's time is one's time, and only God gets to know, and whatever other stupid platitudes spring to mind. You know, I've seen Mr Fox in his cups railing against God, calling Him a vindictive bastard.'

'Maybe Fox had been reviewing the Old Testament, the part shared in common with the Jews and the Muslims. The Book with the mad drunken uncle of a Deity.' Actually, Harriet had recently phrased matters far more strongly than that. She had judged 'the essential wickedness of the character of the Deity'—it was good heretics no longer got executed, John mused—usually no longer, anyway.

She almost laughed again. It was small wonder why the pair of them so often felt shunned by their society, that they still paradoxically and ultimately believed in: it had so much potential. 'I'm just so scared, John. I can't lose you, or my dear children, my other family, even my husband. I cannot imagine how I might bear these things anymore.'

He nodded, a bit lamely, she thought. But when he spoke, it usually helped. 'Just think of the surviving support, then. Think of all those who attended the memorial services for each of the Sterlings. I barely knew Susannah really, but dozens turned out that rainy day, and as for John himself,' and here he had to try and force down the new lumpy feeling in his throat, 'the whole Trijackia came. I really loved the lads for that gesture. We almost never got Sterling to attend our little soirées at the Grote home, but the respect was always there. You could feel it.'

It was strange to hear this man speak of feelings. He sometimes seemed all evidentiary and empirical, like Hume or some conservative legal judge passing sentence onto the accused. At least he spoke of sentiment at all, a far cry from Mr Taylor, and to her growing dismay often from her boys as well. 'I know what you mean, John. Truly.'

Lily arrived, taking turns looking at each while they spoke, not failing at all to take in the 'grandiloquent' terms. 'That is precisely why we make such a good, compatible team, Mr Mill. Philosophy, your expertise, is partly the art of supplying the science of politics into the very practical and morally necessary areas of reform. You and I are attempting to change the world, dear John.'

The girl hardly wanted to be left out of the conversation. 'Uncle John, you yourself told me that an open society only functions with the active participation of its citizens. When we were discussing the Greeks last week, you said that the whole difference between them and what you and Mummy are attempting is that you two, and your friends, are trying to get more of those citizens the right to partici-pate.' She took her mother's hand.

'Speaking of social reform,' Lily added. She had reached a fascinating age: perpetual curiosity, a range of eager questions, tempered by early recognition—John himself had not noticed it until his nervous breakdown—just how full of duplicity, deception, and emotional excrement adults so often were. 'I was hoping to review my notes about Coleridge with you, Uncle John. And you too, Mummy.'

How did a child who still said 'Mummy' also read the feminist politics of Wollstonecraft and de Gouges, and savour the dramatics of Hamlet—she had already queried John about the notion of fatal indecision that might bring down a kingdom—then go back to pointing out museum exhibits such as immense dinosaur bones with the unadulterated and unfeigned glee of someone seeing the world for the first time?

'I shall be glad to do so, of course, Lily,' John simply said. 'If Mummy can leave us to our own devices when we get home,' and he looked up from Lily's shining face up to her mother's, 'unless you have your copies with you...?'

'Actually, I'm still working through Mr Sterling's novels, as per your recommendation. They're quite good. I wish I had known him better.'

'As do I, my little love.' *From the mouths of babes,* John thought, as he knelt down and all but crushed Lily in a fresh embrace. 'That's right, child. That's absolutely right.' He brushed away his last tear of the day. *How did I get so fortunate?* he wondered, hardly for the first time.

* * *

*From The Diary of Helen Taylor:*
So many names, Dear Little Diary, I know, and one never wants one's readers to feel overwhelmed by keeping track of who did or said what.

In the case of Mary Wollstonecraft, her influence upon Mother was profound indeed, and a few decades closer they might have become friends and collaborators—that older lady shared sentiments with her revolutionarily-minded husband Mr Godwin, though they never wrote together as did Mum and Mr Mill. As with Mary

Somerville, she proved one of the last of those polymaths Mother questioned Mr Mill about that day, and Ms Somerville was made an honorary member of the Royal Astronomical Society in '35, along with Caroline Herschel, dutiful sister of more famous brother William, himself the locator of a new planet!

Thus, fret not dearest Reader, about a multitude of names, nor how many Johns and Harriets fill up these pages. Rather, keep in mind the influence of the collaborative ideas of Mummy and John upon our collective times!

# PART FOUR

# Political and Economic Utility

*1848–1851.*

John Mill remained not quite in awe, exactly, but rather dismayed at how close relationships could just decay and rot and fester, like dead bodies. One benefit of knowing so many literate persons—an advantage he usually enjoyed and often tried to take advantage of, since it could feel like getting first choice among proffered sweets—had more recently become something to occasionally dread.

Yet part of that strange and morally weighty question regarding relationships remained. Despite receiving the man's forgiveness, for example, and despite the subsequent financial success of the history of the French Revolution that emerged from having to rewrite his manuscript, Thomas Carlyle had seemed to enjoy further antagonising John Mill, especially where Harriet Taylor was concerned.

John remained defensive about his lady love generally, as one would expect, and the duo had endured years of jeers in public, by former friends and in newsprint as well. Thus, John and Harriet had now devoted several anni difficili to the interesting art of remaining largely out of public view: fewer joint appearances, at least not at dinner parties where they knew most of the participants; fewer explorations of the City, unless these included more widely attended venues where they could blend with the crowds; or locales that simply lay further from the central areas where they lived and were better known. Their own families remained in a perpetual state of tension between trying—often failing—to offer emotional support, or showing hostility accompanied by criticism. John continued to develop his notions of personal liberty—with the caveat attached that persons should remain largely free to pursue their own interests, so long as they refrained from doing harm to others.

Working out what constituted 'harm' precisely remained more difficult, surprisingly so, hardly made easier when one could claim influence from emotional tugs to and fro regarding children or lovers or issues in which one believed or claimed belief. And emotional harm was just one type among several: physical harm, as with—John groaned at the memory, Harriet's sister, resulting from her marriage to a dreadful husband—who himself nonetheless behaved within the limits of the law; financial harm, sometimes just as obvious, but when one worked for a government as John did, the lines often blurred; social harm, including damage to another's reputation—so easy to do, despite laws against libel and slander, another example of a moral offense easier to commit against women.

John still felt dreadful, never having fully forgiven himself for causing such blatant harm to Mr Carlyle for that ashen manuscript, even though it had occurred thirteen years ago now. That certainly qualified as a form of personal harm, though John continued to mentally grapple with how else the fallout might be described. It did not seem like personal or bodily harm—thankfully no one had been injured in the miniature blaze in John's careless kitchen that morning! As for other types of harm, though, John ticked these off again with his fingers as he walked, sometimes unwittingly motivating passersby to offer him a bit more strolling space—those who mumbled to themselves were not to be trusted, while Mill himself took pride in remaining eccentric, knowing that talking to oneself, especially semi-coherently, numbered among the easier methods of becoming labelled thusly. Those with eccentricities might get ostracised—and he largely no longer cared.

He kept enumerating, not paying attention to when or even if his lips might be moving or his vocal cords creating semi-syllabic noises. *Emotional harm*, John considered: Carlyle undoubtedly experienced some degree of that via the loss of so much labour. *Then there was financial harm,* John cringed, *as this was the type I have most feared these years on his behalf: we shall never know how sales might have been affected.* Knowing of his unintended part in such an odd accident, John still felt this keenly, although to his credit Thomas Carlyle had never shown much anger, and had even confessed—albeit after a glass or two of quality claret, still distrusting John's less refined tastes in wine—that the destroyed manuscript about the French Revolution had probably benefitted from a complete rewriting.

*But that doesn't off-set the damage, nor is it the actual moral issue,* thought John now, still navigating London's heady streets expertly. *From a utility perspective, more good, more happiness, accrued from Carlyle's 'second unplanned edition,' but that does not mean the destruction of the first was justifiable.*

He hopped down a kerb, loving the solid yet uneven feel of the ancient laid rocks or newer bricks that constituted London streets beneath his shod feet. *Dear God, I begin to sound like an absolutist after all!*

At Father's insistence long ago, John studied the famous though fanatical devotee to absolute moral principle: any act was intrinsically moral or immoral, he argued, not because God or the ancient deities of Mount Olympus or Mount Kailash said so to a bunch of flawed immoral humans, but because of what reason told those humans. A good human will, this notion went, driven by a heady blend of inborn reason mixed with conscience, alone could lead to the only rational choice. Be prepared for anyone else to behave as you choose, was the over-simplified version explicable to others unprepared to read such dense morality.

Maybe John just wanted elements of both: principles and practicality; rules learned along with mitigating circumstances. *Social harm,* John thought now, tipping his hat to other pedestrians—a rare tribute to vanity, as John's hair had receded greatly within the past few years, and then evading a carriage with the lithe nimbleness of a dancer—*perhaps the most difficult to explain and toughest to justify, but then how easy is it to ever recover one's own sullied reputation?* That was what he and Harriet had faced, even though they themselves had committed social and emotional harm to Mr Taylor. Part of John's mind would continue to admonish him over principles, while the Benthamite portion of his childhood would continue to try and rationalise his own happiness and that of others.

Did absolutists care about happiness? They claimed so, arguing that good rational minds making proper logical decisions would lead to true happiness. But to John it felt forced or wishful, like the unsparing judgement of a religious officiator.

The harm bit remained the clincher, and John had studied, if not outright and directly witnessed, too much of each of these types of harm already. He was still working on a notion with Harriet about the purported wisdom of the mob: there was a classical Greek component of John's mind, which felt quite sceptical about this new modern interpretation of 'democracy,' which the Americans had repeatedly tried to justify despite the hypocrisy and irrationality of their own tendencies to exclude others from the process. The Athenians had also kept most folks from participating, certainly from voting, but John's concern recently had focused more on the collective attitude of the group, the crowds who might demonstrate peacefully and perhaps effect actual change, or the crowds—often composed of the same persons—who might show up to watch a hanging or a dogfight or just set about rioting with a view to short-term gain. And he felt anger at Carlyle for having contributed, John believed earnestly, to this ongoing and very old social ill.

So now here he trotted, all but storming his way without the aid of a vehicle to the Carlyle residence. What did he expect, he asked himself for at least the tenth time now during his walk, which was supposed to have proven more head-clearing than it had become? At least other persons on the walkways no longer glared at him with concern.

As another servant opened the door of the sizable brick home—John could never seem to keep them straight—he consoled himself that he felt similarly, in need of honest pay while remaining at the beck and call of others. Conveniently ignoring the size of the cheques with which the Company plied him, John not only failed again to recall the servant's name but also decided that coming here was a poor choice after all. Sometimes the moral implications of inter-personal relationships just had to be permitted to die, lest they cause—

*More harm?* John thought dully, mechanically asking the door-man to fetch his master. 'Of course, Mr Mill,' the middle-aged man answered, naturally knowing the identities of those likely to come calling.

He should stay. John realised that, standing there feeling stupid and out of place at once, and he was tired of not fighting back, tired of feeling physically inadequate. Strong minds did not often inhabit strong bodies, or such was the insipid trivia with which his father had imbued him. No one would ever take him seriously if he challenged an oaf—a former friend—like Carlyle to a fight, and the whole notion sounded idiotic regardless.

But there were times when he felt inadequate as a man. The love of his life remained married to another, and John hated not knowing for sure if John Taylor left his wife and her paramour essentially alone from some notion of guilt over the syphilis, or some societal sense of decorum, or if he just pitied an intellectually stronger though physi-cally weaker man who had stolen the heart of his wife.

And now here he was, feeling like an imbecile at the doorstep of someone who, he believed, no longer had any interest in him. Even the bloody house was intimidating: Cheyne Road in charming Chelsea ran with three-storey sturdy homes, shouting their wealth to the world. The Cheyne Walk enabled a lovely stroll along the Thames, clear down to Battersea Bridge—aptly named, John considered, as the river ran dangerously in this section, and for decades many had complained about how easily boats and small ships collided with it, and even walkers could slip or trip while trying to cross over.

*Damn these efforts to intimidate me.* John opted to ignore that bridges and homes were erected for purposes other than his personal annoyance, and that he could himself afford one of these luxurious homes if one came on the market, as he recalled Harriet verbally questioning his intention as he announced his plans yesterday.

'You cannot alter another's attitudes, John,' she had admonished, 'nor their beliefs.'

'I know, Love,' he'd answered lamely, then tried humour: 'Which of us taught that immortal piece of logic to the other?'

She'd giggled briefly, though her laughter sometimes proved of shorter duration lately, like it physically pained her sometimes. 'So what, then, do you hope to accomplish by meeting with the man?' She preferred not to mention either of the Carlyles by name: both Thomas and Jane had done too much social harm to the other couple, often as publicly as possible. One could only see one's name smeared in print so often, though the Carlyles always managed to not cross that troubling line into either slander or libel.

'I,' John began, then paused, thinking. 'I just keep thinking that, that—'

Harriet kept looking at him from across the Taylor table. Husband and children were out, and it was ever curious how accommodating the clan had become regarding the privacy of an illicit affair. Immediate family, anyway: the metaphorical jury remained sequestered in refusal to proclaim their judgements about this relationship. John remained unsure whether Mr and Mrs Hardy hated him or not—another note on his lifelong insecurities—and had only ever met Taylor's parents once, years ago, so who knew?

'That—?' she probed.

He sighed. 'Maybe I just hoped he'd "come around," as that inane saying goes.'

'Come around to what? The man largely gave up on utility, like you, and has continued to seek the moral reform of the individual, instead of the farcical and forced effort to reform society from the top down, also like you.'

He had smiled at that, despite himself; then she continued. 'And lest we forget, this is the very person who once described you, in print no less, as, let me see if I can recall précisément: "a slender, rather tall and elegant youth."'

'Dear Heart, no one on this Earth has ever referred to me as tall and elegant, not even in that lost youth spent in France, before I dreamt of meeting someone like yourself.'

Harriet had experienced her own loss two years previously, leading her back into her withdrawing poetry and feeling generally remorseful. John knew how vulnerable she remained to the permanent loss of a loved one, she having informed him quite early in their relationship of how many times she had needed to offer heartfelt farewells. It took her longer to admit how furious and impotent alike she felt standing at anyone's graveside, wanting to throw the anger and the loss and the seeming injustice of death right back at God's face, then recoiling at how others would respond to not only such a heretical gesture but the admission that she didn't believe in supreme Beings anyway.

But back in '46, the news had struck perilously home regardless. Lovely Lizzie Flower, confidant and songstress and dedicated lover of Pastor Fox, had died in her early forties, herself only four years older than her friend, Harriet Hardy Taylor.

By then Fox's little Unitarian journal, the 'Monthly Repository,' had already been shut down for some years, though Lizzie and Fox, and Lizzie's father and sister, had all become regular contributors, offering what John thought had been mostly keen insights into not just the politics of religion but into the more subtle, even sublime, nature of religious faith itself. When he had found out the woman's cruel fate, his subsequent view of his lover had been of her slumped over hand-written draughts of some of those pieces, along with music sheets completed by Lizzie. She had composed some items never published.

Harriet hadn't even looked at John. She was utterly despondent, thick tears dripping onto some of the sheets on the floor of the Fox home, the pastor having offered the space of his own drawing room for 'as long as she needs,' as he'd told Mill upon his entering the bleak house.

She'd mumbled something. He had to request she repeat it.

'I said,' she snuffled, 'what is the damnable point of it all, John? We have some good ideas, share a few laughs, embrace each other in the knowledge that soon the darkness will come... is that all?'

He knew better than to go charging into some blasé platitude about the nature of religion or Divine Plans, partly since he still took care to not flaunt his own atheism the way she did hers. The sanctimonious mob, behaving paternalistically yet often without the slightest modicum of kindness or charitable thought towards each other and the subjects of the Empire, already had plenty of fodder by which to judge this couple.

He just shrugged, helpless. Harriet would never accept a religious response, and while philosophy might strengthen faith, question it, it could not by itself provide it. The foundation must come from some other part of the psyche. 'I truly don't know, Harriet. She was such a delightful person, and of course not just because of her support of us. Whenever I was alone with her, admittedly not that often, she was energetic and bright and constantly able to make things seem better, even if they weren't necessarily so.'

Harriet began sobbing again. 'No one will ever say that about me,' she bubbled through, 'and now I have to feel guilty about that too, making it seem like this is about me instead of about her.'

He had offered what comforts he could, and the two of them had become quite adept at simply holding onto each other through entire evenings, though Harriet had cried again, John shaking his arms in front of Fox to avoid doing likewise—men remained shamed for shedding tears, though he had once told Harriet how he admired how members of certain other cultures, including the Indian people his father never understood as more than caricatures, went unafraid of revealing their true feelings.

John knew that was part of his emotional segue today: that, and desire to avoid confrontation. His father had been better at it; even Bentham would gladly dive into a scrape so long as it remained spoken and did not entail drawn weapons or threat of such.

But that part of the distraction, this sudden remembrance of Harriet's lovely friend, was the occasional recollection of how her music had been performed in India, reminding John of a writer who founded a Hindu college and wrote a text about theism, which John once recommended to Harriet. The text had discussed a style of meditation unknown to Europeans, and delved into the nature of the ancient Vedic texts, and the principal deities—while noting the cyclicity of life and of individual lives.

All was related, that book explained: all people and living creatures were related, and perhaps there was yet some way in which a beloved departed one might remain alive. And that was how and why John knew his notions of harming others had become central.

John remained captive to English sensibilities as much as did his beloved. Fox himself had sobbed that day. He had loved deeply and paid for it dearly.

They had to discuss other minutiae after the service for Lizzie, including such banalities as whether John should even attend the funeral service—yes; and whether Fox should officiate—no; and what Fox should do with himself in his now empty house. His wife was long gone, and Lizzie's sister had found a solid marriage to her Mr Adams, himself still involved with railroads, though John found the man a touch on the boring side when not elucidating on the wonders of locomotive technology and 'how it could bring whole nations together.' Still, stable and non-abusive marriages were surely not to be avoided when available!

John had given Harriet plenty of mental and physical space after Lizzie's forlorn funeral, himself despondent since he could hardly be seen directly next to her or the children, though Haji had made a point, bless him, of seeking him out to offer his own solace, knowing 'Uncle John' and 'Aunty Lizzie' had been good friends. Harriet and

Lily, meanwhile, had dedicated plenty of shared time at the Taylor home at Kent Terrace—the Austins were neighbours, and John knew Taylor had joined them at their favourite holiday spot at Ryde on the Isle of Wight, far enough from the City to mourn and grieve, but not so far as the Continent.

Today, long after the loss of Lizzie and this morning's chat with Harriet, John focused on his destination anew: Thomas Carlyle. John found himself wondering which might be worse: bidding farewell to a deceased loved one, or knowing that an encounter with someone, loved or no—formerly so, in this case—might be the last.

'He once called me "vivid and iridescent,"' Harriet had added, pausing a moment to bat her eyes at him. John had thought only French women could really do that.

But he refused to get distracted. 'As I recall, he also said something about your being a "romance heroine" who nonetheless had a "questionable destiny." Perhaps he saw through us from the beginning.'

Harriet laughed so hard she slapped the table, though John had spoken seriously. She disliked that table anyway, a gift from her in-laws, though they had entertained around it so many times, including the night she first encountered this odd man sitting with her.

'Or maybe it was your delightful Roman nose, or earnest eyes, oh, I don't even recall all the panegyric. The man can truly pile it on as the mood takes him.'

'Agreed,' she said, calming down, wiping her eyes for a moment. Then her expression hardened just a touch. 'I no longer wish to be "lucid" or "calm," John.'

'I think I know that more than anyone at this point, with perhaps the exception of the children.' The Taylor youth, not so young anymore, had continued in their roughly-drawn notions of familial loyalty. Herby still preferred his father's home, and John had stopped wondering if that was simply duty from the eldest offspring. Lily retained her devotions to her mother; Taylor himself attributed that, uncharitably, to feminine wiles. And Haji kept trying to please everyone and not have family squabbles, which in truth had become rarer, though John and Harriet realised Haji's father and older brother both looked down on him for becoming a 'people-pleaser.' John often considered himself likewise, though his patience with his own family had worn thin.

Maybe Herby had read Carlyle's book about heroes and hero-worship, John wondered. He approved of studying the lives of the former, though hated the practice of the latter: if one did not accept one's heroes — or heroines — as they really were, then one became more liable to act irrationally, even belligerently, about the person in question. Even with Harriet he had only a few detailed talks about such implications, both of them concluding that religion had too often become an historic force for evil by this manner: intolerance, racism, colonial justifications, open warfare, the perpetuation of poverty while the 'faithful' lived luxuriously — and even that had scared the pair of them out of discussing it further. John took amusement in the thought: two atheists evading conversation as though a judgemental deity might be eavesdropping.

'I have little wish for unjustified calm by this point either, Love,' he told her.

'Then go: go with my blessing. Just don't overdo it.'

He remained unsure just what she meant by that. She had attended a lecture back in '40 given by Carlyle himself, during which he had spoken of his book, and then proceeded to decry Bentham's utility in no uncertain terms.

And rather unlike his usual calm demeanour, John had stood mid-audience and simply shouted 'NO!' as forcefully as he could. He hadn't known he could be that loud, nor that he still felt some kind of sympathy for his dead intellectual mentors.

Remembering it now, he found it humorous, and began to wonder whatever was keeping the slow-moving butler.

He hastily opted to turn about on his heels and walk away, but he had to try and talk some sense into his old friend. Walking away from utility or the influence of Bentham and James Mill was one thing — John himself had done that, experiencing a breakdown for his troubles — but this new fiasco... Even Carlyle's new title was out-rageously inflammatory, unfair, bigoted: 'Occasional Discourse on the Nigger Question!' How could so few look down on so many, especially when the perspective of the former so often was shaped by privilege, while the latter remained abused, downtrodden... enslaved?

'John? Is that you?' came the familiar but no longer welcome call from the step.

'Thomas.' Still no fan of confrontation, even interpersonal dis-putes, John found himself walking pointedly back towards the steps leading to the imposing house.

Carlyle did not step downward to even their stances, and his pos-ture was taller than that of his former friend anyway. Behind him, his manservant remained at the doorway, glancing with minimal curiosity and deference to his master.

'How fares the hip?' Carlyle queried, perhaps noting a pained glance on John's face. John kept trying to hide his recent rehabil-itation pangs. Earlier in the year he had taken a nasty spill simply strolling semi-absent-mindedly through his beloved Hyde Park. No bones had broken, thank goodness, but Harriet had had to devote more recent time then to her family, leaving John largely on his own to heal. That he had been made to wear a healing plaster for a spell, and that an infection from that had left him temporarily blinded, had not exactly eased his worry, but fortunately by now he was almost wholly back to his rambling ways, though maybe a touch of a limp remained visible to others.

John had to wonder truthfully if part of Harriet's potential reticence with helping to act as his nursemaid recently came down to her own troubles: she had recently presented with her own additional difficulties and strains simply walking, occasionally accompanied by the seem-ingly unrelated symptoms of painful-sounding coughs and headaches. She had rebuffed John's mild interrogations about her overall health, and he had chosen to leave well enough alone, at least for the nonce.

But he remained concerned. He felt she might be keeping some-thing from him.

'It's much better, actually. Thank you, Thomas,' John involuntarily winced. A couple of the London newspapers had somehow gotten wind of the little story—no story at all, grumbled John silently—just more lurid and inane gossip.

The manservant remained obligatorily standing there; it was as though Carlyle could detect the man's presence. 'That will be all,' he dismissed the man.

No reference to the man's name. *No wonder I've forgotten it myself,* John mused privately, admitting that he had endeavoured for many years to improve his treatment of those in service in whatever capacity, beginning with remembering their names.

'Thomas,' John repeated now, anxiously remaining somewhat at a loss for words. 'I've come to beseech you, old friend—'

'Friend?' the older man answered, raising his brow in challenge. 'You dare still cling to that quaint notion, John?'

John made a point of slowly looking up into the man's face, honestly missing the friendship. He promised himself again he would remain calm, different from the seeming madman who had jumped up to shout at Carlyle during that lecture years earlier.

'As I began to say, Thomas, was that I merely hoped you might reconsider some of your most recent work. I realise that draughts of our work so often appear in newsprint, but do you genuinely feel some need to refer to the "Nigger Question?"'

Carlyle crossed his arms defiantly. 'What of it?'

'Does it not strike you as unnecessarily confrontational? And racist?'

'For whom? Remember, John, if you have read the piece already—and for the record, I've always admired how you read things before attacking them—then you must know my intention was to critique hypocrisy. Did that strike too close to home, perhaps?'

John could not tell if the comment about his read-then-critique strategy was intended sarcastically, and did not care. He cared for the unpleasant predatory leer on Carlyle's face even less. 'You would dare?' he all but growled in response.

Thomas shifted from leer to grin. 'It would seem so. But in all seriousness, John my cuckolding acquaintance, believe it or not I tend to side with those in any kind of bondage.'

'Ha!' It erupted just like the prior 'No!' from years past; Thomas knew the tone.

'Look, Mill, the truth is that despite our lovely English-born industrial "revolution," far too much labour remains to be done that our greasy and steamy machines either cannot or never will do, and that's where the physical labour comes in. Your old friend Ricardo would be logically inclined to agree. I suspect your father, rest his gentle soul, would also.'

John Mill could not recall so wanting to lash out in physical assault at another human being in his life. The bloody nerve of this bastard! 'How can you say any of that lunacy?' was all he managed, feeling his fists at his sides. He did not follow Carlyle's glance left and right, nor the few neighbours poking curious heads out of doors and windows to take in the latest entertainment. More cases of gossip willing to misinterpret what was happening, simply by not receiving the whole story.

'They must be servants to those born wiser, John,' Thomas said. 'Some are born lords—or ladies, if you prefer, knowing the intellectual proclivities of your paramour—and that is simply how things are. I don't mean the "divine right of kings," or that "mandate of heaven" nonsense from the Oriental peoples you've studied—same thing, really—I'm merely trying to account for how things are. If the Americans and the Brazilians and the Russians and whomever else still holding others in bondage—which all those peoples still do—suddenly liberate them all somehow, then what happens?'

It was even more infuriating since John did not have the answers to this either. It was like Henry VIII's assault on the monasteries for their wealth, and neither he nor his equally greedy advisors accounted for the fallout of monks and nuns and other Catholics suddenly numbering among the destitute—made worse by the simple fact that those very people had for centuries been the main groups to whom the other

destitute throughout England—from poverty or disease—had traditionally turned for succour! What should a government do if a sizable
portion of its citizenry suddenly, almost overnight, found themselves
with a far greater extension of their personal liberties?

'What's the matter now, John?' This time Thomas had the temerity to look actually concerned, and somehow that made John feel
worse yet.

'Damn you,' John said, not caring in the slightest who might hear
or report it—he had years of experience facing public ridicule—for
his beliefs, his love, his naïve insistence upon getting members of the
public to think without pundits like Thomas Carlyle—but now he
refused to leave without getting something important across.

'This is like another perversion of Herr Hegel,' he added now,
savouring the suddenly confused expression appear on Carlyle's face.
'Your piece years ago about heroes and hero-worship fell apart, but
not because you're a bad writer. Indeed, you're a quite good writer,
which makes the problem worse. But all you do in this new article
is emphasise a master-slave dichotomy, whilst ignoring how Hegel
explained how new ideas come about. It felt as though all you did was
justify the perpetuation of servitude, not its termination.'

'The dualities remain, John,' came the response. 'Like with the
old split in philosophy between mind and body. But in this case it's
master-servant, or even the bourgeoisie-proletariat, if you prefer the
ramblings of that half-mad new German writer.'

John had read Karl Marx, and prided himself on keeping abreast
of whatever appeared on the shelves of booksellers labelled 'philosophy,' for all the weak spots with him remaining in the know with
current events. 'But it's not us versus them, Thomas. That's just adversarial and thus violent, and it's also an oversimplification.'

'History is conflict, John, the setting up of opposing groups,
opposing beliefs. That's something Hegel and this Marx would actually agree upon.'

There was no reaching the man. John was tired, physically and
emotionally tired, of staring at this man and offering his rebuttals,

all clearly to no avail. Yet as with so much else in John's life, he knew he had to try.

But Harriet was right, as she is with so many things, he thought morosely, and also strangely appreciatively, thankful for her — not guidance, necessarily, but talent with seeing some things more clearly than he did or could himself.

He sighed, looking at the old street bricks again. His senses, those bodily receivers of so many endless data, began to take in anew the sounds of the busy and crowded street. 'I shall miss you, Thomas.' And he turned on his heels and began to walk away again.

The only noise behind him, coming from the house, was the sound of the heavy thick door latching. It did not slam, it did not squeak; it merely closed and clicked into place, another barrier between John Mill and some element of truth he continued to seek.

*Damn the man anyway,* John pondered as he continued walking, wondering if it would prove the last time, then realising he did not care. Alert to misinterpretation of someone's words or views, John fretted over a respected intellectual like Thomas Carlyle being utilised for unintended purposes, the occasional fate of writers throughout history.

He felt damned fatigued from being misunderstood, misrepresented; Harriet, too, often felt likewise, and a person could only be ostracised so many times.

John's childhood Francophilia had never left him. A letter to Harriet last year had included the sentimental phrasing: 'Any place in France if it ever be so far off seems too much a home to us.' Maybe it was time to consider a more permanent arrangement.

*While the fine lady's husband lay most likely on his deathbed,* he considered morbidly. He recognised his selfishness, yet found he could not help but consider the intriguing possibilities. Harriet also loved the Continent in general, France in particular, and her talent with the old Romance language had improved during their relationship — though she remained careful to not speak it in front of her family, with the occasional exception of Lily, who had proven something of a natural with dialects and accents.

John confessed, now feeling that slight recent limp returning just a mite. *It's always about them*, he thought bitterly, not for the first time. *We work to educate so many, to take this lofty philosophy and make it simpler, more approachable, something to discuss over a pint and a meal with family, and not the elitist academic fortress mentality, rather like long-dead Mr Hume would have wanted.*

A full revolution was dangerous yet social change was desperately needed, in numerous forms, on multiple levels. Even the Yanks never truly had a revolution, strictly speaking, but a war for political independence, something occurring so far away from home country shores that subduing it became difficult and eventually impossible, and the Colonists had obtained Continental European allies by then. Even so, a fuller revolution might yet await them, since they retained significant issues and bickering over 'states' rights' and economics, and especially slavery and how the colonisers would continue to interact with Indians, enslaved Africans, and as with very recent history, Mexicans.

Violence could hardly solve anything, at least not from a longer-term perspective. Harriet had initially sympathised with the recent would-be revolutionaries in so many cities throughout Europe: Vienna, Frankfurt, Warsaw, Rome, Prague, even Paris — again. But no further west had those short-lived movements come this year, and surely not into the British Isles. People had rioted, with quite good cause: they felt abandoned by their governments, and once food became unavailable, then, as the English horse-racing adage went: all bets were off. Hunger and disease would never be assuaged by logic, John knew. Yet he had also not long ago predicted that the election of a head of state, in this case the underwhelming Louis Napoleon, especially when that head is vainglorious and greedy, could only yield dictatorship.

Harriet had liked his phrasing on that occasion: 'a stupid, ignorant adventurer who has thrown himself entirely into the hands of the reactionary party and but that he is too great a fool, would have some chance by these means of making himself emperor.' She had taken him to task, however, on his rude assessment of these "48 Revolts,' making it clear how she disapproved of him writing that 'the crude opinions and unguided instincts of the working class' must not become 'the directing power of the state.' They could still clash over ideals, and even though John had 'improved' in her perspective about trying to address 'everyone,' to use his own term, she had to show him how his own indoctrinated social bigotry still remained and had to be exorcised. Lily alone approved of that last term.

In the meantime, Britain was too stretched for an empire at this point regardless; she surely did not need to try and put out any more fires, either at home or abroad. An 'Opium War' against the Chinese Qing Empire; two 'Anglo-Sikh Wars,' the second of which had erupted just recently and which particularly horrified John since it involved his own British East India Company against the Indian Sikh Empire and the issue of whether British foreign leadership should be mainly economic or political or religious or a mix; and a recent epidemic of cholera in England, with physicians competing and arguing and yelling about treatments and even potential cures. The '48 urban revolts almost seemed minor!

'Who knows what they'll figure out?' Harriet had demanded of the medical issue, herself quite fed up with doctors and their 'practice' of medicine. 'You should read those journal pieces about that new "germ theory," John,' she recently advised. Even a local English physician had recently advocated the boiling of water to 'clean' it to make it safe for consumption. The literature suggested that not just livestock but also human residents of a filthy if technological city like London had benefitted from that practice, with fewer outbreaks of fewer diseases.

So John kept reading Harriet's recommendations. He had rarely felt disappointment in following up with his lover's choices, and found himself intrigued by how the scientists she'd recommended had put forth compelling logic and empirical evidence — the best of both worlds, John understood — though that remained a large step away from the actual curing of diseases, something which had been dreamt of for centuries but never truly done.

*My, how one's thoughts wander when one tries to limp home, savouring the oncoming dusk whilst simultaneously hoping to not be recognised.*

What a fickle beast fame was! John Mill appreciated recognition in print for his intellectual accomplishments, and not for 'destroying' a marriage, as his sisters still liked to claim. He knew he would have to visit his family again soon, and was dreading it as much as he had dreaded today's visit to the home of a now former friend.

*How do our choices lead us down such strange paths?* John wondered for the thousandth time. Entire lives intersected and criss crossed, sometimes from choice, often seemingly random—a key reason why so many sought the omnipresent explanatory ease of religion—and then might run together for a time like parallel lines, like the railroad tracks John had grown so impressed by, or else diverge, perhaps violently like this afternoon.

*Maybe England needs both our types,* John thought this time: 'progress' and 'order,' to borrow his own terms used in print earlier in the year, claiming that while England might be the 'ballast of Europe,' more romantically-minded France was its 'sail,' the steerer of the great civilising Continent, as with a very old analogy used by Plato to describe the political leaders of the ship known as society.

*And it's all a bunch of biased bollocks,* he concluded, ignoring the memory of the pained look on Harriet's face the last time he had used such a strong term in her presence. He might as well have shouted 'shite!' or 'damn it to hell,' such was its perniciousness.

*Biased bollocks: my dear lover admonishes me to get to know and understand 'the masses' more, but most folks simply do not refer to nations as ballast and sail. They seek happiness and contentment, and while I've whiled away so much time and energy seeking 'higher' thoughts and 'higher' pleasures, here I am, miserable as ever.*

He almost tripped over a break in the road, hearing to one side a pair of skinny dogs scampering about, looking poor and dishevelled but for all that content with their ongoing search for the next morsel of food, the next shelter from English rain, the next friendly pat on the head, and seemingly not fretting about the next kick or the next grocer or restaurateur who refused one of those morsels.

*Perhaps I should have stuck by Father's utility: maybe then happiness would have come calling, not remaining out of reach and the object of ambiguous quest, like the Americans describe it. And myself now labelled a 'windy-wallet,' one who boasts too bloody much, full of 'gum' or other troublesome terms.* John could imagine his parents years ago, washing his mouth out for such deplorable language, so he turned onto another street to finally hail a ride. The hip pain was worsening, and he was damned — more poor language, curse it all — if he would resort to laudanum or the like.

John recalled fondly his meeting a decade ago with that slightly younger aspiring novelist Mr Dickens, who had met with genuine success thus far with his literary career, and now noted that even the authors of fiction could succumb to the temptations of perspectives that might remain only superficially understood. Dickens could also blend opposing forces into a coherent whole, and Carlyle had shown a similar trend in his rewritten history, though John hardly expected gratitude for impelling him to the rewrite! John knew too that Dickens and Carlyle had recently become friendly, and wondered how matters might pan out, while he tended to avoid fiction regardless.

In the meantime, John continued onward and summoned his ride, organising his thoughts, that endless task. He was missing Harriet — no news there — and decided to confront the pain of lost friends since his mood had already suffered today's blow. *No revolution without subsequent civil war,* he reminded himself morosely.

Even now, the loss of John Sterling worked on John's feelings. It seemed natural to turn to him: another missed friend, even more so since Sterling was dead, and had he lived, perhaps John would have fallen out with him, too: how did anyone maintain the asinine notion that they could possibly be in any way 'superior' to others just because of accidents of 'race,' itself a vague notion? Some persons might be obviously dark-skinned or clearly light-skinned, but John had worked with enough fellow humans, even in cosmopolitan London, to understand that this species of mostly bald bipeds displayed colours along a lengthy spectrum, and further, that Europeans could be imbeciles while Asians and Africans could be brilliant, the potential skin-pun therein unintended.

The four years since Sterling's death had flown right by, as the Taylor boys were sometimes wont to say. John recalled Vergil, whom he had not read for decades: 'Sed fugit interea, fugit inreparabile tempus,' as the archaic Roman poet put it, speaking of agriculture and living simply while confronting urban corruption and the inevitable decay of life. 'Time flies,' as the passage was often over-simplistically rendered colloquially.

Loss of Carlyle was one thing; the Trijackia had meanwhile veered all over. Graham still laboured away at the Registrar's office, finding satisfaction in the endless detail. John himself loved research, but the dry data of tracking the major life events of—wishfully—every citizen of the United Kingdom and its Territories, sounded as dull as anything Mill could imagine, choosing not to recall that Graham and Roebuck had chided him for the 'drab drudgery of Empire' that they called his employ at India House. At least Grote gave the impression that he was almost envious of Mill's position, or of his pay. Graham also relayed an amusing anecdote about Mr Peel, whose police constabulary might benefit from increased access to such data sets, the better to 'keep eyes on' those same citizens, though John himself wondered at potential violation of people's privacies and liberties. As for Roebuck, he had served as Queen's Counsel, then got ousted from Parliament, and then recently got voted right back in for Sheffield instead.

John smiled wanly at how Roebuck still opposed private property, the political and economic structure enshrined by Locke, and used to justify slavery and factories and armies alike. Old 'radical Roebuck' would have to keep those views secretive again, especially in light of those short-lived and mostly-peaceful yet still-terrifying—to some—spontaneous economic miniature revolutions last summer. The Continental poor and downtrodden had reminded John of a long-dead baby which still sometimes haunted his dreams, along with thoughts of Malthus and John's never-voiced gladness—not even Harriet knew this—that he had no children of his own. Even she conceded, agreeing with him in print, how as labourers became more educated and economies improved, human birth rates decreased, not welcome news for modern societies, particularly European empires. And therein lay agreement with Locke about property, a belief John yet held.

Something about those 'mini-revolts,' or whatever one called them, had made John defensive; he still wondered what it was. People had risen spontaneously, without advance planning or inter-group communication, and protested the political status quo. These masses differed some from nation to nation: the French—still—wanted better opportunities for jobs in the cities, and to ensure their government would not let them starve during poor harvests or profligate spending; the Germans—and their Prussian cousins—had industrialised as rapidly as the English; the Hungarians and Russians dabbled with getting rid of serfdom; and they all were clamouring for greater representation with their governments, taking their cue from the Americans and trying to address the vast yet finite wealth of natural resources their nations controlled.

John wondered further that such events had not crossed the Channel, a detail political conservatives deemed a sign of English superiority. John had written to John Austin last year, thanking dear 'Mutter' Austin, Sarah, for her continued support of his relationship with Harriet and for her influence upon some of Harriet's close friends. And in addressing the other John, he had written confrontationally that, 'In England I often think that a violent revolution is very much needed, in order to give that general shake-up to the torpid mind of the nation which the French Revolution gave to Continental Europe.'

*Violent Revolution?* he thought again now. What was wrong with him? He had perused that curious text by Marx, which many recent revolutionaries had referred to, and that author seemed content to take credit—falsely—for having almost fomented these uprisings, since his publication date and the start of the revolts coincided closely.

Revolutions had casualties, and would be followed, not always immediately, by civil war. It was a truth of history and no one seemed prepared to admit it.

And now John was en route to the Taylor residence, dreading every clip-clop of his current driver's horse's shod hoofs over this part of the cobblestone labyrinth. He had to admit that his conveyance, a newer carriage design, offered much by way of comfort, but he could not get his lover's recent fiery and unexpected words out of his mind, still carrying her hurriedly delivered last letter. It had proven devastating to read, and she rarely lashed out at him over anything: not during their shared frustrations, hearing or learning later of embarrassing gossip about their improper or impious relationship, not even when either or both of them had taken time to convalesce from their latest ailments.

He fumbled for the paper, already a worn scrap, which seemed appropriate. John re-read the worst part: 'You talk of my writing to you "at some odd time when a chance of subject of thought may be rather a relief than otherwise!" "Odd time!" Indeed you must be ignorant profoundly of all that friendship or anxiety means when you can use such pitiful narrow-hearted expressions... It is the puerility of thought and feeling of any utterly headless and heartless propriety old maid.' Who knew she still cared so for her husband?

John Taylor was dying. Such was the impetus for Harriet's barbed words, and worse, John felt he deserved sanction. It had been years since he felt guilt for cuckolding another man, and the encounters betwixt the two Johns had become few and far between. For the sake of appearances, Mrs Taylor and Mr Mill had continued to carry on—usually—with the veneer of elaborate charade, though no one remained fooled: not the Taylor children, who had more or less 'chosen sides' as those from 'broken' homes often did; not Mill's co-workers at India House; not the male friends in his life nor the female friends in Harriet's, not unless there existed truly talented actors in their social midst. Only Lily had ever made any noise about becoming such.

John smacked the ceiling of the shiny new wooden brougham, alerting his driver. 'Yes, Sir?' came the reply from up top, with a slight trill of the 'r,' as if from a Scot. The very young man, probably the age Mill was when he began his long career, kept trained and gentle hands on the reins whilst flawlessly negotiating the City.

'Next chance you get, young man,' John said, 'turn us about. Take me to India House, please, over at Leadenhall Street. Do you know it?'

John could not hear the near-guffaw from the driver's seat in front of and above him, as the lad quickly took a hard right turn, the clip-clop sound impressively remaining at precisely the same cadence. Most drivers could not manage that, rather how most dogs would tend to speed up even against leashes when crossing a street or entering a park. 'Sure t'be, guv'nor.' John winced at the sudden Cockney, not caring that it made him seem snobbish. 'At's where they 'ave the tile piece, wot? Mosaic?'

*Maybe life would be simpler had I just become a carriage-driver,* John thought briefly but jestingly, since his ability to ride a horse remained practically non-existent, though driving one or two seemed easier. And he could only guess at what this driver might have picked up during time spent at the other end of the reins. Still, most people thought 'the help' beneath them and thus not worth speaking to for any reason.

But this lad sat above him, literally. John grinned at the stupid thought, anything to avoid facing Mr Taylor. He knew it was not cowardice, since Harriet had already warded him off, and his poorly thought notion of visiting the home today was admittedly more due to the selfish need to reconcile with his lady than to offer some empty support for a dying man. Besides, what could he do? He could hardly cure Taylor, who had shown remarkable restraint over the years.

'Yes, that's correct,' John informed his driver, recalling the Roman-era mosaic located during the building of India House, something the upper-level staff took as a semi-omen: as Roman power had spread through three continents, including the province 'Britannia,' so now would British power extend to twice that number, with many times the human subjects.

The lad was proving chatty. John suddenly liked him for that. 'Why d'you need to visit a stuffy ole buildin' like 'at, then, Sir?'

John liked him slightly better now; the choice of adjective was apt. India House was stuffy! He returned to thinking of Taylor. How enraged Harriet had been years ago at the other John's expense—the betrayal, the debilitating disease, how in need of comfort she had been, the last an odd part of what made Mill fall in love with her so easily. And his own attitudes to women had been shaped by all of that, too. His mother and sisters had all turned out so typical: content, even eager, to secure home and marriage and perhaps children, never dreaming of much else. Harriet had opened his eyes to much more, such as the horrible plight of the very women that Mr Taylor had consorted with in the first place. Harriet had shown John an early quotation in her precious diary—which he was not otherwise permitted to read, a condition he still accepted—from a French-Peruvian activist—quite a volatile mix, he thought: 'What a worthy use these English lords make of their immense fortunes! How fine and generous they are when they have lost the use of their reason and offer fifty, even a hundred, guineas to a prostitute if she will lend herself to all the obscenities that drunkenness engenders.'

'Business,' he answered the young fellow at last. 'I work there, actually.'

'Oh. 'Sorry then, wot.'

'No need for sorrow at all. Sometimes I'm the one sorry to still work there after all these years. I've never seemed to find the gumption to seek gainful employ elsewhere.'

'Oh, no, Sir,' came the reply from outside, with less trill this time. Something about that urban accent seemed pleasing after all the formal discussions John experienced. Around India House, he expected few other than the maids and the paperboys to sound this way. 'Sorry I am to 'ear that, I is. Me da, now, 'e's jus' a groom, oroit. In fac,' 'e takes care o' this very lovely lass what's leadin' us to where you gorra go. 'Enrietta's 'er name, an' now I get paid more for drivin' 'an what me da makes groomin'.'

That was an interesting claim, to be sure. James Mill, if yet living, might have a fatal conniption upon learning what India House paid his son these days. There were signs before his death—before John's last promotion—of such jealousy. 'It's good you have a father who hopes you surpass him, or at least finds no threat if you do.'

'Sure t'be,' the lad said. 'Me mum, now, she's a tough 'un, too, like. She teaches fer one o' them charity schools. You ever 'eard o' the "Blue Coats?"'

John was trying to tune out the endless noises of urbanity: not just horses and their conveyances moving about the busy streets, but shopkeepers yelling out their wares; passers-by strolling, shopping, or walking rapidly, purposefully; off to the left the rhythmic sounds of hammering and sawing, John did not know for what edifice; children laughing and running in all directions, rich ones and poor ones alike. Only the former got scolded frequently, while the latter seemed pleased enough just to be scampering about, perhaps thankful they had not been sold nor compelled to work in the nation's collieries or docks or houses of ill repute.

And he had heard of the school, with its 'Blue Coats.' It was one of the institutions Lily and Harriet had checked, but they had decided — Harriet had decided — that her precocious offspring would be better served by continuing schooling at home, largely independently. 'I have indeed. The Blackheath Blue Coat Church of England School, do I have that correct?' Maybe it was the religious affiliation that turned Harriet away: between her Unitarianism-turned-atheism and Lily's Catholic leanings — the girl still made occasional noises about seeking baptism — it seemed small wonder that the youngest Taylor had not become a 'Blue Coat.'

'Aye, 'at's the one. Me mum loves teachin' there.'

'Then yes. My, well, someone I know almost became a student there.'

'Sorry i' din't work out, mate.'

'No need to be.' The younger man kept half-apologising — how very English of him. 'Tell me, are you always this chatty?' John hoped it did not come across as criticism.

'Really depends on'a patrons, don' it?' he said. John liked the term 'patrons.'

'I suppose it would. You're a pleasant conversationalist, young man. I hope that does not sound condescending.'

'Y'know, Sir, jus' las' month, oroit, I 'ad this pair o' dapper blokes, dressed e'en better'n you, if you'll permit me sayin' so. Barristers or solicitors or summat, an' I learned meself the meaning of "condescending" durin' that very ride.' He pronounced the offending word carefully.

'I hope they didn't insult you. It's disconcerting how the folks on whom society often most depends get looked down on by those who have money, and so often for doing nothing to earn wealth in the first place.'

'No insult at all, me good man,' the lad said, trying to refine the last few words into more of a posh accent, but he either could not or would not quite pull it off.

John laughed. 'It sounds like you enjoy your job, then?'

'Rarely borin,' if y'know 'ut I mean.'

John looked outside the cab, glimpsing more of the famed City. Some of it he knew intimately, much he had never encountered. A person could devote an entire long lifetime to London, and would still never know it all. 'Indeed. It sounds like you have some genuine vestige of happiness.'

Laughter from up above now. 'Now at's a word I dunno as well. "Vestige." I gorrit, though. You a professor or summat, then? Nah, ya would'n' be, not at India House.' John swore he could almost hear the sure, deft touch on the reins. The horse looked healthy and eager, too, better than many of the creatures who had to call London home. Maybe that RSPCA group was accomplishing some good work, though John didn't know if they reached out to individual vehicle managers like this man and his father. He wondered if the mother kept pets in her classroom for her Blue Coat girls to fuss over.

The Taylor children sometimes clamoured for pets of their own, their parents always saying nay, and John pondered if that was merely a power struggle. Or if it was awkward to move such animals around, given the seasonal living arrangements of the family, or Harriet's likely inability at this point to care for them, between her ailments and travels, or if Taylor himself really had dander allergies like he had once claimed in front of John.

'No, I'm not a professor, though I know a few of them. I'm a writer.'

'Coo,' the lad called. 'Anythin' I might've read?'

John Mill felt instantly ashamed that he had lived most of his years up to that moment secure in the unjustifiable belief that those from the 'lower classes' would either not even know how to read, or at the least not find any of his work interesting or of merit.

And yet he and Harriet, probably more than any of the numerous literary contacts they had in England, went out of their way to write philosophy — ethics, aesthetics, politics, economics — in as friendly a manner as they could, simultaneously attempting to explain important ideas without either over-simplifying or over-complicating.

So he kept the condescension out of his response. 'I write for a mix of newspapers, and once had partial ownership of one. I also do pieces here and there through editorial letters, and one of my friends is an MP. He told me I should run, but I'm not sure I could serve that way.'

"Ow come? Yer smarter 'an plenny o' them blokes in Parliament. Nicer, too.'

John giggled and shrugged, then remembered his driver could not see the gesture. 'There's only one other person who has asked me that, come to think on it. Some might think I'm too much of a radical.'

'In 'at fancy suit? 'Doubt it, guv.'

John giggled again. 'It's true, believe it or not.' He decided to take the chance: intelligent and curious minds were too precious to waste, whatever their backgrounds. 'My, um, my friend,' he began, still just uptight enough for the times to have trouble pronouncing 'lover' in public, 'she and I have penned quite a number of items. Some of them have focused on parliamentary reform, legislation, ethics.'

'Which papers?' the young man shouted.

'Oh, well, let's see. There's the 'London Review.' Then we've also written for 'The Examiner,' the 'Westminster Review,' 'The London and Westminster Review,' and —'

He paused, hearing laughter from the driver's bench. 'Yes, well,' John added, 'that might sound faintly ridiculous, the commonality of titles and the sheer number of volumes.' And he felt oddly defensive:

'It's quite something to live at a time when there exists a periodical for almost anyone, whatever their interest. Do you read much?' he queried, then anxiously hoped the lad could truly read. Despite the wealth of newsprint, theirs was still a more illiterate than lettered society.

'Me? No, no' much, really. It's 'ard to find the time, ennit? Me parents, though, they follow some o' them papers. Remember, me mum's a teacher.'

'Yes, of course. 'Sorry.'

'No worries, sir. Y'know, jus' las' night, when we 'us 'avin' our supper, wot, Mum was talkin' 'bout summat called 'clersy,' or 'clersay,' an' you talkin' 'bout this stuff now jus' made me think on it again.'

'Clerisy!' John shouted again. 'That's a word we invented. Well, actually the poet Samuel Coleridge coined the term, but we borrowed it.'

'Mum said she liked it, that it was about smart folk like her mebbe runnin' things.'

'Rather than a bunch of often imbecilic politicians,' John finished.

'At's right, sir. Like jus' the las' months, what with that epidemic. Bloody cholera!'

'Indeed. Thank goodness it seems to be on the wane, though it's spread some to Wales and Scotland. And God help Ireland when it hits there: those poor souls are still weak from the recent famine, the ones who haven't fled to America.' *Not the proudest moment in English history, no matter the calls from Dublin and Belfast for Home Rule,* John thought. *How in Blazes can a whole people be compelled to eat absolutely nothing but potatoes while their neighbours import foods from around their empire!* 'We're oddly fortunate that it hasn't become a pandemic, but thousands have died here in London. And yet somehow it seems almost refreshing to contend with some disease other than consumption.' Ironically, it had all come hard on the heels of a recent parliamentary act supporting public health, with safety measures for water and food, rubbish and sewage, while across the Irish Sea subjects starved.

Harriet had followed the recent terrifying news closely, and the children had begun to notice how interrelated world events truly were. No one quite knew the exact source of the cholera outbreak, which of course meant that different nationalities turned xenophobic and blamed each other, a habit deeply ingrained amongst the English. The more reactionary had suggested, as always, that God was yet again wreaking His vengeance upon an unworthy populace, though John and Harriet took some comfort in how Lily chose not to comprehend matters that way, proclaiming that God's love was not about punishment but rather grace through a strong blend of faith and good works. Lily, bless her, had also gone alone to a Catholic church nearby, John could not recall which, to pray for those poor souls in Ireland and to donate food, telling her mother that it might matter a bit more since the Irish tended towards Catholicism themselves. John's newswriting had phrased the situation in more secular terms: 'The Condition of Ireland is the most unqualified instance of signal failure which the practical genius of the English people has exhibited.' He no longer bothered to open anonymous mail received at India House, since it often contained hateful commentaries about his rational insights.

'Never knew a gentleman could 'ave a dark sense o' humour.'

'No one has ever suggested that I have such, lad. In fact I'm sometimes accused of lacking a sense of humour.'

And yet the younger man laughed aloud again at that. 'Well, mebbe you din't mean it like that. An' them poor Irish. We've relatives in Ireland, me da's side 'at is. An' some o' them fled like y'said.'

'To America?' John was intrigued by how those words had become a rallying call for so many in Europe, and other parts of the world as well. He knew the French commentator Alexis de Toqueville had written a mostly positive review of his 'Democracy in America' a dozen years ago after welcoming him to London with Roebuck. And during that very meeting, just weeks before the 'troubles' in the Continent, that perceptive author had presciently warned, as though having just read Marx, that Europe was 'sleeping on a volcano' and that 'a wind of revolution blows, the storm is on the horizon.'

'Aye,' the driver said. 'No' tha' I'm in support o' them Yanks, neither.

And me mum pointed out in some o' them papers 'ow close we came to another bleedin' war with 'em over that territory out west, what's it?'

John silently thanked Harriet again for giving him the impetus to do a better job of keeping abreast of current events. 'Oregon,' he answered after a moment, thinking he had pronounced it properly this time. 'It's between California and British Columbia, which itself is part of Canada. And California used to be part of Mexico, which used to be part of Spain. And "them Yanks" just finished a vicious war with Mexico.' Interrelated indeed!

The lad slowed the brougham briefly to make way for a small group of children, gleefully shouting boys and girls alike playing football in the street, using flower planters — with no plants — as goal markers. John watched them for a speedy moment, foolishly wondering for the thousandth time if he might have enjoyed a happier childhood if he had greater physical coordination, knowing studying had interfered with childlike delights.

'An' we jus' finished a vicious war wit' India, wot?'

John shook his head in disgust, once again forgetting the young man could not witness it, though his comment was correct. The Company had forced the collective hand of the dubiously named Sikh 'Empire' in the northern portion of the Indian subcontinent, and the mess had escalated quickly, with disputed successor-ship in the Punjab region scaring the British, confronted by East India Company concerns over an Indian army that might have led to local rebellion or perhaps something even more consequential. John almost hated admitting to anyone that he worked for an instrument of imperial control, so who was he to complain about the Americans and their self-instigating wars against Mexicans, or those other Indians, or recently, like this lad noted, almost against the British?

'Yes we did, unfortunately. And it seems peace may prove all too short-lived. It's impossible to maintain control over others far from home, something Europeans have been painfully slow to learn.' *Did I actually just say that? Father would have been horrified.*

'I've enjoyed our talk, young man. My own father and his best friend,' John continued. *Was Bentham Father's best friend? And did Father truly have friends?* he wondered, 'co-founded the 'Westminster Review,' a journal "for philosophical radicals," as they described it. The idea was to criticise all the different political parties for infighting, and for their foreign policies.'

He thought the driver had lost interest for a moment, then noticed how smoothly he moved the brougham through a busy thoroughfare. Inner Ring Road was thankfully wide, though that meant it tended to accrue heavier traffic, and John felt glad this was not a market day or holiday. They charged past Finsbury Circus—now a pleasant public garden area John believed to be a far better replacement on the grounds where 'Bedlam' Hospital, or properly Bethlem Royal Hospital, had once stood. He admitted he had few ideas, though, about how to treat the mad beyond what Bentham had written about treating prisoners, most of that focusing on basic hygiene and sympathetic recognition that the residents were still human, whatever their crimes, or in the case of Bedlam, illnesses. Bedlam had been moved to a less visible and less reputable part of London.

The prior commentary went unanswered. 'We're almos' there now, sir. I do appreciate our chance to chat, too. And mebbe you should read fewer o' them papers.'

Leadenhall Street lay south of the old Taylor residence on Christopher Street, and so they, or rather the mare 'Enrietta,' kept trotting towards the Bank of England before turning towards their destination. They truly were just about there; within a couple of minutes they had arrived, John pleased again at not having to weave through a crowd.

'Oroit then, ennit?' The driver looked down at John as he exited the vehicle, and John smiled at the use of such a stereotypical London phrase. John had needed a distraction. Once again, his mind wandered where it would, and he had slowly learned to be less rude to those who found themselves in occupations often looked down upon by their supposed 'betters.' 'Do you have a favourite part of our mighty Capital, young man?' he asked, stepping down from the cab and feeling his way through an assortment of coins, feeling breeze in his thinning and receding and greying hair. He handed off the requisite coinage, which included a generous gratuity.

'The theatres offer some respite,' said the young man, looking at John and taking the payment. He actually winked at his 'patron,' showing off healthy teeth and tipping his cap after pocketing the coins. He was well dressed himself, though of course not in a suit, but looked at home in his flannel shirt    a way from Wales to weave wool, and had what John thought might be an old bruise around one eye — *defending his honour to the neighbourhood toughs?* wondered John, who caught himself once again with that class bias.

'For me as well,' he said, not caring whether the reference to a shared love of theatre was just a joke. The young man was interesting, and had proven a useful distraction to an otherwise gloomy day. He knew John Taylor was having a far worse one, even with his wife in his sickroom.

John typically enjoyed the breezy ride to India House on those occasions when he opted for such, and no longer felt insulted by Harriet's occasional derisive comment about his being 'cheap.' And he was not: his family members could attest to that, which made his feelings of estrangement from them so frustrating. Plus, he did not have to balance the paying off of homes like Mr Taylor did, though he had offered to contribute substantially to the Hardy home before learning it had been inherited — very negatively answered anyroad, and John suspected that Mr Taylor had never even heard of his request through his wife — as well as the Mill family residence of Vicarage Place.

As for the wind that had entered and enlivened the brougham during the ride — it cantered off now to seek another fare — it was laden with the scents of a new age of industry: the omnipresent whiff of horse manure came mixed with faint smoke — fortunately the bigger new factories were in similarly newer cities, like Manchester and Birmingham, such that the 'Dark Satanic Mills' of industry seemed far away — plus a multinational blend of food scents and even a trace of the sea, carried along the wind up the Thames. But the Thames was worsening, and fortunately India House remained far enough north of the mighty river that the odour rarely reached that far. Maybe the recently passed Public Health Act would extend to cleaning up the river, though John could not think of how to go about doing so other than to stop dumping so much sewage into it, a daily mass ritual that probably dated to the ancient days of Roman Londinium.

John had written in the 'Daily News' recently that 'We are living in an age of railroads.' And telegraphs and steamships, he thought now; the world was truly shrinking in a new age of information, as he stared at the huge four-storey classical-looking edifice that had been his alternate home and source of a fine income for a quarter century. 'Nowadays,' his item had gone on, 'rather than not go straight to our object, instead of winding around the hill we even tunnel through it. The spirit of the time requires that its machinery, whether for physical or political purposes, shall be efficient.' He had fretted over individual wording as ever, and Harriet had teased about his never giving up on that notion of trying to encapsulate the 'spirit' of their times, as with their first conversation.

He hated the thought that such spirit seemed to entail looser attitudes regarding romantic relationships, and knowing that the medieval period might have lauded him and Harriet as some doomed Arthurian couple. *No, that's inane. You just have to accept that you feel guilty again after having loosed that feeling for so long.* He would go in to his office, get some work done even though he usually finished by early afternoon, and await Harriet's next summons, mentally preparing himself for anything.

He noticed a slight stoop to his step as he plodded up to his office, still enjoying the view of so much. Few were around this late in the afternoon, and he chose not to bother even checking if there was any tea on the stove. He nodded vaguely towards the staff who remained on site: at this point mostly secretaries and custodians, though he was pleased, recalling the driver, that he knew the names of these other workers. He sometimes asked awkwardly about their lives and families and interests, and occasionally received casual responses, some of them seemingly appreciating the effort, some unimpressed, some clearly feeling that they were still not supposed to chat up their supposed betters.

Sitting at his desk still felt peaceful, even with the endless documents that filtered their way in from the far reaches of the Empire, and he again noted the post-marks on some of these, remembering his prior thoughts about how much quicker communications had become in this modern busy period. His 'Completed' wooden box had his signature or company stamp or both, approving communiqués and other data, some financial.

The desk held separate piles of things of interest: newspapers, fewer of which contained items written by him or Harriet or Ms Martineau or the Austins. Pieces from fictitious serialisations appeared in some, including Dickens's new 'David Copperfield,' and reprinted excerpts of 'Woman in the Nineteenth Century'—Harriet had helped make sure that its American authoress had a following in England. There seemed little that John did not or would not read, and one of his few fears of travelling amounted to bringing the wrong books for the trip or, in other manifestations of whatever silly phobia that might be, arriving with insufficient books or having difficulty finding books at the destination in languages with which he had experience.

He glanced up at the walls of the office, which he kept immaculate. Still, he had struggled with management to permit him to keep certain newsworthy items visible, and while he had a chalkboard for daily notes, he rarely used it, choosing instead to paste such items as reminders, painful as they might prove.

A piece about Ireland appeared there, mocking not just individual readers but every citizen of the Empire. One Quaker observer of both the woollen industry and Irish issues had noted during an 1847 trip with his peaceful though business-supporting father, that 'Of a population of 240, I found 13 already dead from want. The survivors were like walking skeletons; the men stamped with the livid mark of hunger; the children crying with pain; the women in some of the cabins too weak to stand. When there before, I had seen cows at almost every cabin, and there were, besides, many sheep and pigs owned in the village. But now all the sheep were gone; all the cows, all the poultry killed; only one pig left; the very dogs which had barked at me before had disappeared; no potatoes, no oats.' In an Empire of plenty, untold numbers of Catholics so close to and yet culturally so far from England had fled to America.

That keen observer de Tocqueville appeared on Mill's board too, with further commentary on the Yanks. That notion of 'democracy,' taken from the old Greek word with idealistic attempts to update it for the times, did not prove that Americans or British yet had anything other than racial- and gender-based oligarchies, even if elective. Mill nonetheless smiled at Alexis' published hope that Americans would not become complacent, having written how 'Hardly anyone in the United States devotes himself to the essentially theoretical and abstract portion of human knowledge.' That might free up more working hands for labour, especially in newer factories, but de Tocqueville added that 'every new method that leads by a shorter road to wealth, every machine that spares labour, every instrument that diminishes the cost of production, every discovery that facilitates pleasure.' It was harder to determine to which nation he was referring.

So John loitered in his office, occasionally glancing out the generous window, mentally mixing praise and curses of this organisation which employed him; fretted about Harriet's intermittent though sometimes severe aches and pains, then remembered the dreadful state her husband was in; and had a brief moment of self-doubt about the merits of 'A System of Logic'—then feeling a shorter moment's excitement at the prospect of it getting translated into French and German; and then back to self-doubt about the work they had more recently completed for 'The Principles of Political Economy.'

It was a good book, truly. John chided himself for doubting, remembering now that this was the first book—in history, so far as anyone knew—to specifically address women's economic and financial concerns, and to ask, among other sensitive topics, just why women were not permitted more rights—when they were permitted to labour for money at all, of course, and there remained far too many places around the globe where they were not, sometimes under threat of violence or murder—and the book also daringly critiqued the division of labour as envisioned by Smith rather than Ricardo. John and Harriet stopped well short of arguing against personal property as such—even that curious tome by Marx, whilst offering intriguing and often insightfully deserved criticisms of capitalism running rampant, clearly had trouble assessing where private property truly did—or should—end. John and Harriet had noted in their new book that, "'Private property,' in every defence made of it, is supposed to mean, the guarantee to individuals of the fruits of their own labour and abstinence,' though the actual laws of property had 'never yet conformed to the principles on which the justification of private property rests.'

John and Harriet adored public parks, for example, had taught the children to all but worship the growing public libraries, and to be generous to the poor and destitute, though it was Harriet who pointed out that sympathy remained perilously close to arrogance, precisely the sort of dominant thinking that enabled the likes of the British Empire or heavy industry or the perpetuation of castes, like those which remained alive and well and partly sexist in nature in that 'Crown Jewel' of the Empire from which John Mill's employer took its name.

But John and Harriet also understood how terminology often became muddled, particularly within politics. Part of their resistance to the communistic ideas of Marx lay in this issue. As Harriet and John explained, "'Socialism" is the modern form of protest, which has been raised, more or less, in all ages of any mental activity, against the unjust distribution of social advantages.' And they had written of a shared concern about environments, 'from which solitude is extirpated,' and where 'every rood of land is brought under cultivation... every flowery waste or pasture ploughed up, all quadrupeds or birds which are not domesticated for man's use exterminated as his rivals for food.' Even in America wilderness ended eventually.

Still, such concerns did not directly address the growing political rifts, so that 'the healing of the standing feud between capital and labour; the transformation of human life, from a conflict of classes struggling for opposite interests, to a friendly rivalry in the pursuit of a common good to all; the elevation of the dignity of labour; a new sense of security and independence in the labouring classes; and the conversion of each human being's daily occupation into a school of the social sympathies and practical intelligence.' Such were the sorts of passages that John chose to remember as most dear to his heart.

Now, as John saw one of the Company secretaries walking towards his office, he cringed again, both at the realisation that this worker was staring right at him and clearly carrying a folded paper in an outstretched hand; and also at how adamant John Taylor had become regarding one little detail about the latest published text of Mr Mill and Mrs Taylor.

It had grown nerve-racking sometimes just to encounter those souls who inhabited John's and Harriet's daily lives: they could never be sure who might criticise them.

The book's dedication was a case in point: John had wanted to publicly thank his muse, Harriet, for profoundly shaping this work, which at its foundation was largely the working out of his ideas, but she made them more approachable and knew how to write and edit to achieve that, and he knew sales would probably increase from its being easier to read and think about. Even Hume had once reminded his readers that philosophy in any of its various guises would rarely be appreciated by a wider readership unless as many readers as possible could grasp it in its somewhat simplified essence. Such was the balancing act. Even this late, in the summer of 1848 with news of urban revolts throughout much of Europe still echoing in the ears of the anxious, Mr Taylor seemed no less accepting of the truth of tattered marriage. More than seventeen years had passed since John had become the erstwhile third player of the Taylor couple, but the dedication John Mill sought proved another emotional dagger into the heart of John Taylor.

The latter man was having none of it, even though he otherwise strangely seemed to like the recent Mill-Taylor collaboration as well. He even agreed with the book's notion of a 'wage fund' to be shared among the workers of an organisation, partly in the name of greater equality, partly in the knowledge that wealth was finite. He even told his wife that he approved of her noting in the work that 'the distribution of wealth' must necessarily depend upon 'the laws and customs of society.'

But he adamantly refused to grant his consent to his wife's name appearing in such a context, a decision, John and Harriet hated to admit, which was legal, just as Arthur Ley's habit of beating his own wife was. Taylor had proven astonishingly open and forgiving, spending lavishly on a woman he still loved, enduring ridicule from friends and associates and even clients alike — more of the social harm John Mill kept working on formulating — and had already informed his wife that he expected no share at all of whatever proceeds she might net from book sales — an example of self-imposed financial harm. Taylor had previously shown no interest in sharing in the proceeds of the previous John-Harriet collaboration either, and 'A System of Logic' continued to sell well.

Where did this all end? John and Harriet had for years worked to maintain a discreet, loving, and honest relationship, and would have wed long ago had Harriet been permitted to obtain a divorce. There were times when her husband had wanted that too, despite the emotional harm that the Taylor children would surely experience — *I really do have to work on turning off the philosophy*, John thought — and some of which those children had endured regardless. Easier access to divorce would be more practical and realistic: this remained part of the foundation of Harriet's dedication to greater rights for women, including suffrage. She had written commentaries about recent news from New York, where some town that most British had never heard of had witnessed a meeting for women's concerns and rights, with brilliant presentations by ladies named Elizabeth Stanton and Susan Anthony, while John had been most intrigued by how a literate former slave named Frederick Douglass had also attended. Women and anyone of non-European ancestry—those so often in some degree of bondage to those in power—were eloquently and rationally arguing in favour of something better, something the minority with wealth and authority would not give up willingly—one detail that Marx had gotten quite right.

As usual, John continued to try and think of whatever might lift his mood, and as so often his mind kept leading him back to curious blends of ethics and politics. He told the secretary he intended to remain at the office late, and read the proffered note.

\* \* \*

*1849.*

As for Harriet, she could hardly even come to terms with what was happening, nor contend well with her muddled and opposed feelings.

*Damn John anyway,* she thought anew, and it was not her husband against whom she silently raged. *He can be so blasted ignorant sometimes!* came the unbidden afterthought. She did not let herself consider how two men—intelligent, generous, fine role models of adult behaviour for her children—had each dedicated so much of himself to her, yet never before during all these years had she felt so uncomfortably wedged between them as she did now. She stared again at her husband's brow, less sweaty now, and a bit cooler to the touch. The children—more mature now—all continued to make their visitations, never seemingly from duty but from genuine filial love, which both of their parents deeply appreciated. Granted, Herby still lived with Mr Taylor, and had a brief though sadly vicious row with his younger brother, who, while also loving his father, stood accused of preferring the company of Mr Mill. Youngest Lily felt trapped in the whole mess, breaking up said fraternal row by pointing out that she loved both the 'leading men' in her life and refused to accept guilt over sharing her affections with them. It marked quite an independent statement for a young woman.

*Lily accepted it wholly rationally,* Harriet thought, knowing that it was part of her daughter's perceived duty. Harriet took pride in how smoothly Lily navigated complicated adult emotions, trying to ignore her usual resentment over how society told women to feel, and for whom to feel it. Her clinging to the 'Old Faith' can hardly have helped in that regard, despising women as it does, but at least it offers Lily her strong moral compass. She wondered again at how Lily balanced it all, yet her daughter had emerged as probably the most rational, even the most intelligent, of the trio of Taylor offspring.

Harriet ran a hand over her husband's still slightly fevered visage, recalling the first times she ever did so, back when the two of them had shared real passion and hope for an extensive future together. She admitted—only ever to herself—that it might have been easier for all if her husband had simply ignored the jibes and prodding of his stupid club members, or male relatives, or whomever else had suggested that it was acceptable—necessary, even!—for middle- and upper-class men to continue to slake their sexual thirsts, most often at the expense of lower-class women. Even outside of marriage vows. Even if they had found happiness and sexual gratification through those same vows. Even if the men had children. And even if Mr Taylor's own bloody physician had 'prescribed' such activities. 'Modern' medicine clearly had some ways to go just yet; Harriet raged at how the profession emphasised the treatment of male issues, tending to disparage the concerns of women as suffering from 'hysterics.'

But now Harriet empathised with both her husband, and even with the whore—or whores—with whom he had dallied all those years past.

The pseudo-treatments for syphilis still served as an awkward example, and of course had done nothing but alleviate occasional pain, and perhaps helped reduce physical signs of outbreaks—one's shame could manifest itself externally, after all—but the dreaded 'pox' of sexuality remained with Harriet and always would. She had attempted, with highly mixed results, to broach the delicate topic of the disease with each of her children in turn, never very favourably:

Herby had blamed her, then wept, then stormed out of her presence, since men were supposed to remain 'in control' and not cry. Haji had taken the information in stoically, as was his wont; his relative silence on the topic then and later was almost worse. And Lily had cried, hugged her mother tightly, made a point of gently facing her father with the information—Mr Taylor had looked abashed, then ashamed, and then just hung his head in defeat. Harriet had cried herself then, wanting to take away the pain of what was ultimately a simple mistake, a transgression, away from them all. That damnable disease had hurt each of them, and she had finally moved past wanting to blame or hate anyone for it. Even the prostitutes were hardly culpable, not really, existing on the fringes of 'polite' society to offer services mostly against their will, or at least their better judgement. Harriet could not imagine a single little girl anywhere thinking, 'Oh, I cannot wait to be grown up enough to accept money for illicit loveless sex from a stranger who might beat or rape or infect or murder me for my trouble, then take my money as well!' This was just the sort of situation that Ms Wollstonecraft and Ms De Gouges had railed against half a century ago!

*Enough, enough now. Your husband likely has little time left, and still needs you, despite the disaster you've both made of everything.* It felt strange how a marriage might be continued, however precariously, via distance, even in this age of rapid communications—the newer telegraphy was astounding—and Harriet had posted letters to her creative husband from the lovely Basque town of Pau, while she had travelled there with John and Lily. Even on the Continent, news of Mr Taylor's rapidly declining health could reach her with previously unimagined alacrity, compelling a hurried return voyage home. They rushed hectically through the rest of France, sailing from Calais.

Harriet rose, walked into the large, tastefully decorated bathroom her husband had ordered, though she rarely visited it, since this was not the home she had ever shared with him, not the home in which the pair of them had proudly welcomed each of their children in turn, not the one in which she first met John Stuart Mill.

She had to grasp the countertop with the ornate sink, next to the specially built longer bathtub for more relaxing soaks, just to keep herself upright. She was swooning but also refusing to faint. She hated even the thought of fainting: for her, it was too strong and yet too false a sign of the females of the species trying to get attention, though she had once tried to laugh that sentiment off, making a comment about how short of breath the males of the species might find themselves if compelled to wear corsets.

But now Harriet truly was trying to remain on her delicate if sometimes clumsy feet. She glanced at her haggard, exhausted image in the reflecting glass above the porcelain sink, once again unsure of how she should feel about yet another death that had struck close to home, and as usual relegating her own symptoms to the back of her mind. She had syphilis; she had done as much as she thought possible to resign herself to that ugly truth, and her occasional fits of coughing, headaches, fevers, or combinations thereof—including the periodic trouble maintaining her balance walking—would just have to be endured.

They had not made it back across the Channel by the time her father, Mr John Hardy, had himself died during this disturbing year. And Harriet, upon returning home to care for her husband instead, found herself isolated even from family planning of the memorial service! Her mother attempted to bridge the emotional gaps amongst her brood: three of eight of the Hardy children had died by now, and the paterfamilias had left his own house very much in order. Harriet had felt both left out—ignoring crass comments even from her own siblings about just why it had taken her so long to even reach England and the Hardy home—and also relieved to not have to take the key decisions, knowing that such awaited her after the death of her husband.

The guilt that had followed her from port to home dissipated upon entering to find her siblings gazing at her judgementally, her mother thankfully more accepting. Harriet made simple niceties, her own children even pleased to see aunts and uncles and precious few cousins again: modern families seemed to be 'drifting,' a paradox during a time when the world continued to shrink via the steamship and the railroad, but many made excuses to avoid seeing relatives who might live just a village or two away. Now emphasis was placed on going elsewhere to make one's name or fortune or just to escape from family.

Harriet knew that she corresponded to the last of these, though she had in fact worked for years to maintain ties with the Hardy clan, even if it sometimes felt as tenuous as Mill's relations with his own family. The Hardys had come together as a unit at the death of poor brother John way back in '25, strengthening those family ties and yielding vague promises, the same with Thomas four years later in '29; part of Harriet's by now scholarly-level medical research remained driven by the impetus to want to learn more about the consumption that had claimed both young men's lives. And the likes of Easter and Christmas dinners had actually kept the families largely gathered at each other's homes; she and Mr Taylor had hosted more than one of each since then, though she silently chastened herself for the thought: a handful of such parties over a period of decades hardly signals excessive familial loyalty.

Be that as it may, Harriet still had trouble with that trickiest of Christian sentiments: forgiveness. The Taylor children tallied it up to life in the hectic Capital, but amongst themselves knew better, and their preferences for each parent.

That irksome trait of forgiving had eventually helped corrupt Harriet's relationship with her father, and now a fuller reconciliation was of course impossible. It went back to the much less expected death of another brother, William.

*Is it so wrong to confess having a favourite family member?* Harriet had mused in her old room, tears falling onto her diary pages. Dear sweet William, who had looked out for his sisters more than his brothers. Harriet had been in her early teens when illness took those other lads from the family, and she had missed William more than the others. She had wept too, when Will had arrived home to announce his enlistment 'into the proud tradition of the Royal Navy,' beaming and full of pride.

Their parents had made their own reservations clear: military service could of course be hazardous, though no one mentioned that despite stereotypes, more military casualties for any nation occurred from diseases than from the intentional violence of other human beings. Still, Mum and Papa had asked: the Navy? While Will had expressed earlier boyhood dreams of a life of adventure, social stigma remained such that military service in general, and with the Royal Navy in particular, was generally perceived as a rather backward step for a member of 'an up-and-coming family,' in their father's words.

Yet they had come around, realising their third son could use uniformed service as a way into an intriguing medical career—Will had reminded Father of his own curious choice of a health-related profession—and Will became Dr William Hardy, Royal Navy Surgeon.

The family had divided much more sharply regarding the young surgeon's later decisions, however.

Sometimes distant military service led to extended periods of residency in faraway, even exotic, lands. Such was how empires were built and maintained, and William savoured what became several years in Italy. Harriet would regale John whenever a letter arrived home, and took no small pride in the belief—true, as it transpired—that William wrote more to her than anyone else in the family, and John simply loved hearing about more places he longed to visit himself, even if William shared much less interest in the treasures of Roman antiquity than his younger sister and her paramour.

So parental approval might have gotten back on more secure footing, save for Emilia, whom Harriet had been enchanted to get to know during the '39 sojourn to the Continent and their time in Italy prior to venturing into Austria. She was a lovely, charming, unassuming young lass, clearly adoring of her proper 'Eenglish' husband, the world's most dextrous surgeon, to hear her tell it. And Will was already making noises about retiring from the Navy to practice his speciality in his beloved's homeland.

It was not consumption for a change, but Will's sudden death perhaps proved too much for the Hardy couple: all three elder sons now deceased, leaving three younger sons and two wayward daughters. And Harriet had truly believed that she offered a legitimate plea to Father by simply soliciting, 'Dear Papa, what shall you do for poor Emilia?' The young woman's own family was less well off financially, trusting that her well-earning husband would have provided for her: Italian laws regarding women and inheritance were even more backwards and restrictive than English ones, to Harriet's ire. Still, Harriet had not sought a confrontation.

Yet her father's explosion, particularly now with hindsight and years of thought, seemed to Harriet nothing other than another male assault on a woman in need of help, as well as a lesser attack on a daughter only interested in another's welfare.

Thus that sudden dreadful response of Father's: leaving a poor widow to fend for herself; displaying his own latent bigotry towards foreigners — 'bloody typical English xenophobia,' Harriet had ranted at her father, earning incredulous gasps from her sisters and mother, and a potent slap — the first ever — from her suddenly outraged father; and his clear refusal to assist the young woman in any way, had left Harriet dumbstruck. She had taken to sending occasional funds to Italy on Emilia's behalf, opting to ignore the added headache of hoping for responsible currency-exchangers and including folded up notes well secured in sealed letters, though this meant it had to be done less often: coinage would be easier for its lesser value, but the added weight would ironically make it costlier to post, with the added disadvantage of being more obvious and thus tempting within its temporary envelope home. Eventually the replies stopped coming, Harriet wondering if poor Emilia had moved, was too ashamed to reply in thanks, or something else; she had not sent anything towards her former foreign sister-in-law for several years now.

Even then, Lily of all people had understood the situation, as with that facing Harriet's dear sister Caroline, 'Carry' to Lily. Beyond the callous abuse of a wife who had begun to feel a stranger to them both remained her continued defence of the man! This had been the equally callous treatment of Aunt Caroline by none other than Grandpapa

Hardy, Harriet's beloved father, the then-retired male midwife. He had become severe enough after the death of William, and Lily's Mum had worked to forgive her father for such insensitivity, since he had been complaining by then of his own apparent ills. But whatever he may have had, medically speaking, passed without further incident, and his asinine, misogynist, irrational — Harriet had run out of invective adjectives for a spell — horse-arsed — this last coming from Lily — attitude suggesting his daughter might have somehow deserved such treatment at the hands of her husband was far too much. Harriet had barely spoken to him since. And her own mother, Mrs Harriet Hardy, while thankfully not as defensive of her husband as Carry had become of hers, remained too dedicated an apologist for Harriet to feel welcome at her parents' home.

As for Emilia, she had come to feel as far removed from Harriet's father as her own father had. Each person was a lingering shadow, a sometimes pesky and guilty spectre to torment Harriet's feelings.

Harriet toggled her memories, a trick John had helped her to improve, though there remained instances when even he could not pull it off, and there was wry amusement in knowing that they shared the same basic triggers: family members. The worst guilt was reserved for lost family members: John, too, had experienced the loss of beloved siblings, the anguish hardly assuaged by over-bearing parents. And now they had each said farewell forever to their fathers, in each case in absentia.

So Harriet sought solace in other recollections. The rest of that marvellous trip had previously been like a tick-off list of all things great and Italian: Pisa, Naples, Padua, Florence, Rome. Harriet had lost herself in Tuscan art in the famed Florence gallery, and John and Lily had all but raced her to get through the Duomo, the magnificent and easily spotted cathedral. Lily had described feeling closer to God just being in there, especially after they ascended the old stairs to gaze upon one of the Continent's great cities.

Even getting from one place to another was a delight for its own sake, the road linking Florence to Bologna especially so, though rains plagued their side-venture to Venice, not helped by Lily accidentally breaking a piece freshly made by that city's renowned glass-blowers. That old man had proven forgiving, however, and not just because they paid to replace the item and bought a trio of parti-coloured hanging glass balls to 'accentuate the lovely sunlight in my room, Mummy.'

But now memories of such fabled sites could be painful for Harriet: only John could still make her smile, trying with his bungled Italian—his French was so much better!—to remind her of cherished thoughts of her late brother, who had mastered the language, accent and all, to make himself 'fully worthy of such a fine lady as my beloved Emilia.'

That was a bonny way to remember William: at ease in the stiff dark blue naval overcoat, epaulettes denoting his captain's rank, an arm draped just as easily and lovingly around thin Emilia's shoulder, her eyes beaming up at him. It was too damnably insensible a loss, the sort of event that led Harriet to rave at God anew and wonder how her daughter could delusionally find solace in such a Being, whilst she in turn felt sympathy at her mother's wrath.

And thus did Harriet Taylor find herself, some months after the death of her father, distrusting her family and oft-times the whole world, yet curiously anticipating whatever time might be left with the man she had chosen to wed.

*Father may have become a bastard later,* she thought morosely, *but at least he never forced me into marriage. And now my home life becomes a perverse source of comparison with the family life of John Mill...*

*No, as I say, enough! John, despite my lapsing into rage, comprises little part of this.* She recalled how just last year she had visited this home, with a particular purpose in mind. She had naively believed familial troubles had retreated mostly behind them, each person involved settling into some kind of uniformity, and she had further thought her idea a good one, bespeaking that 'shrinking world' that the likes of the new trans-continental telegraph cables had helped to make possible. Mr Taylor and his family had good heads for business, she knew quite well, but sometimes news from afar might shine a light towards new options.

She'd simply showed herself in. Of course she had keys to the house, as did the children. She had located her husband in his study, a fine home office which could double as a smoking or gaming room, replete with dark-stained bookshelves climbing almost to the ceiling; plus a comfortable burgundy-coloured velvet sofa; a sizable globe — illustrated from the early modern period — and a small writing desk. The warm bookshelves contained numerous volumes about Mr Taylor's speciality, including rarer books gathered from the world's materia medica. Under different circumstances, Harriet mused, her husband and her lover might have bonded over a shared interest in history.

It was a lovely room, Harriet thought again presently, looking up from her husband's exhausted countenance to glance about, recalling her ignored recommendations from that earlier day. Maybe Mr Taylor had already wholly distrusted his wife by then.

Harriet recalled that the adventurous — foolhardy? — souls who chose to brave the still wild realm of California — mountains, valleys, forests, rivers, teeming with all sorts of wildlife — needed supplies, no matter how long their stay. Newspapers had given the impression that some folks, probably too many, were grabbing at any form of passage that they could and hoping they would be able to somehow acquire necessities later. But this ignored the most basic principle of supply versus demand, as well as the simple realities of shipping to new and tiny settlements like San Francisco.

'Do you suppose this California discovery will make any change in the value of money for some time to come?' Harriet had asked her husband. He had shrugged, taking a moment to truly acknowledge her. The boys had had the day off, seeing to their own more urban adventures; they both still loved the City's numerous parks, a taste they had acquired as much from Mr Mill as from their father. Lily had remained upstairs, content to pore through her growing collection of books, lately devoting more effort to recent fiction than to the rigours of history and philosophy.

'If said discovery continues I suppose it will lower the value of fixed incomes, but I suppose it may benefit trade? If I were a young man I might go there very quickly.'

Mr Taylor turned, offering the hint of a smile to his stranger-wife. 'You surely do not mean actual supply, do you, Mrs Taylor?' He gave the address easily, with no more tone of betrayal like the phrase once held for them. Certain realities by then were habitual.

'Indeed I am, John,' she answered. 'Consider for a moment just what types of supplies will be needed for all of those. 'The Times' has reported newfound wealth in a relatively unexplored region.'

"The Guardian' has shown more restraint,' Mr Taylor parried. 'Those reporters have suggested that news of all this shiny mineral wealth are likely rather exaggerated. For that matter, the 'Manchester Weekly Times' recently showed the wisdom of wondering what the economic effects of "too much gold" might be on global markets. It reminds one of how Spain once spent its grand empire into virtual bankruptcy simply by importing precious metals too quickly and in great volumes from the New World,' he added proudly.

*He has always been well prepared; one must credit him that.* 'Aside from those amounts "liberated" by English privateers,' she had said, smiling as well, always glad to share in intelligent conversation for its own sake. 'Be that as it may, however, the most probable chance is that the gold will not continue below the surface. Meanwhile there must be fine opportunities of placing goods, and especially drugs, in the placiemento.' She paused for a moment. 'They'll need pharmaceutical agents, Mr Taylor: salicylic acid, glycerol, morphine, quinine. It just makes sound business sense, and it does not seem that the Mexicans or Indians have ever been able to sell such chemicals to Europeans migrating to the New World.' She had no idea what Mexicans or Indians might use as medicinals. Perhaps she should travel so far, a pursuit akin to consumptives being told by their wishful physicians to seek 'healthier air' in drier or damper climes—no one knew for sure—and of course this applied to those who could afford such trips to foreign sanatoria.

Indeed a prior letter from her, Mr Taylor recalled, had asked flat out, 'Are you going to send out quinine?' He preferred not to dwell on that letter, coming as it had from a charming locale overlooking the Pyrenees in Spain. Mr Taylor had long since given up on romantic notions of extensive travels with his wife—they had once dreamt of some Empire Tour together, perhaps with the children—and he still could feel the intrigue of his eminently practical wife with a head for business and sums, as well as one who had become so well read, though much of her reading had come inspired by another John.

He also no longer felt threatened by her extensive research into materia medica in the first place, augmented as it had been for so long by her exhaustive search for a more efficacious treatment for syphilis. She had once promised to share such insights with him if she ever found them, but no damnable physician or chemist had ever come forth with a better solution than the brutality of guaiacum or mercury or even wild pansies, known to his profession as heartsease. Mr Taylor had never arrived at any better treatment, either.

Back in the present, Harriet's journal entry had just received a pained yet honest entry, immediately following one of the minutes-long periods of Mr Taylor recalling his whereabouts and condition, and appearing obviously pleased to be greeted by his wife's warm expression. 'He is in good spirits and today almost free from any pain,' Harriet penned. 'The opium must be right,' as his doctor 'orders him to take it incessantly in almost any quantity.' She paused to consider this: what kind of mental relief must it be to someone who knew they were quickly dying to receive the odd prescription to essentially numb the intense pain as much as they wished, though it dulled the senses?

Harriet continued: 'And though theretofore he could not take any opium without headache, now he takes it all day without any apparent effect, not even sleepiness; there it must be right.' *Let it help soothe his pain,* she pleaded again, refusing to feel guilty as she could hear in her mind the words of her lover about ancient thinkers and old Bentham about pain and pleasure and how to minimise the former while emphasising the latter. She truly hoped such simple hedonism was now aiding her husband in his final days.

Mr Taylor seemed so weak now, a year after his wife's suggestion.

He had not acted on it, and she would not rub salt in the financial wound of a missed business venture, knowing that the 'rush' in California had in fact exploded. Only a select lucky few had returned from the hills and streams and forests with their lustrous newfound wealth — soft and dense by metallic standards yet so curiously prized by humans, but that had done very little to slow the onslaught of humanity into a part of the world previously known really only to groups of those same Mexicans and Indians, and the local wildlife.

Harriet felt wry amusement at how gold had no intrinsic value: no other species cared about it at all. Even now, while the 'rush' still developed its own self-fulfilling speed and prophecy, the Native peoples of parts of California, along with Mexicans who had lived there in a remote part of the Spanish Empire, and even Chinese settlers and traders who had worked with their American counterparts since the Treaty of Paris, all had to compete with the mad and sometimes violent behaviour of those who thought they might get rich by searching in the right place. Mad as hops, Lily might say, preferring the slang of the young.

But for now, here remained the waning flesh of a once proud man, draining too thinly to the horrid diagnosis of rectal cancer. Harriet vehemently disagreed with another asinine medical assumption of their time, having found nothing in the literature, not even in the respected British journal 'The Lancet,' to suggest a connection between cancer and syphilis: no causal link existed for them, only stupid old folk tales. During Mr Taylor's last period of relative lucidity, she had kept working to make him understand that cancer was no one's fault, that neither of them could possibly be culpable for his fate.

'R-read to me,' came the faint whispery voice from the bed. She thought he slept.

Harriet took her husband's cool and clammy hand. 'Read to you?' she repeated, just savouring the words. When had they last shared something so easy, yet so intimate?

A slight nod, clearly an expenditure of energy for the poor disabled man. 'What would you like, John?' she asked, again not noticing the slip into more familiar address.

'Trust,' he struggled, 'trust your j-judgement. Surprise me.'

Harriet could have wept, suddenly wishing all of their children to this room. She thought she could hear Lily's padded steps from above their heads and just down the hall.

'Well then,' she said, 'let me take a look about here,' as she released the hand, offering it a reassuring squeeze whilst placing it almost reverently on the duvet.

'Let's see. Does anything in particular strike your fancy?' It took her a moment to remember that she had not asked him a question like that for years.

'No philosophy, d-damn it.'

His vehemence alarmed her, until she saw him smiling. On his deathbed, and this extremely accepting gentleman—the term had altered with the Reform Act of 1832 so that it referred now more to behaviour and less to nobility or privilege—was making jokes!

'No philosophy, Husband. Understood.' She looked around the small collection of quality-bound books found in this bedroom she had never shared with him, her eyes alighting upon a history. "The Decline and Fall of the Roman Empire?" She smiled as he shook his head, trying not to notice how weak the gesture had become.

'I agree. It's quite detailed, though some are beginning to wonder if the logic might apply to a more recent empire.' She thumbed her way over several other volumes, most still feeling new. She felt vaguely heartened by the books being in the bedroom, suggesting night-time reading without having the books on display in a drawing or smoking room instead: like many children, seen but not heard, sources of pride but without interaction.

Lily had once indicated her frustration with the families of friends. Harriet had mainly been pleased to hear of actual friends, but her daughter had opined that, 'These Catholics: they all have exquisite copies of the Bible, but they never read them.'

Harriet kept smiling, now espying works by Dickens. She'd forgotten Mr Taylor was a fan and had, like Mr Mill, met the novelist, liking the man as well as the author.

She swallowed, her throat feeling lumpy. She and her husband had once debated the merits of prose, himself at the time roughly condemning 'escapist claptrap,' while she had defended stories as offering often more truth than newspapers, especially if one considered that people paid attention to stories, even mythologised them. He'd been horrified at her suggestion that the world's religions had begun that way.

As she pulled down a copy of 'The Posthumous Papers of the Pickwick Club,' still recognising it though its lengthier title had been shortened in this recent edition to simply 'The Pickwick Papers,' she remembered his feelings changing regarding 'simple' stories: as their children had arrived into the world and grown of sufficient ages to appreciate them, she had sometimes found her husband reading translations of the Dane, Hans Christian Andersen, to them at bedtime. Lily loved 'The Snow Queen,' and the boys had giggled over 'The Emperor's New Clothes' and 'The Tinderbox.'

'Dickens?' This time he nodded. She placed the book on her lap, holding it open with one hand while holding anew his still clammy hand with the other, and began reading about a group of male Londoners and their sojourns from the city to get some sense of how their fellow Englishmen actually lived.

Later, as John Taylor fell asleep during Harriet's reading of the hazardous adventures of Pickwick's protagonist, whose talents with firearms and horses alike were sufficiently poor as to become dangerous, she recalled Mr Mill's confessions of similar ineptitudes.

She found herself reassured by her husband's soft snoring, not having stirred during her reading. She sighed, placed the book on the small nightstand by the bed, and turned out the decorative kerosene lantern, itself one of a set: wedding gifts from her parents.

Harriet willingly granted her assent to her husband's request. It felt the least she could do for him by then. John Mill, bless him, never faulted her for it, and never expressed any resentment towards his erstwhile manly competitor, either. So be it: the 'Principles of

Political Economy' would contain no reference to herself as co-author, muse, inspiration, or any such. She had no conception then of how the elimination of her name from a book in which she had actively participated, done, truthfully, to satisfy her husband's relatively mild request, would in fact set an unfortunate later precedent.

That omission to the listing of the book's authorship also had the feeling of a final request, and this would remain with Harriet for the remainder of her own days. Harriet would remember Wednesday, 18 July, 1849. Her husband, beloved by many, dutiful father, tolerant and fiscally liberal husband, loyal son, respected London apothecary, died in relative peace and comfort. His estranged wife had arrived in Paris on May 9, then at the Taylor home at Kent Terrace just five days later, thereby having devoted two months to fretting over him and helping ease his passing into whatever followed the earthly existence of these curious creatures calling themselves humans.

That Harriet had not maintained the slightest faith in certain traditional post-life belief scenarios had sometimes bothered her, and she kept them largely private. John Mill, more socially wise for once, had not discussed the likes of such beliefs with her for some time, guessing correctly that the death of John Taylor could not be interpreted as the impetus for such talks, however intriguing. As ever, though, her well-worn and loved diary received plenty of input on the subject.

'Thank (I was going to say God but cannot use that form so repugnant more than ever to my present feelings)... why should he have these torments to endure!' she wrote in a fury, seeing the point of her pen bending in protest, not caring about the depth of the imprint on paper nor the blots of ink spilling onto it. 'What good to anybody is all this—he never hurt or harmed a creature on Earth.' Harriet's tears fell, mingling with the marred paper. 'If they want the life why can't they take it—what useless torture is all this!'

She slammed the book shut and let the tears come again, thankful no one was there to see her, though the lads were due home that afternoon to help with the arrangements. She had been the only person in the room, holding Mr Tay- —no, John's hand—as the light seemed to slowly wink from his eyes forever.

Stoic as most of the stubborn men in her life, Harriet's husband had seemingly not disclosed just how ill he truly was until rather late in the game, to borrow one of the inept phrases their sons liked to use. Regardless of his frustratingly male disinclination to be more forthcoming, she nonetheless marked his bravery up until the very end.

That of course left the mundane, the practical matters. Sometimes Harriet wondered if the recently deceased had it comparatively easy: at least they did not have to contend with the minutiae of modern post-mortem paperwork. And in the ongoing comedy of errors that Harriet Taylor sometimes regarded her life, she knew that her lover could act as the most rational, and queerly detached, source of help with composing a suitable sermon.

Harriet apologised to John for having castigated him. The day after the other John's death, she had silently railed at Mr Mill for remaining so damnably calm the whole time: neither pulling his hair like the ancient Celts over someone's death, nor weeping, nor, surely, cheering another's misfortune. Still, John wisely opted to avoid the funeral service of Mr John Taylor, Apothecary, Dutiful Son and Loving Father, so Harriet did not have to broach such an awkward topic with him. And she didn't even notice how a phrase like 'Doting Husband,' or some such, had gone absent from the newspaper announcements of the man's passing, and only later wondered who had been responsible. Her father, as she eventually learned, planning early. Even in death, loved ones could surprise.

The service itself proved quiet, given the tension. Unscrupulous newsmen—no women here like Ms Martineau, Harriet hoping female members of their invasive profession would display more sympathy—had naturally gotten wind of the event and made their own forays in the name of a good story. Mr Taylor was known and respected, Mr Mill more so, Mrs Taylor somewhere in between with regard to publicity. Still, while Harriet could at least comprehend gossip, had contributed to it on occasion, she would never forgive these uncouth beasts for attempting to interview family members at the Taylor home.

And the children! Surely they should never be subjected to such tactless questions. 'Mrs Taylor, is it true that your late husband's generous hospitality with this house has gone unappreciated by you? You don't even live here yourself, is that not true?'

Such had proven impudent enough, and Harriet hated that she felt a need to not meet her own children's vaguely accusatory stares as these damnable reporters paced outside the house. They lingered for several days following the funeral and burial, but then finally vanished to pursue their publicly-fed privacy-invasions elsewhere. Harriet had taken pride in Herby for threatening legal action the day before their collective disappearance.

What Harriet needed most of all, though, was not just John's aid, but his quiet and reserved strength. As with his input regarding the recent and painful details of putting a person to permanent rest—for which she adored the man, she had to admit, despite the circumstances—she still had to find a way to deal with her villainous brother-in-law, whose violently spousal proclivities had shown no sign of abating. And that nefarious troublesome issue of the trusteeship had returned with equal force. Her brother Arthur remained in Australia, quite enjoying his new life if letters were anything to go by, despite the more than two months they still required to cross the world's oceans.

But the cursed trusteeship: at its core, the issue remained, Harriet actively and continually campaigning—not necessarily nor always with her sister's aid—to rid that sister, who herself continued to want to both dodge the issue and not stir up any more discord with her hateful husband, of said husband's status as his wife's trustee. In practical terms, this meant that this drunken brute who thought nothing of berating and beating his wife whilst not caring what anyone else thought—such was Harriet's gentle assessment—wielded not just legal power over the ever-more-cringing Caroline, to whom Harriet kept struggling to maintain sisterly fealty, but also economic power over the late Mr John Taylor's settlement of his estate regarding his widow and their three children!

As she had phrased it to John, just days after Mr Taylor's funeral, 'My children and I stand to lose most of what we should have, my Love, and in addition, my loathsome brother-in-law could legally keep battering his wife until she ends up crippled or worse.'

That was the most infuriating part for her: not the financial implications, but that she and her sister barely spoke now, barely recognised one another, and Caroline remained at her husband's mercy. Harriet was beginning to comprehend the American 'temperance movement' they had heard about, the intention to reduce or even eliminate alcoholic beverages; perhaps they had heard of the dreaded Arthur Ley and his vicious propensities! Yet Herby had recently visited America and seemed unmoved by most of the experience, largely regarding 'the Colonies' in the same patronising manner that many in their social circles did, so what matter if they banned liquor?

If wifely abuse wasn't enough, Harriet had further fumed, 'The bastard and Mr Taylor never even liked one another, for goodness' sake!' It was maddening, the most personal issue of women's relative lack of real power that Harriet had ever encountered, and she had been fighting it since '42 — since that shameful day at the cricket park when she had felt so helpless and her sister so embarrassed to be seen. And while Harriet had become quite a dedicated nurse during Mr Taylor's final weeks, whenever she thought of her husband's lack of attention to this issue — 'Be still, dear Wife, Mr Ley is truly dedicated to family, when all is said and done' — Harriet had lashed out at anyone nearby. In truth, part of her fury directed at the hapless John Mill came from that feeling of impotence, of the uncertainty about whether she and her children would be provided for, and if so, how they would manage to finagle financial assistance from the 'drunken brute' who represented, for Harriet, the worst that the 'stronger sex' had on offer.

Matters were hardly assuaged when Herby, despite his typical rational judgement, clearly sided with his uncle regarding this sensitive issue that the family was desperate to keep out of the papers.

He even returned early from his sojourn to America to make sure his voice counted. Perhaps want of privacy was part of Herby's reasoning, and the children knew full well how often the name 'Taylor' had appeared in London papers, tawdry and respectable ones alike. Harriet kept hoping differently, almost praying on one occasion that her seemingly wayward eldest child remained ignorant of the obvious abuse of the inheritance, which might drive the wedge further between himself and his mother.

John had already learned to not refer to Caroline Ley's suffering as an example of what he kept labelling physical harm. 'Of course it is! What else could it be!' Harriet snapped at him once, at that silly cricket match that Caroline had sought to avoid due to the clear evidence of punches on her face. It was the first time Harriet had heard John use the phrase, and she finally just now remembered it. John had kept his mouth shut about the lingering emotional harm done.

Even what comfort she could find in her own battered feelings was not assuaged by the knowledge that John had already contributed much financially to their relationship over the years. Not all of it: they had discussed the assets Mr Taylor had made available in his curious though doomed attempts to win back his wife's affections, and had both concluded that it might make matters worse if John was perceived to be funding the likes of Continental travels himself, even though he could clearly afford to do so. For that matter, he too could have set up Harriet and the children in a new home, but that always seemed more like rubbing salt in the wound of adultery, and now that Mr Taylor had died, Harriet found she no longer felt so secure in that regard. In quieter moments, she mulled and raged over the possibility that part of the reason for attaching herself to this fight might hearken back to her strained relationship with her own father, who had revealed himself less than sympathetic to the plights of disenfranchised and otherwise needy women.

She knew John could fund them all for the rest of their lives, so that wasn't the issue. He likely would have acceded to providing for Emilia as well, though that lovely still-young Italian lass would just as likely refuse, wherever she was. What gnawed at Harriet was not John's focus on physical harm, nor even financial harm with the question of who should underwrite the continued adventures of a wayward wife. No, it amounted to emotional harm—mainly what she was doing to herself! How should she feel: for having strayed; for confusing her children such that they had grown into young adults taking sides; for working to publicly justify a new relationship; for writing 'controversial' work justifying better situations and statuses for women, and the poor, and the downtrodden, and those feeling the intrusive effects of an empire... and for trying to not despise herself for relying on the financial accommodations of two men, each of whom could afford for her to live at a stylish level most Londoners would consider extravagant?

Harriet had never quite gotten around to telling John that while she concurred with his assessment about what she should most likely do with her husband's money, she nonetheless had the same intense reservations about John himself, at least in terms of how he acquired his money. He continued to morally grapple with himself about the Company, even with signs pointing to slowly greater autonomy for the peoples of India—and other parts of said Empire—and his history of doing responsible work for it and them.

'Responsible' work might entail moral compromise, however. *Damn,* thought Harriet, *even I start to sound like that rabble-rouser Marx. Or Bentham!*

And Mr Marx would no doubt take pleasure in pointing out her financial discomfiture: perhaps the communistic solution would be to let Arthur Ley keep the whole messy pile and pay his way elsewhere and keep local distillers and brewers there running profitably until he drank himself to death.

*More social harm,* she could all but hear John say. No, that was no solution.

Harriet eventually confessed, only to John, that familial loyalty or no, she genuinely resented her eldest child taking the side of the reprehensible Mr Ley regarding the ugly trusteeship business. 'From what

I've managed to glean,' she said in tears one exhausting day, 'Herby has actually solicited aid from his Uncle Arthur—in Australia, no less!—apparently after Herby learned that we had looked into hiring a "remittance man."'

John had looked down and shaken his head, his the expression that either acknowledged defeat or offered a pause to countermand with something. Harriet did not prefer either right then. 'So Herbert seeks to maintain Mr Ley as trustee, then?'

Harriet wiped her rebellious eyes and nodded. 'If I understand correctly, a remittance agent tends to be the metaphorical "black sheep" of a well-off family, paid—bribed—to disappear, something now easier as Britain's influence has grown.'

'That sounds accurate,' John had answered. 'But how does that affect Mr Ley keeping the trusteeship?'

Anyone so practical had to prove annoying sometimes, though Harriet found herself grinning for reasons she could not understand. 'My mother's idea was for my brother-in-law to be bought off in a sense, get him sent out like some perverse pensioner, all the way to Australia, where my true brother could, I suppose, keep eyes more clearly focused on him and how he spends what should remain part of our family instead. So my brother, or perhaps some more locally hired remittance man, could fill that role.'

This time practicality offered reassurance: 'That would surely get him away from your sister, which I suspect your mum desires as fervently as you do. It's strange to think of hiring a person just to mind another,' he added, forgetting for the moment that he and Harriet and their families of course came from families that had for decades hired 'help.'

It was also strange how John Mill could mix familiar and slangy terms like 'mum' in with his usual penchant for more formal speech. 'John, just hold me. I'm tired. I'm tired of being powerless, tired of worrying about what others think. My love for you and my children are the purest things in my life. I continually wish Caroline could find the wherewithal to leave that crude waste of food,' she pulled her head away from John's chest to find him snickering at her description, 'but at the moment I'm just too damned tired.'

She fell asleep resting on him in his bed, she too worn out for their own special blends of lovemaking, he just glad to have her back in his home.

*  *  *

*From the journal of Harriet Taylor: December, 1849*
My goodness, what an annus horribilis! I believe I can safely and legitimately claim to have finally calmed down, though I believe apologies are not in order for my behaviour this year, regardless of what certain individuals—names presently withheld—may think.

If anyone remembers my work years from now, perhaps I shall be recalled as some annoying shrew or disloyal roaming wife, or a modern thinker in petticoats or corset, whilst my own preference would be to have someone simply remember me as a dedicated mother and intellectual partner.

Yes of course, dear Diary—the intellectual partner of whom, precisely? All England seems to know the answer, has gone out of its Royal way to remind me and those I care about on a regular basis.

But I also did love my 'first' John—the bright young man who dazzled my parents and then myself—the successful and compassionate apothecary, who accepted credit from clients and patients far more often than I had previously been led to understand, having died in the home he purchased in a doomed attempt to win me back. Bless the man for that, though I recall chastising him for the practice many years ago, when we were first creating our own family together. Now the money seems less important, and the man left behind virtually nothing by way of debt. And now I shall miss him.

Are you surprised, faithful Diary? Perhaps we have different loves—lovers, too—at different stages of our lives, for different reasons. I despised John Taylor for many—too many!—years, and yet at the end, sitting there reading Dickens and Austen to him, mutual forgiveness may have emerged at last. That was how it felt the last time he squeezed my hand and looked at me, not fearful of death or mindful of the Heaven for which he always vaguely hoped—sometimes reminded of such by our precocious daughter—but fearful instead of my still blaming him. I just can't anymore. Sometimes tears no longer flow, though it is equally true to note that occasionally anger no longer comes either.

Rest now, Husband, I beg you. Walk with God, if that be your wish. Accept your fault-ridden wife as she is and find Peace. You deserve such.

Yet I cannot count myself a sinner for the second John either, much as Society may wish to do so on my late husband's behalf, or just because we have lived in sin together for years. I treated John hideously for much of this year, and now both of us must work to put that behind us where the whole mess belongs. To be fair, he never failed when I needed him most, when I would have pushed him away or yelled at him, or transformed guilt over John Taylor into rage at John Mill. My parents and dear abused sister would doubtless say that one must hesitate to trust the rantings of a woman, and for much of my early life I would have agreed. But I have seen men, still the alleged stronger sex, brought to weepy pieces, and often by precisely the same details and events which bring women to their tearful and screeching knees.

For all the news this year, one can hardly credit my husband having made me sole beneficiary of his assets!—homes, the apothecary shop—his parents disapproved, though I say without malice that it was never their decision. The children have all chimed in with their own views, and none of them have proven greedy 'for Daddy's money'—or things—some favourite pieces will of course be carted off by each, which pleases me, since I remain unsure what to do with many of them. It remains difficult enough for a woman to inherit at all: British legislation, from what I can glean of it, offers a piecemeal economic solution to thorny concerns like familial wealth—or in-law trusteeships. We may inherit—some; or own property—sometimes; or gain custody of children—quite rarely, and thank goodness the children are grown now: legally adults, even Lily. Women cannot understand the law, some foolish and unfair men will surely declare, though I do comprehend that the State of New York, recently famed for that magnificent-sounding conference on women's rights, also recently enacted a statute to permit women to inherit, and spend, and collect rents, and enter into contracts, and even file legal suits.

American women in other words, or at least those in New York, that once rebellious Colony where our own General Howe once sent General Washington fleeing, are now being treated as autonomous persons! I almost have to pick up this well-worn little tome of mine and hug it for unabashed joy. When I finish writing tonight I shall treat Lily to that gleeful crushing embrace also. She too has kept abreast of such wondrous events.

 So now I can similarly celebrate my lover's recent success with our curious text on politics and economics and—oh, dash it all, it's a book about everything that keeps a modern society functioning! And it's very little to do with our own philosophical outlooks, making it all the more surprising. It sold fairly well last year but has done much better lately—perhaps the best way to keep a reading audience on its collective toes is to switch tactics, or genres in our case—and then notice how they keep biting.

Production—Distribution—Exchange—such were our broad titles of the key portions, with following sections about potential longer-term outcomes, and the perpetual question of governmental control or influence. We came a long way from the likes of Marx—indeed, Herr Marx referred to our views as too bourgeois—of course he would—and further opined how our separating the means of production from the means of distribution yielded a 'shallow syncretism.' I still wonder if the man even knows that John actually agrees with him about aspiring to freedom from a stifling wage relationship, though they part ways in terms of the moral character of the labourer.

That moral worth—yes, a risky and potentially patronising term, yet necessary nonetheless—of each individual emerges in our distinguishing between 'earned' and 'unearned' income, and we came intriguingly closer to a more socialistic outlook with the likes of caps on inheritances—definitely 'unearned!'—whilst reminding and explaining how taxes are necessary. Where else will money, that social fuel, come from, and we all must pay. We disagreed a bit more with this strange notion of income tax, John deciding that it seems to tax effort and ability, while I tend to remark that a more equitable society would tax its citizens mainly on their ability to pay. And the research into contemporary examples was much more me than John: New Lanark, a village woollen mill—what could be more English than the wool trade combined with factory production?; or the Leeds Flour Mill; the Rochdale Society of Equitable Pioneers—each with their own principles, and I wish I'd more time to interview some of them!

Those were the examples we wrote about, though I privately felt intrigued by other such groups, even if my draughts of news pieces about them we opted not to publish. One was the association of piano-makers, whose 'capacity for exertion and self-denial,' as I described them, enable profit-sharing and group ownership, a utilitarian answer to capital. I further worked on notes about whaling crews—the prac-tice of hunting the large but smart animals disturbs John for moral reasons—plus Parisian housepainters, Cornish miners, and ship crews trading between America and China. I was pleased to get to so many cultural perspectives, but again, we had to leave out something in the end...

Still, John also felt—still feels, truly—that Dear England remains largely unready for some of our ideas. Such is the nature of politi-cal philosophy: plenty of critiques of the status quo—where Marx shines—with an equal plenitude of alternatives, only a few of which if any are likely to be adopted by the society in which the author lives. John and I even had a short item appear in the 'Daily News' logically demonstrating that those who do not follow Christianity—how like us!—are not intrinsically immoral, and we also set about opposing the dreadful 'Jew Bill,' which surprised some, as the Bill would allow Jews in Parliament without swearing Christian faith, so we had to explain how our opposition was not Judeophobic but rather a reminder that said Bill makes no mention of 'sceptics and infidels… Hindoos, Buddhists, and Mahomedans.' We remain so afraid that we cannot come to agreement about how to even spell the names of those we barely understand!

As for empires, they do not permit divisions, never have, a lesson brought painfully home to us again this year, for the second time in just several years. And yet like my inner feelings and emotional attachments to certain men at different times, I dare not voice my opinions of this asinine and second war with the short-lived Sikh Empire in northern India, especially since my nation — my Empire? — no, never that! — emerged smelling like a full bouquet of roses. The Sikh Empire is dissolved, the British East India Company now controls the whole of the Punjab, never mind that its interests are purely mercantile, and most of its staff, including those occupying India, cannot be bothered to learn the first details about those over whom they now lord it all.

I hate this, I bloody well hate this all! And I don't care a shit who knows it! Small wonder John and I get ostracised, and even he hardly knows the true depth of my feelings on this issue. And now I have to struggle to avoid despising my own country and the corporation that has employed the man I love most in the world for many years. What am I to do? My dearest love works for that horrid company, a veritable empire unto itself!

No, none of this blaming will do, and whilst I've only witnessed dear John become truly emotionally worked up a handful of times — still very English, that man of mine, no matter how strong his contagious Francophilia — no, what we continue to seek entails inclusiveness, not leaving out others. John — and I myself, as I must confess at times — continue to learn that diversity is a genuine burden, but that it is absolutely vital as well. All our work, all our articles and editorials, and now books too, shall prove for naught unless we can keep getting others to think, no mean feat in itself. And with politics and economics — much more so than with, say, ethics and aesthetics — it has always been far easier to blame and to rationalise than to come together in shared humanity...

\* \* \*

*From the Diary of Helen Taylor:*
'Genuine concerns, would you not say, Reader? My mother's notes are of a woman indeed later called a mere 'philosopher in petticoats,' or the 'shrew' who shrivelled John Mill's manhood. But Mum was logical to the end: what progress might we make if electors and elected alike behaved likewise?

She did treat me to a 'crushing embrace' on that occasion. She wept whilst doing so, and I pretended not to notice. I would not ask her to suffer more by explaining herself to me.

\* \* \*

*1850 through 1851.*

Thus began a more determined and ongoing collaboration of John Mill and Harriet Taylor, with their unique blending of reason and outrage, a trait commented on by the intrigued Dickens among others, and begrudgingly by some of their political and moral adversaries. Multiple newsworthy pieces attributed to them both discussed current political issues and anything of 'moral worth,' which for John and increasingly for Harriet consisted of just about anything involving human behaviour and decision-making.

After the death early in the year of even more sensational writer Wordsworth, John confessed that perhaps poets, more than philosophers, could best express the states of humans, or at least of their feelings. One fellow philosopher, known for applying logic to linguistics—'Can that even be possible?' Harriet Grote crowed in amusement—had contributed. She had described John as 'born to read, not to write, poetry,' which Harriet found hilarious and brought a knowing grin to John's own mouth.

'True,' he conceded. 'Trust a true philosopher to tell it like it is with no adornment!' He admired that other thinker, another whom he never chanced to meet, and had no idea that said philosopher would become his first biographer.

It was also perhaps an ironic period for the lovers, since they systematically began to make themselves even scarcer to prying eyes, so perhaps opportunities to mix and mingle, even with like minds, became more challenging. They had to admit that not having their names and 'wanton behaviour' bandied about in newspapers offered some relief to the Taylor children, who continued to mourn their father's absence in their own ways.

Herby naturally took it the hardest, as the only one who had made a clear point of living with Mr Taylor for years. He had begun a half-hearted tutelage into his father's profession, but seemed to not wish to pursue it further now his father was gone. And his letter correspondences — often revealing anger towards Harriet and occasional jabs at John, despite liking the man — revealed a curious talent for writing. Harriet acknowledged the hostility and encouraged her son to try his hand more seriously, taking care to not judge ahead of time any specific genre or style. She and John certainly had encountered their share of writers! — novelists, abstract thinkers, poets, historians — whose works might elicit public welcome as inspiring or consequential, or just as often make a nervous public decry such writings as heretical or the work or lunatics or both.

'Plato commented on that once upon a time,' commented John in a festive mood, still liking positive reviews of his (and their) joint work while stepping back from the limelight. 'He fretted that once something was written down it took on a queer life of its own, with author and reader alike unable to really interact.'

'Is that not part of the objective?' Harriet asked.

'Not if people take writing as etched in stone: that's what makes Commandments and Zealots alike.'

Harriet admitted her eldest was his own man now, benefitting most from his father's inheritance, including the lovely home. Yet she heard from him rarely enough that any writing career remained an unknown entity. And she had to admire his filial loyalty, steaming back from America that time just as quickly as the new ships could carry him upon receiving a 'cable' about his father's perilous condition.

But now that he was back in England and seemingly inclined to remain, Herby kept his distance, emotional and spatial, from his mother. His undisguised alliance with the shameful Mr Ley only exacerbated matters, and during their infrequent meetings mother and son opted to mention that issue not at all.

The sense of divided loyalties and taking of sides felt horrible, though Harriet was most concerned with the longer-term effects on the children with each other. 'How will you manage with one another after I too am gone?' she had asked during a forcibly peaceful luncheon in one of the newer eateries near Piccadilly Circus. Meals out remained a largely novel experience, especially for women and especially at mid-day, with John remarking that a smaller establishment with lighter and less expensive fare, minimal if any wait staff, and offering business well before more traditional supper hours, was 'delightfully Roman.' To keep the peace that day, he and Harriet had agreed he should remain absent.

It was remarkable to note that this well-dressed woman — Harriet's presence was already a risk considering the news cartoons lampooning her and John, so she dressed more conservatively to remain semi-disguised — and the three members of her brood, all arrived at the tiny eating-house from different directions, using mixed conveyances. As for the new dining trend, 'It's hardly a restaurant at all!' quipped Herby snobbishly, though he downed his beefsteak on open-faced bread lustily enough when it arrived.

Haji felt embarrassed by the brief outburst, knowing his elder brother had been better reared. Some part of Haji yet honestly wished to have things back 'as they were' during the heady days of trips to museums and zoos and historical sites, unclouded by childlike naivety and the reassuring feeling that they had somehow been blessed by 'two daddies.' He had even grown to feel a touch insecure at eating tables of any sort where conversation was emphasised — thus about something important and hence unpleasant—since he had adopted 'Uncle John's' habit of reading at table, be it a news piece, poetry text, or philosophical treatise. He knew his mother and sister preferred actual conversation, even if trivial, whilst sharing a meal.

As for Lily, she remained as dedicated as their mother to keeping some semblance of family unity, though in her case such impetus may have sprung more for its own sake than for any notion of public propriety. Mum had grown feistier with age, often justifiably so, to Lily's thinking: family affairs were one's own business after all (provided that no real harm was occurring under one's roof—she never escaped her pseudo-uncle's lessons). Further, Lily had studied sufficiently to understand that gossiping about others, whilst perhaps offering some perverse bonding experience and one of which she had, alas, been sometimes guilty herself, amounted to a form of control: nefarious social control, which she had already decided had no place in a 'free' society like theirs.

Mother had taken her to task over that notion of control before, citing the history of the Papacy and Lily's intact if unpublicised dedication to Roman Catholicism, and now she hoped this 'casual luncheon' would not similarly devolve into shouting.

Haji the peacemaker addressed Mother's question, reassuring her that they 'would be well provided for' whenever it might please God to call her 'home.' He did not mean it as an affront, though Harriet stiffened at certain elements of his declaration, earning grins from the other two grown children, elicited by different means.

Harriet refused to be baited that day. 'From a financial perspective, that is surely true, Algernon. I meant more of what you each intended. I am not hear to judge,'—a pleading look from Haji, a derisive sigh from Herby, a tired smile from Lily—'but rather to sincerely listen to your longer-term prospects and interests.'

It took time, plus a drawn out but surprisingly tasty luncheon for the younger adults to recognise that their mother was exhibiting genuine interest. They even reached an unspoken sense that no one wanted to really leave, considering they would head in different directions, though Haji and Lily would be back at home with Harriet soon.

Harriet knew Herby no longer held interest in university studies, though Haji had recently shown some leaning in that direction.
Haji offered encouragement on his elder's behalf—'You could go
into medicine like Uncle Will. You've already got plenty of medicinal background'—but that was at once rebuffed. There had been
talk lately about the educational system linking elements of physic,
surgery, and even apothecary, though that medieval air of physicians
not wishing to have direct contact with patients remained—a risk
in this frightful period of contagious diseases—whilst surgeons got
their hands dirty, symbolically and literally. Harriet felt glad that her
husband had never succumbed to ill patients, some of them walking
into the business with all manner of strange afflictions, sometimes
without doctor's written prescriptions and just hoping for advice.

When the lads turned the talk to their 'baby sister,' Harriet had
to hold her tongue, not wanting the young woman to feel outnumbered. She left it to Herbert to toss subtlety aside: 'What's this lunacy
about the stage, Sis?'

She was prepared, though: in some ways, Lily was the most mature
of them all, having become the widest-read, the ablest linguist, and
the most independently thinking of the trio, for which Herby sought
to blame 'Mr Mill.' John was no longer 'Uncle.'

'It's become a much more reputable profession of late, Brother,
even within the span of our short lives.'

Herby had likewise readied himself for verbal sparring. 'Perhaps,
and while I might let go the usual commentary about the nature of
actors in general and actresses in particular—' Harriet noticed her
daughter did not blush at the implication of harlotry, pleased by her
courage, though old biases remained—'it's unlikely for almost anyone
to truly make it a "profession" at all, living performance to performance,
wandering about like tragedians of old. And it's hardly sanctioned by
any type of formal schooling: the aspirant must apply for an appren-
ticeship of some sort, likely to unscrupulous types.'

'You may seek to write for a living, Herby, and yet despite your abilities and predilections, you've received close to no schooling for that, either.' That did elicit a blush, plus a smirk from Haji, who for once felt less in the middle of matters.

Herby hated being shown up, particularly in front of family, and had grown quite weary of his wayward and disrespectful 'Mummy' with her dallying ways. He had spent so much effort trying to get his father to get angry with this damnable woman, never understanding the man's perpetual command to 'Let it be, boy! You know not what has happened with us.' And that just made matters worse, to Herby's mind: that the most important adults in his life could also prove so blasted secretive.

Herbert Taylor had become an idealistic young man: temperate, responsible, a dedicated voter—Conservative Party, of course—and he further understood the social need for decorum, but damned if he would obey the unwritten and asinine guidelines about family secrets when they extended into family members keeping secrets from each other. Herby's idealism was the need to make his own way in life, something every gentleman should aspire to, as Father had inculcated in him and his siblings, and here he was all but accused of hypocrisy by her!

'Be that as it may,' he growled, eliciting a look of alarm from a passing couple intent on trying out this new type of food service, 'writing, and for that matter working as an apothecary, are simply more respectable.' It was difficult to not spit the word.

Yet he had not expected both women to remain so insufferably calm. 'Dear Brother,' Lily began, 'I love you and value your input, but you must understand that each of us has the capacity, indeed the responsibility, to choose our own paths. Mother agrees with your assessment'—true, though Harriet maintained a neutral countenance—'but she understands that her own instructions to me over the years imply that I must take the decision myself.'

Herby began to wonder whether Mrs Mill, as his friends sometimes called her to goad him, despite his once threatening action just short of a duel, had managed to turn all her children against one another, or against Father. He felt befuddled, hating the sensation, but noticed that Mother had become more rational and logical, annoyingly so, over the years with Mr Mill.

But it offered no satisfaction at all to likewise realise that logic took no sides, and that Mother's reasoning might have worked against her in this instance: she had to accept that her teaching of her intelligent and equally headstrong daughter insisted on the very freedom of choice and action that her sons, and indeed she herself, had emphasised in so much of her written work. And he clearly recalled that Mr Mill might be among the most brilliant thinkers, yet also had the 'pride of Lucifer' that his long-dead mentor had offered as his moniker. Herby suspected his sister might remind them that Lucifer had brought the light of wisdom, like Prometheus.

Algernon, meanwhile, merely felt grateful to not have to currently justify his own comparative lack of ambition. No, that wasn't it really: he just was perhaps engaging in a bit of 'experimentation' with a wandering lifestyle. He was hardly lazy, nor seemingly susceptible to the severe emotional crisis that Uncle John had undergone all those years ago—all three Taylor children knew of it, and while Haji and Lily had always felt sympathetic, Herby had interpreted it as weakness—though he had read widely and considered so many potential life outcomes that it had become paradoxically difficult to narrow his focus. Sometimes too many choices could backfire, something he had tried to explain to Mum and Mill, to no avail. 'Family, please,' he said now, 'let us not, I implore you, resort to infighting now that Father has passed on.'

Lily liked the innocuous-sounding phrase, through Herby bristled, considering it linguistically dishonest: their father had died, not passed on, and they certainly had not lost him. 'Agreed, Haji,' Lily concurred.

And so it continued, each of them realising that, family ties notwithstanding, in some ways they really had diverged onto different paths, based not just on interests but on loyalties. Ever wary of causing harm, Mr Mill would have found the scene a touch disturbing, and as a professional meddler would similarly have wished to somehow amend matters among them. But Herby would have been the first—perhaps only—among them to note that John Mill was not family, a notion not lost on Harriet.

Thusly, the short and indeed feisty Harriet Taylor—all 155 centimetres of her, though she eschewed higher heeled shoes as too confining and thus sexist—suffered the occasional fever these days, but otherwise seemed strong and resilient as ever, just less so in public. She took pride in her children, all of them into their adult years—how did such happen?—but tensions remained. Haji had cast his lot with John and Harriet, often even living and travelling with them, though not as much as his sister.

Lily contented herself with widening her knowledge, still continuing with translations, and helping her mother and John with careful editing. She relished philosophy in all its varied guises, and genuinely believed the three of them were contributing to social welfare during this period in particular, when, for example, the couple finished seven items alone for mass papers merely on the heady topic of what more and more readers were calling 'domestic violence.' She even took over at times as copyist for her mother, since Harriet had presented with more of those frequent fevers lately.

The articles continued unabated: about labour relations—the recent Factories Act had cut work weeks down to sixty hours; the ongoing struggle to truly eliminate slavery once and for all; how society dealt with 'eccentrics'—John had commented about this, mentioning something about 'tyranny' of the 'common perspective,' though Harriet seemed in disagreement over that idea. Even listening to would-be revolutionaries and those with odd—no, 'eccentric'—ideas in a corner of Hyde Park which had previously been home to the dreadful Tyburn Gallows could prove a respite from home, though Harriet at least had plenty of access to diversions—and funding—than most women of her station.

John had recently suggested, perhaps half-jokingly, of donning incongruous disguises and bringing some of their combined ideas to the public from that park spot, which had already taken on the unofficial moniker of 'Speaker's Corner.' It was one thing, he explained, to publish ideas that some would take as odd, radical, or in between, yet another to appeal directly to whomever might be passing by a park, and London fortunately benefitted from its public green spaces being open to all, at almost all hours.

Harriet half-jokingly replied that maybe he could position himself at said corner, quoting insights from 'Principles of Political Economy' without identifying himself or the text. They both wanted a more literate populace, after all. Perhaps Harriet's greatest fear, voiced only ever to John, lay in the possibility that women would finally obtain the power of voting, yet find themselves ill-prepared for the responsibility. They both hated the idea of the foolish or the under-educated having such social power. Perhaps they were Platonists after all!

If happiness — the actual social goal, though John, and less often Harriet, kept insisting that it had to be qualified more than quantified — had to be sacrificed in order for the potentially 'unlimited increase of wealth and population,' to quote their book, then what was the point? Perhaps they were Malthusians, too!

It remained easier to emphasise the need to destroy slavery — a 'simple sell' at home, but more challenging to explain to British trading partners, especially American ones — or the need — 'not merely desire,' Harriet stressed — to add women to the Reform Bills.

Were these precious social benefits, which the pair understood as inborn rights but which most of the world still perceived as threats, steps towards some more equitable social system? Were they just dreams after all? So much literature and poetry and philosophy of their time and place in history suggested otherwise, but their productivity in journalism implied steps, more steps, endless steps in a more moral direction.

It was so tiring, Harriet considered again, admittedly glad to have a break from the children after the luncheon. Her relationship with John had suffered so much in recent months, via time apart, the death of Mr Taylor and the settlement of his last wishes, and a certain widow feeling like she carried too much psychic weight upon her petite frame. It was high time for the two of them to get back on track, and what better way than to continue with one of those steps? This would prove a larger, more difficult one to surmount to be sure, but worth the effort, and when On the Enfranchisement of Women went to press in '51, Harriet would take more pride in her work than ever before, and not only for having the lead with the writing.

* * *

'Twas always better to begin a new year on a metaphorical high note, Harriet thought, having reached a stage when she felt more intellectually independent and simultaneously bodily weaker with each year. This combination was hardly her first choice, but if increasing debilitation was the price to pay for living as she chose, then so be it.

She had prised Caroline Fox away from her habit of haunting both small local libraries and the National Archive for the simple pleasure of both sharing something, and, Harriet had to admit, simply showing off. *Bookish girl,* Harriet thought again, considering the proclivities of her own daughter, who had taken the initiative to call on Caroline several times, and the pair of them had begun to organise informal but entertaining reading groups, aspiring to the French salons that had gone out of vogue with the Revolutions. The young women's difference in age was even less than that which had existed between Caroline and Lizzie Flower, so perhaps some heroine-adulation might be called for. Or maybe it was just the pleasure of having an intellectual and emotional mentor; whichever the case, the pair of them had become fast friends, though Lily remained at home presently.

Caroline had largely eschewed the grandness of the Great Exhibition, though admitted she enjoyed some of the cultural displays, despite the racism shown by trying to 'exotify' other peoples. As Harriet met with Caroline near Kew Gardens—they had only visited once previously, though the now world-famous public botanic park had been open over ten years—she thought—hoped—that perhaps copies of what she carried in her handbag might find their places on the shelves of the Library, or even the Archive.

Yet the famed Archive, repository of All Things Great and English, had recently paled in comparison with the 'Great Exhibition of the Works of Industry of All Nations.' The Exhibition would last nearly six months, more than many observers initially believed or thought possible. John and Harriet attended and genuinely enjoyed themselves, though preferred to remain as in cognito as possible. Dressing more formally than usual seemed to accomplish this, as no one in London was prepared to recognise John in particular with a black felt top hat, carrying Bentham's walking stick 'Dapple' as they strolled about.

The only instance that John took an amount of time that began even to bore Harriet, who herself felt entranced by so much, came while visiting the India Exhibit. 'Lovely, but too small,' he critiqued, 'and it's shameful to think of how little my father truly understood this astonishing culture, more ancient than our own.' He ran his fingers along one of the velvety wall hangings, reminded of medieval tapestries, then grinned, recalling that the Indian piece was indeed older.

Harriet held his arm snugly, finding the display room delightfully colourful and taking in costumes and wall hangings amidst ornate furnishings which made one blush for their magnificence. 'There seem fewer "actors" in here,' she mused, thinking how Lily would adore the pageantry, certainly not limited to this room. The children had opted to visit on their own schedules, Herby and Lily together one day, Haji bringing along a lady-friend whom he promised 'to introduce to you, Mum,' though that had yet to transpire.

'And why is it so exotic?' John pondered, frowning that judgemental glare of his, even though just a handful of other souls occupied it then. 'This is the "crown jewel" of the glorious Empire,' he added, voice loudening with frustration about too many details that the India room elicited, 'and we might just be standing in some fancy furniture shop.' A stuffed elephant stood lifelessly in the middle of the display room: the taxidermist had performed a neat job, and the ornate howdah on its back impressed. It took a few more minutes to decipher that few of the international exhibits benefitted from live cast members: several persons of each far-off nationality were on hand to answer questions, but the mostly White visitors to this fabled semi-living museum of the whole world remained content to point and murmur 'ooh' and 'aah.' There remained an other-ness to this approach: John had castigated his fellow English for their xenophobia, and such behaviours seemed confirmed, as putting things and peoples on display enabled the perpetuation of their alien-ness while rendering them harmless.

A display found by Harriet mentioned the amazing Koh-i-Noor Diamond, a recent gift from the Maharaja—a ward of the East India Company—to Queen Victoria, and when John walked over to read it, he drew glares from other visitors when he loudly wondered what the selling rather than gifting of such a stunning gemstone might do to alleviate Indian poverty.

Harriet had no answer for him. She did with many other subjects, and for the first time found herself regretting that she would very likely never see amazing India: it had been a passing childhood fantasy, actually gaining the approval of her parents if the teasing of her siblings; John loved the idea, but had trouble articulating the blend of feelings involved—*John Mill, at a loss for words?* Harriet had once considered—overseen by Guilt.

They opted not to visit the Koh-i-Noor exhibit after all; they would have been depressed to find that it just 'didn't sparkle enough,' despite its more than 105-carat size. But it had yet to be cut into smaller, almost as priceless pieces. The even larger pink Daria-i-Noor diamond, of Persian origin, lay in another display, receiving more visitors.

Truth, John would later confess he was as much impressed by the first-ever pay toilets—a penny per visit, with hundreds of thousands of visitors gladly offering their copper coins for the privilege—as by some of the international exhibits. Each was large—'the country displays, not the loos,' John was heard to declare—and showed off something of the natural as well as cultural glory of the nation in question, but the minimal 'staffing' of such by foreign citizens remained quite wanting by both him and Harriet.

Yet Dickens and Tennyson raved about the Great Ex, Dickens writing of finding himself 'amidst the heterogeneous masses,' Tennyson rhapsodising about 'all of beauty, all of use, that one fair planet can produce.' Prince Albert, seemingly no longer under suspicion by English xenophobes of harbouring nefarious Germanic schemes, played a key role in the entire production, though he had endless help, and some began to refer to the lining of the land running past the Crystal Palace as 'Exhibition Road' and to the area of South Kensington as 'Albertopolis,' which the Prince did not mind. Many wrote fondly of new technologies and devices on display, including refinements made to telescopes, ceramics, textile looms, and daguerreotypes: some visitors kept their patience long enough for the fascinating 'photographs' to be taken of them, though children could rarely remain sufficiently still. Harriet mused that perhaps some of their co-written news articles would be enhanced if newspapers could begin to use such images to help get their points across.

Statistics alone represented Imperial grandeur: the Crystal Palace lay 2000 feet in length, 100 feet in height, though it seemed more spacious inside for both sheer magnificence and the amount of sunlight that could penetrate the overhead windows, and it had been built to surround some of the trees in Hyde Park, rather than their getting chopped down to make way. A grand total of some £186,000 would be amassed by the chief planner and designer, slated to go almost entirely towards new museums in the area. Said designer envisioned such cultural exhibitions to remain gratis, as the great British Museum was, testament to wanting to show off British accomplishments whilst simultaneously appearing humble; John and Harriet thought him in agreement with their own emphases on greater education; John quipped that the man would receive a knighthood ere long.

Some six million visitors, from six continents, flocked to the glass Palace to witness in person some 13,000 exhibitors and their proud demonstrations. As Harriet and John learned later, the Indian display had been encountered by them merely at an off time, with workers from the Sub-Continent frantically trying to make repairs to some of the items, others meeting with dignitaries, still others merely taking an all-too-brief luncheon break. It had hardly proven a ghost-town after all.

Charlotte Brontë wrote of the Crystal Palace, 'It is a wonderful place—vast, strange, new, and impossible to describe. Its grandeur does not consist in one thing, but in the unique assemblage of all things. Whatever human industry has created you find there... It seems as if only magic could have gathered this mass of wealth from all the ends of the Earth... The multitude filling the great aisles seems ruled and subdued by some invisible influence. Amongst the thirty thousand souls that peopled it the day I was there not one loud noise was to be heard, not one irregular movement seen; the living tide rolls on quietly, with a deep hum like the sea heard from the distance.' She outdid the likes of Dickens and Tennyson in her appraisal.

Strolling arm in arm away from the Exhibition that day in June, when it remained crowded, John and Harriet concluded that their habit of largely extracting themselves from public view had definitely been for the better, confessing to each other near voyeuristic feelings.

Harriet tried to lighten matters. 'Many of the people in national costume seemed pleased to be there, to show off some of their culture.'

After some moments, John nodded. 'I think you're right. I just wonder if some of them also felt like the animals who so thrilled the children in the London Zoo.'

Harriet gripped his arm tighter, glad for such a delightful memory. A near perfect day, she thought, sighing yet remembering that all families had their episodes of unity and disunity, favourite recollections along with moments perhaps better forgotten.

John collected his thoughts. 'Do you recall our discussion of whaling when you were so proud of describing business collectives?'

'Of course, Love,' she answered. Standing there, looking back at Hyde Park with its grandiose glass structure now starting to reflect a fading sun, she recalled it in detail, like so many of their discussions. 'It proved a touch sensitive, as I recall.'

He nodded. 'Bentham once offered a marvellous idea about that, though he was speaking more generally. He said, "The question is not, can they talk, nor, can they reason, but—'"

"'Can they suffer?'" finished Harriet.

John nodded. 'Jeremy took the emotive idea of Hume and made it rational.'

'Jeremy? I've never heard you call him that.'

'I have decided to become less formal regarding my memories.'

She grinned. 'So how do you mean?'

'Well, Mr Hume barely delved into ethics at all. Roughly, he said that you feel sympathy or even empathy for a fellow living creature—regardless of its species, gender, age, habitat, proclivities—or you do not. Rather like falling in love, one supposes.'

Neither of them knew that a new American novelist was about to witness his book go to press, about the whaling enterprise critiqued and graphically described, via a rightly vengeful whale and a fanatically vindictive ship captain. Like Bentham but appealing to a wider audience, it would raise similar questions without overtly asking them. Such were the merits of literature compared to philosophy, Harriet would think once she read it.

They continued ambling, enjoying the City anew without being recognised, pleased that others had their own cares and distractions, whether in the huge glass superstructure or elsewhere. And they always made a point of discussing what they had just done and explored during a day, whether it was a beach at the base of a cliff in Italy, a patch of forest outside Paris yet to succumb to industrial appetites, or the displays in Hyde Park.

John returned to voicing his thoughts about the train exhibits, explaining that there came new rumours of expanding upon the now extensive British rail networks. He might rhapsodise about how they were living in a period of new modes of travel, a theme which Harriet enjoyed—though they had still only ridden a single train together—yet which she had wearied of eventually. But the stock market bubble created by railroad expansion, reaching its explosive zenith back in '46 only to leave share-holders devastated and poor, suggested that British confidence would have to return first. Still, the Exhibition showed off a new locomotive, with descriptions of up-and-coming passenger and transport cars, John gawking at the display like a boy in a sweet shop. Parliament was starting to admit that no modern empire could be maintained without ready access to communication and transport, and that rail lines could provide both throughout the whole world.

The would-be boy in the sweet shop slowed—he knew better than to halt abruptly when walking with Harriet, his old habit—then stopped, taking Harriet's hands and gazing as deeply into her eyes as he could. She no longer tensed when he did so. The City quickly dissolved away, she feeling that they might be the only persons left in the World. She had to come to a stop more frequently during their walks about the City these days anyway, though thankfully her rheumy joints remained stronger than the parts of her that still ached—face and head—or that became numb for short periods—mainly her hands.

'It's good to be out and about again, Dearest,' he said simply.

'Indeed,' she countered. 'These old legs have been less betraying all day! And have you been watching others as I have these hours?'

He had been: it could prove astonishing how much one might glean of other persons—non-humans, too, considering their previous discussion—merely by looking about, though not invasively. No one in Britain likely took personal privacy more seriously than did John Mill, an attitude that Harriet copied, albeit more from her own experiences. And yet a person's pace, or stride, or dress, or style, or direction of their own glance, or their responses to external stimuli such as urban noises and voices—these details all revealed much to anyone patiently observing. John tended to favour emotional details: did a particular person present with some sense of happiness? That question remained at the foremost of his thoughts, and continued to guide his own attitudes and writings.

Harriet paid more attention to women generally, regardless of class or race: how did they seem; were they happy; did they present as anxious or giddy or fretful or hopeful?

And she still stared at John, not noticing the stares they got back from others: even lovers should not stand at street corners like children or dogs awaiting commands.

'We're almost finished with the project, John,' she said.

He sighed, looking downward. Sometimes his smile did not quite meet his eyes, though it came easily in her presence. 'Our basic though crucial concern is "that the principle which regulates the existing social relations between the two sexes—the legal subordination of one sex to the other—is wrong in itself,"' he repeated from the manuscript.

Harriet added, '"What is now called the nature of women is an eminently artificial thing—the result of forced repression in some directions, unnatural stimulation in others." I'm quite glad we've kept that passage intact, John. Oh, and "It may be asserted without scruple, that no other class of dependents have had their character so entirely distorted from its natural proportions by their relation with their masters."'

At this, a passing woman actually huffed in disgust and strode away from them, having considered asking this odd-looking couple about the Exhibition and if it was true that prices had reduced to make it more accessible. They did not know, though Harriet wryly observed earlier in the day that sometimes sexism might work in women's favour: season tickets for men—for those who simply could not get their fill in one curious day—came to three pounds, three shillings, but two pounds, two shillings for women.

And they would have wholly endorsed the fact that prices varied depending on the day for single admits: from a single shilling up to a pound on some days, though John and Harriet would have worried at the logic of such a scheme. Regardless, the sometimes lowered fees had already brought in countless members of the lower economic classes.

Two men strolled by them next, then obviously altered their route as they overheard John: '"What is now called the nature of women is an eminently artificial thing—the result of forced repression in some directions, unnatural stimulation in others..."'

Harriet replied: '"It may be asserted without scruple, that no other class of dependents have had their character so entirely distorted from its natural proportions by their relation with their masters.'"

The lovers had never intentionally memorised so much of a project before, but both had obsessed with the intricacies and meanings of individual phrases and words. John knew from his over-loaded childhood that Latin and Greek could convey more accuracy, whilst English, much as they loved it, remained a better choice for poetry or prose, all the more reason for precision.

The new project would shortly go to print, with no one to restrict their names or dedications, no one to tell them what could not be done. 'On the Enfranchisement of Women' remained the title, as they had decided that subtlety was just not the way to go. All the years of writing for 'radical' papers, and sharing their views, and publicising rational ideas whilst getting lambasted for the same, had come to this: beyond the intricacies of logic and the necessities of economics, their new book would call for nothing less than what its title boldly declared: suffrage should indeed expand further, as was the century's trend, at least in Britain, and should once and for all include the 'gentler sex.'

For all John's disquieting attitude regarding actual revolution—his Francophilia tempered with disgust over the latest upstart 'false Emperor'—his term—along with trepidation about both English readiness for such, and the disturbing truth that any true political revolution created casualties—a lesson learned by England two centuries earlier and which he feared the Americans were about to learn—he nonetheless perceived nothing whatsoever wrong with the prospect of women voting, nor with the potential for perhaps even some violence relating to such.

*Perhaps this is some latent sexist intimation on his part,* wondered Harriet, as though John might think—though he would hardly ever admit so—that a feminist revolution would somehow intrinsically offer less violence and bloodshed. Gentler sex indeed!

Whichever the truth, Harriet felt bold, unafraid, and she removed one hand from his so they could walk, but squeezed his other hand fervently, never wishing to release that comforting grip, surprisingly strong in a man satirised in newsprint as feminine.

And as they kept walking towards home silently, London offering its endless cacophony of sounds, Harriet mused to herself their most radical shared ideas yet.

'The mental companionship which is improving, is communion between active minds, not mere contact between an active mind and a passive. This inestimable advantage is even now enjoyed, when a strong-minded man and a strong-minded woman are, by a rare chance, united: and would be had far oftener, if education too the same pains to form strong-minded women which it takes to prevent them from being formed.' The words remained their own: shared, discussed, debated—sometimes hotly, sometimes leading—strangely, to an equally potent undercurrent of raw sexuality.

How many lovers write together, then get naked together, then return to writing whilst still sweaty? Harriet thought now, easily recalling the betraying image of John's eager manhood beneath his britches during one such especially eager session of multiple types of creativity. And she loved how he had roared—most unfemininely!—at her drawing some forced yet funny analogy to the pitching of a tent during a wilderness excursion, though the sexual guilt that pervaded their quirky period of civilised history immediately led her to consider that they had never truly gone camping together. It seemed primitive, but she had to admit that the sense of passionate longing invading her usually rational thoughts gave such a scenario appeal.

John felt the stronger squeezing of her hand, not knowing what prompted it, simply savouring the natural sensation of it. And he had no inclination as to her thoughts, his own having remained on the technical wonders that accompanied the spirit of their age.

"'It is neither necessary nor just to make imperatives on women'," Harriet recalled proudly, "'that they shall be either mothers or nothing, or that if they have been mothers once, they shall be nothing else during the whole remainder of their lives.'"

*Oh, but I—and we—have already made something of the remainder of our lives!*

* * *

*From the journal of Harriet Taylor: December, 1851.*
Were I a woman of faith, I might offer gratitude to a deity for such a blessed year, indeed, the greatest of my unconventional life thus far! Lacking such respected traditional belief structure, I can nonetheless—and have done so, gleefully!—shout my happiness from the rooftops (two thus far, despite rheumatic pains!), and proclaim that I love him, I love him!

John's proposal was delightful, even more romantic than I give him credit for possessing, and I believe nothing stokes the fires of love more than the ability of a lover to keep surprising a partner. Whilst some predictability is good and necessary—another description of trust—that John not only crafted such a creative proposal, but that he managed to catch me unawares, despite how often we had discussed it, was lovely. While Mr Taylor yet lived, it remained of course taboo, but then became a living option!

An interesting and crucial thing, trust: so challenging to construct, yet tragically so easy to destroy, often irreparably. Yet John and I have shared so much in trust: blends of comic as well as tragic in life; hopes, dreams, aspirations, and also the banality of finances and managing a home and attending to family. In some ways, it's as though we received a jump start on running a home together—our own sanctuary, no interference, children already grown with no possibility of having more. It's delicious to ponder it all.

To review the 'text' of this document makes me feel like those in possession of the world's sacred papers and papyri and clay tablets must feel—like something recorded for the ages!—privy to the most intimate of secrets. How does one respond to one's 'last' will, and further, one's 'testament,' a final chance to leave for posterity one's aspirations, wishes, desires, perhaps blending the fulfilled with the still longing or even regretful?

Dear departed Lizzie, bless her soul also—and yes, one can believe in a living creature's eternal essence without conforming to religion, thank you!—would have hated it: she'd have taken poor Mr Mill to task for offering something so dry and boring, even if heart-felt. 'But Harriet,' I can still hear her voice in my mind, 'where finds one the poetry, the declarations of love ever-lasting… did he even offer you flowers or a ring?'

I silently answer her Ghost, as though she lurks in the room with me. Fret not, dear diary: none of those silly Continental séances to help me commune with the deceased! And damn them for abusing people's memories and sentiments, anyway. Besides, despite John Taylor's various qualities, he was simply not a poet like you. And I believe I completed my late husband's parting requests to the fullest, though one must wonder why I write of such this late—because I was emotionally unprepared to do so until now!

Thus do I speak to Lizzie's memory, letting her know that flowers and sonnets were hardly necessary, and that John's choice of a ring confirmed his tastes: simplicity and value over all. Eighteen-carat gold has become curiously more easily obtained thanks to that 'rush' for gold in California, only even more recently all but matched by another rush down in Australia—one wonders if one's brother might exploit an idea one once gave to her husband to 'cash in,' as the Yanks say, on the need to supply the adventurous and foolish.

And that gold—not a fortune's worth, surely: that would be gauche and unlike John, though he could afford the large and gaudy—but rather artistically wrapped about a pair of colourful stones I had not previously known I would love. An amethyst and an emerald, competing with yet also complimenting each other, rather like the two of us. As for that proposal, I took the time to record it here anew, since John keeps asking me to burn his correspondence: whatever will future historians and biographers think?

Even our trio of children acknowledged that, and they all miss their father, finding their own adult ways in the world. And the time will undoubtedly come when Herby and I shall have to discuss further his lack of happiness—indeed, of his notable absence from—my second marriage. Thank goodness Haji and Lily attended and signed the documentation as legal witnesses: 21st April, 1851, now my favourite date, with none of us much caring about the fact that the nuptials took place within the cramped Register Office in Melcombe Regis way over in Dorset. 'Lovely county and scenic area, offering a chance to forget for a time the wagging tongues back in the City who no doubt would have welcomed the chance to try and shame our eccentric marriage.

Yes, we signed our own private documentation, understanding marriage as a contract. All human societies created marriage at some time in their otherwise unique histories, and indeed, it has always been contractual—but our own 'take' on the archaic institution was modern and independent: no arrangements, no dowry, clearly no waiting until the 'big day' for bride and bridegroom to first set eyes upon one another. Just our special day, with limited family, in a wholly secular ceremony. The only witnesses were our officiate—we still regret Dear old Fox having been unavailable, though we understand his reasoning—plus Haji and Lily.

A glorious spring day, after the heavy snows from this past winter: the poetic symbolism of such a suddenly energetic spring was not lost on us! 21 April received little localised interest in the press, with all the fuss and to-do about the 'Great Exhibition.' Still, 'The Times' noted how, 'Considering the immense number of educated foreigners'—John and I had to confess later that this sounded like us speaking of our own countrymen!—'we are likely to have upon us in a very few days, and the splendid buildings, the antiquities, the galleries, and the treasures of art they leave behind them in their own capitals.' It was exciting, and we thought it might serve as sufficient impetus to draw us out of our social shell: after all, we are properly wed now at last!

'The Times' continued rhapsodic, noting local historical buildings and related institutions worthy of visits from those self-same 'foreigners,' especially the ones with some free-spending income—the socialist writers might be horrified by such profligate spending, particularly in light of how various cultures would be made to seem 'exotic' by being on display, so hopefully it will be tasteful like we hope and not worthy of John's condemnation, as with Carlyle's racism. 'The moral of all this is,' that newspaper added, 'that we ought to make the best of what we have,' and that it may yet still be 'necessary to prove to foreigners that London really is the ancient city'—and thus worthy of study and visits—'it pretends to be.' Huzzah for national pride for once!

Then came responses to our nuptials, from John's family and mine. Dearest John had already become so estranged from his mother: younger sister Mary, writing for the news and becoming as much a peacemaker for her clan as Haji is for mine; the other sister Harriet—another Harriet, like my own mum!—and older sister Clara, have been less welcoming, clearly struggling for politeness on the remarkably few occasions when I have been in their presence. To a certain extent I can sympathise, as my own parents had nothing to do with John, though alas that has altered little now that I find myself re-married. And I have yet to meet sister Jane, who has become as much the Francophile as her brother, and so far as I know, remains on the Continent as I pen this entry. As for previously friendly Wilhelmina, I confess I know not her current whereabouts.

Poor John: there we were, attempting to celebrate our gladness at last, as he described yet another 'vulgar and insolent' letter from young sister Mary, who was in fact merely trying to keep the family together. My loyalty remains steadfast to my new husband, though in truth he has been such in sentiment and spirit these many years, and I at once fear that his opposition to his family's opposition—one of those damnable double negatives found in mathematics and logic alike—will only serve to produce a permanent breach in his feelings towards them.

Unfortunately, the same may apply to their feelings towards him. Far better, it seems to this modern woman, to rewrite his own take on the whole institution:

'The whole character of the marriage relation as constituted by law being such as both she and I entirely and conscientiously disapprove, I, having no means of legally divesting myself of these odious powers… feel it my duty to put on record a formal protest against the existing law of marriage, in so far as conferring such powers; and a solemn promise never in any case or under any circumstances to use them.' He published this 'Statement on Marriage,' and in one of the more widely read 'papers, too.

With families, no one likes the suggestion that they might be paying 'insufficient respect' to another, especially when they may feel disinclined to offer a genuine welcome to that person in the first place. I have worked to ingratiate myself with the Mills, as John has attempted with the Taylors, especially with my children, but one cannot compel feelings in another. If that were true, we could emerge from our self-imposed retreat from much of society—alas, how John and I do miss the theatre!—and simply force others to feel some modicum of support for us and our now official relationship.

But that was what John told his family, including his mother: that they all had paid me too little or merely begrudging respect. Now that our fathers are both gone, perhaps we should get our two mums together for tea and insist they come to terms, though I don't believe they actually have a problem with one another—just with the circumstances.

Our young Queen, too, received opprobrium for her choice of husband, and Albert is as German as Victoria is English, but are both strong, and the public has gloried in their children, heirs to the throne. England has had monarchs of Danish, Norman-French, part-Welsh, Scottish, Dutch, and German ancestry, so what matter such minutiae if their relationship prospers?

Had I a mind to offer prayers to deities in Whom I do not believe, I might beseech an Almighty figurehead to not let me clash so violently—permanently?—with my children as they seek their own matches. Herby and Lily show no such inclinations to my knowledge, though Herby might not inform me while Lily seems genuinely disinterested, and I can only hope—not pray!—that this aspect of her character does not result from her parents' own troubled union. As for Haji, he at least has shown some eagerness in the Fairer Sex—his outmoded term, not mine—yet no marriage inclinations. All my dear cubs have entered their twenties, old enough for the responsibility. Perhaps part of me merely seeks the solace of grandparent-status: all the fun with none of the mess or sass.

As for the Mills, younger brother Henry died years back, another poor consumptive case, damn that infernal disease—though John's old friend Mr Sterling had, near the end of Henry's life, introduced the latter to Sterling's own physician, whose treatment I don't recall what—almost saved the day. For that matter, John's sister Clara met Caroline Fox during that same time and setting and became friends, the only other positive relationship I can name to emerge from the odd links between Mills and Hardys.

No, no more dwelling on about that, like some hospitalised depressive. And as with Mr Taylor's will, which merits its own security within our solicitor's sizable client files, I must reproduce—in my own handwriting, letting the passion and attachment to someone guide my hand—some of Mr Mill's own loving proposal, as unorthodox as our ceremony. A flirtier or more fashionable woman would have welcomed it not, but I must write it again here, solely for my own dreamy, occasional perusal:

'Being about, if I am so happy as to obtain her consent, to enter into the marriage relation with the only woman I have ever known, with whom I would have entered into that state; and the whole character of the marriage relation as constituted by law being such as both she and I entirely and conscientiously disapprove, for this among other reasons, that it confers upon one of the parties to the contract, legal power and control over the person, property, and freedom of action of the other party, independent of her own wishes and will; I, having no means of legally divesting myself of these odious powers (as I most assuredly would do if an engagement to that effect could be made legally binding on me) feel it my duty to put on record a formal protest against the existing law of marriage, in so far as conferring such powers; and a solemn promise never in any case or under any circumstances to use them. And in the event of marriage between Mrs

Taylor and me I declare it to be my will and intention, and the condition of the engagement between us, that she retains in all respects whatever the same absolute freedom of action, and freedom of disposal of herself and of all that does or may at any time belong to her, as if no such marriage had taken place; and I absolutely disclaim and repudiate all pretension to have acquired any rights whatever by virtue of such marriage.' —6 March, 1851—

Life beckons anew, or so it feels. The '40s felt like such a wretched decade of peering past death's door: dear brother William, John's brother Henry, whom he was getting to know again, my former mother-in-law, bless her for not despising me as she might have, my own father, and, the most heart-wrenching loss of all—forgive me, Father!—dear Lizzie Flower... yet life moves on, with our consent or approval or no.

As I pen this I hear carollers outside, probably flawlessly dressed in evening wear with hats and bonnets, looking like Welsh revolutionaries, one supposes. I briefly reminisce as they work their way through 'The First Noël,' my childhood favourite, back in those years prior to my interpreting what Scriptures said in absolutist terms. Now the tune is become just a lovely melody, and I must confess—even John does not know this—that I once sang it to our children as they took turns throughout December opening our—yes, laugh now, you judging public!—Advent calendar for treats.

I cannot blame our charming Queen either, nor her paramour the handsome German Prince, who despite English concerns from the '30s remains not only smitten with our home-grown female monarch but with their children—four princesses and three princes already, and all healthy if our plethora of newspapers offers accuracy. And the royal brood likewise adore these new Holiday traditions: expanded song-fests, balls, feasts worthy of Henry VIII himself (in his later years, anyway), and a resurrection of a practice of his despised contemporary, Martin Luther, who turned the classical and Pagan Yule log into the indoor Christmas tree. One hopes homeowners and servants alike will remain vigilant about all those lit candles in homes! And after enough Christmases, those well-bred youngsters will no doubt take over much of Europe and perhaps other parts of the world via the ancient art of dynastic marriages.

I fear—hope?—that the Empire, for all its strange glory, its lost or false humility—cricket and rugby enthusiasts bandying about 'fair play' and making it seem so English whilst thousands of miles from home our 'subjects' may find themselves repressed or starving—will transform into wretched Ebenezer Scrooge, terrified into morally upstanding behaviour by the restless spirits of those the Empire has crushed in its rush to Greatness.

The charitable jongleurs, or whatever they name themselves, have now shifted to the newer 'It Came Upon a Midnight Clear,' and I have to pause for a few minutes, both to listen to them and then to wipe away several rebellious tears. I cannot shake the belief that dear old Lizzie, bless her, would have adored it. It seems much her own style: praising and soft yet haunted around the edges, like her doomed relationship with Pastor Fox, whose own marriage remains in shambles after the scandal and who yet refuses to keep to himself these days, like the ancient religious hermits. Instead, he went from watching Lizzie's body enter the ground to quickly entering a different kind of public service, as a Member of Parliament for Oldham, part of the Liberal party. Perhaps he has calmed somewhat from the more vociferous though less organised Radical party. We've seen little of him recently, but applaud his political efforts: he even suggested to John that he should run someday, which John laughed off, but then I noticed a curious gleam in my Love's eyes as we bade goodbye to the pastor that day. William and his dearest Lizzie never did visit Scotland. Never the time nor the money, nor a shared simultaneous inclination: how many opportunities for excitement do we permit to vanish like that?

'O Holy Night' made its tranquil debut just the year following Lizzie's death, too, another hymn she likely would have found solace in—Fox as well, for that matter—though neither of them could have worked their own laborious way through what is in truth a four-octave tune. I wonder if that group outside the house knows it, then mostly stop listening. For now and for the coming year, I shall content myself less with new holiday habits and more with relationships and attempting to track the effects of my continued philosophical work with my husband…

* * *

*From the Diary of Helen Taylor:*
My, but those feelings do run the gamut, do they not? Dear Mum, I wholeheartedly applauded your genuine happiness, allowing Dear Mr Mill to analyse that quirky term howsoever he might have wished. You deserved it. You both did. And no, I have yet to find my own reflected happiness in a man, never having sought it, in truth. My own most beneficent feelings have other sources, at least thus far.

I only interrupt here to note how Mother could shift so easily betwixt a horrible year covering several pages of her diary to one that clearly numbered among the finest of her life among the next few pages. Let it not seem, Dear Reader, that Mum could spin her feelings so easily, and recall that her inserts summarise so much at a time. As do mine, I suppose.

She needed those less refined, more casual words, as I do mine here in my own lovely leaves of rich paper, a place to reflect and not have to write for an interpretating public who, as Plato indeed warned, would inevitably render judgement along with meanings which might differ from those of the writer regardless…

# PART FIVE

# God Is a Utilitarian

*1854–1858.*

Haji and Lily had become outstanding participants in the soirées that John had begun sponsoring. The Grotes remained courteous hosts when it was their turn, though it had become ever more challenging to get the whole Trijackia, plus the Grotes, plus Harriet's few female friends, all in the same place, though the Mill home seemed to garner a larger draw than any other. And the children—adults, John had to keep reminding himself, still deciding what to 'do' with their lives—kept conversations lively and hors d'oeuvres plentiful, and chats at these small parties ranged the full gamut of topics. Nothing remained off-limits: economics, politics, racial issues, gender issues, religion, and there remained unspoken rules—on occasion vociferated loudly yet rationally by any of the 'three Jacks'—that no matter the disagreement, respect for the speaker came first. 'You're welcome to silently believe that the rest of us are wrong,' added Roebuck one night.

Again came the subject of Parliament finally lifting restrictions on Catholics and Jews in government jobs, their houses of worship receiving less vandalism in recent decades, and the faithful were free to pursue most other occupations.

'Look at Disraeli,' George Grote added during one of these evenings. 'He's part Jewish, though I don't know how much exactly.' Some polite chuckles at this, though guests that night were themselves unsure if one could be a 'portion' of a religion, like one could be part French and part Egyptian.

Harriet Grote tried to lighten the mood. 'Disraeli's all over the place, whatever else he does in the Commons. He's favoured greater British intervention in remote places like Afghanistan and South Africa, and yet he's also on the forefront of that new company tasked with building a modern and more thorough shipping canal through the Suez.' She stole a glance at John Mill. 'And the poor sod clearly loathes our dear Mr Mill.'

Ignoring the public jibes that truly had been aimed at him by MP Benjamin Disraeli, John Mill posed the question, 'Why do we feel the need to intervene in the affairs of the Afghan Emirate or the Kingdom of Zululand?' It sounded like he was finally taking more interest in current events, though for him these faraway lands had established cultures and governments, and his concern was less with British policy, more with the political autonomy of sovereign powers. 'As for an updated canal, Napoleon gave that up during his invasion of Egypt, thinking separate water locks would be necessary.'

John Roebuck shook his head, knowing from previous experience that these salons of theirs were intellectually safe. 'Don't underestimate Disraeli. He's at least as tough as Peel, God rest his soul, and side-stepped the religious question by converting to the oath and traditions of our dear old Church of England.' Peel had served as Home Secretary, and his London police force had gained international renown for its modernising successes with law enforcement, though London's gaols remained barbaric and despairing locales, despite Bentham's critiques.

'I met Disraeli before leaving Parliament myself,' Roebuck continued.

'Long live the "independent member of that house!"' shouted Harriet Mill, referring to Roebuck's description of himself upon entering service as MP for Bath, way back in '32, not long after they first met at a more formal and uncertain gathering.

Roebuck grinned at her. He and Mrs Mill had often clashed over their views, usually in a friendly and respectful manner, though on one occasion she had called him 'an ill-bred Canuck,' to which he responded that the supposedly derogatory term was actually compli mentary, and in fact an Americanism for their northerly neighbours. He remained a utilitarian at heart: his voting record confirmed that. While not the racist Carlyle was, he had publicly agreed with the American Southern states and their purported right to govern themselves, even if that entailed maintaining slavery. 'Make no mistake,' he said, 'Disraeli is as dedicated to his principles as, say, William Gladstone, perhaps more so since he started as a High Tory, then broke away with Peel and others to become Conservative members. There are noises now of him helping start a "Liberal" party, too!'

Ah, politics: shaper of ideals while shaped by them, and offering nary a dull moment at social occasions. In between serving their elders and listening to such discussions, the Taylor offspring—adults though still the youngest attendees—shared a glance, trying to ignore the now louder animation involving which issues Liberals and Conservatives agreed and disagreed about. Haji and Lily still possessed some of the strict moral dualism of youth—things must be Right or Wrong, as parents tended to teach—yet also displayed a wisdom beyond their years, even beyond some of what was on offer at these parties. Their own conversations had logically built on the foundations of their mother and stepfather, and they remained curious and alarmed by how such open-minded parents holding such progressive beliefs could still unwittingly turn blind eyes to the likes of religious questions.

Like his younger sister, Algernon Taylor freely admitted to a fascination not just with Christianity in general but Roman Catholicism in particular, and had recently even spent some contemplative 'researching' months at a Barnabite monastery in Rome—the 'Clerics Regular of Saint Paul,' who emphasised the medieval vows of chastity, poverty, and obedience. They remained numerically a tiny order, partly due to a fourth vow to never pursue higher office. Haji opted to return home after his ascetic period, having decided that the priesthood was not for him, sharing a laugh with John about the ancient phrase attributed to Saint Augustine—'Lord, make me chaste... but not yet!'—and cracking about how the nuns at the adjacent convent were 'lovely.' He broke that up with an admission that he 'might be open to marriage for the right lass,' though had no one presently in mind.

At least his Italian had improved, and he had made noise about teaching English to Italians, perhaps becoming a vintner and selling his bottled wares back to a demanding English, whose endless thirst for ales and ciders remained classist: the rich preferred wine. Stepfather John imagined the business aspects, knowing his stepson to be a passable connoisseur—but rather uninterested in the daily details of managing a labour force. Still, the thought of someday sipping a Taylor Vintage 1861 or the like offered its own appeal, if Haji ever pursued it.

As for dear Helen, she might prove more able to manage those business aspects of developing a career, and her own tentative plan had thus far received no support from her mother, even though John rather liked it. 'But you're biased by your love of the performing arts,' Harriet had chided him.

'Dearest love,' John defended his step-daughter to his wife, 'if you've learned nothing else from me, then at least acknowledge that everyone is biased, from some source. We had to explain that in our intriguing book, if you recall.'

'How every argument must begin with at least one premise that is uncontroversial, another way of saying that we have to take it on a certain amount of, dare I say it, faith. That was a strange term to have to explain in a book about logic.'

He grinned, in that knowing way that most people never witnessed in him. 'So what, then, is the problem with Lily's idea?' He thought he knew the answer, but had also made sure the young lady was not around during this conversation. John had never attempted to get between Harriet and any of her children, on any topic. All of those young adults had at some point thanked him for it, even Herby.

'John, it's acting!' Harriet had cried. 'It's disreputable! There are reasons why women were forbidden from acting on stage for so long.'

'Yes, and those reasons hail from the same sort of sexism against which you and I have railed for so long now: the notion that women need to be protected from immoral actors, or that the profession is filled with scoundrels.'

She finished for him. 'Or because acting is based on lying, and because women have enough trouble being trusted by society as it is.'

He sighed, holding back his comment, which she had already heard, about how professions based on intrinsic dishonesty seemed limited to dramatics and politics; it seemed less funny now. Even some of the ancient Greeks, those inventors of theatre, had opposed their new social art at times: it was too false, too emotionally manip-ulative, too overtly political, no place for women, or some mix of these. Yet Harriet enjoyed theatrical performances as much as John. Londoners had, after all, re-invented the theatre for early modern audiences.

John and Harriet had loved attending a revival of 'Cinderella' at Drury Lane, and 'Othello' at Covent Garden, early in their court-ship. Harriet considered the shows nearly frivolous expenses until the intermissions, when she and John had strolled arm-in-arm, never mind the knowing or judgemental glares from the other well-to-do. She had also liked the fresh fruit for sale at performances, though she thought it the height of rudeness how so many patrons talked while the cast members were exhibiting their talents, an annoying habit which generally met with far less tolerance when a performance was opera. John still dreamt of attending an opera at the famed La Scala theatre in Milan, or partaking of Mozart's 'Die Zauberflöte' in Vienna, then recalled that the latter featured a mother trying to rescue her daughter, and chose not to belabour the point with Harriet. That

Austrian theatre might even be dangerous — the 'Old Price Riots' of 1809 over tickets remained in the memories of many, though John and Harriet had discovered wry humour in realising that perhaps society had made strides after all, if those decried as 'peasants' not long ago could nowadays riot over limited access to theatrical events.

'Harriet, within our lifetimes, even writing by women has undergone nothing less than revolution. Think of how many women writers there are, how many we know.'

She recognised at once where this would lead, but did not try and silence him. 'John, on that touching note which is doubtless a jab at my alleged hypocrisy with women working for pay, have you heard of this lady, Catherine Spence?'

With his mesmerising memory, John considered, knowing that Harriet was losing ground in their discussion, so he accommodated her. 'I cannot say that I have.'

'I don't know her, either.' John raised an eyebrow, which some found off-putting, but which Harriet knew for silent praise, encouraging a speaker to continue. 'Born in Scotland, emigrated to Australia at an impressionable age.'

'Does she know Arthur, then?' Harriet shook her head, though her brother, still loving his adoptive southerly country, had heard of her, and via a surprising channel.

'They don't all know each other, Dear,' she chided him. 'Besides teaching and acting the suffragist,' and she could tell she had John fully hooked now, 'Ms Spence recently had her first novel published. And it sounds like she's not yet thirty!'

'Fascinating,' he conceded, 'though I remain unsure where you're heading.'

It was her turn to feel exasperation. 'Two details, Love: first, this is someone who knows of our work, at least according to recent accounts from dear Arthur, even if the pair of them do not know each other directly.' She sighed deeply, finding calm and clarity. 'And second, Mr Taylor played an instrumental part in getting her published!'

John dimly recognised this was supposedly a chat regarding Lily's future, and the late Mr John Taylor was rarely a topic of discussion for them. Not that he remained a forbidden subject by any means: it was just that Harriet still, John knew, occasionally mourned the loss and sometimes still missed what had been, for all its mutually destructive tendencies, a promising friendship and, prior to Harriet's 'trouble,' a solid familial basis for three independently-minded youngsters, if not always a meeting of minds for their parents.

That did nothing to alleviate the confusion, though. 'How?' he said. It was rare for him to try and cheat one word into a full sentence, and his mouth looked like it wanted to keep moving, like it so often did.

'That's just it: I don't know all the details. Can you imagine? Somehow, in all our conversations and letters abroad to absentee siblings, Mr Taylor managed to help "bankroll"—is that the term?—part of the requisite funding for Ms Spence's book. I've actually been looking for it on London bookshelves, have been told by the staff at Hatchards bookshop that "it's expected soon," and by that newer shop on Paternoster Row that "we cannot find any record of this publication, Miss." At least they no longer address me as 'Mrs Taylor.'

'Maybe they just have no wish to order copies.' John tried not to sound bitter, but some London booksellers remained hesitant to carry copies of his and Harriet's 'radical' or 'contentious' or 'controversial' works, never mind that the staff of these otherwise fine shops—Harriet and John had made their joint bookshelves sag a mite from shopping at them—had not actually read their works.

Besides, 'controversy' sold books, just like it sold newspapers. Their first book on logic, while thankfully not having been received as solely a scholastic text, was admittedly dense at times, though hardly controversial—unless one considered John's condescending attitude towards the 'uneducated masses,' even if this was tempered by his ongoing pleas for the widening of education, to match or surpass the widening of enfranchisement. If there could exist 'an exact science of human nature,' then it must apply to all.

As for their work on political economy, it too sought to detail the understanding—and implications—of different approaches to a society's economics and politics—and therein lay the potentially controversial parts, so John and Harriet believed—that must support such.

Their own new text indeed caused stirs, and penetrating conversations in Continental salons, and the religious conservatives—not Pastor William Fox!—would revisit images of perdition masquerading as morality in condemning it. They had discussed this concern at length whilst debating another new book—already on the shelves of those self-same shops—of which John's only initial critique had been its cumbersome, medievalist title: 'The Elements of Social Science; or, Physical, Sexual, and Natural Religion. An Exposition of the True Cause and Only Cure of the Three Primary Social Evils: Poverty, Prostitution, and Celibacy.' John could almost picture its author getting arrested merely for adding his name to the cover, reminding John of his own arrest for peddling brochures back before Harriet even came into his life.

Plus, John had purchased a copy of the book for Harriet's birthday, knowing she would hardly put it down until she finished it. She would probably have her daughter read it afterwards, perhaps Haji as well, though it might frighten Herby a touch.

Getting back to Lily, John had wanted to let the matter go, though Harriet could tell by his familiar expression that he did not consider the issue to have lessened in importance, and he still loved the theatre even more than his wife. Mrs Mill hardly wanted her only daughter consorting with the likes of prostitutes—which in fairness some actresses were, though actors sometimes sold themselves in a variety of ways, too—or, Heaven forbid!—become one herself. John just wanted his stepdaughter to find her own path in life.

'Well, good for Mr Taylor, and for Ms Spence, then,' John said. John had tried to reassure Harriet by noting that under altered circumstances, he and the late John Taylor might have become friends, and was surprised—he still had occasional misunderstandings about the workings of female minds—that the effort made Harriet weep again.

*So long to wait,* John thought for the thousandth time, *but entirely worth it.* He had never wished ill upon successful Mr John Taylor, apothecary. They had other things in common, too: John failed to hide his amazement that the supposedly literarily disinterested Taylor had gone to such lengths to support this Ms Spence in Australia, or that he had kept abreast of the news writings of Ms Martineau in England, for example.

As for Harriet, she had—thankfully!  remained mostly symptom-free for several years, with only occasional 'flare-ups' of issues like headaches—usually not so debilitating, though once in a while they would leave her feeling light-sensitive and irritable—with a bloody nose, or a fever, though usually not all at once. She had decided to count her blessings and appreciate having lived a mostly happy and healthy life, all things considered. John knew she still awoke some-times, sweaty and tearful, worried about a return of the partial paral-ysis that first struck over thirteen years earlier, and then sometimes weeping softly for several minutes, grateful that she at least had never contracted consumption.

But what to do about Lily? John's own focus—obsession, Harriet would say, not quite meaning it as criticism—upon personal liberty meant that he felt both logically and morally compelled to support his stepdaughter's plans, whether they matched his or Harriet's or not. That was the tack he presented to his wife, having learnt at least enough about how her alert and brilliant mind functioned to realise that suggesting she might be clinging too much to her no-longer-little girl would prove counter-productive.

'But how does she find happiness that way, John? And how does she avoid falling in with the wrong crowds with a lifestyle constantly on display?'

John gazed right at her and simply said, 'As to your second query, we've made sure for so many years that her judgement is measured and as sound as possible.'

She rubbed her eyes, staring back. 'What then of my first query?'

He hooked an arm behind hers. 'That's the question we've spent our entire lives together attempting to answer for ourselves and for others. Lily will have to answer it for herself.'

* * *

Helen Taylor, aged twenty-three in 1854, rubbed her arm again where the sting remained, though the slight bleeding had quickly stopped beneath a clean white dressing and bandage. Lily took pride in keeping updated with news, a veritable duty instilled in her by her headstrong mother, and to a lesser extent her rational yet often dreamy stepfather.

While the Compulsory Vaccination Act of the previous year remained applicable in force only to infants, Helen had already debated with these elder adults in her life of how, logically, if babies must be prevented in this new and amazing medical manner from acquiring certain diseases, then adults should surely follow, even if the general public still had trouble comprehending how intentionally giving someone a miniscule amount of a disease could make the person immune to it. Public welfare, always a prime focus for Mother and Stepfather, was becoming more of an issue, though perhaps Mr and Mrs Mill were simply afraid of the thought of being willingly stuck by a metal needle.

'Like der savages in die Pacific islands, wit' their tattoos, one supposes,' Herr Gomperz had commented last year, his Germanic drawl noticeable on certain consonants, one of the numerous guests of the Mills at their shared home at Blackheath, near the namesake school. Lily and Haji sometimes made themselves scarcer, but enjoyed the setting of Mother's 'radical' round table—'like Camelot's own, with everyone meeting equally!'—Stepfather John had exclaimed upon making the purchase, after behaving more systematically with regard to practicalities on that occasion, carefully measuring the space for such a costly and difficult-to-deliver purchase. But there were also times when Lily and Haji preferred their own tête-à-tête, especially away from racist ramblings from the likes of Gomperz and others who believed they behaved in the common good, like utility demanded.

Lily had tried to explain this to Mother once: that part of the younger woman's attraction to Roman Catholicism lay not in youthful rebellion nor seeking to be a radical in Church of England society, but because its moral code—like those within all religions, Lily believed—could be found more within one's own conscience than in philosophy books.

Then again, Lily also understood that some persons seemed to truly lack a conscience, and further had versed herself with the more sordid components of Catholic history, from Crusades and pogroms and persecutions, to more recent and disturbing justification for purely political and economic imperialistic expansion.

Lily continually impressed house-guests and family members alike with her prodigious memory; her stepfather once admitted that it was at least as adept as his own, or that of the late Mr Bentham. And some months earlier, Lily had gently if firmly returned Dear Stepfather's own words to him.

'Father,' she had taken to calling him, though never in front of her brothers, at least not Herby. Nor aunts, nor uncles, nor Grandmama. 'Did you yourself not write once in the 'Westminster Review,' that "no government can now expect to be permanent unless it guarantees progress as well as order; nor can it continue really to secure order unless it promotes progress?" It seems fair to me to conclude,' and the other guests had looked admiringly at this young woman, then at Mill himself to find him both reddening and smiling, 'that the enforcing of a new statute clearly in the interest of the health of the nation via the health of its subjects—very young and,' a wink at Mother, 'slightly older.'

'Very vell put, young lady,' Gomperz added approvingly. Theodor Gomperz was a classicist, and hopefully, though no one mentioned it that otherwise fine evening, he might outgrow his racist sentiments someday. John Mill, after the unpleasant loss of Thomas Carlyle's friendship, remained wary of extremist views from anyone. He admitted he had indeed written that passage, and then, typical of him, led the discussion to justify it.

Haji, bless him, had been at Blackheath during those heady days as well, before returning to his own home. Harriet and John delighted in having the children entertain other esteemed guests, as the couple also began to regain their old confidence regarding selection of friends and—dare I say it? thought Lily sometimes—public appearances. Such guest-lists had included Italian and French writers—veterans of the '48 urban revolts—and radical advocates of officially sanctioned cooperatives to guarantee employment for the lower economic and social classes. One of them said outright that Jesus of Nazareth had, after all, numbered among the most fanatical socialists in history. Mother had shot Lily a glance of her own at that, with a hint of a smile, but Lily took it in stride, realising the strange truth of it, despite centuries of Catholic acquisitiveness in His name.

Such guests were never boring, and Lily had the chance to balance her own perspectives and beliefs with those of the curious company her parents kept. She at first blushed when Gomperz—roughly her own age, a bit into his cups that night, perhaps letting his glance linger towards Lily a bit too long—said he hoped to have more philosophical disputations with his hosts, and with Lily. He aspired to study at the University of Vienna, and Lily wished him well.

During those same fascinating months at the retreat of Blackheath, John and Harriet encountered and considered and began to incorporate into their ideas and ideals such vital events as never before. They had grown weary of feeling 'in the middle,' betwixt radical thinkers who thought they had gone 'soft,' conservative writers and politicians who sometimes suggested openly they should be 'muzzled,' and liberals, politically more or less displaying a mix of radical and conservative attitudes. John and Harriet continued to remain in the forefront of what they understood as something very simple: how to get as many as possible to engage in that activity that throughout history had proven so radical in itself—to think, to approach topics from the perspective of reason rather than passion.

That was what the politicians and writers who ignored or despised them never understood. John and Harriet Mill did not favour increased suffrage or greater rights and protections for certain groups or limiting imperialist ambitions per se; instead, they followed logic and ethics and took the next steps.

Accusations of being too liberal or radical or utilitarian or anything else amounted to red herrings from detractors: label or libel, Lily grasped that showing irrationality in anything her mother and stepfather had written was very challenging, even if one tried to do so merely as practice for a logic course. Maybe part of the discomfiture from others amounted to intellectual jealousy; some reporters had learned of John's intense upbringing from who-knew-where, and used that either to laud a brilliant mind shaped from youth—the tabula rasa of Locke, elaborated upon by Hume, showing the merits of a 'proper' education—or to illustrate how too much 'book-reading' might damage someone, especially one who was also a bit frail of body.

Having acknowledged all that, however, Lily found herself strangely envious instead of her brothers—both ensconced under their own roofs by then, as she suddenly had to witness dear Mr Mill's much less rational lashing out at certain other parties. Harriet would later attempt, repeatedly, to attribute her husband's viciousness towards his own family by recalling his pale and sombre countenance in early 1854, upon greeting her and an eager if sober Lily, before sharing his own dreadful truth-telling.

Emotional storms quickly but not quite satisfactorily dissipating, Blackheath could offer its own balm, and Mrs Mill, while remaining free as of late of some symptoms, had nonetheless received her own diagnosis lately of broken blood vessels in her lungs, with a bit of bleeding occurring with slight coughs. Any internal haemorrhage was terrifying to contemplate, and to pull one's silky handkerchief from one's mouth and nose with blood and mucus in it had led Harriet straight to a physician in Nice. Her much-improved French stuttered slightly from apprehension, and so Lily had to interpret while gripping her mother's hand and trying not to give into fear herself.

It was hardly reassuring on its own, as so many by now understood that bloody sputum was also a tell-tale signature of consumption, itself taking as many citizens of Europe as malaria took from many parts of Africa and Asia. It had thrown Harriet into a panic one morning to find herself adjusting slower than she would have liked to a strange room, with her daughter in an adjacent bedroom, then recalling their location — without John, who had been informed by the Company that he could not, for once, be spared at that time. And she was as startled as she had been at her first womanly bleeding to have found blood on part of the bedding, but this time on the pillowcases and not the sheets. She and Lily had fled home, to be greeted by John's equally disturbed visage, though he knew more of her recent ailment than she of his.

'What do we do now, John?' his wife had demanded of him, perhaps of all Creation. They had both lost so many to a single disease, and knew so many other families had also. It was what made familial strains that much more wrenching.

He just held her, reaching for Lily for a triadic crushing embrace, all three letting tears come on their own, dignity or servants or carriage drivers feeling embarrassed be damned. 'I wish I knew,' he answered feebly, almost ashamed he could not offer more.

Just enough of the traditional patriarchal attitude remained in this 'effeminate philosopher' to lead John to ask, 'How was the trip otherwise?' mostly to Lily, always wanting to keep her involved.

'Charmant, Papa,' she said, John feeling another pair of rebellious tears find their path onto his dampened cheeks, delighted by how easily she addressed him thusly.

'Est-ce que ton voyage s'est bien passé? Dites-moi sur Nice.' He enjoyed that she continued to practice the language, and looked forward to hearing about a French port that he had never visited, even in his youth during travels with his family. It would help ease the conversation towards his own diagnostic admission.

He found it easier, after they had unloaded the ladies' luggage and sat down for an afternoon tea — 'Never more welcome than now,' mused Harriet — to read from his own little journal, kept recently and thus far only in reference to all things medical and unusual.

Harriet was touched that day. John had dismissed the servants after verifying that Harriet was doing as well as could be expected, and a physician friend of her late father could be summoned quickly anyway if she again worsened—when her husband chose to take over the running of the household. At least for a time, and at least with details and rituals that he found more manageable than ensuring a winter's supply of heating coal, or remembering to store certain foods in the ice box, especially after the servants returned from their shopping excursions to secure groceries. It was more like him to note the evolution of terms—ice boxes were becoming known as 'refrigerators,' and better insulated, such as their own stained pine box lined with Cornish tin and Irish cork—than to pay much attention to its price when they bought it.

John could more than afford high-grade produce, and London markets remained replete with exotic foodstuffs, too—Harriet adored ginger, insisting on using the freshest for baked treats, as well as a non-English additive sometimes to her tea. The couple had once joked about the purported sexual benefits of ginger consumption—John had laughed about an ancient notion that it might aid men's libido, Harriet surprising him by knowing that the Chinese used it medicinally. Her medical readings over the years had taken her to some unexpected places.

Now John continued 'fussing' over the women, adding an agile touch to the afternoon service, one setting of tea with ginger, the others without. It might seem to a casual onlooker like Mr Mill was merely pandering, but Lily, perhaps even more so than her mother, understood not only the intimacy of this caregiving gesture, but also the overt reversal of 'traditional' service roles. Lily knew her 'birth father' never would have waited on women like this!

And there was John Mill, almost anonymously, flagrantly disregarding societal decorum by tending to his exhausted and potentially still ill wife, and doing so with genuine tenderness, even with his stepdaughter available in the same room.

'Spot of milk with no sugar, yes, Lily?' he asked after ensuring that Harriet had her own, smiling up at him as he turned to her daughter.

'Hmm?' Lily mumbled. 'Er, yes please, Father.' She still felt surprise by what she was witnessing. *No wonder the papers have satirised him for being the 'feminine philosopher!'*

He walked into the kitchen purposefully, yet with a grace that some took as weakness, a flawless stride that emerged from almost daily rambles through parks: John Mill sometimes truly still did twenty miles on a Sunday, something Mother never begrudged him, though she had developed a certain envy at his ability, as it simultaneously fled more and more from her formerly robust self. His hip rarely bothered him lately.

'We've no scones nor biscuits,' John called out from the other room, 'though if you don't mind, I'll gladly fetch some toast with honey or jam, as you wish.'

*Toast, too?* Lily wondered, now glancing at her mother, who returned her gaze over a warming sip from the floral china, part of a set comprising a wedding gift from her first marriage. Wonders hardly ceased: jam was old, of course; the Tudors often ate it straight, but toast was, well, peasant food, at least the heavy, brown, grainy material that John and Harriet preferred, or such was the conventional 'wisdom.' Honey remained costlier, and Lily knew that John loved it, the fresher from the hive the better, a taste strengthened by those childhood summers at the Bentham estate in France.

'Lily?' came the kitchen voice again.

She moved her glance from Mother to Stepfather, seeing a countenance that betrayed nothing and yet also felt full of warmth, a welcoming curiosity lacking the judging that was so much a part of their world. Lily had to remind herself that she could recall no episode of John Mill becoming truly angry, though she had missed his clashes with former friends.

'No, thank you. Would you like some help?'

A giggle as he turned back to finish. 'Perish the thought! It's good to serve; we should all do so at times. That's another lesson from the Asian lands; well, at least the Japanese. The Indians still have their castes, despite a belief in reincarnation.'

Again the befuddled look at Mother, who shrugged, her lips curling into the closest thing to an actual smile since their return from Nice. Was that the same Mr Mill who had trouble comprehending how much to pay a driver for a ride into another part of the City; the man who formerly had trouble recalling the names of 'the help,' or even to pay them at times; the 'saint of reason' so lost in texts and 'feminine wiles' by the notorious 'philosopher in petticoats' sitting across from Lily, slowly sipping her tea; indeed, the very same who had once utterly forgotten to order coal for his home as winter lay in wait?

References to other cultures came upon the man suddenly, that was nothing new. And yet this notion of serving others... it seemed more utilitarian than his liberty-of-the-individual philosophy, but still...

Returning from the other room, and having dutifully handed off the tea service, earning a kiss from Mother and a loving smile from Lily, the younger woman watched, feeling her heart thud one of the strongest loves it would ever know, as John rose a few minutes later in the collective and contented silence, strolled over to that cumbersome piano she and Mother alike had once decried for its expense, and quietly sat while his long, skinny fingers began to lovingly and ably pluck out 'Für Elise,' the romantic Beethoven piece, reminding Lily of her abortive, if nonetheless pleasing, childhood attempts to learn ballet.

Lily was stunned into maintaining that silence, and not only because her stepfather was playing the piano well. *When and where did he acquire the skill?* she wondered, surprised partly by her prior ignorance of this side of him and partly because it was such a demonstrative, feminine gesture: formerly Georgian and now Victorian England insisted that 'genteel' talents like cooking and cleaning and singing must remain overwhelmingly the provenance of women.

Lily caught the subtle, inviting scent again, rising into the room along with the soothing musical notes. 'Mother, don't you prefer your old Darjeeling?'

'I still do, Lily,' Harriet answered in a near whisper, 'though your stepfather has also introduced me to "gunpowder green."'

True shock now, Lily's expression falling like Ms Austen's literary mother fretting over finding her daughters suitable husbands, her interest in suitors guided mostly by their incomes. Austen's heroines, however independent and intelligent, did not serve. 'Should I even ask?'

Harriet grinned, truly feeling better, her handkerchiefs remaining cleaner lately. 'Think of it as a more potent form of traditional green tea, Love.'

'Just what you need, Mother: more stimulants.' Harriet laughed at that, as John glared at them, an almost serious countenance suggesting that performances by fine artistes should be appreciated quietly.

In truth, Lily savoured this scene along with the tea — and toast with a delectable peach jam, though she still preferred stronger orange marmalade, before wondering briefly if the latter represented more British imperialism: oranges hardly grew locally, after all, and their harvest probably required cheap labour; she'd have to check that later.

Harriet beamed as the first piece concluded. 'You should hear him with Chopin's 'Nocturne Two, in E Flat Major," she said softly to Lily, 'but he only plays that for me.'

Lily could hardly feel jealous, considering the old belief that only women possessed the digital dexterity for such compositions, then mentally chided herself for clinging to demonstrably false and sexist appraisals, shifting her weight back into the comfortable chair. She closed her eyes, smelled the steamy tea in the cup held just in front of her face, and let herself feel.

These queer adults who had both shaped her life so profoundly, often but not always intentionally — and more so than her 'real' father had, bless him — Lily realised that Harriet and John Mill had accomplished truly impressive things. Together. Few couples read so voraciously — though part of Lily's more independent self-education had reminded her that reading time equalled leisure time, which in turn necessitated not just the ability to read for its own sake but the funds to engage in it.

*That is something Mother has never truly understood,* Lily thought without bitterness, knowing that part of the incentive behind all this emphasis in her parents' still-developing thought included something that remained unwritten: that one can never actually change the thoughts or beliefs of another. A core part of Lily's thoughts and beliefs included the ancient Roman Catholic notion of 'good works,' still often practiced by her nation's Protestant organisations—they just labelled it otherwise—which in turn included helping those who lacked the education to learn to read, and funds the buy books, and leisure time and access to comfortable parlours and drawing rooms to keep up literary skill. Lily wondered if Mother and Stepfather realised how radical even these notions were, which they applauded but had not directly argued for themselves.

Fewer couples wrote, much less published: pamphlets, newspapers, some of which John had played a part in acquiring or editing or both, and books. Still fewer—Lily silently moved her fingers as she mentally ticked off her strange checklist—wrote philosophy, and dabbled with radical politics, and studied the economic implications of such.

And now here the strange duo seemed utterly relaxed at home, ignorant for the moment of those who jeered them in print—or in person—and who wondered too publicly if Harriet was a deviant wife and John a liar or lecher or some other deviant. They shared glances between measures of the piano music—Lily finally almost felt just a touch of envy, since John's playing was probably approximate in ability to her own—and they had seemingly learned how to live with a unique blend of fame and notoriety.

But that was altogether different from a man, usually sympathetic to a fault, castigating members of his original family for disrespecting a person they still frustratingly referred to as 'Mrs Taylor.' Lily gently touched John's tiny tome, knowing how personal and private a diary could feel to its owner, and read bits and pieces, occasionally looking at the older adults for their reactions. The book looked fatigued but strong.

That the other Mrs Mill—the elder widow, John's mother, had witnessed her health deteriorate just weeks earlier, finally becoming yet another casualty of illness, would not help mend the familial breach, Lily knew at once, her eyes scanning several pages of notes. Some of these had clearly been composed under duress, and Lily likewise recognised the indelible stains of occasional tears on the pages.

Similarly, John's remaining family members might not trust any further the simple facts that his mother had of course yet been in England while her son had — once again — gone gallivanting about the Continent — finally released by the Company and ostensibly for the improvement of his own problematic health — as the older woman had grown worse.

One could argue, Lily feeling guilty for thinking such titbits like a legal solicitor hunting sordid details, that John's requesting via Continental letter-writing that his mother officially designate some- one else as executor of her will — and thus of much of the family's remaining estate — 'either instead of me, which I should prefer, or as well as myself,' was misguided. Hopefully he had enjoyed Brittany and Normandy, as Lily tallied the dates of the entries with what she knew of her stepfather's recent itinerary, but she found it insensi- tive that he could have reached this state with his family, his Mum in particular.

Even that was not all. As near as Lily could determine, both from the worn diary pages and her own recollections, the worst friction had begun last year. John had long before decided that he found relations with immediate family members all but untenable. She supposed that much of it had begun with something of a mutual antipathy — among John and his siblings — that dated to his childhood. Lily had some understanding of just how deeply and permanently anyone's upbring- ing would inevitably shape the rest of one's life. Babies and children who were loved and fed and generally healthy clearly fared better later on, yet physicians and other commentators sometimes noted the exceptions: the child raised in abject poverty who acquired an advanced education or became some useful and valuable contributor to his — or her — society, contrasted with — and to Lily's thinking, these latter remained alarmingly more pernicious in English society — those who grew to adulthood with every 'advantage' yet still emerged with intolerant and abusive attitudes towards others.

John Mill, meanwhile, had turned himself into a noted scholar and social critic when one might suppose, upon learning of his younger years under the well-intentioned but emotionally and intellectually extremely daunting tutelage of his father and godfather, that he could have easily turned into a hostile tyrant.

But he cared about others, including those thousands of miles away whom he would never meet. Those who had shared impressionable youthful years with him seemed the only exceptions, though one might understand his shorter temper with those who had lashed out at him and his ideas in the press.

Thus remained one crucially short fuse with this man: Lily's mother.

The younger of the Taylor women had never solicited personal information regarding John's family, not wanting to pry despite curiosity; some details should remain out of the reach of others. Nor had she ever witnessed discussions, debates, or debacles within the Mill homes through the years, but it was clear an impasse had been reached even when Lily had been in swaddling clothes. Whomever was 'right' in any logical or moral sense was long since eclipsed by John accusing 'those damnable women' of offering 'insufficient respect' to Mrs Harriet Taylor, now Mill. Again, Lily could not confirm nor deny this, and for that matter Mother herself had little experience with her paramour's kindred, yet hesitated to broach the sensitive topic or to visit anyone else named Mill.

So an alternate executor had been located, Mother having once observed that such a sordid adventure resembled her own issues with her abused sister, and Lily had thanked God more than once that her brothers never abused her, and had confessed to no one but her priest — Mother did not know she attended the occasional Mass — and her own diary, that part of her considering entering a convent school had developed not only from legitimate interest in an education, but also for having a method to explain why she never wished to marry. Too many risks remained for women in marriage.

But there were other ways of hurting persons—*dear God,* Lily thought, *indeed I am picking on Father's 'harm principle!'*—besides punching and kicking and pushing down staircases, and John, for all his sympathy for many and empathy for those he cared about, had ravaged his kindred. Lily fretted it would mar his own logical and moral legacy.

Lily knew that there had been some brusqueness and even name-calling, the sort to which she and her mother had taken pains to inure themselves over the years, as the then Harriet Taylor was painted as anything from trollop to wanton to home-wrecker.

Still, Lily suddenly wished very much to drop John's little journal like a hot potato, wishing she could alter a public and emotional yet no less generally true condemnation of Mr John Stuart Mill for so shaming his family. She further wondered how many others had ever seen this smallish and usually very quiet and unassuming man roused to such wrath, yet also silently admitted that there existed a chivalrous spin to it: making amends for his prior selfishness regarding Harriet when Mr Taylor had received his final diagnosis, the penitent Mr Mill had addressed his true love in letters as 'dearest angel' and 'dearest love.' Even more potently, Mill had openly referred to himself and Harriet as 'one,' such declarations dating to the early '30s. And this came from the man who also wrote, upon the occasion of his nuptials, of his 'duty to put on record a formal protest against the existing law of marriage, in so far as conferring such powers' of patriarchy within a legally-defined relation, matched by his 'solemn promise never in any case or under any circumstances to use them.'

That was the only remembrance now to make Lily smile, just slightly: none of the heroines of the 'English century's' prose writers had wed instigators of women's liberties!

Lily appreciated John's willingness to share another excerpt from his recent travel diary—she had not known he kept one, nor had Mother—though he described it in terms only relevant to his most recent trip. Lily still found it odd that both her parents had visited the Continent lately, though at different times and without one another.

Still, she took her time to read the passage to which John had called her attention.

From that spring, he wrote about feeling 'bitterly how I have procrastinated—'*procrastinated?*' Lily thought dully: this from a man who read two lifetimes of philosophy in their original languages before his age reached double-digits? But she did not judge: feelings were feelings, honest in themselves if sometimes lied about later.

'Procrastinated,' she re-read, 'in the sacred duty—' another odd phrase—'of fixing in writing, so that it may not die with me, everything that I have in my mind which is capable of assisting the destruction of error and prejudice and the growth of just feelings and opinions.'

Lily looked at her stepfather, his own countenance still seeming raw and red even in the drawing room's candlelight now that night had returned, knowing that he was surely as angry with himself for becoming so annoyed with his own relatives as he was with them for allegedly driving a frightful wedge between him and other persons he loved.

The urge to continue reading, to slake that perpetual intellectual thirst, remained. Like her parents, Lily took solace in the conviction that this was not the childlike gossipy sort of inquiry, the judgemental attitude of others whose drab lives might suffer from unwillingness to try different or forbidden things. No, Lily promised herself that she was continuing to better herself, and her relations with her stepfather, by learning more about him. Besides, he had not just approved but requested what in just slightly different circumstances would doubtless qualify as an invasion of privacy, yet another of those utilitarian terms John Mill had modified. He wanted Lily to read his travel journal.

She already knew he had benefitted from a shared relationship of trust with no less a personage than the Queen's own physician, one Doctor James Clark. That was the sort of tawdry detail to toss freely about at social gatherings, Lily understood.

Dr Clark, however, whilst seemingly discussing Mother's own case—she did not have consumption, despite her frustratingly quirky and random-seeming symptoms—but Clark nonetheless confirmed that John did have it.

The word glared at Lily from the page. John had displayed no apparent anxiety in penning it, the eleven-letter word of such dread to their time looked like the other words surrounding it, and Lily was already practised in deciphering John's penmanship: often hasty, with closely composed and narrowly drawn characters, plus lengthy crossings of the 't's' and curly tails for the 's's.'

John Mill could not have, must not have, consumption! The horrid wasting disease, the plague of modern times, feller of so many, including relatives of Lily's whom she had never met because of their appalling deaths. It was too heart-wrenching to contemplate.

She must shut her eyes. The piano-playing continued. 'Lily?' came the soothing voice, never sharp or overtly critical, like his nay-sayers claimed.

Lily winced, looking up to find the two older adults gazing at her.

Maybe it was John's perception of others that annoyed some of them. 'You've found Dr Clark's diagnosis?' he said.

The young woman swallowed, wishing for a handkerchief that was not upon her person. Only Mill—Taylor grim humour would get her through this. 'How on Earth does—forgive me, Father—a rank commoner and critic of monarchy, both ours and those across the Channel—possibly become a patient of Britain's royal physician?'

Harriet roared at that, long ago having given up caring about social niceties like privileges of birth—'meaningless bloody accidents,' Lily had once heard her exclaim in a fit of pique—since those very ladies, and gentlemen too, who were most educated, tended to be the very same who rudely frowned at upstarts like Harriet Hardy Taylor Mill, who ironically sought greater liberties and privileges for those very same people. 'Your stepfather has benefited from similar good fortune, Lily, just not based on the randomness of blood,' she said now. 'And he's been careful to cultivate,' sneaking a prideful glance at her husband, still engrossed in his piano skills, 'good connections.'

The timing seemed auspicious, as the sonorous keystrokes brought themselves to a melodic and peaceful end. 'Thank you for taking so long to interrupt,' John said.

'No, no,' Harriet added, 'you know I, we, would never interrupt, especially someone with actual talent. My own playing never progressed much past age twelve or so.'

'Perhaps that's why you failed to marry better,' John jested.

His wife threw a pillow at him. *Most unseemly of her,* Lily thought, hiding a new smile behind John's travel diary.

'At least I know why you remain so hell-bent on your daily walks,' Lily said finally.

'Hmm?' he intoned, dutifully picking up the satiny pillow and pretending to wipe dirt and dust from it. 'Oh, with the illness.' His tone was casual, but it made sense as he added, 'Exercise helps all, Lily.' As Harriet was still looking towards her daughter, John exploited her inattention to hit her playfully on the head with the pillow, then set it down. 'Why do you think I sometimes do so many miles on weekends?'

'To avoid church?' Lily asked, still feeling the need for playfulness. Some were even suggesting that laughter, that oft-elusive and subjective response to the world, might perchance help sufferers with whatever ailed them. It could hardly make things worse.

And it helped ease an otherwise awkward and tense moment, of which all three of this curious trio had grown weary. Leave it to Lily's older brothers to forge more 'traditional' paths. 'May I ask, Father,' Lily began, 'was the diary intended as therapeutic, or was it perhaps something you'd meant to work with previously?'

He came over and joined Harriet on the sofa, Lily still occupying a padded upright chair, what she thought of as almost decadent luxury. 'Both,' John answered. 'Plus, since we were unable to travel together that time,' he took Harriet's hand in his, holding it with a blend of tenderness and an expression like she was the air he breathed, 'I wanted your Mum to have something enlightening to read, to maybe compare with her own travel notes.'

*That might be,* Lily thought, *but Mum's own travel notes tend towards the bland and mechanical:* 'Day Nine—too hot, missing friends at home, but the food shows promise.'

John wrote otherwise. He may have failed as a poet, but his

attention to nuance and details left Lily wondering if he had missed an alternate calling as a novelist. Maybe he numbered among the poor souls who thought storytelling peaked with Homer.

He had scoffed at that, insisting his purpose was to avoid writing fiction, adopting an attitude similar to what Mother evinced regarding the acting profession. Still, his diary style displayed the playful tags of the creative writer. Lily skimmed ahead some pages, hoping that the odd job offer briefly mentioned had already been brought to Mum's attention. 'Did the faculty at the University in Corfu truly offer you a teaching post, Father?' she asked.

He grinned, then turned and offered a brief kiss to Harriet, propriety be damned. 'Yes, Daughter,' he liked calling her that, never having grown accustomed to using 'son' with either of the lads. 'Corfu is lovely, Greece the most central component of what some call the "Western Tradition." But my Greek is not what it was years ago, and even if I felt inclined to bring it back "up to snuff," as the adage goes, moving about the world seems an adventure for the young.'

'No, no,' Lily said, 'you hardly escape that easily, Sir. The two of you remain fine travellers. I may have relatives in the South Pacific, but they remain quite sheltered, hardly exploring the tropics or deserts that exist down there.'

Looking at them, she realized her mistake. 'Oh, dear no. I'm sorry!'

'It's all right, Lily,' continued John. 'Relocating to another country would likely place too much strain on us both, from the perspective of our health.'

Lily glanced down, hoping to hide in the pages, ashamed to have not considered the obvious. 'I like your description regardless, Father. Here: "I do not believe there is a more beautiful place in the world and few more agreeable."'

She sneaked a quick look back as John said, 'It was a most delightful day when I wrote that, and I was missing the pair of you painfully.'

Lily continued reading. '"The burden of it to us," that faculty job, I presume, "would be that we could not," let's see, "have the perfectly quiet life, with ourselves and our own thoughts, which we prefer to any other." Nicely put, that. Is that essentially what you told the university personnel?'

'Yes,' he conceded. 'I really am a better writer than lecturer. People say I have such a soft voice, anyway.'

'Father, please don't. You have nothing to justify to me!'

He sighed. 'I know. Perhaps I secretly wish such an offer had come along years back, before all these blasted medical concerns.' A knowing hand squeeze to his wife.

He was not about to allow this to devolve into melancholy, however. 'During these recent trips: France, Italy, Sicily, and of course Greece, I almost collapsed from laughter when I got to Rome to learn that the King of Naples and the Pope had recently removed much of the nude statuary!' He started laughing again, Harriet joining him. Lily thought Mum's first husband would have blanched or reddened or felt otherwise traumatised by mention of naked statues being hidden away from curious eyes.

She also knew it was not a poke at her own religious inclinations. 'Did some nudes remain in view, then?'

'Some, partly. It just made the visiting school children want to see them more!'

They all laughed at that. What was it about children that made them sexually curious? Some adults were writing how humans, like other animals, were essentially sexual beings. Lily had not dived so far down the hole of potential convent life to feel bothered by that, though she comprehended how one's own insecurities — whether truly one's own or if they were external, products of a more or less repressive and socially conservative society — might lead one to seek an escape from such distractions.

'In Sicily,' John added now, 'the mule-riding was fascinating. I think I did better with them than ever with horses.'

'I still would relish seeing you ride a large stallion or workhorse!' Harriet mused.

'No, no. The mules proved pleasant enough company. Maybe it's just that they're slower and lower to the ground that made it easier.'

'Tell Lily about your infection,' Harriet goaded.

Raised eyebrows from the younger woman. *Please do not—we were just discussing things sexual!* 'Oh, I took a scratch from some local flora, never learning the precise species, and the thorn made me want to scratch off my whole arm.'

'We're so glad it did not become infected,' said Lily, only half-joking. Untreated infections could prove fatal, she knew.

'Well, it did, though it resolved in a few days on its own. The fleas in the cheap haylofts and deplorable "inns" were much worse, believe you me.'

Lily gaped at her mother. *Really? This man who sometimes griped about the musky odour of horses whilst conveying through giant London had stayed of his own will in barns?*

'Really,' he said, as though reading Lily's thoughts. 'Would you believe further that I took on as a travelling partner in Athens—a pleasant gentleman from Manchester—and that near the border of Greece and Turkey, said companion had been gracious enough to hire no fewer than ten armed men to ward off bandits?'

Her look said it all. 'This is when one wishes one had one of those new photographic cameras,' John lamented, still amused. 'The whole trip came to almost seven months, which wears one out, plus it marks the longest your mother and I have ever been apart.'

'When did you miss her most?' Lily wished to know.

'Easy: next to the fabled Pnyx, back in Athens after thankfully not encountering bandits. I was recalling the glorious speeches made there of old, reminding myself of my ideals. And your mother's, too.' This time she leaned forward to kiss him. What would London's papers say about such untoward behaviour?

John grew serious for a moment. 'Ladies, the statue example in Rome was indeed comical. But when you cough up blood from your own laughter, you begin to wonder if your best travel days might lie behind you.'

Lily genuinely hoped that John spoke truly about all these matters, and again that his recent treatment of his kindred would not prove some horrid blot on his overall character. She had suspected for some time now that future writers would rummage about and thereby rearrange their lives: Lily had read enough biographies to know that, once asking Mother about her own early foray into that literary genre.

'Do you think this is truly what Caxton thought and believed?' she had solicited that day. 'I mean, you've offered a window into the late medieval English period, after all.'

Harriet had felt proud of that work, but also understood that no matter the attention to detail and depth of research, an observant writer centuries removed from the subject would inevitably have to invent some of the finer points: what exactly did the person say on one occasion, even when a precise date and place might be known? What did the person wear, or eat, or drink? What did she or he truly care about most?

So Lily returned to the diary. Her 'true' father, her late Daddy, while she missed him and thought of him often, would nonetheless have never tolerated such a candid insight into his thoughts. And John Mill could have hardly objected less, even welcomed the chance to share with 'his ladies.'

'I seem to have frittered away the working years of life in mere preparatory trifles,' that passage continued, and then Lily handed the book, the same size and apparent make of her own, she noticed, to Mother instead.

'You're wrong, Father,' she said now, feeling her Mother's touch briefly as the diary changed hands. 'You two are the most driven individuals I have ever had the good fortune of knowing, and I remain proud to call you parents.'

Lily stood up, making to move away, wanting to give them some moments together. 'There's just been so much death, Lily,' came Mother's voice. 'Your stepfather and I have chosen to cling to life, but one never knows when it might be snuffed out.'

The younger woman stopped in the doorway and turned to face them. 'I shan't pander to you by suggesting that only God knows when each of our times comes, nor how often our wills may disagree with

His.' She collected her thoughts. 'But the fact remains that the two of you, so strong on your own, have become something truly formidable together. You have been since you first met, but now that your relationship has become legal and more socially acceptable, you can continue the humble task of changing the entire world, one curious mind at a time.'

It was too delicious an afternoon to dwell on such concerns. An English person's home was their castle, after all, or such was the influence of British thought, that particular ideal going back at least to Locke, Lily knew. Because her stepfather knew, and of course gone out of his way to impart that bit to others.

Her parents marvelled at this precocious and sombre young woman, a reflection of their own independent thoughts and attitudes. Harriet still dearly hoped that Lily was not sacrificing her own impending happiness by remaining glued to her reading and travels and religious faith—which clearly did not conflict with her own from spite but from careful, rational forethought—then watched as her daughter slowly turned again and strolled out of view, leaving Harriet with the man who loved her fervently, body and mind.

Harriet closed her eyes, feeling dreamy despite the stimulation of strong tea, offset some by a contented belly and the loveliness of the music. Lily tried to force out of her mind for now the issues that awaited them all when they faced the World again: Mother trying to write and reconcile with family, especially her sons; Lily's own career aspirations; and a sudden memory from some months earlier of a meeting at John's Company, to which he had gone uninvited somehow, regarding how 'Company stock must not be permitted to drop further, regardless of what happens in India.'

That was morally disconcerting, to say the least. British exports had reached a peak in 1850 and had dropped somewhat since, though hardly enough to warrant economic panic.

Still, there were already signs even within Company offices that some would do whatever might be deemed necessary to maintain British political and economic interests strong, not necessarily in that order.

As late in that year as his admission of illness had come, John Mill had indeed found himself again travelling to his beloved Continent, as he and his wife had oft-times before, sometimes solo, sometimes together, sometimes with a younger Taylor in tow, usually Lily.

That latest time, however, witnessed John not only wondering if this would be his last such journey, but also, to his chagrin yet from the sheer seemingly logical necessity of doing so: wandering on his own.

Such a decision might have appeared taken for the same purportedly selfish reasons that had by now all but alienated Mr Mill from his blood family, but in truth Harriet remained a bit infirm for such a voyage, with Lily—and sometimes the Taylor 'lads,' even Herby on occasion, who had made slight inroads with his mum—acting as primary caretaker.

Additionally, one might further think that a person of such financial acumen and means as John Mill might travel with an entourage, making a Grand Tour accompanied by followers, adorers, and other hangers-on, but he had a become a man with a truly unusual talent, all the more remarkable for a rich individual who hailed from an equally solvent nation and empire: John had taught himself to live well below his means. Those early lessons in Classical thought had not merely yielded a tightly focused and rational mind, but more recent thinkers like Malthus and Ricardo had, through their well-argued if sometimes alarmist chapters, instructed others in how not to go into staggering debt. Those authors had intended such fiscally responsible readers to include whole governments, but the smaller personal scale worked as well. Yet John's homeland lived beyond its means.

Britain had committed, again, to a morally questionable—and easily bankrupting—war in a peninsula on the north of the Black Sea—fighting with France rather than against her, despite centuries of mutual antipathy, with both imperial powers having combined their impressive forces with the Ottoman Empire—the strangely matched trio locked in the latest sabre-rattling and musket-loading lunacy against a foe in the form of the Russian Empire.

John had penned a surprisingly short and concise argument in support of intervention in the Crimean crisis, using as a key premise his own well-articulated disillusionment with Tsar Nicholas I and his part-European, part-Asian Empire, but then, since politicians and philosophers alike sometimes never seemed to learn, matters escalated quickly. Lily had sharply rebuked him for that support.

'This idiocy grew mostly out of access to the Holy Land for Christian minorities!' she yelled at him one day.

John thought that a shallow perspective. 'What of control of the Black Sea,' he answered, 'and access to the Hellespont?'

Lily had anticipated that, especially since her stepfather possessed knowledge of Classical history, including an understanding that the 'Greek Bridge,' or 'Hellespont,' was that upon which Constantinople sat on its ancient western portion, while the gateway to Asia Minor lay on the eastern. It had been a cultural and not just literal bridge, a traditional demarcation point between East and West since the time of Homer's Iliad.

Which John could read in its original Greek, and which now Lily chose to elaborate upon further. 'Control of old ports is a side issue, Father. What of the religious issues?'

She was briefly pleased to see the question put him off balance, though still crushed by the need to pose it. 'Perhaps I missed something in the news, Daughter.'

Lily continued to grow pleasingly accustomed to that address, at least. 'It's like with the Crusades, Father: a critical issue through these tense "negotiations" concerns access to some of the ancient pilgrimage sites.'

'Do you think that explains our sudden and strange alliance of necessity with the Ottomans?' John did not treat this as mere mental exercise; he really wanted to know.

For all his brilliance, however, the man could still prove exasperating. If it was not a religious question answerable by ancient Pagans and their deities haunting Greece's Mount Olympus or India's Mount Kailash, then he simply wasn't interested. 'No, Father,' she added now, 'the Ottoman Muslims and the Palestine Jews don't seem to have much more concern than usual. This is more about the old Catholic—Orthodox split.'

John took his time mulling this over, nodding in his sanguine way as he considered it.

What Lily knew from her recent readings was that the whole mess was growing quickly out of control, like so many other ill-conceived conflicts throughout history. 'All of them!' quipped Harriet, while John remained unsure, or at least more sure of some inter-ventions by force having been, if not morally inspiring, then polit-ically necessary. Yet even he acknowledged a deepening frustration with the powers involved, quickly grasping that this was becoming a huge battle of established empires against each other, hardly enabling the furtherance of more socially progressive ideals. And Lily's quip about East and West gained credence as the Greeks were siding with the Russians, and the Italians with the irrationally-formed English-French-Ottoman alliance.

And that, for Lily, made little sense indeed: the might protect-ing the Anglican Church, mixed with mostly Catholic, mostly post-revolutionary France, along with officially Islamic Turks from the one of these three empires that had existed since medieval years? She hated the cynicism, but it would seem to require compulsion or greed to unite such a disparate group, even if just temporarily.

Plus, whatever the fallout, England's fine young men were there. Plus a few women, judging from recent news reporting: a cadre of nurses had been hastily drawn up to deal with the now inevitable ill-nesses, injuries, and deaths. John's recent sojourn to get devoured by insects and terrified by bandits had left at almost the same time. It made one wonder how much national shipping might get co-opted into sailing 'the lads' into harm's way.

'Even this new-fangled telegraphy, with its rapid communications, seems not to be helping,' John admitted, interrupting Lily's thoughts, himself wondering if these conservative monarchs and emperors even bothered to try contacting one another more quickly in an effort to dissuade the coming violence. Thus far it had not helped.

'True enough, Father,' Lily collected herself. 'Do we know if heads of state are taking advantage of these new wonders? God knows the railroads are already getting exploited to transport men and munitions into the fray.'

Maybe she was just feeling emotionally short, angry even. Lily tolerated much: the sexist comments her mother had endured before her and still did; questions about her faith—Catholics remained a minority in dear Olde Englande; other concerns regarding the profession she still wished to pursue. Even finding acting classes in glorious London had proved difficult, which might likewise pertain to her sex. And maybe another fruitless war was irking her further. Morality aside, England had pursued military engagements of dubious merit with China, India, and now Russia, within the past fifteen years, and such a lengthy series of campaigns was not sustainable by any measure, moral or monetary.

Plus, Lily had re-read that letter to her from John from that recent trip of his, something she continued to debate sharing with Mother. Lily hoped her Mum kept up her intimate conversations with her husband, something never done to significant extent with the man she still referred to as 'Mr Taylor.' And while John Mill usually appeared to others as wise, serene, or at least rather quiet considering how altering his thoughts could be, he sometimes revealed a different self via written correspondence.

'Nor would I' he had composed, in part of the same letter in which he castigated himself for procrastination, 'for anything which life could give, be without a friend from whom I could learn at least as much as I could teach. Even the merely intellectual needs of my nature suffice to make me hope that I may never outlive my companion.'

*Noble,* thought Lily now, even chivalrous of a kind, but those who bemoan the purported 'loss' of chivalry in these modern times forget—or simply did not learn—that it was based on a mix of abuse of those without power or money, a violently militant attitude towards foreigners, and the enforced denigration of the Fair Sex.

Lily knew John to be at work on an autobiography, which just

served to confuse her. Such a project—he admitted he had liked the
one penned by that rebellious Yankee Benjamin Franklin—hardly
seemed a priority for one who might be interpreted as having rather,
well, such dark thoughts regarding his wife. Maybe John was merely
acknowledging his abortive and ignorant efforts at housekeeping. Lily
might have to assist with that at some point. And maybe Lily herself
was simply denying the harshness of her parents' conditions: John
was surviving a disease that brought down so many, whilst Mother
had such varied and worrisome symptoms from a separate illness.

* * *

S urely 1855 would begin more auspiciously, at least such was
the consensus at the Mill-Mill-Taylor residence. It lasted until
Caroline Ley's—nee Hardy's—'worthless husband,' as Harriet
described her sister's drink- and violence-loving spouse, returned
home inebriated once again, and injured his wife once again.

Lily heard the latest account of abuse from her mother—who
received it from her mother—and both were stunned by its candour,
horrified with no doubt about the fate of a formerly lovely, vibrant
woman Lily still sometimes called 'Carry.' And Lily devoted as much
effort to considering just how the poor frail woman could willingly
lay with such a man. Had Aunt Carry truly grown up so desperate
for confirmation as a person that she had willingly entered such a
marital contract? Had Mr Ley—Lily refused to call him 'uncle,' just
as Mum categorically would not refer to him as 'brother'—done such
a fine job acting the role of good provider that Aunt Caroline and
others had been duped?

*Is that part of the price and power of acting?* Lily thought now, of a
sudden concerned again about her lingering ambition.

Then again, under the law, said marriage hardly had to include
willing aspects in the first place: husbands could take their marital
pleasures as they saw fit, whilst remaining unwed—as the situation
existed for women, anyway—offered its own mix of relative lack of
legal protections. And Lily found herself alternating between wishing

to have it both ways for herself: to somehow integrate the wholly incompatible hopes of pursuing life in the convent and the theatre. Something would have to give.

She and Mother had recently travelled anew to Ryde, both women loving the wind in their hair and on their faces during the ferry ride to the pier serving the town on the Isle of Wight, joking that it felt as exciting as a full boating adventure across the Channel, with less risk of seasickness. The pier might be showing its age, but a walk through the medieval town of Ryde helped lift the spirits, for Lily more so when she took off for a spell to visit St Mary the Virgin's Church, with its archaic tower and well-kept memorials in the immaculately-tended cemetery. She enjoyed a brief confessional with a charming young priest—younger than myself, even?—while Harriet had contented herself in the sunny day on a nearby public bench.

It might be comical, both women feeling guilty for not attending to each other whilst taking a few moments to be alone, or almost alone in Lily's case.

Lily walked out of St Mary's feeling refreshed, in more ways than one. Mother wasted no time. 'You know, my dear, I think I grow now as weary of my own clan as John has of his.'

'Thank you for asking, Mother. I did quite enjoy my short visit to this lovely historic church, and feel my soul more in order.'

Harriet bowed her head. 'I'm sorry,' she choked out, then felt her daughter's reassuring and strong fingers on her shoulders. Something else not to do in public!

'Mmm,' she added, 'thanks.'

'Mum, it's all right,' Lily kneaded, feeling the continual tension in her mother's shoulders and neck, thankful the woman had never grown hunch-backed. She was short and frail as it was.

'So what more of charming clan, then?' Lily hoped it wasn't her brothers.

Harriet replayed the recent frustrations about Aunty Carry, finally telling Lily to stop as Lily had ceased realising just how much pressure her frustrated fingers were exerting.

They both hated feeling in such a manner for any reason, and society placed such high expectations upon family loyalty. But these women and the man who shared their home had largely decided that loyalty, while superior if freely given, nonetheless had to be respected: it was easy to destroy as love or trust. For now they leaned back on the bench and just sat, Lily shedding her bonnet and Harriet her hat, suitable for race-day, thought Lily, sitting and feeling the sun's delightful energy on their skin.

John had remained behind, much as he wanted to join them. He had initiated a half-hearted attempt at research into his contemporaries, something at which he excelled when the subjects were long dead. In this case it included colleagues at the Company, and he had grown alarmed at that previous comment regarding 'Company stock price' remaining stable and ideally continuing its two and a half century steady climb. Immediately concerned that this might prove an allusion to foreign policy, he remained suspicious enough of any system by which an economic and financial organisation effectively ran a government, and in this case of a culturally different foreign nation.

It was disconcerting, to phrase it politely. As with kin, John grew ever more distressed with his professional 'family,' feeling the same concerns about loyalty that the women in his life—not those with whom he grew into manhood, notably—felt about relatives. In his own case, he experienced content aloofness from his own kindred, but the unabashed ambitions of the Company had extensive political connotations.

He had, as usual, shared his concerns via the Royal Mail service with the love of his life. As he described the growing and no longer masquerading tyranny of the East India Company, she made him laugh while at the same time slightly bursting his emotional bubble by pointing out that Continental politics had hardly improved much, either. Napoleon III was a 'crafty French despot,' showing a disdainful vulgarity, or so Harriet felt, during his recent visit to London with the Empress, strangely named Josephine: Harriet half-jokingly wondered about history 'repeating itself,' a phenomenon John understood well. Their book had mentioned this in a more roundabout way: how similar circumstances, whether for a person or a nation, would yield similar results via similar decisions.

For all that, they wrote of their intrigue by how much the world felt shrunken, attributing this not merely to the experiences of age—younger generations were 'always' more or less wise or some such—but also of the technical changes. Telegraphs, steamships, railroads: all had brought so many much closer, and should have the side effect of allowing would-be rational minds sufficient time to consider more sober decisions before leaping into the breach. Harriet remembered John's meticulous computations of how long it should take a letter or package to reach various corners of the Earth from England.

They shared witticisms via continued writing, knowing from books' worth of experience that the exercise did not just display affection: they actually word-mined their letters later for their next collaborative projects. These letters read unlike many of their contemporaries', full of insight and philosophical debate, though they kept disputes for in-person occasions: even with reduced mailing periods, days upon days remained too long for hurt feelings to corrode love.

Happiness had returned, at least in terms of their shared intellectual and moral quest. Time apart offered the chance to revisit the topic, which had never managed to appear in 'System of Logic' nor even 'Principles of Political Economy.' One of John's letters contained a summary that he was hoping to put into their next book, which would be intended to address this 'happiness' question once and for all. What was it, anyway? The Americans, idealistic if misguided, had attempted to not codify it exactly, but nonetheless offered a breach of the social contract to England by claiming that people had not a right to happiness, but the right to pursue it, like the object of some medieval romantic quest.

That never sat contentedly with John and Harriet, who remained suspicious of the notion of chasing after something intangible, and which might not wish to be 'found.' They understood this was not some inborn bias against the former colonists who had revolted.

No, this was entirely the opposite position of the greedy Company, which now regarded itself largely as its own government, acting independently of both Crown and Parliament. As for the Indian people, John and Harriet admitted—privately—their respect for them, sometimes imagining the Indians acquiring political and economic independence from a paternalistic nation which had as different a culture as the American Indians had from the Europeans who had landed on their eastern shores and begun moving westward.

But they knew that an analogy of the head of a family also failed completely. It was facile, self-righteous; the Americans might say patronising. And it hardly brought anyone any closer to an answer to the question.

So John tried again. 'Quality as well as quantity of happiness is to be considered,' he had begun in that letter, 'less of a higher kind is preferable to more of a lower. The test of quality is the preference given by those who are acquainted with both. Socrates would rather choose to be Socrates dissatisfied than to be a pig satisfied. The pig probably would not, but then the pig knows only one side of the question: Socrates knows both.'

Harriet had shared that letter with Lily during this getaway to Wight. Lily suddenly understood part of John's frustration: how could one possibly explain that happiness could never be the object of quest or hunt, like some elusive deer prancing and then fleeing for its life in one of Britain's old game parks, forests protected by law that reserved hunts only for those of rank and riches? Happiness emerged for Lily most often when she felt at peace, calm, not fretting about what others thought, knowing that she had recently done nothing significantly wrong. For her it remained that simple; thus the visit to St Mary's. Acting could do that for her in another environment, and so she craved it, wanting to contribute to the shared happiness of others, understanding the appeal of staged performances. That was a project worth pursuing, she believed, with happiness as a side-effect, not a goal.

But then the old circular logic re-emerged: how did one develop a taste for the theatre, one of Lily's stepfather's 'higher' pursuits?

What about the old English love of 'blood-sports,' and not just those mounted hunts in restricted areas? And what of those who sought 'happiness' at the expense of others, whether said others served as prostitutes, or had the misfortune for having been born as other help-less animals, like those sacrificed in the interests of the desperately gambling, rich and poor alike? Or even the pig compared to Socrates: pigs were clearly intelligent and feeling creatures.

At least old 'Papa' Bentham—Lily's later nickname; she of course had no memory of him—had raised that question of other members of the animal realm suffering. She wondered again what else had been left out of Stepfather's lessons about the brilliant thinkers that preceded and shaped him, especially those he had known personally.

Parents edit material for their children, she thought, with less anger than usual, but what has dear Mr Mill not told me of his father and godfather?

Interestingly, John himself found some impetus for the new work through his correspondence with Auguste Comte, that feisty French philosophe, whom John had still never met in person, and the man's idea of 'praxeology.' It referred to purposive action, and John admit-ted he had largely brushed it off previously because it seemed, well, tautological: of course actions had purposes! Did not all of them, including other animals such as satisfied Socratic swine, have some purpose, even if the creature embarking on said course might not be fully conscious of such at the time? It would explain everything from meticulous planning and rehearsal down to raw instinct and auto-nomic bodily responses.

John had learned of Monsieur Comte via their mutual networks of social contacts, and had politely expressed written interest in meeting someday, but anyone dedicated to 'reading between the lines' would quickly realise that mutual admiration in this case was feigned. Still, thought Lily, one thing her study of theatre and plays had taught her was that a person resented or even despised by someone quite often turned out have a great deal of character similarities with the person doing the loathing.

Loathing might be too strong a term in this case, and John, when feeling honest, would grudgingly admit that some of the ideas of Comte had come across in John's own work, and the reverse had also become true more recently. Initially reading and reviewing the careful praises of the American social experiment by that other famed Frenchman de Toqueville, John had discovered Comte's work, and had agreed with Comte, and with Coleridge also—that creator of clerisy—that the potential solution to the risks of increased suffrage was the intelligentsia, something taken almost from Plato's 'Republic.' John obviously favoured the principle, especially since he and Harriet continued to work on its expansion to include women, but John—partly on his own, partly with his wife—had come to believe that education remained more important than greater suffrage.

The wed writers had been misunderstood, taken out of context, reviled publicly, and Comte was part of the problem. Harriet had dismissed Comte's notion that women's purportedly smaller brains entailed smaller intellects. Most of the man's correspondence with John had taken place during the '40s, and while Comte had written of his ideal of a new science, with a new subject—politics and economics and even ethics—called sociology, he had remained steadfastly closed-minded to criticism. John meanwhile had received more hostility via multiple public avenues and instead reached dedicated open-mindedness, believing essentially that the greatest sign of intelligence and maturity was not the ability to read Plato in Greek at the age of five—or ever—but to admit when one had made a mistake.

Meanwhile, Lily no longer felt surprise or shame by just how far her thoughts could propel her. Maybe it was the Holy Ghost working through her mind, and she could still feel and faintly smell the coppery tang on her fingertips, like blood she supposed, from having dropped a few good British pennies into the St Mary's donation box, then lighting a candle in prayer for Mum, for John, for her brothers. She lit a separate one for herself, silently thanking God for helping to keep all their ideas clear.

Now, sitting still outside and watching the tourists amble about,

Mum naturally saw right through her. 'Did you pray for anything in particular?'

Lily grinned, still feeling strength in those same callused fingers, resuming kneading her mother's achy muscles like so much leavened dough, and found herself briefly thinking of the Body and Blood of Christ. The Holy Carpenter, for all His gifts, had not been the only one in history to suffer for truth, and Lily's attitude to her faith, while strong as ever, yet waxed and waned with regard to the perverse question of divine wrath and judgement.

'Oh, merely to avoid heresy, Mother,' she said, refusing to believe that a loving God could ever be capable of torturing for time evermore the questioning and debating tendencies of His strangest, possibly smartest, and mostly hairless bipedal creatures, who after all only exhibited the very curiosity with which He had imbued them.

Harriet leaned forward, then turned on the cast-iron bench to face her daughter. 'I was unaware any of the family thought of such.'

'I'm merely concerned, Mother, about the consequences of us all speaking our minds. Why do we do it, Mum? You, John,' she only used her stepfather's name with her mother, 'the thinking minds of history.'

Harriet was pleased for them to be meeting on emotionally neutral territory like this. Recent rows had erupted between them, John staying wisely out of the way, partly since he could logically side with either woman depending on his mood and what points each of them raised, still having trouble realising that sometimes a person—and a woman, Harriet would remind him—just needed to be heard and acknowledged.

But these sharply worded disputes between mother and daughter remained not just about issues of faith—interestingly, those had begun during Lily's childhood, and Harriet had never truly pushed very hard, terrified lest her little but very smart girl experience the psychic collapse that John Mill had, something which Harriet still tried to understand. Her own depressions lately had deepened, and not for reasons to do with her impending mortality.

No: rather, these fights remained mostly about Lily's decisions, and the two women had reached a sort of détente, Harriet realising that her daughter had the same independent streak that she possessed herself. So it was refreshing to speak peaceably like this.

'My dear daughter, if I've taught you nothing else, then hopefully I have at least imparted the importance of struggling to be heard, especially for us of the "gentler" gender.'

Lily laughed, though her own amusement never manifested as more than a smiling giggle. Except when she was on stage, and properly motivated: in truth, the seemingly mild Helen Taylor could guffaw or shout or weep with the best of them in a theatre, but she still fought with herself just as mightily to do so on cue, like any actress or actor should.

'I know, Mum. That's what I've loved most about you. Even with our differences.'

Harriet embraced Lily, at first lightly, then more fervently, as though afraid to release her. 'Now, if we can just get your brothers to accept those differences.'

Lily accepted the closeness. She might miss her father, but John Taylor had not been the most demonstrative of men. John Mill, on the other hand, sometimes comically ventured far into the opposite direction, though Lily understood his clumsy effort to make up for what had gone missing from his childhood.

And she knew Mum had not wanted her relationships with her children to feel distant like that; children were not simply miniature adults. 'Agreed. Have you had any word from "the lads" lately?'

Harriet released her, easing back into a more sedate sitting position. 'No,' she sighed. 'Haji does come by periodically, but hardly calls on us as often as I'd like. Perhaps mothers just hope for more contact.'

'No, don't do that,' Lily admonished. 'I know Haji's busy, but I receive little contact from him these days, either. What of Herby, then?' She thought she knew the answer.

Mum just shook her head. 'Like I said a little while ago: "family."'

'No, Mother, please don't do that, either. Those differences are one thing, but we've reached a level of, well,' she sought an appropriate description.

'The dynamics of the nobility?'

This time there emerged more genuine and heartfelt laughter, Lily forcing herself to close her mouth after a few moments to regain self-control. 'Heaven forbid! Are we become that troubled?'

Even Lily had felt difficulty accepting her beloved Church's recent notion of 'officially' and divinely sanctioning the faith of the Immaculate Conception, or that the Pope had made noises about ending the Papal States and replacing them with something more resembling a modern nation. And that remained above and beyond the 'quirky'—one of John's terms—or 'odd'—one of Harriet's—dealings and behaviours of Europe's noble and royal families. They were beginning to seem less sacrosanct, and the growing prevalence of newsprint and accompanying cartoons sometimes let them know.

Harriet laughed along with Lily, though in her case it felt slightly forced. She loathed how matters had gone finally with her own sister, had fretted about John's family too, and with some members of the Hardy and Mill clans deceased, it was too late to make amends with them. She emotionally went to and fro with feelings about her father—his shameful treatment of widowed Emilia, somewhere in Italy—offset by her own recognition of the times when she thought herself a less than dutiful daughter. But how did one evaluate one's own behaviour? Even the great John Stuart Mill had plenty of difficulty with that question!

*  *  *

Harriet had, by the closing days of '55 and heading into '56, become a more public and less private writer. Her diary still travelled with her, never left behind—she remained more likely to forget to pack sufficient changes of clothes, or for inclement weather—she believed the Continental clime generally would prove more suitable for her constitution than the 'dismal dampness' found so frequently in her homeland—than forget the little subtle book with its battered corners, faded cover, yellowed pages, even ink colours that ranged so widely in age as to seem different, though she always used the same.

Fewer entries now appeared within regarding the health of anyone, not just of herself. It had come to feel burdensome to make such notes, almost as though to do such might amount to tempting Fate, Greek-style. She would not share this weak logic or what her father might have called 'womanly fretting' with husband, daughter, or sons, but the risk felt real for all that.

She recorded more minutiae instead, that might appeal to those foraging through her personal effects for clues about how she thought. Obvious pride for John emerged in the reference to his 'final promotion!' at the East India Company, which amounted to £2000 per annum, enough to pay off, well, anything. Like his father, John had become 'Examiner of Correspondence,' in charge of communications with executives within the Company, and in India, approving all communications 'except the military, naval, and financial.'

The money meant they had their own conveyance now, plus horses—'Thank goodness,' John had cried, 'that I still have no need to try and ride!'—and staff to care for them, and could write off the expenses of their homes. Beyond that, much remained to begin more dedicated annualised contributions to various charities. Lily had immediately suggested the RSPCA, seconded by John. He might not be able to ride, and in truth none of them were very accomplished equestrians—only Herby had shown much promise in the family, but had not ridden with his siblings or parents for many years—and horses and other creatures in need of succour and food and shelter and simply not being abused by potentially vicious and cruel humans could benefit from the Mill's generosity.

So too could poor and abused humans. Admittedly, so much of the thought behind donations was the old notion of Christian charity, which had become more popular during the past few years as donations themselves—gifts of food, clothing, shoes, or actual specie—could now be more easily made anonymously. Donation bins and boxes, usually secured via lock-and-key, had begun to appear near churches and government offices, though many of these remained small enough that only coinage could really be left with them.

Harriet, in these private notes, shied away from judgement regarding the often sharp and hostile public disagreements over the ongoing question of what, if anything, 'the poor' might merit. Even definitions proved controversial: the old first Poor Laws had attempted to delineate between the 'impotent' poor — those who truly were unable to do much if any labour, whether from injury, illness, age, or all three, and the 'able-bodied' poor, who might be able to perform in workhouses — some encouraging, others prone to various abuses, or, more recently, create 'poor law unions.'

Just wanting to help out had become a confusing question, and some persons of more means — not really the nobility, of course, but the 'middle' classes, or 'middling' classes, if one accepted the satire of them in the papers — to volunteer some form of labour. Lily had developed an affinity for helping less fortunate children how to read, since the new public schools remained a topic for similarly divisive attitudes as charity in general, but the grand book collection at the British Museum — Lily kept petitioning for a British Library, but that would have to wait — remained open and gratis, so the areas outside, where mixed such a blend of British citizenry, could lend themselves to a young literate person to help others.

In her journal, Harriet had also all but glossed over another horrid opium war, which had led her and John to question again his commitment to his imperialist and exploitative employers. He could no longer remain there with a clear conscience, and British and French troops had united again — still a strange thought — along with American forces, to land on the Asian mainland and take on its Chinese defenders. At least the Crimean madness had finally ended, and Harriet confined her comments about that to the intriguing Ms Nightingale, who had mostly single-handedly and drastically reduced military fatalities by improving hospital conditions. The British public lauded the work of the 'lady with the lamp,' referring to her practise, shared with nurses under her leadership, of 'making the rounds' at all hours, comforting the troops, changing their clothes and bedding, making sure they received adequate hydration and nutrition. The military higher-ups had naturally found amusement in such 'feminine' cares, until Ms Nightingale's own statistical measures verified the accomplishments of these 'mere' nurses.

For Harriet, the woman and her accomplishments might have been catnip: someone dedicated to changing health care from its foundations upward, who was unafraid of heading into harm's way for the benefit of strangers, who argued publicly not only in favour of fundamentally modifying nursing and medical care but also in support of the 'contagionist' theory of the passing of diseases... Harriet was hooked at once, wondering in the diary if her combined social contacts with John might enable a meeting.

It had proven much less satisfying to make what Harriet wondered might be her final entry about Caroline, her beloved, abused sister. Potential future readers of the diary would simply note that one sister had informed another that despite the former's efforts to help, the latter's interests would have to be pursued independently. Harriet, in other words, could not force Caroline to leave, try for divorce — *still extremely difficult, damn it!* — or anything else.

Harriet only hoped she had not truly abandoned Carry. John explained repeatedly that she had not done so, that a person had to want help, seek it out, and actually make the attempt, but Caroline seemed content with her abusive arrangement. The Mills never understood it, tried in vain to accept it.

More uplifting was the hand-copied verse Harriet had lovingly added opposite the last notes about her family. Like the nurse returned from the Crimea, a fellow curious English citizen, Mr Livingstone, had ventured into some of the most inhospitable portions of Africa, the whole continent prized by the major European powers in a final global land-grab of grotesque proportions and greed, motivated partly by the sheer exotic nature of Africa and partly by how the rest of the world was either colonised already by Europeans or Americans, or had struggled for independence from such — especially in South America and parts of Asia. Thus England, to the chagrin of the Mills and others, had to stake its claim to stay competitive with its own version of what the Americans labelled 'manifest destiny.'

'It's a grotesque perversion of both the message and the intent of true Faith, Mother,' Lily had quipped. Harriet noted the Yanks tended to be staunchly Protestant, unlike Lily or the recent massive influx of Catholic émigrés like the starving Irish: for Lily, the message was more about potential divinity within the human species and its capacity for goodness, not politics.

'I know, Dear,' Harriet had answered. 'It's certainly not "destined," any more than it appears as something "manifest!"'

That was not what interested Mrs Mill, however, who kept her focus, like that of her husband, much more on the local and thus perhaps partially attainable. As for Livingstone, amalgam of physician, explorer, and preacher, he had developed a penchant for vocally and rationally arguing for the final elimination of slavery, and he had been witness to its shameful continuation in parts of the 'Dark Continent.' Most telling for Harriet, though, was his lovely description of having found the source of the mighty Nile River.

The magnificent Victoria Falls, as he related, 'had never been seen before by European eyes; but scenes so lovely must have been gazed upon by angels in their flight. The only want felt is that of mountains in the background. The falls are bounded on three sides by ridges 300 or 400 feet in height, which are covered with forest, with the red soil appearing among the trees.'

Harriet had closed her eyes dreamily upon first reading that, knowing John would love it just as much. They had never more than fantasised about an African trip. The toughest lesson for a dedicated traveller was that one could never hope to see everything.

'If one imagines the Thames, instead of the Zambesi,' Livingstone continued, 'filled with low, tree-covered hills immediately beyond the tunnel, extending as far as Gravesend; the bed of black basaltic rock instead of London mud; and a fissure made therein from one end of the tunnel to the other, down through the keystones of the arch, and prolonged from the left end of the tunnel through thirty miles of hills; the pathway being 100 feet down from the bed of the river instead of what it is, with the lips of the fissure from 80 to 100 feet apart; then fancy the Thames leaping bodily into the gulf; and forced there to change its direction, and flow from the right to the left bank; and then rush boiling and roaring through the hills—one may have some idea of what takes place at this the most wonderful sight I have witnessed in Africa.'

'John,' Harriet said quietly now, watching him heat a kettle of water for afternoon tea. She retained her fondness for 'gunpowder green,' and loved the attention in this form from her man, him realising that her ability to even locomote about the house had suffered again over past months. 'John,' she repeated, 'have you read these pieces yet?'

He walked over to the breakfast table, serving her then sitting. Between them, per usual, lay an assortment of newspapers, books, and hand-written notes covering a myriad of topics. One never knew when the metaphorical Muse might come a-visiting, as Lily said, so pens and blank sheets could be easily found in every room of the house. Where most of their class—and higher—would rage about spilled ink from a hasty if inspired grab at the nearest bottle with a suitable quill, the Mills had become more proficient at cleaning rugs, or creatively arranging furnishings, or simply purchasing darker items in the first place.

'Which ones?' he asked, glancing about the pile. He was pleased to offer some simple eggs and bread, with no help from the staff.

'The more impressive seems this item called 'Notes on Nursing.' It's written by a young and quite enterprising woman, freshly back from the Black Sea region.'

'She served in the recent horrible-ness?' John sometimes plastered words together, German-style, to refer to things of which he had low opinions. The Crimean War certainly qualified.

Harriet nodded. 'Ms Florence Nightingale. She's taught herself a new method of statistics and then upsetting the established order of medical health by arguing coherently that even basic changes in sanitation and hygiene actually save plenty of lives.' Harriet's admiration was unfeigned, and her interest in news about health care in any form had continued to hold her attention. Thankfully the syphilitic sores had not returned for many years now.

'I did. We should try and meet her, although I hear that she prizes privacy perhaps even more than we.' Harriet exhaled wistfully, retaining her appetite for encountering strong and smart persons, especially women, though she too had heard that the Angel with the Candle, who would gladly chat up any enlisted man whatever his condition, shied away from meetings with the nobility and an adoring public. It seemed Ms Nightingale just wanted to keep doing her job, casting about for a new and revolutionary nursing school in London.

Sipping his tea, John mulled over other recent news. Certain topics had already been glossed over a mite, such as Harriet wanting to renew writing book reviews, something she'd done little of recently. She had enjoyed the recent 'Madame Bovary' for its honesty, appreciating the descriptions of an idealistic young French physician trying both to find a professional niche and keep his wife content, with said young wife coming to resent their rural lifestyle and seeking sexual gratification elsewhere.

But it hit too close to home, so to speak. True, John and Harriet had been careful, and the situation in that Monsieur's sensational novel had been different—despite its frank appraisal of human sexuality, nowhere in its titillating pages were descriptions of the other hazards of sex like diseases, and Harriet found the story a bit facile while others condemned it for being too risqué. *If only relationships could be resolved so easily!* Harriet had mused.

Maybe reviews amounted to pandering. The stereotype remained: reviews of novels were for those whose writing proved inadequate, while reviews of non-fiction were the province of those who could not secure professorships or official posts. And John no longer edited 'The London and Westminster Review.'

'On the topic of women and claims to privacy,' Harriet continued, seeing the playful gaze from her husband, 'what news from your
"Mutter?" Did you not just receive word from her?'

He seemed to just glow at the mention of certain personages,
Lily noted as she walked in. Maybe that is what gets him reviled in
the masculine press: a willingness to feel.

'Mutter' referred to the ageing Sarah Austin, now in her early
sixties. Her husband John, the formally fiery commentator on juris-
prudence, had produced work decades earlier with Bentham, arguing
for what they referred to as 'legal positivism,' recognition that laws
were artificial rules created by human beings — thus Harriet's interest, who kept insisting that gender roles were equally artificial — and
that legality and morality, while potentially overlapping, remained
distinct intellectual arenas.

'She's well,' John said simply. 'She continues with translations,
though I'm not sure precisely what she's working on these days, other
than keeping up with Guizot.'

'And she's the bread-winner in that household, is she not, Father?'

'She mostly always has been,' John replied. 'Poor old John has
entered a depression lately. His own works seem to only have been
appreciated by specialists — those annoying lawyers and ethicists,' Lily
grinned, 'and I sometimes wonder if part of him may still be fighting
in the wars against Napoleon, poor man. I know little of his military
service, though.'

Lily prodded again. 'You don't think he feels frustrated by having
his living mostly paid for by his wife?'

Rather than look perturbed, like his stepdaughter had sought to
upset the natural order, John just looked askance. 'I shouldn't think so.'

Harriet nodded, mulling that over. Part of what her own detractors seemed to not comprehend was that she, like Wollstonecraft
before her, did not actually argue in favour of either gender being
dominant within a marriage or a household, recognising instead that
in most circumstances, a family would primarily have a sole wage-
earner, with the other person remaining more available for running

that home, especially if children lived there. 'What has Guizot himself been working on?'

'Oh, let me think.' François Guizot remained among a small number of souls John Mill had never managed to meet in person, despite mutual interest. It wasn't merely due to the man being French; despite having served as French ambassador to Britain, and living in England for a year, they had still not managed to meld their schedules, that time in London coinciding with some of John and Harriet's own Continental travels, ironically.

Still, anyone who had been Prime Minister of another country during the '48 revolutions throughout the Continent had to have some interesting insights, to phrase it mildly. Indeed, while some maintained that Guizot's attempts to ban the Campagnes des banquets: local meetings, especially within Paris, that had become much more overtly political in theme than the earlier salons, had furthered the '48 uprisings, others held that the urban revolts of that year had made Guizot more conservative. Whichever lay closer to the truth, it was well known that the man had pursued expansion of 'public education' throughout the République française. 'I think "Mutti" should be nearing completion of her translation of Guizot's work on the history of the English Revolution.'

'Our revolution?' Lily wondered.

'Indeed. My father used to say that if you truly wished to know what went on in your country, you should read another country's newspaper, or a foreign author's history.'

'The idea being, presumably, to minimise bias?'

'Yes, though of course one could become just as biased in the other direction.'

Harriet joined in again. 'Lily, who else have you been following these days?'

Lily understood the nuance of the question, her mother referring more to female authors, and Lily opted to tread carefully, since Mum had little taste for English novelists.

'Well, I'm surely no Mary Anning, Mother,' she said at last, citing the English woman who had begun selling 'fossils' of seemingly very old creatures near her home in Lyme Regis, raising questions not only about extinction and monsters but also the potential of women making contributions to natural philosophy. 'I choose to utilise my talents elsewhere.'

Rebellious youth notwithstanding — Lily was twenty-five — Harriet felt daring enough to venture into one more component of feminine territory, confident that John would not shy away nor change the subject. She waited until Lily chose to retire to her bedroom upstairs, probably writing in her own diary or reading. Mother and daughter often shared book-lists, and while Harriet had no fear that Lily could handle what she wanted to discuss, she did not want John to feel embarrassment, his progressive views notwithstanding.

'John,' she said, looking at him as he raised his head from his teacup, 'your mention of Mrs Austin reminded me of something, and perhaps I feel I must proffer some warning, since I think I'm,' she took a breath, 'going through the Change.'

Bless him, he wore that expression of masculine confusion in the face of feminine mysteries, but then she discerned comprehension dawning. 'The menopause?'

She nodded. 'It's cheery to see you taking it so well. Most men either have no wish to discuss something so outside their experience, or if they listen, are more likely to lament not being able to procure more children.'

'You know that has never been my focus. Your own children have been a marvellous fit for me, and I've never felt that odd pull that drives so many animals into brief madness. Nor do I evince any need to "pass on the family name" or the like.'

Harriet just gazed at this eccentric man who had crept into her life, all due to an almost forgotten dinner invitation over a quarter century past, which he had almost declined, so he admitted later. 'It was terrifying,' he confessed, 'I thought all the guests would be "attached."'

John had developed a slight stoop over the years, odd for one not much taller than Harriet herself, and who walked almost daily

as if from religious obligation. He found wry amusement in his defi-
ciencies: no sportsman whatsoever; content to remain largely in the
background at a career that he still described as a job whilst others
climbed the metaphorical rungs to 'success.' Yet within the rare head
that newspaper cartoonists drew as bird-like, akin to a waiting vul-
ture, Harriet knew there lurked an astonishing mind, capable both
of perceiving ideas that never occurred to most, and comprehending
another's perspective and attitudes.

'I'm also sorry if this row with Lily has kept you up lately.' That
was putting it gently: mother and daughter had clashed one final epic
time over the acting decision, but Harriet had at last conceded, and
Helen—'"Lily" is no proud thespian name, Mum: too redolent of the
disreputable women you keep thinking occupy the stage'—had ventured off on her own. John had rationalised matters with both women,
but in his own time, and each out of sight of the other. Harriet often
found that annoying, but recognised the peace offering—laced with
good rational sense—that it was. Plus John continued simply to loathe
direct confrontations. It wasn't fear: this was someone who had taken
prime ministers and cabinet members and scions of multiple royal
families to task in public reporting, after all; it was just that he didn't
like how it felt.

Harriet's mood had not improved as she and John shortly thereafter also had to wave goodbye to Haji, again more of a fixture in the
Mill home, as he sailed off for Italy. 'You're sure?' she had asked him.

'One cannot pass up the chance for a traditional "Grand Tour,"
Mum,' he had said.

She grunted. 'That's your stepfather talking, that is.'

But her middle child had a glorious smile, and he had kept waving
from an open window in the railcar as the train pulled out from its
cosy and smoky station, John there as ever to ease her back homeward.

'He doesn't have to know what he seeks,' John said on the way
back. 'The quest is so often its own reward.'

'Oh, do shut up and kiss me,' she answered. He gladly did so,
having never minded her forwardness.

Time seemed to speed up. John had read accounts both ancient and medieval describing this sensation. He had never found anyone who ascribed the feeling to the supernatural or spiritual, just recognition from commentators in ancient Greece and China alike that age should not be feared, partly since it was of course entirely natural, and further that longevity had a near-universal correlation—so traditional thinking went—with greater wisdom.

John's fear was, rather, that such a traditional perspective might be on the wane, and not merely in England. 'Life expectancy' was clearly increasing—part of the prophecy of Thomas Malthus made real—and what nobody seemed to have anticipated was a corresponding attitude among some of the young that maybe the elderly were not necessarily as wise as archaic stereotypes suggested. Or maybe it was just a reflection of the young not wanting to become old—another human near-universal—and rebelling in the equally ancient tradition of the young thinking they were smarter than they might truly be, the old suspecting that the next generation might yet be too rash.

*What had Plato described Socrates as saying,* John thought again: *not only that the unconsidered life is hardly worth the effort, and also that his philosopher-rulers had to be at least, oh, what was it? Sixty-five, like the Papal minimum? Is there a Papal minimum?* He felt wry amusement for not remembering these queries, and would have to take them up with 'his ladies' when they returned.

Scotland this time, and a recent wire—John still marvelled at the abbreviations in communications these days—indicated that both Harriet and Lily had been 'ill,' though neither had elaborated further. Each word added to the cost of a telegram, he knew, but a man considered as rich as he had become hardly needed concern himself with it.

*Does it remain better to be a dissatisfied human than a satisfied pig?* John wondered again. He recalled the thin dogs he witnessed outside the Carlyle home when he and Thomas had their final falling out, and neither man had evinced any effort at a reconciliation. John thought that just represented his emotional exhaustion after betrayal; he found he could still barely hold a grudge, though in honest moments of reflection he guiltily remembered that his immediate family members proved the exception to that.

What then of those dogs? As with the Poor Laws, new groups like the RSPCA might try to aid them, and it was hardly their fault for being thin and desperate and scrounging through urban trash. Farm dogs, as with farm pigs and farm horses and farm sheep and farm cattle, seemed happier. At least they might savour joyful lives, even those toiling for human overlords. Even those facing slaughter at the end of those lives for their meat, leather, bones, tendons — John had read some about the American Plains Indian tribes using virtually every imaginable part of their hunted bison carcasses to leave the impression of extremely dedicated and non-wasteful industry — at least for a few years could taste enjoyment.

John did not want to tangle with the utilitarian ghosts of Jeremy Bentham or James Mill, but John had never truly escaped from their shadows: Bentham had been sympathetic to so many, and Hume would have approved in that regard as well.

So was happiness found in the alleviation of suffering after all? John did not imagine those tough city dogs philosophising — *perhaps they're happy just for that!* he thought grimly — but any creature which could feel could experience pleasure and pain, right? Was that the key component of happiness? And if it was not, then why had John developed and then doggedly — he grinned at the strange near-pun — hung onto the four-fold criteria of his 'harm principle?'

*Or perhaps I make my mind wander anew, listening to birds and squirrels outside the house, forcing myself not to think about what 'ill' might mean in the case of the two most important women in my life?*

Back to Harriet and Lily, then. The Romans had discussed the hazards of metaphorically and socially burning one's bridges, since the literal practice of such comprised a consequential part of their history, especially when they ceased being a republic and became an empire. Despite the risks, Harriet and John had both chosen to burn bridges of their own this year. As with Carlyle, John attributed it to fatigue rather than ire, but that failed to erase the guilt, even though he had almost stopped wondering how the Carlyles fared. He'd heard that Thomas was busily at work on a massive biography of Frederick the Great of Prussia — one of the 'benevolent despots' of eighteenth-century Europe — the sort of person John had ceased to admire.

Truth was boring, John had learned, and perhaps nowhere was this truer than in subjects like politics and ethics. He no longer felt any moral kinship with dictatorial figures in either his century or the last, much preferring the sober and sedate, but hopefully stronger and more lasting pace, of the Houses of Commons and Lords. Imperialist leaders might make decisions faster, but that also made the decisions more challenging to check.

*Maybe I grow apathetic,* he mused, *or perhaps jokes at our expense are just unamusing.*

In Harriet's case, she simply could not summon the energy to try and help her sister, especially as Caroline remained obstinately unaccepting, even insulted by the effort. Harriet's last letter to Arthur in Australia had noted how she had 'suffered more than you would perhaps imagine from the rupture with her and its cause.' She cried when leaving home to post the letter, John embracing her and agreeing that it was necessary. But that hardly lessened the dreaded sense of finality. News from the remote continent remained sporadic, and when it did arrive was so often negative and frustrating.

As for John himself, there would be no mistaking the intent of his own recent communiqué with his sister Mary, penning that he did 'not know why you write to me after such a long interval if you cannot show more good sense or good feeling than are shown in this note.' Harriet remained ignorant about the contents of whatever Mary's intent had been in that instance, but had opted to not push the issue, knowing how sensitive she and her husband had become where family was involved. Haji had seemed understanding, though Herby, when he learned of it, briefly used these writings as ammunition, mostly against his mother, only breaking off again when Lily intervened.

There were times when John Stuart Mill remained genuinely glad he had never fathered children, much as he loved the Taylor trio, even hostile Herby. All three were mature enough to realise when their efforts led to genuine emotional harm. And John sometimes failed to grant himself sufficient credit. He had his own causes; he gave his life to the pursuit of knowledge, the more practical the better; he was a prolific writer, and could have earned a cosy living from that alone, yet had kept his ever-advancing position with the East India Company, telling himself for decades that his work there was important, that it helped others, before admitting, as the company had again fallen into such disrepute, that his logic there had failed him, that it was akin to what Smith had written in support of 'capitalism:' that the pursuit of wealth by individuals and whole nations alike would support the 'unfortunates' in all societies. John had missed the point, at first pleased that the logical structure was similar to what Bentham had said about happiness, even defending the Company indirectly, arguing that its alternative would prove too militaristic. Selfishness was acceptable, even necessary, and happiness would be served. Spending any amount helped someone, it was assumed, part of the equation consisting in that even the 'lower' classes, including persons hired by John and Harriet to help run their sometimes very busy and sometimes quite uneventful home, would benefit.

The other area in which John fell short in his honest self-appraisal lay simply with what plenty of commentators throughout England had chided him for many times: his patience with the woman who became his wife, and his own sexuality—or, as papers had hinted at or even openly said in their otherwise prudish society, lack thereof.

Neither of them could quite comprehend how little privacy seemed to matter in this new age of increasing public access to information. The irony of it was also frustrating: the greater literacy and education that John and Harriet so prized and argued for, in public venues like newsprint, was also leading to more persons learning intimate secrets of those who might wish to keep a metaphorical lid on matters. When did it cease to be 'news' and start to become 'gossip?'

Thank goodness few had ever learned the true nature of Harriet's illness: such was one example. Thinking about it led John to sigh, again hoping that Harriet and Lily would shortly return home from Scotland safely. Even now, few persons knew that the poor woman had syphilis, a detail that the papers would never stop dissecting if they learned.

Harriet had taken a nasty fall just before their trip, brushing it off as John had tried to ignore his own collapse when he had hurt himself in Italy. She still displayed some trouble walking, though thankfully did not require crutches or a wheelchair, but her physician had indicated the return of trouble with blood vessels in her lungs — consumption? — they had both thought at once, but that was not the case. The other symptoms remained an odd collection: the old numbness in her hand, an occasional fever, fortunately running its course quickly each time. Yet it was maddening to experience symptoms, even short-lived, when they did not seem to add up to a coherent working diagnosis.

It was early in the afternoon the next day when the women arrived home, tired but in good spirits. They had raved about the 'fabulous Celtic Highlands,' and the marvellously imposing Edinburgh Castle, and Lily had found she had a taste for Scotch whiskey, bringing several bottles south to have John try. Despite temperance movements in England and America, at least drunkenness was one vice that had passed by the families Mill and Hardy and Taylor.

Mother and daughter smiled to find John asleep in his favourite chair, a newspaper on his lap. He barely ever snored, to Harriet's relief — Mr Taylor had at times kept her awake through entire evenings — and looked so peaceful right at that moment.

Harriet noticed him first, and turned to Lily with an index finger to her lips. Lily smiled again, taking both their travelling cases upstairs herself, having loved the trip but looking forward to a cleansing bath and a meal cooked at home. She knew the staff would not interrupt her stepfather wherever he might find himself napping.

Reading the piece John still seemed to point towards even in slumber, Harriet began to read. It was about the very recent 'Sepoy Rebellion' in India — of course! she cried inwardly — and wondered who the author was. She could only get through an excerpt before quietly picking up the paper and gazing longingly at her husband, who seemed peaceful despite the news.

'... you could see members of human bodies, legs and arms sticking up browned and withered like those of a mummy. But there was no putrid smell or anything of that kind I could perceive. Those dead arms of our murdered country people seemed to be making a mute appeal to us from the darkness below; far more eloquent than words they called to Heaven for vengeance on the ruthless perpetrators of untold atrocities...'

Harriet swallowed, yet still notice how an Indian heroine had helped lead the resistance against the British.

Harriet joined Lily upstairs so they could unpack, and wondered just what the legacy of the English, and their Empire, and their home-grown philosophy, might be.

* * *

The key detail about one's final days was that one so often had little sense they might be approaching. John, Harriet, and the Taylor trio had acquired, willingly or less so, a sense that recognising one's inevitable end was neither morose nor morbid: rather it could serve, should serve, as John would repeat, as an impetus to cherish whatever time might remain. One with a fatal illness could potentially gain some feeling of when Death might come, but Harriet's aggressive and eager spirit—a curious combination that would go misinterpreted by commentators then and later—continued to drive her.

As ever, one could find grim assessments of humanity or wry amusement in the news of the day, even when abroad. And the Hôtel d'Europe had become their favourite haunt over the years. Avignon was a marvellous riverine city, and Lily too had adored it at once, even joking about the Church Schism from the later Middle Ages, when the city had its own papacy to compete with Rome's. As for the hotel, it dated to the later sixteenth century, remodelled in the eighteenth in the style of a hôtel particulier, comparable to a British mansion, though it remained unprepossessing. It featured an exquisite court-yard and private bathrooms, almost overlooking the Rhône, and John and Harriet always enjoyed the delectable nearby restaurants which featured the freshest fish, succulent onion soup, roast duck à l'Orange, plus tasty and slightly tart hippocras to wash it all down.

Sometimes news could be interesting when presented neutrally and from far away, and John and Harriet discussed the potential implications of the 'Restoration' occurring in Japan, about which neither knew much. John had studied India through his work and his father's bigoted legacy, China through ancient thinkers and his own interests, but so much of Asia remained mysterious despite his penchant for study. He remembered Bentham once describing the samurai as a far-Eastern version of armoured knights, but were often 'more chivalrous,' so Bentham claimed, than their far-Western counterparts, even though they shared in common personal oaths of militaristic loyalty to lieges.

'Plus, they bathed far more often,' old Jeremy had opined. 'Imagine grooming being of central importance to blooded warriors.' John had liked the imagery. He had further savoured the notion of noble warriors being continually encouraged to develop artistic skills besides martial ones: calligraphy, poetry, a musical instrument, or the curious Japanese obsessions with creative paper-folding or flower-arranging; European knights from before the Crusades forward tended to be crass, unrefined, and illiterate.

He was reminded of that bathing and grooming imagery as he found an article in the 'London Times,' which he had to seek out here in Avignon; it was all over Paris, read by expatriates who had little French, or just chose not to learn, an attitude John loathed.

But his light-hearted nature erupted as he read aloud to Harriet of the 'Great Stink' back home. During the later summer, a horrid and toxic blending of the effluence of industry with human bodily wastes had accumulated more than ever before in the Thames. An ancient sewer system still tried to keep up with modern demands and simply could not do so anymore, even with newer expansions. The moniker had appeared immediately, sparking satiric critiques from around the world, including many Imperial territories.

But inside most grown men lurked immature boys fascinated by toilet humour. John remained convinced that women and girls were just as susceptible to 'such poor taste,' but for now merely said, 'Hopefully no one struck a match near the river during the past few weeks.'

A smile, followed by a playful smack, though Harriet could barely reach him. John adored the soul behind that smile. He would never tire of seeing it, still able to clearly recall the first time he witnessed it in the old Taylor home on Christopher Street. 'Such a catastrophic explosion would at least clear the air, and also add credence to miasma theory.'

Harriet laughed now as dedicatedly as she could. 'I think that dated miasma notion is wrong, though,' she said. 'True, air can be tainted with all manner of disgusting things, but if air always carried disease, it seems we all would have grown sick and died centuries ago, along with all the plants and other animals.'

'Agreed, Love, though the cholera outbreaks have continued in the City recently.'

*Just what we need,* moped John, *another epidemic.* But he recalled how a curious physician had isolated cholera to one faulty well in the City back in '54, receiving due laudatory adulation for his work in identifying how tiny impurities actually caused disease.

"The Press:' "Gentility of speech is at an end: it stinks, and whoso once inhales the stink can never forget it and can count himself lucky if he lives to remember it."'

More giggling, which John was briefly elated to witness, as he grew ever more desperate to keep it going. 'You know, Harriet, just three years ago one curious scientific observer noted that the Thames had become "an opaque pale brown fluid."'

'Ow, that's disgusting!' Harriet cried, but her body betrayed its attempt to continue laughing. Part of living in their modern period of history entailed developing a strong—if dark—sense of humour, or perhaps go mad instead. After mutually recognising they should feel some sympathy for the sufferers of the latest epidemic—though they had both known so many taken by the scourging diseases of their time—they grew a touch more serious.

'That letter in 'The Times' was meant for Parliament,' John continued, 'though rumour has it the Royal Society got wind of it,' more giggling, and a crude repeat of the word wind, John himself trying not to smirk, 'and a copy arrived at the Company as well.'

And then he stopped laughing, recalling how one callous co-worker at said Company had suggested that now Londoners knew what it was like to live in the foreign land which inspired the corporate name. John hated the blatant racism at once, telling the man that, 'When your shit-house stinks, you get nowhere by calling it names or acting like another mindless British bigot. You need to clean it!' And he had stormed out of the office, ignoring the murmurings behind him from colleagues who had always regarded John Mill as 'the quiet studious one.'

'At least Disraeli got Parliament to rush that needed legislation through,' she whispered. 'What was it he called the river again?'

'Oh, "a Stygian pool, reeking with ineffable and intolerable horrors."'

'Sounds like Parliament itself, Darling. Don't let Disraeli rile you.' The Prime Minister was still no fan of John. If he only knew how much of Harriet's mindset appeared in 'his' work!

Harriet turned to him, smiling, still weakly. 'What was that other piece you mentioned during the train ride, again, Sweeting?' she asked, her voice actually working on roughly two of every three syllables.

John wished to make no mention of it, since some were protesting his latest observations, though occasionally John could adopt the tone of a dedicated journalist, as with his recent 'The Partition of the East India Company.'

Simply put and unbeknownst to Harriet—though Lily had some suspicion, as she had proofread the work in question—John could no longer contemplate working for the Company, after some thirty-five years of dedicated service. Upper management had come to perceive him as naïve, often leaving him out of decision-making, though John had never attended many of those policy-altering meetings anyway. He had the draught with him, though, always one—like Harriet and Lily—to have and be able to take more notes whilst travelling, and he unfolded a scrap now to finally read to his wife.

'That your Petitioners, at their own expense, and by the agency of their own civil and military servants, originally acquired its magnificent empire in the East. That the foundations of this empire were laid by your Petitioners, at that time neither aided nor controlled by Parliament, at the same period at which a succession of administrations under the control of Parliament were losing to the Crown of Great Britain another great empire on the opposite side of the Atlantic.'

'Ouch,' Harriet said simply, but then they laughed. Truly, it did feel like a lifted weight for John, who had already decided to devote his remaining life and energy to his wife.

The problem, though, was that even with this warmer clime, and the loveliness of Avignon, which they had visited previously together, Harriet had her cough return, and John thought she felt a bit warmer than good caution recommended, though she denied feeling chills one would expect from fever. She continued to exhibit trouble sleeping, and now had difficulty lying down. This last sign concerned John most, since it was new.

He fervently continued to hope that he had not harmed this woman he so loved, whom he prized above all other persons encountered through his busy and unorthodox life. *Have I been a good husband? Did I contribute to the strife of her first marriage, even though she—and Mr Taylor, oddly—both roundly denied so?*

He knew he had become a very adequate provider. On his income, that was simple.

Nonetheless, John had taken the precaution of contacting a local physician, an English expat, also without Harriet's knowledge. Dr Cecil Gurney had treated Harriet successfully back in '53 for the trouble with her lungs, which had included the haemorrhaging that so terrified them. That had been during the trip further south to Nice, though the doctor was spending his holiday here in Avignon as they were.

So that night, 2 November 1858, John remained in their room at the famed Hôtel d'Europe. A typical pile of pages lay in front of him, and initially all he could notice were phrases that came from Harriet: 'sufficient warrant;' 'price of diversity;' using 'tyranny' to describe the inevitable state when a numerical majority of persons had their way at the expense of the minority, and it was she who further had argued initially more strongly in support of safe-guards to prevent that from happening.

*She must pull through,* John thought again. *Dr Gurney is a fine physician, and I cannot finish our works without her input!*

He watched tears fall upon the heavy small desk in their ornate hotel room. It was the first time he had ever so specifically thought that statement through.

*Wives may inspire husbands,* he mused silently, *but I have a collaborative partner, as well informed as myself, who finds the flaws in my ideas and helps me find a clearer way.*

He knew sleep would come haphazardly tonight if at all, so he read through the most important pieces. The duo had already selected the tentative and simple title, 'On Liberty,' for this new seminal work. It would contain some references to their previous collaborations, include some ideas that had appeared here and there in print previously, but this would also become a wholly new project, intended as the most tightly composed and logically supported treatise in defence of human and individual liberty, but without the social chaos that the reactionary and conservative believed would result.

First, John went to check again on his slumbering wife, who looked quite peaceful. She continued to breathe regularly, not requiring much by way of covering: the floral sheet and her satin nightgown were enough.

The sheet had been removed from the bed, however, due to her continued difficulty with fully reclining, in either a prone or supine position. The long rocking chair she reported as quite comfortable.

John watched his beloved for several minutes, satisfied that she would feel at least somewhat refreshed come morning, and took solace in the knowledge that Dr Gurney had cabled him back to report that he was en route. Just after their supper, John had also walked purposefully down the street to send a telegram to Lily, refusing to sweeten it and knowing she could take the truth: 'She is not better—or perhaps worse—have written to beg Dr G to come.' Lily had heard of the doctor's talents, too.

Even that wire was calm compared to what he had said to the good doctor: 'My wife is lying at the Hôtel d'Europe—so very ill that neither she nor I have any hope but in you to save her—I implore you to come immediately. I need hardly say that any expense whatever will not count for a feather in the balance.'

So now, having communicated with those who most needed to know, he pored over the documents again, wondering whether these deceptively simple paragraphs would constitute the bulk of their legacy.

'The only purpose for which power can rightfully be exercised over any member of a civilised community, against his will, is to prevent harm to others. His own good, either physical or moral, is not a sufficient warrant.' They had dabbled with 'his or her own good,' but agreed that for now this would suffice: it would no doubt prove incendiary enough.

John recognised that the next section would take a little more re-writing, though he still pictured Harriet, pacing past the piano while he sat watching her, transfixed as ever. Just witnessing her move proved impetus enough for his intellectual inspirations; for her, she adored gazing at her lover sitting upright in a chair, once describing his posture as far more 'magisterial' than his actual stance could be.

What would be known as the 'harm principle' existed as 'one very simple principle as entitled to govern absolutely the dealings of society with the individual,' they had written. In adjudicating this, 'no person is an entirely isolated being.' Person, not just man. And what might be simple 'inconvenience' for society, 'which society can afford to bear, for the sake of the greater good of human freedom' includes such alleged offenses as 'gambling, or drunkenness, or incontinence, or idleness, or uncleanliness,' which might be 'injurious to happiness,' but had to yet be allowed for the individual.

Education earlier was far superior and effective than instilling bans later, a similar logic to that used by the world's great faiths, something Lily had indicated. And we rebel against authority when it patronises or preaches. This is the price of diversity, thought John. 'With the personal tastes and self-regarding concerns of individuals the public has no business to interfere.'

That was it, the bare version of what they tried to impart: individual freedom and its expression were central, but such had to be tempered by the moral barrier of harming others, whether other persons, animals, forests, oceans, mountains, mines, factories, governments…

John looked over at the lovely still-breathing form just feet away. She had shifted position in her sleep, though continued to breathe normally.

The other accent to this moral and political outline was what Harriet labelled the 'tyranny of the majority,' a phrase John took some getting used to. This manifested as 'a social tyranny more formidable than many kinds of political oppression, since, though not usually upheld by such extreme penalties, it leaves fewer means of escape, penetrating much more deeply into the details of life, and enslaving the soul itself. Protection, therefore, against the tyranny of the magistrate is not enough: there needs also protection against the tyranny of the prevailing opinion and feeling.'

Personal liberty alone was not enough: a person had to have space in which to bring it to fruition. And Harriet had taken the greatest pleasure in this scheme by using a term repeatedly invoked against both herself and John. 'Precisely because the tyranny of opinion is such as to make eccentricity a reproach, it is desirable, in order to break through that tyranny, that people are eccentric. Eccentricity has always abounded when and where strength of character has abounded; and the amount of eccentricity in a society has generally been proportional to the amount of genius, mental vigour, and moral courage which it contained. That do few dare to be eccentric marks the chief danger of the time.'

It was not about being odd for oddness' sake; it was about society's not interfering with the creation and protection of new ideas, even when those ideas might be, well, odd.

John later shook himself awake, his head having fallen onto the hard desk. He normally required a much softer setting in which to slumber, so he knew at once he had been truly exhausted. He yawned, stretched and felt his now quite sore neck and shoulders, and only glanced at the pages in front of him before turning to Harriet in the chaise.

Something was different. John could feel it at once. The tears were already forming at the corners of his eyes as he reached over to check for breathing, then for a heartbeat, and found neither. His wife's eyes remained closed, giving the indication that she had simply slipped away, like a boat on a calm sea with a sole passenger.

\* \* \*

The good doctor had been unable to make it in time to Harriet's side, though John would never blame him, both men realising that there was nothing he could have done anyway. Harriet's treatments—partly self-sought and self-administered—had ranged quite a gamut over the decades, from the horrid mercury and hot baths—both given up many years ago as ineffective—to the continued travel to warmer climes, imbibing of certain judicious tea selections—her favourite choice, as she got to dabble with different concoctions—to various chemical admixtures to reduce or dull pain, though Harriet fortunately never developed a habit for alcohol or opium or aether.

The couple had known one another for almost twenty-eight years, rarely apart, and benefitting notably from access to ready funds, from

John's hefty salary to Harriet's inheritance from a first husband who had proven, as she admitted later, much more noble than she had often thought while he yet lived.

But John had felt like an outsider for most of his life to that point, and even often perceived his relationship with the only woman he ever truly loved from the perspective of what was socially acceptable. 'For seven and a half years that blessing was mine,' he told his step-daughter shortly after Harriet's death, 'for seven and a half years only!' This emerged as the culmination of devotion that would appear later in Mr Mill's autobiography, in which he described 'the lady whose incomparable worth had made her friendship the greatest source to me both of happiness and of improvement, during many years in which we never expected to be in any closer relation to one another.'

Ensuring that a statement made its way into newsprint, John kept matters surprisingly succinct: 'It is doubtful if I shall ever be fit for anything public or private, again. The spring of my life is broken.' For once the newspapers offered less ridicule.

Mrs Mill's mortal remains would be lovingly interred right there by the Hôtel d'Europe, with Lily in attendance, 'the boys' unable to make it, though in the case of Herby, John felt unsurprised. John collected their papers and notes, wrote directly to the Mayor of the city of Avignon, and ensured that the city was paid for the burial, with another thousand francs to donate to the poor as the Mayor saw fit.

Lily moved in with her stepfather, after what even she admitted was an 'abortive exercise' in the hectic and ever-competitive arena of the theatre, though the curious pair would enjoy performances of various types for years to come, mostly musical. The manuscript about Liberty was promptly sent off to John's publisher, with his loving dedication on the top page which mentioned 'the friend and wife whose exalted sense of truth and right was my strongest incitement, and whose approbation was my chief reward.'

Lily notified Herby herself, though her own sentiment was reserved for Haji instead. 'O dear Haji,' she penned, trying to maintain her usual composure, 'it is all over but I too was too late too late too late... It seems to me I can never sign "Lily" any more. I was her Lily—now I am no longer anybody or anything but a miserable wretch.'

And yet history moves in curious and often unintelligible ways, for even if the spring of his life had broken, the British Empire and the world of philosophy were hardly finished with the widower Mr John Stuart Mill.

# Avignon, France

*Early 1907.*

(From the unpublished memoirs of Ms Helen Taylor, the longer entries dated shortly before Christmas, 1875):

My stepfather was correct, of course: after so much love and difficulty and the frustration felt by him, and Mother, and my biologic father, John and Harriet Mill truly only did have just a few years together, at least as husband and wife, though their intellectually productive time together prior to their marriage was breath-taking and indeed still radical, even if societies were acquiring more understanding of how racism and sexism and the destruction which often accompanies industrialisation all have moral implications. Perhaps this last prejudice should be labelled 'landscapism' or the like. All continue into the present of course, though most of my own work has favoured the second of the three.

As for myself, having read the curious early-century novels by Ms Austen but not the mid-century ones by that eccentric trio of Brontë sisters—one of whom became quite a vocal critic of 'The Enfranchisement of Women,' I might add!—it remains difficult for

me to imagine such total longing for another person, such a true partner, an ideal mate, or at least someone willing to not just tolerate but
even accommodate all of another person's faults and foibles. I even
had trouble bringing such characters to life on the stage, through my
slight career as an actress. At least Mother displayed the fortitude to
permit me, even to encourage me, to try—not just auditioning and
pretending to be someone else in a professional capacity, all the more
daring since actors—and actresses, too—have so often been held in
social disdain by so many others, never mind how popular theatre has
been in so many cultures for so many centuries.

Politicians are actors, too—perhaps that is why so many find it
easy to despise them—to get paid to lie, paid to shape policy, paid to
influence the feelings and beliefs of others, an alarming yet ancient
trend commented upon by varying thinkers, though philosophers tend
to differ hugely about the best approaches to politics in practice. But
my stepfather understood it—the need for the lie, though one must
never mistake him for approaching the topic from the perspective of
a pessimistic doomsayer like Plato—for if a society decides that more
instead of fewer should be allowed to vote, and if there exist simultaneously no educational nor moral nor social requirements to exercise
the practice and responsibility of voting, then those who vote with
their hearts rather than their heads will have to be lied to—else the
liar has no chance of gaining election in the first place!

My mother comprehended this also, knew that John's long-term
employer, the fabled though infamous East India Company, was itself
built on a lie, which helped enable and then perpetuate another lie:
the idea that empires can last. The Company finally entered its overdue death throes the year Mother died, and so many saw it coming,
though those who lament its passing tend to be the same who remain
the most fanatical about the preservation of our Empire itself, conveniently ignoring that all empires fade. The cultures that support them
are much more important, and Mother and Father understood that
the English have far more to offer the world than the self-defeating
grip of political control.

The mighty India House was unceremoniously destroyed in 1860. I do not believe my father-figure ever shed a tear over its loss, perhaps since he retired with a large pension—far more than most of us could hope to ever receive as annual pay. Even the more talented stage personalities I have encountered could never hope to receive so much.

I confess I had to chide Father (my stepfather, the man who occupied my heart more strongly and for a far longer duration than my own biologic father—forgive my saying so, Papa Taylor!) when he finally opted to try for Parliament. He ran for City and Westminster—good neutral territory, he decided early, full of conflicting views and exciting history for its proximity to both the centre of government and the religious influence of the world-famous Abbey of that name. And he clearly possessed sufficient funding from his days of imperial employ to finance his own campaign. For John Mill, that was more honest.

Within government, Disraeli still loathed John Mill. What would one expect? Disraeli served as Prime Minister twice, was succeeded by Gladstone—both times!—and like Gladstone was officially a Conservative, though of a more Tory than Whig bent. What was it Father once wrote—and said in public—about Conservatives? Oh, yes: 'I never meant to say that the Conservatives are generally stupid. I meant to say that stupid people are generally Conservative.' Perhaps I was premature in my judgment about his status as raconteur after all, and Mother would have loved that statement had she lived to hear it. He probably said it to her at some point through all their years of debating.

Yet Disraeli was idolised in the Lords, even made a member of the Garter by our aging and morose Queen, who has occupied the throne so long herself. Disraeli had all the marks of a great statesman—member of the Privy Council, and even the Royal Society, though his scientific contributions were, well, non-existent so far as I can ascertain—Ms Anning's fossil-collecting was of greater scientific merit—and he will remain unloved for his skill as novelist and poet, too, as Mother herself learned—enough reasons for him to distrust Mill the upstart MP, the son of some far-too-radical thinker from nowhere, and who, whilst running for public office, made mention more than once of how political candidates must either fund their own campaigns or else not run at all.

But Gladstone, serving as PM thrice—what a model of the democratic process, methinks!—once called John a 'saint of rationalism.' Also on the Royal Society—also for reasons unknown, at least to this writer—President of the Board of Trade—Father's old friend Graham was an admirer!—but also a walking muddle of contradictions. Gladstone supported Irish Home Rule but also, in keeping with similar logic, the American Confederacy that Father railed against, though for concerns more to do with race and personal liberty and less with international relations. Gladstone could oppose the morally dubious 'opium wars' affecting—infecting—both our Empire and that of the Chinese, yet remain an adversary to the Ottoman Empire and to Egypt. Like Disraeli and his support for armed intervention in Afghanistan and South Africa, Gladstone could argue for force. For Father, such arguing retained just a touch of the old utilitarian streak, probably the last such for John Mill, and probably due simply to the number of souls affected by any war.

That was partly where my stepfather proved so different, and often so irritating. He won his parliamentary seat—even after his old arrest record was 'accidentally discovered' during the 1865 campaign—but it exhausted him as much as Mother's death had some years earlier. He could never hope to become the Great Orator as he so often had wished—much too quiet a voice and too respectful of others to sink to the shouting matches that one finds within the world's great buildings where political issues are decided. Sometimes one could get a sense of jealousy, since the Great Empire simply did not receive a voice in other countries finally disposing of the evils of slavery, or with the Russian Empire selling something frigid called 'Alaska' to the Americans—so close to where we almost fought it out again over the 'Oregon Territory'—or with the unifications of Italy and then Germany into newly independent nations trying to struggle with the medieval and then modern major players of England,

France, Spain, Holland. And yet we remain involved—mired?—in Africa and Asia. Indeed, one may wonder which parts of the world remain truly self-determining, free of intervention by Europeans and now Americans.

Father once asked, when we were strolling about Greece during our last trip together, what I thought of the story, maybe legend, of a Roman orator practicing to become a clearer, more audible speaker by filling his mouth with beach pebbles and then practicing speaking to the sea. He bent over then and picked some pebbles up, as I watched the surf recede, feeling wistful that I could see no seashells right there like the ones Mr Sterling had once sent to me and my brothers, and I admit I could not believe my eyes when Father placed some of those salty stones into his mouth! But instead of painstakingly trying to talk he started to laugh, that high and nasally and strangely lovable laugh of his, and opened his mouth to show me that he was just pulling my leg. Let the shouting matches continue, he told me—politicians and voters and philosophers and scientists and theologians will all keep shouting, while truth gets laid aside, often to struggle on its own, though it rarely wins on its own.

English society remained unready for some truths even once Father took his seat in Parliament: whilst the issue of women's suffrage would continue to get tabled—witness how some of us remain denied of voting, regardless of how much influence we may have over the minds of men and of society as a whole—he nonetheless succeeded in ways that no one had imagined possible. Not a soul, including himself, expected his appointment as Lord Rector of the University of St Andrews—he confessed having little interest in his ancestral Scotland generally, even if sympathetic as always to the underdog, in this case the Scots of old, sending forth William Wallace or Rob Roy McGregor or Bonnie Prince Charlie to fend off the greedy English—some have seen a bit of Americanism in John Mill for that alone—and he likewise admitted to feeling hopelessly ill-prepared for such a prestigious job title, not even possessing a university education. He felt sad too that Mr Fox and his lovely partner

Ms Flower—I must struggle to recall either of them now—never made their sojourn north.

Then again, John Mill spoke more languages than many members of the St Andrews foreign language faculty, understood philosophy more thoroughly than their philosophy faculty, and could draw ancient parallels to modern issues and questions more appropriately than any among their Classics faculty, so if the position title was mostly honorary—and hardly adding much more income to the post-retirement India House windfall—professors and students alike up in Fife remained in awe of him and his works. He had to rein in his own surprise upon finding his writings on course syllabi of philosophy professors, and with greater frequency than those of his own father and godfather.

Still no great orator even that late in his life, he nonetheless offered a memorable 'inaugural address' to that fine Scots university. Journalists and other dedicated note-takers—including students and faculty—sat there enraptured by what he said. Education, John informed careful listeners that day in 1867, 'is one of the subjects which most essentially require to be considered by various minds, and from a variety of points of view. For, of all many-sided subjects, it is the one which has the greatest number of sides.'

I took pride in memorising some of that speech, occasionally fantasising that perhaps I could recreate it on the stage somehow, like how some actors or actresses might simply perform excerpts taken from famous plays, especially rousing and inspirational ones by Shakespeare—'once more unto the breach, dear friends'—but this time unto the hallowed halls of academia for the ancient philosophical ideal of self-improvement.

'Whatever helps to shape the human being,' John had continued, 'to make the individual what he is, or hinder him from being what he is not—' speaking to one's liberty in determining one's self—'is part of his education. And a very bad education it often is; requiring all that can be done by cultivated intelligence and will, to counteract its tendencies.'

Dear God, that might have been my own mother speaking! Never have I encountered two such souls, both on the same quest to define their own morality and their own humanity on their own terms, whilst simultaneously becoming the most decent persons I have ever had the good fortune of knowing.

They had their fights, God knows, and surely their flaws, and yet for all their work — satirised, caricatured, lampooned — they were passionate yet rational with their views and their attraction and devotion to each other, especially regarding decisions and policies and how to live and treat others. I still wish I could have witnessed more keen faces in Scotland those years ago as the small, thin, mercurial and unassuming former member of Parliament explained that logic itself exists chiefly 'not so much to teach us to go right, as to keep us from going wrong.' One had to learn to think, and then to reason and reach conclusions — whilst keeping passion aside for the nonce, perhaps the most challenging task — then realise even then that conclusions may be temporary, superseded by later truths or discoveries.

Imagine it: a new lord rector of a large medieval university, a bastion of wisdom and tradition, who had himself received remarkably little by way of 'formal' education, telling his scholastic audience that they remained as liable to error as the most undereducated souls occupying the Stews and Whitechapel in London, or in their case, more like the Great Junction Street and Muirhouse neighbourhoods in Edinburgh.

(A leaf or two of the journal appears to be missing at this point, but the writer resumes, seemingly beginning on a later day. — ed.)

That final trip to Greece was stunning, to put it mildly, and I confess I have not found the wherewithal to do much travelling since, other than to return here to Avignon. Biographers might eventually comment about the symbolism of this small French city and its history of once headquartering a second Papacy — what marvellous internecine conflict! What drama, even — especially? — for us Catholics! — but it was simply the place my stepfather came to love most during a childhood spent partly away from his homeland.

For someone often eschewing comfort during travel, our final camping trip in the summer of 1862 proved amazing. The Grotes declined the trip for concerns over their health, and en route we had to endure impressive late-season snows in northern Italy, incessant rain in Corfu, and seemingly equally endless fog within mighty Athens itself, the last precluding otherwise magnificent views from the Acropolis, though we of course trudged up it anyway. Father prided himself on his adventurous spirit by then—Mother, bless her, would have hated trying to keep up after her own adventures, occasional injuries, and later manifestations of illness. So Father was thus able to find amusement at our guides' unfounded concerns over wolves howling 'too close' to our group's horses in wilder parts of Greece, or the piercing—I thought quite fetching, really—sounds of jackals and owls at night.

It still took us quite a while just to get there, especially for our not opting to sail into the Mediterranean but going overland after crossing the Channel. This included a visit to Herr Gomperz' residence in Vienna, that early promoter of the 'Logic,' who, if I may be permitted to say so, might have been in love with me. Father let him down gently, and while I felt some faint flattery such as any actress might, I remained disinterested. No doubt readers of this journal will pick over this or other titbits and decry my sexuality much as they might John Mill's, yet it does not matter. The hypocrites of our society will judge as they wish regardless, and endlessly quibble over whether Father or myself were virgins, or otherwise asexual, whilst completely missing the point about what we accomplished.

* * *

Previously I had mentioned Father's foray into the endless and biased conflicts of politics. Of course he ran and served as a member of the Liberal Party, even if he had friends—past and present, and adversaries—also past and present—whom he respected, who were members of Labour or even Conservatives. The Whigs had served their purpose, and were truly defunct shortly after Mother's death, having also faded into history within America, especially after their monstrously destructive civil conflict in the years just after her passing; and the Tories—truly, they've been gone so long I cannot remember them myself.

Yet Father—again, while I loved and do still miss my genuine literal father, 'Father' herein refers of course to Mr Mill, not my Papa—would have warned of the dangers of voters perceiving the existence of two sole parties, and how the interests and needs of the nation could easily get lost within internecine and often infantile disputes between the two. Despite a lifetime as a Francophile, Father recognised that such a situation might become as corrupt and morally stagnant as the États Généraux had in France—meeting only under dire threat of a revolution which came anyway, and while designed to have officially consisted of three groups, had so often been dominated by the nobility and the clergy, forgetting the other ninety-six percent or thereabouts of the populace. Again as with the Americans, there existed multiple parties, but dualistic thinking—or perhaps because perceiving the world as so many dualities—black / white; male / female; rich / poor—tends to preclude thinking, is what helps to perpetuate this foolish and very often destructive sense of us versus them.

Though I digress it was never about conservatism nor liberalism per se—rather, it was about people, many with newly acquired voting powers, not just expressing freedom of suffrage but taking responsibility for such power, and thinking about issues and candidates rationally. John Mill recognised that human societies require both conservative and liberal elements alike: preservation of morals and standards and positions are as important as creativity and prose and new ideas, especially when the latter are offered in the service of the state. We can always improve. All these years later, I understand that that was what he hoped to teach me, what he felt utilitarianism as espoused by his father and by Bentham could no longer address, so that it too needed improving, though it was surely radical itself when those older men were first so thrilled with it—or older women, for that matter.

The endlessly frustrating part, however, remains how much not just women are misunderstood, nor how much I or my mother may have been misunderstood, but how much John and Harriet Mill remain misunderstood! I got my stepfather's 'Autobiography' to press shortly after his death almost two years ago, something he and Mother had both hoped might 'stop the mouths of enemies hereafter,' though such did not occur. Some of the reviews and comments I found devastating. 'Fraser's' magazine—'unconscious egotism;' 'The Times'—insinuations of femininity, even foreignness—John Mill was often applauded for remaining a Francophile but that certainly never made him an Anglophobe!; or 'The Edinburgh Review'—dozens of pages of the manuscript used to try and undercut Mr Mill and his rational and thought-provoking philosophy. Even Carlyle could hardly face his demons from a broken friendship at the end, calling this, his former friend's last and posthumous work 'the life of a logic-chopping engine.' As for poor Mother—sometimes being ignored is the unkindest cut of all—many now doubt whether her influence upon her second husband was genuine or even existed. Even those who disagree with or loathe John Mill, like that rascal Disraeli and his ilk, yet tend to agree that his views at least are somehow uniquely masculine and not the products in any way of some feminine whimsical mind getting overly worked up over God-knows-what. This, despite the clear dedications to the original versions of the books for which John Mill was becoming famous while still alive, but alas, after Mother had already died. Many of the same persons who had the temerity to question Father's sexuality—and this is one modern woman who shan't shy away timidly from speaking earnestly of perhaps the most basic component of the human condition!—had taken apparent pleasure in attacking a straw man, one of John Mill's most railed-against fallacies, and upon his death attacked his work instead of him.

* * *

Feeling slightly calmer now. I walked past the Hôtel d'Europe again just earlier today, and visited their graves, little Kalos along for the stroll. Father always loved dogs—cat Phidias remains at home, though at times walks with me on his own leash, drawing amused glances from the townsfolk! The horizontal tombstones contain lengthy quotes immediately attributable to those familiar with their works, so I shan't dwell on them here. And yet while many seem to understand my mother's death at 51—even if syphilis remains c'est inderdit in polite social circles—many more seem unaware of what finally sealed the fate of John Mill, just shy of his 67th birthday. And I admit I had to do my own amateur medical research, using some of Mother's old books that she acquired whilst looking into her own affliction to learn much.

Perhaps never quite at home back in England—a sentiment I have sometimes shared!—now they may stay at each other's sides in perpetuity. I remain committed to the belief that those with genuine religious conviction, such as myself, must temper such with an equally strong and real sense of the humorous, in this case the idea that these two souls wished to remain together 'forever,' even though both remained throughout their lives, so far as I could ever determine, atheists, or at least sufficiently undecided or annoyed by the minutiae and confusion and violence so often resulting from religion that they had perhaps become, to borrow the still new term, agnostics. I have tried to retain my own Catholicism throughout adulthood, my loving parents understanding as best they could—both appreciating the moral lessons of the world's religions while frustrated at how religion falls short and lapses so easily into hatred and intolerance and homicide. I have even noted such during Confession. But if religion fails, it must be because man—and woman—fails, and not because of the shortcomings of a Deity—or Deities, as with the Hindus in India, our Jewel in the Crown. Such remains my sincere hope.

And dear Father: I could never chide that would-be atheist for visiting—every year after Mum's death until his own—Avignon, and her gravesite, always staying at the Hôtel d'Europe, with me and Kalos and Phidias, the pets proving calm and curious travellers.

On that note of humour—Mother did appreciate the joke in my once observing that at least the practice of Catholicism was legal in Britain again, having been made so only a year or two before she met 'the second John,' as I once jokingly referred to my future step-father. And not only could I grow up Catholic if I so chose, but there might be more opportunities to further my education within that more ancient Church tradition than existed for women within her own—Mother never quite forgave the Church of England tradition, God bless them anyway—for refusing to educate her or her siblings, and thus my maternal grandparents became Unitarians; and thus they met the late Pastor Fox; and thus he could wed my mother to John Taylor yet also serve as a key instrument in introducing her to John Mill—one can get dizzy considering all the loops and circles and entangled webs that we not only create but get created for us, so it seems small wonder how we come up with religion to explain the grandiosity and mystery of it all. And I recall the look on Mother's face when I suggested I could always become a nun: fine education, life dedicated to good works. In truth, I likely would have found it too restrictive, and not only for the limited options for one's wardrobe.

Perhaps that new term is safer, then: agnosticism—perhaps, in the face of the fabulous Natural world, achievable through the simple and underrated act of walking, as Father and I, and sometimes Mother too, so often did, Father with his faithful 'Dapple' tapping along—and feeling the sublime among all the majestic living things in this end-less wonderful Creation—a sense of agnosticism, a polite and humble refusal to enter the arena of religious posturing, is the most rational response. At least, that is how I imagined my parents describing it, as I stood there this afternoon, ignoring the slight touch of gentle rain, and foolishly hoping the pair of them could indeed remain together in perpetuity. My God, how I miss them! I wept not whilst gazing at their graves but when I turned and walked away, that light rain feeling itself like tears.

So much death—a theme often appearing in Mother's work, though usually only in her poetry, most of it remaining unpublished in her own lifetime, though some of her better pieces found audiences. Perhaps I shall look into something of a posthumous poetic publication on her behalf, and, better still, ensure that no clumsy pseudonym appears with such. Currer Bell has proven a rewarding novelist, though how many know her as Charlotte Brontë? It would seem all the more fitting since so much effort has been undertaken to keep Mother's capable name from the later editions of Mr Mill's works. It was so clearly her influence that kept him going so often, and then the memory of her after her too-soon death. The political, economic, and most importantly, moral thoughts of John Stuart Mill simply would never have matured so much, nor accounted for so much, without the refining and feminising flourishes of my mother! Only an atheist-turned-poetess could have possibly observed how 'religion and poetry address themselves to the same part of the human constitution: they both supply the same want, that of ideal conceptions grander and more beautiful than we see realised in the prose of human life.'

So many of the others from my parents' network have passed on now, and while my parents savoured and flourished under a series of close friendships—plus the occasional one which may have ended unfortunately badly!—I confess that I in fact know little about how some of them may themselves be remembered, and will have to endeavour later, perhaps, to shed some light onto their lives. Graham and Roebuck are more public, still alive to cause trouble, for that matter, so I shan't mention them more herein, though I know Father wished he could have seen more of Graham later in life, while Roebuck remained too attached to simple teleology / utility for Father's taste and temperament—and critical of his relationship with Mother—and they certainly clashed over the issues and political divisions which manifested during that Yankee Civil War. For Father the issue therein was slavery and the happiness—there, the one magnificent utility-term that he never forsook!—of so many people, while Graham insisted upon the strength of a group which asserted itself politically, in that case the Southern Confederacy with its unofficial not-quite-recognised friendship with Great Britain, engaging on a course which to Graham seemed akin to what the White colonists had attempted to do eighty years earlier by rebelling against English taxes. One can never predict the multi-national exchange of ideas either, in this shrinking world of ours—I have it on good authority that the survivors of a doomed mass charge of those Confederate troops at some town in Pennsylvania which might otherwise have secured the whole War for them sang Ms Flower's 'Nearer my God to Thee' as they tended their wounds afterwards—of the flesh and of the spirit alike.

Yet again I digress, however—it has always amused me how we are willing to distract ourselves when confronting uncomfortable topics. Let me see… I barely knew George Grote, for example. By my time, meetings at his home of the Athenaeum or the 'Trijackia' or whomever else seemed to have dropped off, and Grote truly did use his own curious pseudonym—for the avoidance of public opprobrium—to question not whether God existed, but whether the existence of God contributed anything to happiness. That was dangerously similar to Father's own take on the question earlier, the sort of topic he must have grappled with during his breakdown—about which I knew almost nothing whilst Mother yet lived. Father and Grote alike might have revelled in that strange blasphemous question posed recently by a new mad Prussian: whether humanity was God's major mistake, or God was humanity's major mistake. Sin it might yet be to think such, though I confess it made me smile too, partly since I think the metaphysical jury remains out on that question.

Yes, I continue to read philosophy. It calms me. Most do not understand that.

Yet Grote wanted to reform Parliament while publishing a cogent if superficial history of the ancient Greeks. I think his widow Harriet yet lives, and has achieved some status as a biographer, thus showing how women with my mother's name could continue to write for effect and publication. 'Twas she who once observed how Mother 'was tired of him (John Taylor, my father), and cared for clever people,' and was a 'very pretty woman.'

The Aunty Carolines, as I sometimes called them, have both been promoted to Heavenly status now as well. Dear Ms Fox recorded, as I try now to do so long after the relevant facts, many of the goings-on of her life and times, and she too had a flair for the dramatic. Still, Mother always considered her amongst one of her two closest friends and confidantes, the other of course having been Ms Flower, who died sadly so young, and so long ago now. Both these lovely ladies would, one thinks, be pleased by how one's written words can perpetuate not only one's own thoughts and memories, but a sense of one's place as one was writing. Perhaps I may yet get the opportunity to peruse whatever other personal records either or both of them may have kept during their lives.

That leaves my true aunty, then, Caroline Hardy Ley. That damnable trusteeship issue never seemed to truly go away, and the poor woman, always working so hard to put on a brave face at least in my presence, died at almost precisely the same age as did Lizzie Flower. If my parents had been more open to the possibility—occasional necessity?—of direct violence, they might have visited upon her abusive drunken wretch of a husband something other than the force of law, something still so wanting with regard to the protections of so many members of our polite society. Women, children, animals — so many of the downtrodden still suffer at the hands of men, who in turn yet manage to escape without justice on so many occasions and in so many ways. Yet this foolish survivor, Aunty Carry, unwittingly offered so much philosophical ammunition to my parents over the years—so many of those news articles, and public appeals, and Father's speeches to Parliament, and grist for the logical mill of works like Subjection of Women—had been inspired by anger and a crying out for justice and a sense of frustrating helplessness for those like my aunt. May she rest now, and may her husband experience at least a century or three in Hell to learn the lessons he could never acquire in his mortal life.

My, how this mind of mine wanders. Such is the benefit of

recording one's own innermost thoughts—not so much an exercise in the vain hope of posterity's remembrances, but to help one organise. Those who talk to themselves seem doomed to accusations of madness, or at least of that favourite term of father's—eccentricity—yet keeping a diary as I have done intermittently, as my mother before me, is in truth the same thing, just with physical evidence left behind. And we theatre-people are always dramatic as well as eccentric, are we not?

These two individuals in so much of my life, never attending formal schooling—although Mr Mill, long before I came along, might have studied more at the newer University College in London had he been willing to swear to uphold the Thirty-nine Articles of Faith of the Church of England—offered such insights, whether they had readers or listeners or encountered blatant hostility instead. How could we make ourselves better, they kept asking. And presenting insight was something I attempted in vain to do with my foray into stagecraft. I admit now, though I failed to then, I never could become much of an actress, yet the desire appeared so early in my life—not so much to appear as the centre of attention, something for which Mother chided me more than once—but instead to... how should one put it? To take the brave chance to inform attentive listeners of truths they might not consider otherwise... That is when theatre might become something great indeed.

These two such brave souls published over four-hundred newspaper articles together. And yet one might wonder at the apparent hypocrisy, or at least the all-too-English irony, of them both writing so much about the plight of the underclass, in England, Jamaica, India, Ireland, America, anywhere, while so often also failing to fully acknowledge, or help to liberate or further educate, their own servants. Sometimes I had a more rewarding relationship with the latter individuals, or at least sometimes assisted with the labours necessary to operate a healthy household. For all that I and my parents have loved This Englande, it remains yet a highly class-conscious society, something de Tocqueville railed against while praising the opposite in the Americans. The horrid conflicts between White Americans and the Africans they enslaved, the Indians they stole from, the Mexicans disputing them, and all of these not so long ago — only the latter group knowing the ways of Europeans and their different ideas of land ownership — often went unremarked upon by that French writer and others of his intellectual ilk. But I was mentioning my parents — and how it was Mother who dealt with the servants for by far the majority portion — including instructing them and even seeing to their pay. I have never believed Father did not care — he simply occupied a different world, and for all the talk of social reform, he surely had far more trouble recognising any need for it within his own household.

I admit also that only with difficulty can I find it within my torn heart to forgive my stepfather for having burned, apparently, all the letters Mother wrote to him, and then feel another tug at my emotions in the knowledge that she had requested such drastic action. John Mill remained a passionate devotee of history in all its forms, even taking his own father — and others — to task for positing historiography that suffered from overt racism or sexism or even, borrowing from the sentimental but necessary thought of Bentham, what one supposes might be labelled landscapism — animalism? — as I suggested. Regardless of valid concerns such as privacy, the rules changed when one was no longer with us.

Even stranger, much more recent history largely eluded John Mill, and to some extent my mother as well. Witness his amusing if embarrassing encounters with law personnel in London for expressing his well-reasoned views, like less harm to women and also to the babies they might produce yet remain unable to properly care for, and even follow-up critiques of the men who of course most directly placed the women in those positions to begin with. The same applies to those destroyed letters, and also to the daily and immediate needs of the East India Company, and the millions of lives affected by its decisions. No, Mother and Father remained more engaged with the what-could-be rather than with the what-was — a logical-moral legacy pointed out by Hume before any of us were born — even while recognising that the latter offered endless lessons for the former. My own supposition is that the quirky Mr Mill felt so frustrated by the history of Hume or his own father that he never got past the belief that the discipline was always biased. Even his beloved field of 'Classics' remains defined in Mediterranean and thus largely European terms, though he knew the rest of the world had so much to offer.

Still, I perhaps proceed too fast. The calendar indeed seemed to advance more quickly after Mother's passing. I could fill pages with notes about other women writers like Ms Nightingale, herself never married, though her photographs illustrate a lovely and intelligent countenance, who proved with her own work how the most basic personal hygiene literally saved lives. And Father remained too distracted by Mother's passing to read the astonishing conclusions of Mr Darwin until some years later, when natural selection expanded the already largely accepted ideas about evolution, and when some were perturbed to think that the development of life might be random and might not even require the aforementioned Deity. But ideas must adapt also — Mother would have loved reading about that.

(Note: the younger Ms Taylor began keeping her diary perhaps as early as 1842, when she was only eleven years old, and it was previously believed by historians and other scholars that the surviving remnants of this diary only went until 1849 or thereabouts, so we are thankful indeed to have located this additional section.

On a sadder note however, Ms Helen Taylor also outlived both her elder brothers, Herbert and Algernon, by some four years. Only Algernon is known to have had any issue of his own, after his marriage in 1860 to Ms Ellen Gurney, daughter of the very physician who once treated Mrs Harriet Mill, though of these latter children — Harriet Hardy Taylor Mill's grandchildren — daughter Elizabeth died 'paralysed but sane;' son Cyprian would 'suffer for about forty years from religious mania of Folie circulaire;' — an earlier name for manic depression — and another daughter Mary died 'after having been certified' mad, though for a period when 'madness' remained open to interpretation, we are alas left with speculation. While careful readers may wonder or question how such conditions are either ambiguously named and described, or perhaps offer tacit support to the late Mrs Mill's contention that she had acquired syphilis from her first husband Mr Taylor, then passed this dreaded disease to her descendants, what remains known with greater certainty is that the Hardy–Taylor line may have ended with Helen, and that Mr Mill never had biological children of his own.

Sometimes fate operates in such a manner that it might lead one to believe in the notion of karma, something that John Mill himself had tried to dismiss, though he had studied it somewhat in his growing appreciation of the society most appropriated from during his Company career. In this sense, Dr Gurney would emerge for the Mills once more. In 1873, whilst once again visiting Avignon and Mrs Mill's gravesite, that physician was summoned by telegraph to find Mr Mill presenting with 'an enormous swelling, over his face and neck,' leading Gurney to diagnose erysipelas, a skin infection with notable oedema potentially anywhere, though in Mill's case mostly about his upper body, including the face and neck. This was years before the bacterium that caused the disease would be identified, indeed some time before scientists could even agree on the new germ theory of disease, and Mill was grateful that he had escaped some of the more unpleasant symptoms, like severe headaches and vomiting. Fever and chills and fatigue predominated instead, and he faced his end as any good Stoic, with what Dr Gurney noted as 'calmness and resignation,' even more thankful that his brilliant and curious mind never failed him, not during his years in Parliament nor as the head of a Scottish university.

Perhaps not a humourist as some claimed, Mr Mill near the end joked how a commoner like himself could at least contract an illness which had previously despatched Queen Anne, along with two of George III's children: the Princess Amelia and Prince Augustus

Frederick. 'At least I found myself in fine medical company,' he quipped mere days before his death, 'just like my inspiring wife.'

As for Mr Mill's final moments, it is worth noting the extreme peace he found in Nature, continually advocating for direct experience of it as a human necessity, that the notion of humans as separate from the rest of the world was illusory and artificial, another idea taken from ancient Indian thinkers. Upon his arrival, Dr Gurney noted how the garden near Mill's window had become occupied by nightingales 'so tame that when I paced up and down between my visits to his bedside, they followed me from tree to tree' like animal messengers from a fairy story.

The remainder of Ms Taylor's memoirs partly reproduced herein, meanwhile, appear barely legible or are believed destroyed, though her final known thoughts have been appended below. Whilst continuing her work on behalf of women's suffrage, Ms Taylor did live to learn of its formal adoption in nations that became part of the new British 'Commonwealth'—including New Zealand in 1893 and Australia in 1902—though Ms Taylor did not, unfortunately, have the opportunity to witness women being permitted to vote at long last in her own country in 1918, with the conclusion of the Great War—ed.)

What a century it all was, then! One can only wonder what amazing things and events will be ushered in during the twentieth... As my dearly departed stepfather said so elegantly in the book named for the philosophy he could never quite hope to escape from, 'A certain infusion of the laughing philosopher... is a prodigious help towards bearing the evils of life, and I should think has saved many a person from going mad.' Admittedly rarely publicly comedic, and noting further that Mother and Father could just as often weep together as laugh, they knew humour helped open minds as much as philosophy could, and I end here my entry in the genuine hope that they both understood that they did change things, that they did begin reform and even revolution—of ideas and of persons alike—and that their relationship and marriage might inspire others as much as their writings have. I shall always miss them, more than anyone else I have ever known.

(Final Note: It seems that not all correspondence between John Mill and Harriet Mill was destroyed, despite their sometimes conflicted mutual requests about such. Among Ms Helen Taylor's diary was the following hand-written note from her mother to her future step-father, dated to 1832—ed.)

'Far from being unhappy or even low this morning, I feel as though you had never loved me half so well as last night—and I am in the happiest spirits and quite well part of which is owing to that nice sight this morning…, and so I shall go adieu darling  How very nice next month will be. I am quite impatient for it.'

www.ingramcontent.com/pod-product-compliance
Lightning Source LLC
Chambersburg PA
CBHW070152120726
47909CB00001B/77